PRAISE FOR

The Secret Keepers

A *New York Times* Bestseller

An *Entertainment Weekly* Best Book of the Year

An Amazon #1 Best Book of the Year

"Genuinely **haunting** and **ingenious**."
—*The New York Times*

★ "Stewart…has created an **exciting, fully imagined world** filled with **mystery and danger**, where children can have real adventures without parental supervision. He **keeps readers on tenterhooks until the final page**."
—*Publishers Weekly* (starred review)

★ "Fans of Stewart's Mysterious Benedict Society and series like it will devour his latest novel. This **epic story filled with adventure and twists and turns** is certain to **keep readers' interest from beginning to end**."
—*School Library Journal* (starred review)

★ "**Children will be caught up in the mystery**, trying to decipher the clues as they follow Reuben and his new-found friends in their race to save the town from a dreadful future.…All in all, **this is another winner from Trenton Lee Stewart**."
—*School Library Connection* (starred review)

"There are enough **hidden tunnels, concealed traps, enigmatic secrets, hair-raising surprises, quirky characters, and ethical dilemmas to keep the plot buzzing**. Fans of the Mysterious Benedict Society series will welcome Stewart's latest puzzling adventure, **whose seemingly ordinary hero proves quite extraordinary**."
—*Kirkus Reviews*

"**This adventure easily lives up to the high bar.…The Smoke is an excellent main villain, creepy and oozing menace**."
—*The Bulletin*

The SECRET KEEPERS

By TRENTON LEE STEWART

Illustrated by DIANA SUDYKA

Megan Tingley Books

LITTLE, BROWN AND COMPANY

NEW YORK   BOSTON

Little, Brown and Company
Hachette Book Group
1290 Avenue of the Americas, New York, NY 10104
Visit us at LBYR.com

Originally published in hardcover and ebook by Little, Brown and Company in September 2016
First Trade Paperback Edition: September 2017

Little, Brown and Company is a division of Hachette Book Group, Inc.
The Little, Brown name and logo are trademarks of Hachette Book Group, Inc.

The publisher is not responsible for websites (or their content) that are not owned by the publisher.

The Library of Congress has cataloged the hardcover edition as follows:
Names: Stewart, Trenton Lee, author. | Sudyka, Diana, illustrator.
Title: The secret keepers / Trenton Lee Stewart ; illustrated by Diana Sudyka.
Description: First edition. | New York : Little, Brown and Company, 2016. | "Megan Tingley Books." | Summary: "When twelve-year-old Reuben finds a peculiar, magical watch that has the power to turn its wearer invisible, he's propelled on the adventure of a lifetime." —Provided by publisher.
Identifiers: LCCN 2016006406| ISBN 9780316389556 (hardcover) | ISBN 9780316389563 (ebook) | ISBN 9780316319126 (library edition ebook)
Subjects: | CYAC: Adventure and adventurers—Fiction. | Secrets—Fiction. | Magic—Fiction. | Invisibility—Fiction. | Clocks and watches—Fiction. | BISAC: JUVENILE FICTION / Mysteries & Detective Stories. | JUVENILE FICTION / Fantasy & Magic. | JUVENILE FICTION / Action & Adventure / General. | JUVENILE FICTION / Science & Technology. | JUVENILE FICTION / Family / Multigenerational.
Classification: LCC PZ7.S8513 Se 2016 | DDC [Fic]—dc23
LC record available at https://lccn.loc.gov/2016006406

ISBNs: 978-0-316-38954-9 (pbk.), 978-0-316-38956-3 (ebook)

Printed in the United States of America

LSC-C

10 9 8 7 6 5 4 3 2 1

For Arjun and Bhairavi

CONTENTS

PART III: HOME AND NOT HOME

PART I

THE TICKING CLOCK

WALKING BACKWARD INTO THE SKY

That summer morning in the Lower Downs began as usual for Reuben Pedley. He rose early to have breakfast with his mom before she left for work, a quiet breakfast because they were both still sleepy. Afterward, also as usual, he cleaned up their tiny kitchen while his mom moved faster and faster in her race against the clock (whose numerals she seemed quite unable to read before she'd had coffee and a shower). Then his mom was hugging him goodbye at the apartment door, where Reuben told her he loved her, which was true—and that she had no reason to worry about him, which was not.

His mom had not even reached the bus stop before Reuben

had brushed his teeth, yanked on his sneakers (a fitting term, he thought, being a sneaker himself), and climbed onto the kitchen counter to retrieve his wallet. He kept it among the mousetraps on top of the cupboard. The traps were never sprung; Reuben never baited them, and so far no thieves had reached up there to see what they might find. Not that the wallet contained much, but for Reuben "not much" was still everything he had.

Next he went into his bedroom and removed the putty from the little hole in the wall behind his bed. He took his key from the hole and smooshed the putty back into place. Then, locking the apartment door behind him, he headed out in search of new places to hide.

Reuben lived in the city of New Umbra, a metropolis that was nonetheless as gloomy and run-down as a city could be. Though it had once enjoyed infinitely hopeful prospects (people used to say that it was born under a promising star), New Umbra had long since ceased to be prosperous, and was not generally well kept. Some might have said the same of Reuben Pedley, who used to have two fine and loving parents, but only briefly, when he was a baby, and who in elementary school had been considered an excellent student, but in middle school had faded into the walls.

Eleven years had passed since the factory accident that left Reuben without a father and his mother a young widow scrambling for work—eleven years, in other words, since his own promising star had begun to fall. And though in reality he was as loved and cared for as any child could hope to be, anyone who followed him through his days might well have believed otherwise. Especially on a day like today.

Reuben exited his shabby high-rise apartment building in the usual manner: he bypassed the elevator and stole down the rarely used stairwell, descending unseen all the way past the lobby to the basement, where he slipped out a storage-room window. The young building manager kept that window slightly ajar to accommodate the comings and goings of a certain alley cat she hoped to tame, enticing it with bowls of food and water. She wasn't supposed to be doing that, but no one knew about it except Reuben, and he certainly wasn't going to tell anyone. He wasn't supposed to be in the storage room in the first place. Besides, he liked the building manager and wished her luck with the cat, though only in his mind, for she didn't know that he knew about it. She barely even knew he existed.

From his hidden vantage point in the window well, which was slightly below street level and encircled by an iron railing, Reuben confirmed that the alley behind the building was empty. With practiced ease, he climbed out of the window well, monkeyed up the railing, grabbed the lower rungs of the building's rusty fire escape, and swung out over empty space. He hit the ground at a trot. Today he wanted to strike out into new territory, and there was no time to waste. When they'd lived in the northern part of the Lower Downs, Reuben had known the surrounding blocks as well as his own bedroom, but then they'd had to move south, and despite having lived here a year, his mental map remained incomplete.

Of all the city's depressed and depressing neighborhoods, the Lower Downs was considered the worst. Many of its old buildings were abandoned; others seemed permanently under repair. Its backstreets and alleys were marked by missing shutters, tilted light poles, broken gates and railings, fences with gaps in them. The Lower Downs, in other words, was perfect for any boy who wanted to explore and to hide.

Reuben was just such a boy. In fact, exploring and hiding were almost all he ever did. He shinned up the tilted light poles and dropped behind fences; he slipped behind the busted shutters and through the broken windows; he found his way into cramped spaces and high places, into spots where no one would ever think to look. This was how he spent his solitary days.

It never occurred to him to be afraid. Even here in the Lower Downs, there was very little crime on the streets of New Umbra, at least not the sort you could easily see. Vandals and pickpockets were rare, muggers and car thieves unheard of. Everyone knew that. The Directions took care of all that business. Nobody crossed the Directions, not even the police.

Because the Directions worked for The Smoke.

Reuben headed south, moving from alley to alley, keeping close to the buildings and ducking beneath windows. He paused at every corner, first listening, then peering around. He was only a few blocks off the neighborhood's main thoroughfare and could hear some early-morning traffic there, but the alleys and backstreets were dead.

About ten blocks south, Reuben ventured into new territory. He was already well beyond his bounds: his mom had given him permission to walk to the community center and the branch library—both within a few blocks of their apartment—but that was all. And so he kept these wanderings of his a secret.

Despite her excessive caution, his mom was something else, and Reuben knew it. He wouldn't have traded her for half a dozen moms with better jobs and more money, and in fact had told her exactly that just the week before.

"Oh my goodness, Reuben, that is so sweet," she'd said, pretending to wipe tears from her eyes. "I hope you know that I probably wouldn't trade you, either. Not for half a dozen boys, or even a whole dozen."

"*Probably?*"

"Almost certainly," she'd said, squeezing his hand as if to reassure him.

That was what his mom was like. Their conversations were usually the best part of his day.

Crossing an empty street, Reuben made his habitual, rapid inventory of potential hiding places: a shady corner between a

Nobody crossed the Directions, not even the police.
Because the Directions worked for The Smoke.

building's front steps and street-facing wall; a pile of broken furniture that someone had hauled to the curb; a window well with no protective railing. But none of these places was within easy reach when, just as he attained the far curb, a door opened in a building down the block.

Reuben abruptly sat on the curb and watched the door. He held perfectly still while an old man in pajamas stepped outside and checked the sky, sniffing with evident satisfaction and glancing up and down the street before going back in. The old man never saw the small brown-haired boy watching him from the curb.

Reuben rose and moved on, quietly triumphant. He preferred bona fide hiding places when he could find them, but there was nothing quite like hiding in plain sight. Sometimes people saw you and then instantly forgot you, because you were just a random kid, doing nothing. As long as you didn't look lost, anxious, or interesting, you might as well be a trash can or a stunted tree, part of the city landscape. Reuben considered such encounters successes, too. But to go completely unnoticed on an otherwise empty street was almost impossible, and therefore superior. He was reliving the moment in his mind, exulting in the memory of the old man's eyes passing right over him without registering his presence—not once but twice!—when he came upon the narrowest alley he'd ever seen, and made his big mistake.

It was the narrowness that tempted him. The brick walls of the abandoned buildings were so close to each other that Reuben saw at once how he might scale them. By leaning forward and pressing his palms against one, then lifting his feet behind him and pressing them against the other, he could hold himself up, suspended above the alley floor. Then by moving one hand higher, then the other, and then doing the same with his feet, he could work his way upward. It would be like walking backward into the sky.

No sooner had he imagined it than Reuben knew he had to

try it. Glancing around to ensure that he was unobserved, he moved deeper into the alley. He could see a ledge high above him—probably too high to reach, but it gave him something to shoot for, at any rate.

He started out slowly, then gained momentum as he found his rhythm. Hand over hand, foot over foot, smoothly and steadily. Now he was fifteen feet up, now twenty, and still he climbed. Craning his head around, Reuben saw the ledge not too far above him. Unfortunately, he also saw how difficult it would be to climb onto it—his position was all wrong. He frowned. What had he been thinking? He didn't dare try such a risky maneuver, not at that height. He'd be a fool to chance it.

That was when Reuben felt his arms begin to tremble and realized, with horror, that he had made a terrible mistake.

He hadn't anticipated how drastically his arms would tire, nor how abruptly. It seemed to happen all at once, without warning. Now, looking at the alley floor far below him, Reuben became sickeningly aware of how high he had actually climbed. At least thirty feet, maybe more. The way his arms felt, there was no way he'd make it back to the ground safely. He probably couldn't even get back down to twenty feet.

Thus the action he'd just rejected as being foolishly dangerous suddenly became the only choice left to him, the only hope he had. He had to make the ledge, and by some miracle he had to get himself onto it.

With a whimper of panic, Reuben resumed his climbing. The trembling in his arms grew worse. He could no longer see the grimy, broken pavement of the alley floor below. His vision was blurred by sweat, which had trickled into his eyes and couldn't be wiped away. He was burning up on the inside but weirdly cold on the outside, like a furnace encased in ice; the alley's quirky cross breezes were cooling his sweat-slick skin. Beads of perspiration dripped from his nose.

In desperate silence he pressed upward. He heard the wind fluttering in his ears, the scrape of his shoe soles against brick, his own labored breath, and that was all. He was so high up, and so quietly intent on climbing, that had any passersby glanced down that narrow alley, they'd have noticed nothing unusual. Certainly none would have guessed that an eleven-year-old boy was stretched out high above them, fearing for his life.

As it happened, there were no passersby to see Reuben finally come to the ledge, or to note the terrible moment when he made his fateful lunge, or to watch him struggle for an agonizingly long time to heave himself up, his shoes slipping and scraping, his face purple with strain. No one was around to hear Reuben's gasps of exhaustion and relief when at last he lay on that narrow ledge—heedless, for the moment, of his bruised arms and raw fingertips. If any passersby had been near enough to hear anything, it would have been only the clatter of startled pigeons rising away above the rooftops. But in the city this was no unusual sound, and without a thought they would have gone on with their lives, reflecting upon their own problems and wondering what to do.

Reuben lay with his face pressed against the concrete ledge as if kissing it, which indeed he felt like doing. He had such immense gratitude for its existence, for its solidity beneath him. After his pulse settled and his breath returned, he rose very cautiously to a sitting position, his back against brick, his legs dangling at the knees. With his shirt, he dried his eyes as best he could, wincing a little from the smarting of his scraped fingertips. His every movement was calculated and slow. He was still in a dangerous predicament.

The ledge was keeping Reuben safe for the time being, but it was only a ledge, spattered here and there with pigeon droppings. When he tried to look up, the wind whipped his hair into his eyes; to keep them clear, he had to cup his hands like pretend binoculars. The rooftop seemed miles above him, and might as well have been. Beyond it the early-morning sky was blue as a robin's egg. A perfect summer morning to have gotten stuck on a ledge in a deserted alley.

"Well done, Reuben," he muttered. "Brilliant."

He knew he couldn't get back down the same way he'd come up. He would have to edge around to the back of the building and hope for a fire escape. Otherwise his only option was to follow the ledge around to the street side, try to get in through one of the windows there. If he was lucky, perhaps no one would spot him. But if he couldn't get in, he would have to shout for help. Reuben imagined the fire truck's siren, the fierce disapproval on the firefighters' faces, the gathering crowd—all of it terrible to contemplate, and none of it even half as bad as facing his mom would be.

His mom, who thought he was safe at home in their apartment, reading a book or watching TV or maybe even back in bed. His mom, who even now was on her way to slice and weigh fish at the market, her first and least favorite work shift of the day. His mom, who had never remarried, who had no family, no boyfriend, no time to make friends—meaning Reuben was all she had, Reuben the reason she worked two jobs, Reuben the person for whom she did everything in her life.

His mom, who would not be pleased.

"Oh, let there be a fire escape," Reuben breathed. "Oh, please." Swiveling his eyes to his left, he studied the precious, narrow strip of concrete keeping him aloft and alive. It appeared sound enough; there was no obvious deterioration. A brown crust of bread lay nearby (probably some pigeon's breakfast that he'd rudely interrupted), but that was all—no broken glass or other hazards. His path looked clear.

Reuben began shifting himself sideways, moving left, toward the back of the building. He kept his shoulder blades pressed against the brick wall behind him, his eyes fixed straight ahead on the featureless wall of the building opposite him, just a couple of yards away. He tried very hard not to imagine the dizzying drop below him.

He had progressed a few feet when his hand came down on the crust of bread. Without thinking, he attempted to brush it away. It seemed to be stuck. Glancing down now, Reuben discovered that the bread crust was actually a scrap of leather and that in fact it was not resting on the ledge but poking out of the bricks just above it. What in the world? Why would this scrap of leather have been mortared into the wall where no one would ever see it? Was it some kind of secret sign?

Reuben pinched the scrap awkwardly between two knuckles and tugged. It yielded slightly, revealing more leather, and through his fingers he felt an unseen shifting of stubborn dirt or debris, like when he pulled weeds from sidewalk cracks. He tugged again, and a few loose bits of broken brick fell onto the ledge, revealing a small hole in the wall. The brick pieces appeared to have been packed into it.

Reuben took a firmer grip on the leather and gave another tug. More bits of brick came loose. The scrap of leather turned out to be the end of a short strap, which in turn was connected to a dusty leather pouch. Carefully he drew the pouch from the hole and up into his lap.

Not a secret sign. A secret *thing*.

He should wait to open it, he knew. It would be far easier, far wiser to do it after he was safely on the ground.

*Why would this scrap of leather have been
mortared into the wall where no one would ever see it?
Was it some kind of secret sign?*

Reuben stared at the pouch in his lap. "Or you could just be extra careful," he whispered.

With slow, deliberate movements, Reuben brushed away some of the brick dust. The pouch was obviously old, its leather worn and scarred. It was fastened with a rusted buckle that came right off in his hand, along with a rotted bit of strap. He set these aside and opened the pouch. Inside was a small, surprisingly heavy object wrapped in a plastic bread sack. It was bundled up in yet another wrapping, this one of stiff canvas. Whatever it was, its owner had taken great pains to keep it safe and dry.

Reuben unbundled the wrappings to reveal a handsome wooden case, dark brown with streaks of black. Its hinged lid was held closed by a gray metal clasp, the sort that could be secured with a little padlock. There was no lock, though; all Reuben had to do was turn it. He hesitated, wondering what he was about to find. Then he turned the clasp and felt something give. The lid opened with a squeak.

Inside the case were two velvet-lined compartments, both shaped to fit exactly the objects they contained. One of the objects was a small, delicate key with an ornate bow; the other appeared to be a simple metal sphere. Both had the dark coppery color of an old penny and yet, at the same time, the bright sheen of a brand-new one. They were made of a metal Reuben had never seen before. Something like copper or brass, but not exactly either.

Reuben very carefully lifted the sphere from its velvet compartment. It felt as heavy as a billiard ball, though it was not quite as large as one. He turned it in his hands, gazing at it in wonder. What was it? He'd expected that the key would be needed to open it, but there was no keyhole. Looking more closely, he noticed a seam, scarcely wider than a thread, circling the middle of the sphere like the equator on a globe, dividing it into two hemispheres.

"So you *can* open it," he murmured.

Holding the sphere in his left hand, Reuben tried, gently, to open it with the other. He used the same gesture he had seen in countless silly old movies he'd watched with his mom, in which hopeful men drop to a knee and open tiny velvet-covered boxes, proposing marriage with a ring. He imagined he felt every bit as hopeful and excited as those men were supposed to be.

The two hemispheres parted easily, smoothly, without a sound, as if their hidden hinge had been carefully oiled not a minute before. The interior of one hemisphere was hollow, like an empty bowl. It served as the cover for the other hemisphere, which contained the face of a clock. What Reuben had found, evidently, was a pocket watch.

And yet it was a pocket watch of a kind he'd never seen, to say nothing of its quality. Its face was made of a lustrous white material, perhaps ivory, and the hour hand and the Roman numerals around the dial gleamed black. It was missing a minute hand, but otherwise the parts were all in such fine condition the watch might have been constructed that very morning, though Reuben felt sure it was an antique.

A wild fluttering started up in his belly. His pulse boomed in his ears. How much, Reuben wondered, might such an exquisite device be worth? Indeed, the watch seemed so perfect—so perfect, so unusual, so beautiful—that he almost expected it to show the correct time. But the hour hand was frozen at just before twelve, and when he held the watch to his ear, he heard no telltale ticking.

The key! he thought. Reuben's mom had a music box that his father had given her before Reuben was born. You had to wind it up with a key. It must be the same with this watch. A closer inspection revealed a tiny, star-shaped hole in the center of the watch face. Could that be a keyhole?

A glance confirmed his suspicion. The key lacked the large rectangular teeth of normal old keys, but rather tapered to a narrow, star-shaped end, small enough to insert into the hole. This was the watch's winding key, no question.

Reuben was tempted. He even laid a finger on the key in its snug compartment. But once again a warning voice was sounding in his head, and this time he listened to it. He might fumble the key, drop it, lose it. Better to wait until he was in a safe place. Better, for once, to resist his impulses. This was far too important.

Reluctantly he closed the watch cover and put the watch back inside the case. He was about to close the lid when he noticed an inscription on its interior: *Property of P. Wm. Light.*

"P. William Light," Reuben muttered, gazing at the name. "So this once belonged to you, whoever you were." He closed the lid, fastened the clasp. "*When*ever you were." For whoever P. William Light was, Reuben felt sure he'd stopped walking the earth long ago.

Reuben rebundled the case and tucked it back inside the pouch, then stuffed the pouch into the waist of his shorts—no small feat in such an awkward, precarious position. Now he was ready to move.

He took a last look at the hole in the wall, wondering how long the watch had been in there. It had been put there by someone like him, someone who found places that were secret to others. It could only have been *found* by someone like him, as well, which made its discovery feel very much like fate.

Just don't blow it by falling, Reuben thought. *Boy finds treasure, plummets to his death. Great story.*

It was with exceeding caution, therefore, that he began to inch sideways along the ledge. A wearisome half hour later he reached the back of the building, only to find that there was no fire escape. No windows, either, and no more ledge.

"Seriously?" Reuben muttered. He felt like banging his head against the brick.

His bottom and the backs of his thighs were aching and tingling. Another hour on this ledge and he'd be in agony. Yet it would take at least that long, and possibly longer, to reach the front of the building.

There was, however, a rusty old drainpipe plunging down along the building's corner. Reuben eyed it, then grabbed it with his left hand and tried to shake it. The pipe seemed firmly secured to the wall, and there was enough room between metal and brick for him to get his hands behind it. He peered down the length of the pipe; it seemed to be intact. He had climbed drainpipes before. Never at anywhere near this height, but if he didn't *think* about the height...

It was as if someone else made the decision for him. Suddenly gathering himself, Reuben reached across his body with his right hand, grabbed the pipe, and swung off the ledge. His stomach wanted to stay behind; he felt it climbing up inside him. Now that he'd acted, the fear was back in full force.

Clenching his jaw, breathing fiercely through his nose, Reuben ignored the lurching sensation and got his feet set. Then, hand under hand, step after step, he began his descent. He went as quickly as he could, knowing he would soon tire. The pipe uttered an initial groan of protest against his weight, then fell silent.

Flakes of rust broke off beneath his fingers and scattered in the wind. Sweat trickled into his eyes again, then into his mouth. He blew it from his nose. Every single part of him seemed to hurt. He didn't dare look down. He concentrated on his hands and his feet and nothing else.

And then the heel of his right foot struck something beneath him, and Reuben looked down to discover that it was the ground. Slowly, almost disbelieving, he set his other foot down. He let go of the pipe. His fingers automatically curled up like claws. He flexed them painfully, wiped his face with his shirt, and looked up at the ledge, so high above him. Had he actually climbed all the way up *there*? He felt dazed, as if in a dream.

Reuben withdrew the pouch from the waistband of his shorts and gazed at it. This was no dream. He began to walk stiffly along the narrow alley, heading for the street. One step, three steps, a dozen—and then he felt the thrill begin to surge through him. He'd made it! He was alive! He'd taken a terrible risk, but he'd come back with treasure. It seemed like the end of an adventure, and yet somehow Reuben knew—he just *knew*—it was only the beginning.

The DELICIOUS SMELL of FEAR

In the alley behind his apartment building, Reuben once more stuffed the pouch into his waistband. He climbed up and over the iron railing around the storage-room window and peeked in through the grimy glass. All clear. He scrambled down into the window well, stuck his legs through the slightly raised window, and worked his way forward, arching his torso as if doing the limbo. His toes found the floor just as his head cleared the window. It was all routine.

After stealing up the empty stairs to his apartment, a small two bedroom on the fifth floor, Reuben emerged minutes later wearing clean shorts and carrying his school backpack. This time he left the building by way of the lobby, where three people stood in line at the desk, waiting for their turn to complain to the nervous young building manager. She kept saying, "Sorry, I know. I know. Sorry." Evidently, there was a problem with the hot water again. Or possibly just the water, period.

Reuben passed through the lobby unseen. He didn't even have to make an effort.

He spent the entire time at the laundromat sitting in a corner, gazing into his backpack. If anyone noticed him, the way he sat with his hands plunged into the open pack, staring fixedly at something hidden inside it, they probably thought he was reading a book he wasn't supposed to be reading. When the buzzer sounded on his washing machine, Reuben carefully closed the pretty wooden box, rewrapped it, put it back inside its pouch, and zipped up the backpack, which he carried with him to the washer. He had never been so careful about anything in his life.

When his clothes were dry, he stuffed them into his backpack and went out into the late-morning sunshine. He was only a few blocks from the community center. Along the way Reuben passed few stores open for business, and even fewer people. There weren't a lot of employment opportunities in the Lower Downs; most people who had jobs or were looking for them spent their days in other neighborhoods. The market where Reuben's mom worked, for instance, was situated near the Southport ferry dock in Riverside, and her part-time evening job took her to a neighborhood called Ashton.

"It's all part of my master plan," she'd told him once, with a scheming look. "After I've memorized every single bus route in the city, I can get a job as a substitute driver. They'd be fools to turn me down! Ha-ha!" And she had raised her fists triumphantly, as if becoming a substitute bus driver were the surest path to riches.

"Have you ever driven a bus?" Reuben had asked.

She'd waved him off. "Don't get bogged down in the details, kid."

The community center was a two-story brown-brick building that housed a dingy basketball court with perpetually bent rims, a few warped Ping-Pong tables, a reading room with out-of-date magazines, and other similarly depressing features. Reuben usually spent his time there gliding along the walls and hanging about in quiet corners, observing without being observed. But sometimes, like today, if he determined that the staff office was empty and all the staff members scattered throughout the center, he slipped into the office, snatched a key from a nail behind the door, and snuck up onto the roof.

Nobody ever disturbed him up here. They couldn't. The door locked automatically behind him, and he had the key.

A featureless plain of asphalt and sun-bleached gravel, with a bank of air-conditioning apparatuses that roared continuously, the roof, Reuben thought, was an ideal place to do some serious thinking. Though he often peeked down over its low perimeter wall in search of anything or anyone of interest to watch, today what he wanted to think about was right here with him, hidden inside his backpack.

Still, for a moment he stood gazing over the main thoroughfare in the direction of Riverside, where his mom worked, where the buildings were somewhat taller and less decrepit than those in the Lower Downs and where occasionally, on very clear days, he would spot the huge Southport ferry gliding eerily along the river. From this distance it looked like a building that had come unmoored and was drifting among the other buildings. Which, in a way, it was, Reuben supposed. A sort of floating parking deck. His mom had told him that from the market she could hear its horn blast at full volume, twice every hour, all day long. That never got old, she'd said.

"Not even a little?" Reuben had asked, and to clear things up,

21

she'd followed him around the apartment like a demented goose, imitating the horn while he covered his ears, fleeing in circles and giggling. "You're right!" he'd cried. "How could that ever get old?"

"That's what I'm telling you!" his mom said, honking again. Then their neighbor had banged on the wall, and they'd had to quiet down.

Standing on the roof, Reuben could hear that faraway horn now, its sound rendered soft and spooky by distance, like the lowest note on an organ. He settled down with his back to the perimeter wall and the backpack between his knees.

With laborious care, Reuben removed the wooden box from its pouch and its wrapping, then took the watch from the wooden box. The sunlight on the coppery metal was absurdly brilliant, making him squint. He opened the cover. The black numerals on the watch face glistened like freshly applied ink. He wondered what had happened to the minute hand, for in all other respects the watch was perfect, unblemished, gorgeous. He loved the weight and solidity of it in his palm, where it fit snugly, as if custom-made for his small hands.

Reuben felt another shudder of excitement. He couldn't stop wondering how much he might sell the watch for. It was surely worth a great deal of money, he thought—maybe even enough to turn things around for him and his mom. Why not? There was no harm in dreaming. Yet the thought of parting with his secret treasure already gave him a pang of regret, so he let himself day-dream about vast sums of money without dwelling on the part about handing the watch over.

What was it his mom had said? *Don't get bogged down in the details.*

Twice Reuben took the key from its velvet compartment and examined its elegant bow, somewhat clover-shaped, its metal finely twisted like wrought iron. Both times he held the other end just over the star-shaped hole in the center of the watch face, then shook his head and put the key away. He felt nervous about winding the watch. He worried he would break something.

When at length the muted sound of the ferry horn broke in on his thoughts, Reuben blinked, stretched his neck, and noticed how much warmer it had gotten on the roof. He had a vague realization that he'd heard the horn a little while ago, too, perhaps more than once, without consciously registering the fact. His bottom was sore, his legs were stiff, and his stomach growled insistently. Could it be lunchtime already? He put everything away and stood up. The first thing he noticed was a group of four men walking along the main thoroughfare. He crouched down again, clutching his backpack. The Directions.

Now Reuben knew what time it was. Today was Wednesday, so it must be noon. That's when the Directions visited the businesses along this stretch. He had observed them any number of times. Always nervously, though. It was tricky to spy on Directions.

For this was how the Directions had come by their nickname: in every group of four, each man was always looking a different way. One looked ahead, one looked left, one looked right, and one kept an eye out behind them. They chatted as they walked along and would glance at one another as they spoke, but always their gazes drifted back to their appointed directions. They were like sets of wandering eyes, seeing everything there was to see.

They had other nicknames, too. Even though you weren't really supposed to talk about them, at one time or another Reuben had heard them referred to as Wanderers, Rounders, Gatherers, Compass Men, Knockers, and Boots. Every now and then, someone dared to call them simply "the Counselor's men," since it was to the Counselor that they reported. This was considered unwise, however, and was especially frowned upon by superstitious types, who feared that even whispered conversations would

23

draw unwanted attention. Certainly no one wished to receive a summons to the Counselor's mansion. A meeting with the Counselor almost guaranteed that he would mention you to the man he worked for—the very last man on earth you would want to be thinking about you, for any reason, ever in your life. The Smoke.

If indeed The Smoke was a man at all. A lot of kids believed that he was something else. Exactly what, no one knew. Something bad, though. Something terrible. Because it was forbidden to talk about it, naturally when children were alone there was a great deal of discussion on the subject, and Reuben had overheard countless conflicting rumors and speculations. One story that everybody seemed to agree on, however, was that once, years before Reuben was born, a madman had run screaming through the streets of the Lower Downs. He had been, by all accounts, terrified, and it was widely accepted that his terror—and perhaps even his madness—had had something to do with The Smoke.

This was all Reuben knew about that particular story, but it was more than enough to give him the shivers. As a general rule, he tried not to think about The Smoke. He was generally successful, too, except at times like these, when he saw the Directions making their rounds.

Every neighborhood had its own set of Directions; some of the larger ones had two or even three sets. The Counselor's decrepit mansion in Westmont had a crew all to itself, or so Reuben had heard. In the Lower Downs there was only one. Reuben didn't know their names, even though supposedly they all lived somewhere in the neighborhood, but he'd given them nicknames. Lefty and Righty were brothers, both of them short and blond and fidgety. Frontman, tall and lanky, set the group's pace at a saunter and wore a sardonic smile. Lookback, bringing up the rear, had a fleshy, bored face that contradicted the way he checked over his shoulder every few seconds. If you never saw his expression, you'd think he was paranoid. But keeping an eye out behind him was simply his job (and no doubt also a long-ingrained habit, as he'd been doing it for years). He never looked as if he actually expected to see anything of interest. Perhaps he never did.

Supposedly they had families. Supposedly they were just regular men. Still, to Reuben that seemed hard to fathom. Once, in a grocery store with his mom, he thought he saw Frontman picking through the wilted produce. Seeing Frontman alone there, without his three associates, was like coming across a disembodied head living a life of its own. And what was it doing in a grocery store, anyway? Reuben had doubted his eyes, and his mom had abruptly turned down a different aisle, preventing a closer look.

(Only much later did he recall how crowded most of the store's aisles had been, yet how utterly empty the produce section was. His mom hadn't been the only one whipping her cart around, pretending to have missed some item on her list.)

A lot of kids his age probably didn't know what the Directions really did, didn't know how it all really worked. But Reuben had known since the previous summer, before the rent had gone up and he and his mom had been forced to move.

Their old building had been just around the corner from a little bakery, which they'd liked to visit on Saturday mornings. Reuben would have a doughnut, and his mom would drink coffee with extra cream. They always took their time, nibbling and sipping at a tiny table in the corner. They loved the bustle of the place, which did a brisk business, and even more so the smell, which was indescribably wonderful.

("Like being tucked into a warm bed by an angel," his mom had ventured, and Reuben had suggested it was like sipping from a pool of honey at the end of a rainbow. But they had to admit that their descriptions fell short.)

The baker was a friendly man, always winking at his customers and loudly teasing the nieces and nephews who worked for him. He even remembered Reuben's favorite doughnut (Bavarian cream), and whenever Reuben approached the counter, the baker would raise his wiry eyebrows and say, "The usual for you today, young man?"—which saved Reuben from having to speak up in front of a lot of people. For a time, because of this man and his heavenly shop, Reuben had wanted to become a baker himself.

One day when his mom was at work, Reuben was sneaking along the alley behind the bakery and its neighboring businesses. Alleys are not generally the best-smelling places on earth, but thanks to the bakery this one always had a pleasant aroma, and Reuben spent more time there than he did in others. He liked to creep up to the screened back doors and listen to the murmur of voices inside, trying to make out what was being said, darting off to hide behind trash cans whenever he sensed someone coming out. On this day, though, he discovered a rusty, industrial-sized metal sink lying upside down behind the bakery. Milk crates had been arranged around it like stools, and on top of it rested a deck of cards, a portable radio, and three hands of cards lying face-down. He had come upon an interrupted game.

His eyes were drawn at once to a big, rusted-out hole in the side of the sink. Or not big, exactly, but big enough. He didn't hesitate. He dropped to the ground and wormed his way through the hole.

Almost at once he was rewarded by the sound of the back door opening, laughing voices, and footsteps approaching the makeshift card table. The players sat on the milk crates again. Huddled in the darkness under the sink, Reuben could hear them talking (by their voices he recognized the baker and two of his nieces) and the cards being shuffled and tapped against

26

the metal above him. Someone switched the radio on, and polka music resonated all around him. Soon the card game was back in full swing.

Reuben felt ridiculously pleased with himself. He'd found a perfect hiding place. He pretended he was a spy listening to a coded conversation among criminals, memorizing every word so that later he could decipher the code. Although the villains *seemed* to be talking about nothing more interesting than the older niece's upcoming wedding, Reuben the spy knew that they were hatching a plot of incomparable wickedness. Once he got his hands on their secret codebook...

Just then a new voice entered the conversation—a man's voice, full of false friendliness. A screen door creaked open and banged closed. Hurriedly the radio was switched off, and milk crates scraped against the pavement as the players quickly got to their feet. Reuben felt prickles rise on the back of his neck.

"Sorry to interrupt you," said the stranger's voice. "But you weren't in the shop. The boy offered to come fetch you, but that would have left your counter unattended, and of course we hate to interfere with the proper running of your business. So we came back here to see what you were up to. We do like to know things."

Reuben, shifting to his left, peeked out through the rusted hole and saw several pairs of men's shoes. The baker's and four others. Reuben felt his heart quicken. He had never been so close to the Directions before.

"And now you know," the baker said, his own voice just as empty of real friendliness as the first man's had been. "We were taking a break."

"Must be nice," said the Direction who had spoken. "Ourselves, we can't take breaks whenever we please. Ourselves, we have the Counselor to answer to. We have to keep a tight schedule. Which is why we're wondering why you're back here when you knew we were coming. Why you'd want to make us wait."

"I'm sorry," said the baker in a choked voice. "My watch seems to have stopped. I didn't realize it was so late."

"You haven't lost track of anything besides the time, now, have you?" said the same Direction. "You weren't hoping we'd just move along and come back next week? Is that what we're going to have to tell the Counselor?"

"No, no, of course not! I'm not such a fool as that, and you know it. I have your envelope right here, with the full percentage, as always."

"And no report of anything unusual?"

"I would tell you if I'd seen anything. Come, I'll show you the ledger, and you can be on your way. I know you have your schedule to keep."

Five pairs of shoes stepped to the back door of the bakery. The door opened and closed, and Reuben was left alone with the nieces, who sat down again in dead silence. After a minute the younger niece began to speak, but the older one hushed her. The silence stretched on. Then the back door opened, and Reuben heard a single pair of shoes approaching. The baker sat heavily on his milk crate again.

Reuben crouched beneath the overturned sink, absently listening to the baker and his nieces pretend to enjoy their game, although the happy mood had clearly been destroyed. He felt the same about his own game, and no longer pretended to be a spy. He was only a boy, impolitely eavesdropping on a family conversation. The instant the card players withdrew, he wriggled through the rusted hole and walked stiffly out of the alley. For the rest of that afternoon he lay in his bed in the empty apartment, flipping through a comic book he didn't much like, wishing he didn't know what he knew.

Reuben never wandered through that alley again, and after he and his mom moved, he never returned to the bakery at all. She had once suggested that they go back, but he had said he didn't feel like walking so far, much less taking a bus. The truth was that the place made him sad now. He couldn't stand the thought of someone like the baker being forced to answer to those men, to hand his money over to them and pretend that everything was fine. Even the delicious smell of baked goods troubled Reuben now. He had come to think of it as the smell of fear.

Time to Plan, Time to Dream

Aﬞter Reuben watched the Directions make their rounds and move on to a different street, he went back inside, drinking in the cool air with relief, for it had grown quite hot on the roof. He scurried into the office with the key, scurried out empty-handed. On his way to the water fountain he changed directions twice to avoid bumping into kids from school. There were days when it was unavoidable, when someone would nod at him, and Reuben would nod back, averting his eyes. That was about as close as he had come to making friends.

Partly the problem was that he'd switched schools. At his new school everyone already knew each other, had known each other since the days of snacks and nap times. No one had made any real effort to get to know him. The friendly kids already had friends, and the shy kids kept to themselves.

Anyway, he knew he couldn't blame everything on the new school. Even at his old one, the closer he'd come to middle school, the more things had changed. His friends had stopped wanting to play hide-and-seek with him, and not just because he always won. The boys he'd known had become more interested in sports, and the girls, even more mysteriously, had begun to cluster in impenetrable groups, engaging in coded conversations. Somewhere along the way Reuben realized that he was still playing hide-and-seek, was in fact playing it all the time, but by himself, without a seeker. No one was seeking him.

Reuben gulped so much water from the fountain that he could hear it sloshing in his empty belly as he walked home. There was little shade on the street, only a few dilapidated awnings. He squinted in the fierce brightness and kept his head down, listening to his belly. He was caught off guard when someone spoke to him from the doorway of a hardware store.

"Young Pedley! What are you so mad about?"

Reuben started and turned toward the voice, which he instantly recognized as belonging to Officer Warren, one of the Lower Downs' beat cops—the only one who didn't make Reuben nervous. There he stood in the dusky doorway, his blue police uniform faded but carefully pressed, his boots polished, his smile as friendly as ever. Officer Warren was a tall man with walnut-brown skin, close-cropped hair just visible beneath his police cap, and eyes that always seemed to be studying Reuben, as if trying to figure out something about him. Yet he was so kind that in his case—a very rare case—Reuben didn't shrink from the attention.

"I'm not mad," Reuben said, returning the smile. He raised a hand to shield his eyes from the sun.

"That so?" Officer Warren cocked his head to the side. "Why were you frowning, then? Looked like you were furious at that sidewalk." He gestured toward the ground at Reuben's feet.

Reuben chuckled. He jerked his thumb up at the sun. "It's just bright."

"That it is," said the policeman, stepping out from beneath the store awning. He took a pair of sunglasses from his shirt pocket and put them on. "We need to get you a pair of these, young man. Then you don't have to go around looking like you hate the world. What do you think?"

Reuben nodded and said it was a good idea.

Officer Warren was studying him, as usual. "Tell you what. I need to get a new pair soon. When I do, I'll let you borrow these. Sound like a plan? Yeah? All right, then, it's a plan."

The sun glinted painfully off the policeman's well-polished badge, but Reuben kept looking at him. He liked Officer Warren immensely. Every time they spoke, Reuben wanted to become a police officer.

"Well," said Officer Warren with a sigh, "I suppose I'd better move along. I need to check in on some people." He laid a hand on Reuben's shoulder. "You say hi to your mom for me, okay? She doing fine? That's good, that's good. All right, now, take care, young Pedley." He moved off in the direction of the community center, whistling for the first few steps, then falling silent.

Reuben imagined the cheerful look fading from Officer Warren's face. No matter how friendly he was with everyone, the policeman generally looked very serious, even sad, when he was alone. Reuben had watched him often enough to know. It was for this reason that, after they parted, he always had second thoughts about becoming a policeman. For if you really wanted to be a good one, how could you ever be happy in New Umbra?

The fact that the police in New Umbra had to look the other

way whenever the Directions came around, that they could do their jobs only up to a point, beyond which they dared not go (for "Police officers have families to worry about, too," Reuben had once heard someone say), was surely enough to depress even the liveliest spirit. A few rare types like Officer Warren managed to be especially kind and helpful, but that didn't mean they were happy, and for every friendly officer in New Umbra, there was another who was bitter and defensive. Most just seemed beaten down, however, as if their job involved going outside every day to be kicked.

Reuben took one last look at Officer Warren, then turned and continued on his way home. Despite what he knew, his encounters with the young policeman always left him in a good mood, and this time was no exception. This time, in fact, he'd been in a brilliant mood to begin with. Indeed, he was perhaps the only person for blocks in every direction who at that moment was feeling hopeful.

At home Reuben had two bowls of cereal, eating sloppily, his eyes fixed on the lustrous contents of the wooden box, which he had opened and set before him on the kitchen table. He was in a terrific mood. He hardly knew what to do with his excitement, or for that matter the watch and key. He spent the entire afternoon doing little more than gazing at them. For variety he carried them with him into his bedroom, then into the bathroom, where he looked at them in the mirror, and then back out to the living room couch. He pondered, more or less continuously, what they might be worth. Hundreds of dollars? *Thousands* of dollars? More?

Reuben wondered, too, about P. William Light. Had he been a collector? Was he rich? He'd had this case custom-made for the watch and key, so he must have valued them greatly. But it wasn't P. William Light who'd hidden the box in the wall above the ledge, was it? Reuben didn't think so. The man who'd had his name engraved in this beautiful box would not be the one who had wrapped that bundle up in a plastic bread sack. No, that had been someone else, someone from a more recent time. P. William Light was from further back.

In any case, the bundle had been inside that hole in the wall for a long time. No one had come to claim it. To Reuben the laws of ownership were therefore perfectly clear: finders keepers. He had his doubts about whether his mom would agree with him, though, and there was also the sticky business of explaining how these things had come into his possession. And so, though part of him was bursting to share his discovery with her, a far greater part counseled secrecy. He knew, at the very least, that he would not be telling her the truth anytime soon. He needed time to think. Time to plan. Time to dream.

That night was one of his mom's evenings off from her cashier job in Ashton. As usual on such evenings, she came home from the market with a package of fish, even though she was sick to death of fish. Reuben still liked it, and she got an employee discount.

Reuben carried the package into the kitchen as his mom wearily dumped her handbag onto the floor and kicked off her shoes. She beckoned him back over. "Come and hug your mother, child," she said in a husky, pretending-to-be-formal tone, and Reuben laughed. Her clothes smelled of fish, but Reuben was used to it. He gave her a long hug. She was just tall enough, and he was just small enough, for her to rest her chin on the top of his head.

She scratched his back affectionately. "Your day okay?"

"Sure," Reuben murmured, closing his eyes. He loved having his back scratched.

"Anything exciting happen?"

Reuben shrugged. Having stared all afternoon at the watch and key, he was seeing them even now, burned in his mind's eye. He'd hidden everything in his closet mere minutes ago, behind a cardboard box of old toys.

His mom kissed his head and released him. Only then did she notice his bruises and scrapes. Reuben saw the anxiety blossom on her face, a rare sight. His mom had elfish features with, typically, an elfish look of mischief and confidence about them—except when she was worried about her son.

"Reuben," she gasped, "what on earth happened to you?"

"Oh! I'm fine," he said, trying to sound casual. As a matter of fact, his arms did ache and sting, but he wanted to put out this fire as quickly as possible. "I tripped down the steps at the library. I looked like an idiot, but I'm okay. They don't hurt that much."

His mom bent over to make a closer inspection. "We should put ointment on these scrapes." She searched his face, her hazel eyes narrowed with concern. "Were you embarrassed?"

"What? Oh. No. Actually, I don't think anyone saw me." Reuben wished he hadn't said that about looking like an idiot. She was already worried about his lack of friends.

"People fall sometimes, Reuben. It doesn't make them idiots."

"I know," he said, nodding. But he was thinking, *If you only knew.*

When his mom was satisfied that he truly was all right, she went to take a shower and change her clothes. Reuben darted to his closet, wanting to take another long look at the watch. But no sooner had he unbundled it than he heard his mom launch into a loud and elaborate complaint—evidently, the hot water was still out. The pipes in the wall fell silent. Reuben put the watch away with a sigh.

After he'd set the table, Reuben sat with his legs tucked under his chair to avoid tripping his mom as she moved about the tiny kitchen. Her hair, still pulled back in its workday ponytail, had gone frizzy in the heat. Now she stood over the stove with a spatula, reminiscing aloud about their old place.

"I mean, it wasn't the be-all and pinball," she said, flipping the fish in the pan, "but at least it had hot water. Plus the stove had decent burners."

"'The be-all and pinball'?"

She looked over her shoulder at him, feigning annoyance. "Yes, the be-all and pinball. It's an expression."

Reuben rolled his eyes. "Mom. No, it isn't."

"I'm pretty sure it is. What do you know? You're just a kid." She twisted her torso one way and then the other, stretching her back.

Reuben shook his head. His mom cracked him up. Other people called her *spunky*, a term she despised. *Spunky*, she said, was what you called people who acted like they were bigger and better than they were. "I don't think you should judge people by their size," she'd told him. "Or their quality, either, for that matter."

Reuben had asked how you were supposed to judge people if not by their quality.

"By their hair," his mom had replied. "Their hair or their clothes. And that's it."

Over dinner Reuben endured the usual questions about how he'd spent his day, answering with the usual stories—comic books at the library, a few games of P-I-G with the community center's underinflated basketballs, a conversation or two with kids he knew from school. As usual, his mom seemed slightly suspicious about the "talking with other kids" part. She didn't challenge it anymore—she'd figured out that it only made him feel bad, as if not having friends was somehow his fault, a flaw in his personality—but he could still see the doubt and concern in her eyes. It was a relief when dinner was over and the daily catch-up conversation officially ended.

"Well," his mom said when the dishes were all washed and put away. She swatted Reuben's shoulder with the drying cloth. "Dream house?"

"Absolutely," he said. "I'll get the graph paper."

"I'll grab the pencils."

Reuben went into his mom's bedroom and reached under her bed, pulling out a stack of papers. He glanced over two or three pages and called out, "Old one or new one?"

"Up to you!" his mom called back. She always did. Reuben always asked, and his mom always deferred to him. After the first few times, the exchange had become a sort of unacknowledged joke. Then, over the weeks and months, it had taken on an almost ceremonial quality. Strange as it might seem, it made Reuben feel closer to his mom, and he was sure she felt the same way, though they'd never discussed it. Talking about it might ruin the effect.

"New one," Reuben said to himself with satisfaction. "Definitely a new one today." He took a couple of blank sheets from the bottom of the stack and returned to the kitchen table. His mom sat sharpening pencils with a little plastic sharpener. She nodded approvingly when she saw the blank graph paper. That was part of the ritual, too: Reuben always made the right choice.

"I want this one to have a climbing wall," he said, settling into his chair.

"Nice." His mom handed him a pencil. "Will there be a safety harness?"

"No need. I'll have the wall come up out of the swimming pool."

"Clever," his mom said. She pursed her lips. "However . . . have you ever experienced a belly flop, Reuben?"

Reuben shook his head. He'd never actually been in a swimming pool.

"Well, I have. It feels like getting slapped by the *world*."

He snickered and bent over the graph paper. "I'll try to avoid belly flops, then. And you can use the safety harness. I'll put one in."

"Thank you." She tapped her pencil against her teeth, thinking. "I'll bet we could use it to move heavy things around, too."

Designing and modifying dream homes was their favorite thing to do together. It had started at their old place, when the rent went up and his mom began looking for a cheaper apartment. When Reuben had asked if in the new apartment he would still have his own room, his mom had made a big theatrical fuss about how spoiled he was, wanting his own room of all things, and didn't he realize that if he got his way, he would never stop wanting more? First two rooms, then a whole apartment, then a whole house? Somewhere in the midst of their pretend argument, Reuben had declared that he *did* want a whole house—a mansion, in fact—and he expected her to have it built for him.

"Fine!" she'd said, throwing her hands up in exasperated defeat. "Just show me what you want, Your Majesty!"

And so it had begun. The idea was that the mansion couldn't be built until Reuben had made up his mind, which was proving to be an exceedingly difficult task, given all the possibilities. It might take years, he'd admitted. In the meantime, it wasn't lost on him that his mom had spent weeks scouring the newspaper and making phone calls, trying to find a two-bedroom apartment they could afford.

Reuben worked awhile in silence. He usually did most of the drawing, with his mom offering input and colorful commentary.

They had dozens of designs. The homes always had secret passages, doors hidden behind bookcases, trapdoors beneath rugs, fireman's poles between floors. When situated in warmer climates, the houses typically had swimming pools with underwater entrances, high dives, and tunnel slides that descended from Reuben's upstairs bedroom. The designers' guiding principle was never to say no to any suggestion but rather to figure out how to make it work.

"There's always another way," his mom would say when Reuben got frustrated with some complication in his design. She also insisted on making even his most whimsical ideas practical in some way. His tunnel slide, for instance, might double as a laundry chute. The clothes hamper would be a sealed plastic container with handles that could be snagged with a shepherd's hook kept poolside—a brilliant touch, in Reuben's opinion, as it transformed a chore into a game.

They both liked to think they made a good team.

"Here's a question for you," Reuben said, after having worked quietly for a minute.

His mom gave a slight start. She'd begun to doze off. She blinked exaggeratedly and contorted her face, as if a bug had landed on her cheek. "What's that?" she asked, trying to focus. She cleared her throat. "What's the question?"

"I'll ask you later. You should go to bed, Mom."

She frowned and drew herself up straighter in her chair. "No way. I'm awake." She pointed at her ponytail. "Look, I haven't even let my hair out yet. What's your question?"

Reuben shrugged. "I was just going to ask what you would do if you got a lot of money."

"You mean other than build the mansion?"

"I mean really, if it really happened. Like, I don't know, if a mysterious stranger sent you a box full of cash. To thank you for a long-forgotten kindness or something."

"'A long-forgotten kindness,'" his mom repeated, the corners of her lips twitching. "That's a new one. Okay," she said, crossing her arms to indicate seriousness, "a box full of cash. What would I do? Well, I would probably quit one or both jobs, depending on how much money it was, and take classes at the city college."

Reuben looked at her askance. "Really?"

"Yes, really. That used to be the plan," she said. "When you were a baby, that was the plan."

Reuben knew what this meant, and he knew that it usually made his mom sad to think of that time when his father was still alive. But she wasn't showing it, and he knew she wouldn't.

Once, when he was much younger, he'd caught her crying and had gotten very upset himself. He'd pressed her to tell him what was wrong. Eventually she'd admitted that she missed his father, was sad that Reuben had never known him and even sadder that he hadn't been given the chance to know Reuben. "He would have loved you so much," she'd said, crying harder.

It had all been rather mysterious to Reuben, having been so young at the time, with no memory of his father. But he was distraught nonetheless, and his mom had struggled to pull herself together in order to comfort him. The next morning she was bright and smiling, offering no trace of the disconsolate person he'd glimpsed the night before. Studying his face, she told him that he didn't need to worry about her, that she'd simply been overtired.

Not once since then had she complained to Reuben about anything truly serious. Not once. But he'd never forgotten that night.

"Classes," he said, shaking his head. He flipped his pencil around to use the eraser. "If you got all that money, you would take *classes*."

His mom raised her chin defiantly. "That's right."

"You can't think of a more boring answer?" He bent over the paper and blew off the eraser rubble.

His mom covered a yawn. She shrugged. "After the classes I could get a better job. We'd have more money. I wouldn't ever fall behind on the rent."

"We're behind on the rent?" Reuben looked up.

His mom's expression grew suddenly alert. "No, I'm only saying that if I received this miraculous money, it would never happen. That's all. The bigger thing, the main thing, is that I could be home with you more."

Behind on the rent. So they were doing even worse than he'd thought. Pretending to let it go, Reuben pointed his pencil at her. "Okay, I grant you it's a good answer. It's still boring, but it's a good answer."

"Thank you. Of course, I'd also get a motorcycle."

He chuckled. "Is that right?"

"I'd let you ride in the sidecar. We could paint flames on the side."

"This motorcycle of yours has a sidecar?"

"Can you imagine *not* having one?"

"A sidecar," Reuben murmured, nodding thoughtfully. He bent over his drawing again. "Now you're talking sense."

Soon they had to call it a night. His mom could scarcely keep her eyes open, and Reuben wasn't doing much better. He was excited, though, and more than a little nervous. It had occurred to him what his next step with the watch would be, where he needed to take it and how to go about it, and as he got ready for bed, every yawn was followed by an involuntary tremor of anxious anticipation.

Today was a big day, he thought. But tomorrow would be bigger.

KNOWING OTHERWISE

Late the next morning Reuben got off the subway at Brighton Street station, holding tightly to the straps of his backpack. He'd waited until after rush hour to avoid being seen on the train by any neighbors who might happen to work here in Middleton, the neighborhood in which New Umbra's busiest retail district was located. Even so, the station platform was fairly crowded, and Reuben made his way up the steps into daylight along with a dozen other passengers. He stood with his backpack pressed to the station wall and looked up and down Brighton Street, where all the best shopping in New Umbra was done.

Everything about Brighton Street seemed to shine—the

shop windows, the chrome on the passing cars, the clicking shoes of well-dressed pedestrians. Reuben was aware that even run-down cities have their share of wealthy people, their lawyers and doctors and factory owners, and in New Umbra such people did their shopping on Brighton Street. Though certainly not as fancy as some places Reuben had seen in movies, it nonetheless made the Lower Downs seem all the more squalid in comparison. Most of the people who shopped here, Reuben supposed, wouldn't think his own neighborhood fit for human dwelling.

He was somewhat familiar with the area. He'd come here with his mom just a few months ago, when she'd needed new clothes for a job interview and had seen a big sale advertised. The outfit she bought, and the way she wore her hair with it, had made her look like someone who ran a company or worked with the mayor. On the morning of the interview, Reuben felt intimidated just eating breakfast with her. But she hadn't been hired for the position, because she had no experience.

"I thought I might win them over with my charm," she'd said. "Evidently, they were immune. They must have cast some protective spell." She spoke lightly, as if it were only one interview among many, and nothing to make a fuss about. She hadn't been to any since then, however, and Reuben understood that she'd been forced to rethink her prospects.

Still, it was thanks to that shopping trip that he knew of all the jewelry and antiques stores in the Brighton Street area. He and his mom had poked around a couple of the latter places, trying to decide what sort of exotic cabinets and canopy beds they would want in their dream home, and had stopped to look into the display windows of a number of jewelry stores. (His mom wouldn't enter those stores, though. She didn't care to be coldly ignored by employees who would judge her—correctly, alas—as a browser only. Definitely not a buyer.)

Reuben started walking, unsure where to begin. He thought

he might just go inside the first place he came to, which turned out to be a jewelry store about two blocks from the station. He stopped and stood outside the display window, trying to work up his nerve. Ten minutes later he was still standing there, seized by that familiar dread.

He frowned at his reflection in the glass. He needed to find out how much the watch was worth. He couldn't guess how bad it was that they were behind on their rent—his mom tried to keep these things from him—but he knew it was bad enough. She already worked two jobs. What else was she supposed to do? If Reuben could sell the watch for enough money to keep them afloat, or maybe even put them ahead...well, he had to do it. He knew he did, and this was the first step.

Behind him in the reflection Reuben could see the cars and pedestrians coming and going. No one was paying him any attention at all. The tall buildings echoed with the sounds of horns honking, bus doors squealing open and closed, a thousand shoes clattering and shuffling on sidewalks.

It was just discomfort, he told himself. That was all it was. He had to push through it. Reuben pivoted on his heels. A bell above the door jingled invitingly as he entered. Then the door closed behind him and all was quiet.

The jewelry store was a small place, a single room with half a dozen display cases and a well-dressed young man leaning back against a counter at the rear. The man's legs were crossed at the ankles, his weight on his heels. With his nice suit and glossy brown hair so artfully combed, he looked as if he might be posing for a fashion magazine. He was gazing at his fingernails with a bored expression that betrayed a faint amusement.

"Wondered if you were coming in," the man said without looking up. "You've been out there long enough. I thought maybe you were planning a stickup. How about it? You here to rob me?"

Reuben felt his cheeks reddening.

The man yawned and looked up. "Don't look so serious, kid, I'm only joking. So what is it, then? Looking to buy something for your sweetheart? Not sure we'd have anything in your range."

Reuben took the pouch from his backpack and stepped forward. "I wondered if you could tell me how much this is worth." He moved to set the pouch on one of the display cases.

The man straightened abruptly. "Don't put that there," he snapped. "I'll have to clean the case." He sighed and beckoned Reuben over to him. "Set it here on the counter. I'll have a look."

Reuben stood at the man's elbow as he drew the bundle from the pouch and unwrapped it. At the sight of the handsome wooden case, the man pursed his lips but said nothing. Then he opened it and looked at the pocket watch and winding key for several seconds without moving. Reuben glanced back and forth between the man's face and the beautiful objects in the box.

Presently the man took up the pocket watch and turned it in his hand. His thumbnail found the seam, and in a moment he had opened the cover to reveal the watch face. He made a small noise in his throat, the meaning of which was impossible to guess.

"You're wanting to sell this?" he asked, without taking his eyes from the watch.

"Not me," Reuben said. "And not today. It belongs to my uncle. He just told me to ask what it might be worth."

The man's eyes flicked in Reuben's direction. "Your uncle, eh? Why didn't he come himself?"

Reuben shrugged, trying to seem casual. "He's working."

"I see." The man carefully returned the watch to its velvet compartment and examined the key. "Well, you can tell your uncle that what we have here is a sort of novelty item. Not much market for it, I'm afraid. A watch that looks like a ball? Missing its minute hand? It's pretty, but then so is a lot of costume jewelry." He put back the key, then pointed to the inscription inside the lid of the case. "This is a problem, too. Nobody wants to buy a case with someone else's name inscribed in it. Honestly, this would be a hard sell, kid."

"But the—but isn't the metal alone—isn't—?" Reuben stammered. He jabbed his finger toward the case, in his agitation almost poking it. "But surely it's worth *something*, isn't it?"

"Hey, take it easy." The man bundled up the case and slid it back into its pouch. "Listen, kid, I don't even know what the key and the watch are made out of. Not gold, if that's what you were thinking. Not even copper." He shook his head, sliding the pouch in Reuben's direction, though only a few inches. "I can try to help you out, but I couldn't do much."

It took Reuben several uneasy moments to realize what was happening. The man wanted to buy the watch and the case. He wanted to pay less than they were worth, so he was making them out to be essentially worthless. Perhaps he didn't believe Reuben's story about an uncle.

Reuben slid the pouch closer to him, watching the man's eyes, which were watching the pouch. "Like I said, I'm not here to sell anything. My uncle—"

"I can give you a hundred dollars for the whole package," the man interrupted. "Case, watch, and key. Just to be nice. You seem like a good kid."

"Thanks," Reuben said, after a pause. A hundred dollars was more money than his mother made in a whole day of work. "I can't sell it, but I'll tell my uncle. Maybe he'll want to." He quickly took the pouch from the counter and stuffed it into his backpack.

"You know what?" said the man, taking hold of Reuben's arm. He smiled in a friendly way. "Now that I think of it, I'll bet I could find a collector who'd be interested. Wouldn't be easy, might take me a while, but I could probably make a sale eventually. Which changes matters a bit. A minute ago, I figured I was doing you a favor. Now I'm realizing I might be able to make some money at some point. Not a lot, mind you, but a little. So how about this? I'll give you *two* hundred dollars. Still probably more than any of it's worth, but I'll take the risk. What do you think? You can buy yourself a nice bike for that much and still have plenty left over. I noticed you were on foot."

The man was still gripping his arm.

"May I use your phone?" Reuben asked with difficulty. His mouth had gone pasty. "I could call my uncle at work."

Now the man laughed, letting go of Reuben to put his hands on his hips. "Are you really giving me more of this uncle business? Do we have to do that? Do I have to listen to you pretend to get permission on the phone? Can't I just give you the two hundred dollars and be done with it, no hard feelings for lying to me?"

Reuben looked down at his feet.

"Oh, come on," the man said teasingly. He was beaming now, excited. "How about I show you what two hundred dollars looks like, and then you can decide whether or not you need to use my phone." He tousled Reuben's hair and went behind the counter, where he stooped to take a handful of bills from a low drawer.

When the doorbell tinkled, he straightened with a start, as if he'd been caught committing a crime. But there was no one entering the store. In fact, there was no one in the store at all, for Reuben was already out on the sidewalk and fast disappearing.

⁓

After this encounter with the crafty man at the jewelry store, Reuben took a long walk down Brighton Street to settle his jangling nerves. He would never forget the greedy gleam in the man's eyes. What if he had simply taken the watch? What could Reuben have done about it? He needed to be craftier himself, he realized. The watch was obviously valuable—a fact that made it hard for him to calm down—and he was on his own.

He still had no idea of the watch's true value, either. He would need to visit other places, and if they were anything like the last one, he might have to visit several before he received an honest assessment, to say nothing of the risk of losing the watch altogether. He decided that from then on he would always make sure other customers were present—and he would never allow anyone else to handle the watch.

And so, stoking up his courage, Reuben began again, stopping in at several of the jewelry stores and antiques dealers along Brighton Street. In some places he was treated with suspicion; in others, with courtesy or condescension. In one he got the impression that his life might be worth less than the watch in his hands, and from this place he made a hasty exit, followed by a lot of deep breaths. He needed a new plan.

Glancing around to make sure he wasn't being followed, Reuben veered away from the bustle of Brighton Street. On the adjacent block the storefronts lost their gleaming façades, and within a couple of blocks they fell away altogether. He came to a small park. It was rather a sad park—a neglected patch of grass, a nonfunctioning fountain, and a handful of plane trees, one of which overhung a bench. But it was quiet and empty and therefore perfect. Reuben settled onto the bench in the shade.

He unzipped his backpack, unbundled the wooden case. He set it on his lap and stared probingly at it, as if it might contain the answer to his most pressing question: What now? He was just a kid. A kid couldn't expect to get a fair price for some rare object he'd found; he'd learned that much, anyway. He couldn't even find anyone to tell him the truth about its value.

Reuben opened the case, hefted the glossy orb of the watch,

and saw in its strange coppery metal his own distorted face gazing back at him. His reflection made him look goofy, he thought. But was it any wonder his face showed such wide-eyed admiration? He'd spent the morning watching other people tremble at the sight of this beautiful object in his hand.

He was about to return the watch to its case when the door of a nearby building banged open and four men strode out. They were in mid-conversation, arguing in loud voices. Reuben had never seen them before. Yet he knew at once that they were Directions. One man in front, two walking abreast just behind him, the fourth bringing up the rear. Eyes everywhere.

Reuben sat like a statue, watching them. It hadn't occurred to him that he could be caught off guard like this. It should have— the Directions in this neighborhood were unfamiliar to him, their habits unknown. Yet here he was, sitting like the worst of fools with this exquisite pocket watch in his hand, right out in the open.

He knew they would take it. He hadn't the least doubt. Maybe if there were witnesses around, the men would show restraint. Maybe. But there were no witnesses; nor did Reuben have a good explanation for how he'd come to possess the watch. Even if he had one, it probably wouldn't matter. A watch like this? The Directions would take it. They did not answer to the law.

Reuben followed their movement with his eyes. So far no one had seen him. The men were skirting the park, keeping to the sidewalk some twenty paces to his right. They were arguing about something to do with the Counselor, some urgent inquiry making them delay their lunch. Maybe in their hurry they would be less careful, Reuben hoped, less thorough in their observation. He fought a desperate urge to hide the watch. He knew better than to move. Movement was the enemy. He imagined himself to be part of the bench, part of the shadows.

The gaze of the leftmost man, sweeping across the park,

drifted past Reuben. He looked elsewhere, not having noticed the boy on the bench. The Directions progressed farther along the sidewalk, and then the one in the rear glanced back over his shoulder. He, too, failed to spot Reuben sitting in the shadow of the plane tree. Or perhaps he did notice something without quite realizing it, and the afterimage gnawed at his brain, for when some moments later the man dutifully looked back again, his eyes went straight to that bench.

The bench was empty, however. Nor was Reuben anywhere to be seen. He stood on the far side of the plane tree, his back pressed to the peeling bark, listening to the diminishing voices, the diminishing footsteps, and finally the blessed quiet.

He was holding the open case in one hand, his backpack in the other. He'd made the decisions without thinking: put the watch into the case, grab the backpack, move around the tree. It had taken him three seconds.

Reuben slowly felt the tension leaving his body. Even his jaw hurt—he'd been clenching his teeth. He opened and closed his mouth a few times like a gasping fish. He retrieved the canvas wrapping and the pouch, which he'd abandoned on the bench. They had gone unnoticed or else had been deemed insignificant, rubbish left over from a sad little picnic.

Shaking his head at the close call, Reuben bundled everything up. He should go home and rethink his plan, he thought. His dream of selling the watch for a grand sum might have disappeared, just like that. He put on the backpack, relieved to know that now he just looked like a random kid again, nothing special or even interesting about him.

He set out for the subway station, taking the backstreets, knowing otherwise.

Hidden Movements

On his way to the subway station, using the less-traveled sidewalks south of Brighton Street, Reuben noticed a sign in a display window that read *Clocks and Watches—Sales and Repairs.* He stopped walking and stared at it. Now *this* was the kind of place he should visit, he thought—not some snooty store on Brighton Street but a simple little out-of-the-way shop. *Repairs* meant he would find an expert here, rather than some crafty sales broker with both eyes fixed on the day's profit. Maybe that close call with the Directions had actually been a stroke of good luck. If not for them, he would have taken a different route and never have seen this sign. Reuben peered in through the window.

The shop was small and looked empty. No one sat behind the counter, but a sign on the door had been flipped around to say *Open*. He took his usual steadying breath and went inside.

A bell chimed as he entered. Then all was quiet, or what passed for quiet in a room whose walls were lined with shelves of clocks and watches, most of them ticking, ticking, ticking. He imagined an enormous army of insects marching through the room.

Behind the counter, a door opened. An elderly woman in a light yellow summer cardigan appeared, holding a steaming teacup. She set the teacup on the counter and reached for her glasses, which were hidden in the mass of curly gray hair on her head. She blinked a few times, then fixed her gaze on Reuben. She had watery cornflower-blue eyes.

"Yes?" she said simply.

"Um, hello," Reuben said, taking the pouch from his backpack. He gestured at the counter. "May I set this down? I'd like to ask your opinion on something."

With a little frown, the woman moved her teacup to the far end of the counter, careful not to spill it. "What is your name?" she asked. She spoke with an accent Reuben could not identify. His first thought was Swiss, but that was probably because he'd read that the Swiss were known for making clocks. It might just as easily have been Italian or Hungarian and he couldn't have told the difference.

Reuben gave her his name—his first name—and said, "It's about an old pocket watch."

"And this is what is in your wallet?" the woman asked, pointing to the pouch. Her precisely manicured fingernails glistened with transparent polish. "This pocket watch? Yes, you may set it then on the counter."

Reuben removed the case from the pouch, unwrapped it, and opened it to reveal its contents. Watching the woman's face for signs of the admiration he'd grown accustomed to, he was curious to note instead a look of mild alarm. But perhaps that was how she expressed admiration.

"My uncle asked me to find out what I could about it," he said. "How old it is, what it might be worth, that sort of thing. He found it in his attic with some other old stuff."

The woman gave no reply to this. Lifting a hand to hold her glasses in place, she bent to peer more closely at the case and its contents. She made no move to touch them, though, and presently she straightened and indicated with a subtle gesture that Reuben could put the things away.

Feeling somehow as if he'd been unfairly dismissed, Reuben did as he was directed. The woman, meanwhile, pushed her glasses back into her hair and squinted at the opposite wall. Reuben followed her gaze and noticed, for the first time, that every clock in the shop was set to exactly the same hour and minute. That must take some doing.

"Would you permit me to examine this pocket watch more closely?" the woman asked.

Confused, Reuben said, "You want me to take it out again?"

"Soon, yes. Not now. First I must meet briefly with the four men—you know whom I mean, the four men who go about? Looking always to different corners?"

"Oh. Yes," Reuben said, suddenly uneasy. "The Directions."

"If this is what you like to call them, yes," the woman said, nodding. "Probably it is better. I use a less polite name, but that is not for you. Yes, I must meet with these Directions, Reuben. They will be here in two minutes, or no longer than three. It is the only thing that I respect about these men, that in this way they are like clockwork." She frowned. "But this is rude of me. Perhaps your uncle is one of them."

"No, he isn't," said Reuben, smiling to reassure her. He was beginning to like this woman. "Shall I come back later, then?"

"You may if you like." The woman pointed at the door behind the counter. "Or, if you wish, you may wait in my rooms. I ask only that while the men are here, you do not enter."

Reuben chose to wait in the rooms behind the door. They turned out to be the woman's home: a sitting room, a workshop, her bedroom, a kitchen, and a bathroom—all of them tiny, all in perfect order and perfectly clean. Mrs. Genevieve, as she told him to call her, suggested he make himself comfortable on her sitting room sofa. But no sooner had she returned to the front than Reuben heard the chime of the doorbell, and without hesitation he jumped up from the sofa and put his ear to the shop door.

Mrs. Genevieve's greeting, though muted, was clear enough. "Good afternoon," she said, and that was all.

"Same to you," said a man's voice, gruff but casual. "What's the news?"

"No news," Mrs. Genevieve replied, "unless one of you wishes to purchase something. That would be news indeed."

"You've made that joke before. It still isn't funny." Reuben heard floorboards creaking. He imagined four large men nosing about the little shop, most likely the same men he'd seen from the park bench. "So do you have our—? Oh, good, you do."

Reuben heard two brisk, businesslike taps. (He pictured the man receiving an envelope full of money, tapping it a couple of times on the counter, and sliding it into a pocket.)

"And just a glance at your books...Very good. Anything unusual to report, Mrs. Genevieve? Right. A shrug. That's all we ever get from you. Fine, you can get back to your tea. Though I don't know how you can drink that stuff—tastes like dirty water to me. Only coffee for yours truly, and gallons of it. Fact, that reminds me: I need to use your bathroom."

Reuben recoiled from the door but could still hear Mrs. Genevieve telling the man that this wouldn't be possible. "It is out of order," she said, which was surely a lie. She hadn't mentioned any such thing to Reuben.

"Is that so?" the man retorted roughly. "And you never have any need of a bathroom yourself? Maybe I should have a look at it for you."

Reuben snatched up his backpack and cast about the sitting room for a good place to hide. There was none. He could hear a tone of protest in Mrs. Genevieve's voice, though he could no longer make out her words over the pounding in his ears. The man responded in a tone of rising anger.

Then Reuben had an idea and hurried into the bathroom. Moving fast, he removed the porcelain top from the toilet tank and lowered it noiselessly onto the bath rug. He reached inside the tank and jerked loose the flush chain just as he heard the shop door open.

Reuben stepped into the bathtub, retreating behind the bath curtain until the backs of his knees pressed against the faucet handles. He hugged his backpack and held his breath. The man's heavy footsteps came in from the sitting room.

The man grunted, then muttered, "Well, what do you know?" Reuben heard him jiggle the lever, cursing under his breath. The footsteps clumped out of the bathroom again. A moment later the shop door closed.

Reuben sat down on the edge of the tub. He felt a little faint, perhaps from holding his breath while his heart was pounding away. He put his head between his knees and breathed slowly until he felt better. When he heard the chime of the doorbell—that would be the Directions leaving the shop—he went back into Mrs. Genevieve's sitting room and took a seat on the miniature sofa to wait.

Mrs. Genevieve came in, closing the door behind her. She looked at him with a puzzled expression. "You heard this that I said about the toilet?"

Reuben nodded.

"And you thought to save me by breaking the chain? That was a quick idea. Almost too quick. I was making ready a different explanation when he returned and told me it was only a broken chain. He said, 'Surely someone like you must be able to repair a flush chain? Or is this more difficult than watchmaking?'"

"I don't blame you for not wanting to let him in," Reuben observed. "He was rude."

"He is the worst of them," Mrs. Genevieve said. "We dislike each other, he and I. But how is it that he did not see you?"

"I hid behind the bath curtain."

She frowned. "Very risky."

"I'm a good hider," Reuben said, somewhat defensively.

"So it would seem," said Mrs. Genevieve, and her eyes betrayed a twinkle of amusement. "But this was a risky act nonetheless, and I thank you for it, Reuben. Now then, let us examine this pocket watch of yours," she added, and without waiting for a reply, she opened the door to her workshop and went in.

The workshop was essentially a very deep closet. Its walls were taken up with cubbies and shelves, all perfectly organized, and dozens of tiny labeled drawers. On a narrow counter that ran the length of the left wall lay a single, partially disassembled watch under what resembled a transparent cake cover.

"Set it over there," said Mrs. Genevieve, indicating a clear stretch of counter. She laid out a few small tools and a soft cloth, then tugged on a pair of white gloves. "You may stand nearby, but you must keep your shadow away, okay?"

Mrs. Genevieve settled herself onto a stool. With careful, meticulous fingers, like a gentle nurse removing a bandage from a wound, the watchmaker took the case from the pouch and unbundled it. She studied the case a moment, then opened it. Her expression upon seeing the pocket watch this time was not one of alarm but something else altogether. Her eyes grew heavy-lidded; her head swayed ever so slightly, as if to music. Reuben was reminded of when he and his mom used to go to the bakery—of the look on his mom's face when she first smelled the delicious aromas.

"It is beautiful," Mrs. Genevieve said softly, and for some time she sat gazing at the watch and key as if that were all she ever intended to do. "I do not know this metal," she murmured presently.

"Me either," Reuben said. "Do you know what the case is made of?"

"The case?" Mrs. Genevieve said, pointing to the pocket watch still resting snugly in its compartment. "It clearly is the same metal as the key. Oh! But you mean this box—which of course is wood—I do not know what kind. " She pointed again to the watch's gleaming coppery sphere. "This exterior of the watch, you see, we call also its case—the watchcase. And the key and the watchcase are of metals I have never seen, though I know metals very well. It is...surprising."

Mrs. Genevieve returned the key to its compartment and lifted out the pocket watch. She turned it slowly in her hands until it had made a full revolution. Then she opened it, and with a quick intake of breath, she glanced at Reuben. "It seems impossible," she whispered, "the condition of this piece. How can it be so perfect?"

"It's pretty great," Reuben agreed with a grin. "The minute hand broke off, I guess, so maybe not perfect, but still—"

"It never *had* a minute hand!" Mrs. Genevieve snipped. "The pocket watches of this time told only the hour!" She pushed her glasses up into her wiry gray hair, then reached for her watch-maker's loupe and put it to her eye. She appeared to be scowling furiously. Reuben, abashed, hoped this was just how she looked when she peered through her loupe, which she held in place using the muscles around her eye.

"So no minute hands," he ventured after a pause. "That seems odd."

Mrs. Genevieve had set the pocket watch onto the cloth, still open to reveal its dial, and was turning it slightly this way and that. She let Reuben's comment go unanswered for a long minute before interrupting her examination to look at him. To his relief, when she removed the loupe from her eye, her scowl seemed to fade.

"In the early days of clocks there was no use for a minute hand," Mrs. Genevieve said, clearly making an effort to sound patient, and almost succeeding. "Such precision was impossible at the time. Even with the hour hand there was much inaccuracy."

"The early days," Reuben repeated. "When are we talking about, exactly?"

Mrs. Genevieve shrugged her thin shoulders. "There is no 'exactly.' But I would tell you that this pocket watch was made in the late fifteenth or early sixteenth century. It is for this reason that I am so amazed at its fine condition."

"Because it's five hundred years old!" Reuben cried, and Mrs. Genevieve flinched. "Sorry," he said, lowering his voice, "I guess I'm just excited. I never thought it could be that old. How can you tell? Because of the minute hand?"

"This, yes, and also the shape," said Mrs. Genevieve. "Such watches of this time, they were called 'clock watches'—not 'pocket watches,' do you see, for they were not always kept in pockets. They were a fine decoration, to be worn by wealthy persons about the neck or hung from a chain, though sometimes, yes, they were carried in pockets. And many were in the shapes of little barrels, or sometimes of eggs, or of spheres like this one." She shook her head wonderingly. "But I have never seen another such as this."

Mrs. Genevieve returned then to her examination of the

60

watch, and Reuben excitedly pondered the significance of her words. The fact that she was so struck by the piece's beauty and rarity suggested that he might truly be in possession of an extraordinarily valuable artifact—perhaps even a priceless one. Mrs. Genevieve was an expert, and she seemed to think the watch was one of a kind. Was it possible, he wondered, that he was on the verge of becoming rich? He was suddenly finding it difficult to hold still.

At last Mrs. Genevieve put down her loupe. She turned to him with a troubled expression. "Very well," she said, "I know some things, and some things I do not know, and both for the same reason." She pursed her lips, thinking, then went on. "I cannot examine the movement of this watch—the movement is what we call its inner workings, its mechanism, do you see?— because there seems to be no way to open the watchcase. There are no visible screws and no visible seam. Because I cannot examine the movement, I cannot determine its condition, or whether the movement is unusual, different from those of other clock watches. But because of this I know also that the watchmaker was a genius. No ordinary craftsman, no, not even a remarkable one, could have fashioned such a watch. Before now I would have said this was not possible. And yet here before our eyes is proof of its possibility."

"Why does it seem impossible to make a watch that you can't open?" said Reuben, very softly, as if he were in a library or church.

"A clock, Reuben, is a device. And devices are constructed of different parts, yes? Parts which must be joined together. How then can we not see, even with a magnifying loupe, these places where the parts are joined? A clock is not a ceramic bowl. It must have seams, screws, joining pieces of some kind. Yet this one does not. " Mrs. Genevieve clicked her teeth together, as if biting the air. "I dislike mysteries, Reuben."

Reuben was fascinated. "So do you think it doesn't work anymore? Can we wind it up and see? That's what the key is for, right? To wind it up?"

Mrs. Genevieve nodded. "And possibly also to set the time. If one cannot open the watch to do so, the key must be the answer. You have never used this key?" When Reuben confirmed that he had not, the watchmaker considered before saying, "I am afraid that the mechanism may be very delicate and easily broken. I cannot take the responsibility. This you may tell your uncle. If he wishes me to, I will explain my idea to him. He can choose then to wind the watch or not, as he wishes."

"My uncle's really busy," Reuben said. "Why don't you explain it to me, and then I can show him?"

Mrs. Genevieve gave him a shrewd assessing look. "You intend to wind the watch yourself."

"You're right," Reuben admitted, after a pause. He figured he had little to lose. "I'm going to try it either way. But if you tell me how, maybe I'll do a better job of it. And I'll take full responsibility if I break it."

Though Mrs. Genevieve made a show of disapproval, it was plain to Reuben that she was eager for him to try it. She wanted to see what would happen as much as he did. And sure enough, after much frowning and muttering, she relented.

"Very well," she said, and after bidding him to put on a pair of gloves like hers, she took up the key to demonstrate. "My idea," she said, "is that this exterior"—she circled a finger around the small, star-shaped end of the key—"will slide very tightly into a place where it may be turned, and by its turning you will move the hour hand, do you see?"

Reuben nodded.

"Good. And my idea also is that this *interior*"—Mrs. Genevieve turned the key to show how the star-shaped end was actually hollow, its interior worked with irregular grooves, something to which Reuben had given little thought—"if you slide the blade of the key deeper into the watch, this empty place will fit precisely over a very small nut or bolt, do you see? And then you may turn it—"

"Like a socket wrench!" interjected Reuben. "That's clever. Okay, I'm ready to try it." He took the key from her.

"You must be gentle," Mrs. Genevieve warned him. "Very slow and careful, yes?"

"Yes," said Reuben, already fitting the end of the key into the matching hole in the center of the watch dial. It took him a couple of tries—his excitement was causing his fingers to tremble—but then he had it, and with the slightest pressure he could manage, he slid the blade of the key down into the hidden shaft. It went easily, without the least bit of resistance, for about an inch. Then Reuben sensed a subtle change, as if the shaft had narrowed. His eyes swiveled to Mrs. Genevieve, who was biting a knuckle and frowning at his fingers with great intensity. "I think I'm to the first place," he said.

Mrs. Genevieve nodded. "Try then to turn the key. But do not force it! If it does not wish to turn, you will know. You must listen to your fingers."

Holding the watch steady with his left hand, Reuben began to turn the key with his right. There was a faint—a very faint—feeling of friction, but the key turned, and as it turned, so too did the hour hand, moving past the twelve o'clock position and on to one o'clock before he stopped and looked excitedly at Mrs. Genevieve. "It works!"

"I see this," Mrs. Genevieve said, and that was all, but with one gloved hand she touched Reuben lightly, briefly on the shoulder. Whether she intended this as a gesture of approval or of shared excitement, Reuben couldn't say. Perhaps it was both.

"Okay," he said. "Now for the socket wrench."

Holding his breath, Reuben applied pressure to the key again.

It slid smoothly but with a feeling of slight resistance, like a book being squeezed into a tight space on a bookshelf, until it had been inserted all the way up to the bow. This time Reuben didn't hesitate. He had developed an unshakable feeling that the watch was in perfect condition, that there was nothing more fragile about it than a brand-new watch fresh off a watchmaker's bench. Thus when he began to crank the key and heard the familiar ratcheting sound (anyone who has ever wound an alarm clock or wristwatch would recognize it, as well as the vibrating sensation in the fingers), he was not at all concerned that he was breaking anything. He knew he was merely winding up the mainspring, just as he knew to stop when the winding grew difficult.

Feeling as full of hope and wonder as a child listening for the ocean in a seashell, Reuben put the watch to his ear. But if it was ticking, he couldn't hear it.

Mrs. Genevieve whispered, "I think perhaps the spring will not unwind until you withdraw the key, at least to the setting position."

Reuben did as she suggested, pulling up on the key until it stopped, then tweaking its angle until he felt it slide snugly up into the setting position. He raised the watch to his ear again, and this time he heard it: a tiny, tinny ticking. With wide eyes he looked at Mrs. Genevieve. She was gazing eagerly back at him, eyebrows raised in expectation. "Would you like to hear it?" he asked.

"Please," whispered Mrs. Genevieve, and stooping forward, she turned her ear to him.

Reuben carefully extended the watch until it was almost touching her earlobe. He saw her check her breath, her slender frame rigid with attention. She broke into a delighted grin. "I hear it!"

"So it's perfect," Reuben murmured, his heart beating double time. His mind raced ahead to a future he had scarcely dared to hope for. His mom could quit her jobs, take classes—whatever she liked! They could do anything! Go anywhere! They might even actually build a dream house! He had only to figure out how to sell it, and he felt sure the watchmaker would help him with that.

"A watch like this must be worth a fortune, right, Mrs. Genevieve?" Reuben asked eagerly. "I mean, how exactly do we decide how much it's worth?"

Mrs. Genevieve, who had been listening to the watch with such obvious pleasure, slowly straightened, her smile fading. "Oh, such matters are determined by dealers and collectors," she murmured with a distracted air, and to Reuben's surprise her expression grew quite troubled. "But, you see . . ." She winced slightly, as if suffering from a toothache, then glared at the watch in his hand as if it were the cause. "Reuben, I am sorry, but I must tell you something you will not wish to hear."

Reuben stared at her, suddenly overcome with dread.

"This . . . watch," Mrs. Genevieve said in a heavy voice. "Certain persons have been looking for it for a very, very long time."

Reuben was dumbstruck. He took a step back, gripping the watch tightly, as if some unseen person were already trying to pull it from his grasp—as if Mrs. Genevieve herself might try to do so. But the watchmaker was only looking at him sadly.

"I didn't at first wish to tell you," she said. "I did not wish to frighten you. And, yes, it is true, I had a desire to examine this watch, which I had not believed I would ever see with my own eyes, if indeed it existed."

Scarcely any of her words registered but one. "What are you talking about?" Reuben whispered. "Why would I be *frightened*?"

"Because, child, one of the persons seeking this watch"— Mrs. Genevieve closed her eyes and shook her head regretfully— "is the one known as The Smoke."

MOMENT OF TRUTH

*T*he Smoke?"

Mrs. Genevieve removed her glasses and, closing her eyes, pinched the bridge of her nose. "Surely you know whom I mean. Perhaps you call him by a different name."

"I know who he is," Reuben muttered, though this was only partly true, for no one truly knew who The Smoke was. No one but The Smoke's representative, the Counselor, had ever even seen him—or anyone who *had* seen him hadn't lived to tell about it. But everyone knew that The Smoke secretly ruled New Umbra. It was considered a secret only because his authority was unofficial and because no one dared speak of it.

Reuben sat down on the floor. He was feeling faint again. Worse than that, actually—he felt the way he had when he was high above that narrow alley, when he'd thought he would fall. A sickening sort of fear, a rising panic. He drew up his knees and pressed his forehead against them.

"I am sorry," said Mrs. Genevieve. "But you should not be frightened, Reuben. All can still be well." Though she tried to sound comforting, she might as well have been saying *The Smoke wants the watch, The Smoke wants the watch, The Smoke wants the watch*—for that was all Reuben could think.

He looked miserably up at her. "Who exactly is he, anyway? Do you know?"

"Ah!" The watchmaker flapped her hand as if at a bothersome gnat. "Who is to say? Who knows that he is even a man? I have heard some say that he is a monster!" She rolled her eyes contemptuously. "A monster who wishes to possess valuable things. He would not be the first."

"But how do you know he's looking for the watch?"

Mrs. Genevieve frowned. "How do you think? He communicated his wishes to Cassius Faug—" She paused. "Do you know of this Mr. Faug?"

Reuben nodded grimly. He had heard the man's name mentioned only rarely, but he remembered it. "The Counselor."

"Yes, this is the one," said Mrs. Genevieve. "And naturally the Counselor has instructed his men—the Directions, you understand?—always to be 'on the lookout' for such a watch. They in turn ordered me long ago to inform them if such a watch appears. This is true for the other watchmakers in the city as well. There are but a few of us anymore."

"I just can't believe it," Reuben muttered. "How does he even *know* about it?"

Mrs. Genevieve shook her head. "It is said that he knows things that no one else can know. But in this instance he is not the only one," she said, rising from her stool. "Wait here a moment."

As soon as he was alone, Reuben felt his eyes stinging. He buried his head against his knees again. Not two minutes earlier he'd been so excited. His hopes had been so high. He was surprised by how much it hurt to lose them. Mrs. Genevieve didn't want him to be frightened of The Smoke, but Reuben hadn't even thought about his own safety. It was the simple fact of losing the watch that upset him, the watch and what it represented.

For of course he would lose it. Mrs. Genevieve wouldn't dare help him sell it, and even though it was Reuben who had found the watch—a discovery that had seemed so fated—he couldn't even *keep* it. Because what sort of fool would hold on to something he knew The Smoke wanted?

He understood now the watchmaker's look of alarm when she'd first seen the watch. She'd recognized right away that it was the one sought by The Smoke. Yet she hadn't mentioned it to the Directions when they came to her shop, and she'd kept Reuben's presence in her home a secret. She'd even *lied* to them. That could have been disastrous, and it very nearly was. Reuben considered this. Mrs. Genevieve had taken a big risk, either for the watch's sake or for his sake. Possibly both. He had a feeling it was both.

Presently Mrs. Genevieve returned holding a newspaper. She spread it out on the counter. "This advertisement in the classified section," she said as Reuben rose to join her, "it appears in all the papers every day and has done this for as long as I can remember. You see, it is not only The Smoke who seeks the watch."

Mrs. Genevieve had penciled a circle around the advertisement:

LOST: ANTIQUE POCKET WATCH AND WINDING KEY FASHIONED OF UNUSUAL, COPPER-LIKE METAL. WATCH IS SPHERICAL IN SHAPE; IVORY DIAL HAS NO MINUTE HAND. LARGE REWARD OFFERED.

"A large reward!" Reuben said with a rush of hope.

"Oh yes," said Mrs. Genevieve. "Such a clock watch would merit a reward, but who is this who offers it? There is no name or address listed, only a telephone number. Is this a person to be trusted?"

Reuben frowned. "Well, they must have a lot of money if they can afford to take out all these advertisements. I don't see why they wouldn't be able to pay a reward."

"There must be a great deal of money indeed," said Mrs. Genevieve, "or a great deal of power. These advertisements have run for many years. But do you see? Why does this person want the watch so badly? Why does The Smoke? How do they know of it? And do you really wish to become involved with either? I would not advise this."

Reuben felt himself getting irritated. "So what, then? What am I supposed to do?"

Mrs. Genevieve studied him. "Is this true what you say about your uncle?" Reuben hesitated, which was all it took. "I cannot tell you then what is best to do," she said, sighing. "You could perhaps return the watch to where you found it—"

Reuben thought of the ledge above the alley and uttered a low, bitter laugh. "I really can't do that, Mrs. Genevieve."

"In this case," the watchmaker continued (and not a little sternly, for having been interrupted), "it may after all best for me to turn over the watch to The Smoke. I have been told that he will pay handsomely for it as well."

Reuben thought about this. "Do you think he actually would?"

"Perhaps," said Mrs. Genevieve, though she looked dubious. "And if he does, and if his men do not privately decide to distribute this reward among themselves, then I will give it to you."

This course of action did not seem the least bit promising to Reuben. The Smoke had no need to keep his word to anyone, let alone some elderly watchmaker in her quiet little shop. Regardless, Reuben thanked her for the offer and said he would consider it.

Mrs. Genevieve looked at him, clearly troubled. But after a pause she said, "Of course." Then she said she must reopen the shop, which she had closed for the sake of their private discussion. "Perhaps," she added with a melancholy smile, "we may first listen one last time to the ticking."

Reuben agreed. But when he held the watch to his ear, he heard nothing. "It stopped."

"No!" Mrs. Genevieve breathed, and muttered something in a language Reuben didn't know. "The spring—!"

Reuben was already sliding the key back into its winding position. "It makes no sense," he said. "Why would it have broken when it was working so perfectly?" He turned the key. Everything was the same as before—the raspy ratcheting sound, the familiar feeling in his fingers. He cranked the key until the watch was fully wound, then withdrew the key and held the watch to his ear. It was ticking again.

Mrs. Genevieve listened to it herself, her face darkening. She looked extremely displeased now. "But if the spring is intact," she muttered, "why must it be wound again so soon? And why"—her voice rose as she held the watch out at arm's length to stare at the dial—"why has the hour hand not moved at all? Not one millimeter, Reuben!"

Reuben, who had been very relieved to find that the spring was not broken, needed a moment to absorb Mrs. Genevieve's complaints. "Well, it's an ancient watch," he said resignedly. "Maybe it just doesn't work properly anymore."

"No!" Mrs. Genevieve snapped. She shook her head. "You do not know watches, Reuben. This is not understandable behavior! It's as if this watch has been fashioned merely as a showpiece—a novelty, do you see? An exquisite watch, a masterpiece, but one

*He cranked the key until the watch was fully wound,
then withdrew the key and held the watch to his ear.*

which does not tell time! But why? This watchmaker of such genius cannot make his watch to tell time? It is preposterous!"

"You're right, it's weird," Reuben agreed, though he didn't understand why Mrs. Genevieve seemed so angry. "Still, it's kind of amazing, isn't it? The fact that you can still wind it up, even if it doesn't do what it's supposed to?"

"But this is what I hate! This mystery!" Mrs. Genevieve moaned. She seemed truly distressed. "Reuben, still do you not see? What if this watch *is* doing what it's supposed to do?" She looked up at the ceiling and shook her gloved fists theatrically. "And we do not know what that thing is!"

⁓

So the watch had a secret.

All the way home Reuben could think of nothing else. Except, of course, The Smoke, thoughts of whom kept him glancing over his shoulder and quickening his pace. He took the stairs in his building at such a rate he was left gasping for breath as he staggered down the hallway to his apartment. Never had its musty, dusky interior felt so welcoming, nor had he ever been so quick to lock the door behind him.

After wolfing down a hastily constructed sandwich and gulping milk from the carton (it was well past lunchtime now), Reuben hurried into his bedroom and opened his backpack. He was going to figure this out.

In moments he had the watch in his hand and an eye on his alarm clock. He wound up the watch. After fifteen minutes, it stopped ticking. He tried again, with the same result. A watch that had to be wound every fifteen minutes was ridiculously impractical, so of course Mrs. Genevieve was right. The spring must have been designed for some other purpose—a secret purpose. But what? And did The Smoke know the secret? Was that why he wanted the watch so badly?

Reuben felt a sudden need to double-check the lock on the apartment door.

He came back and dragged the old cardboard box of toys from his closet. He hadn't opened it even once since they moved here, but he was pretty sure he still had a windup toy robot. Sure enough, he found it at the bottom of the box, among a jumble of action figures. He wound it up and set it on the threadbare carpet. The robot managed a couple of awkward steps with its block-like feet before toppling over. Reuben remembered why he'd never been fond of this toy. It always ended up that way, with its feet churning uselessly, like a beetle on its back.

His plan had been to pry it open and study how its spring mechanism worked. But as he dug through the box looking for something to use as a prying tool, he came upon an old jack-in-the-box and had a sudden inspiration. Mrs. Genevieve had seen no way to open the watch from the outside, but what if something made it open up from the *inside*? What if it was like the jack-in-the-box, which opened unpredictably when you turned its crank?

Maybe there was something valuable inside the watchcase, and the only way to get to it was to set the watch to a certain time and then wind it up—rather like the combination lock on a safe. Why not? The more Reuben thought about it, the more convinced he felt he was right. He jammed the cardboard box into the closet and sat down on his bed.

Taking a breath to steady himself—his heart was racing now—Reuben eased the watch's winding key back up into its setting position and turned the hour hand from one o'clock to two o'clock. He pushed the key all the way in again and wound the watch. Then, tense with expectation, he pulled the key back up to allow the spring to unwind. Nothing happened. He held the watch to his ear and confirmed that it was ticking. Perhaps the secret mechanism would be triggered at some unpredictable point during the unwinding.

And so Reuben stared at the watch in his hand, waiting. A minute passed, then two. He found himself growing more and more excited. He couldn't tear his eyes away. He hated even to blink for fear he'd miss something, and he began to feel jittery and hot. The purpose of a jack-in-the-box, after all, is to fill you with mounting anticipation, the tension increasing second by second as you wait for that startling moment when the hidden figure pops up—and Reuben was waiting for something far more dramatic than a little clown puppet. By the time ten minutes had passed, the tension had grown almost unbearable. After fifteen he felt ready to collapse. And indeed, when the watch stopped ticking, he sank back onto the bed with an exhausted and disappointed sigh.

Ten more positions to try. What if nothing happened until the last attempt? He would have to endure over two hours of nerve-racking waiting. And of course it was possible that nothing would happen at all. Reuben didn't choose to believe that, however.

He turned his head toward the wooden box sitting open on the bed. He gazed at the inscription inside the lid. "Hey, Mr. Light," he mumbled, "what's the secret?" For he felt sure now that P. William Light had known it, whatever it was. But if the man's ghost was hanging around the watch, it certainly wasn't whispering any hints to Reuben. He was going to have to do this the hard way.

He rolled onto his belly, set the watch to three o'clock, and tried again. Again nothing happened. Fifteen minutes of pointless ticking, that was it. Reuben groaned and pressed his face into the mattress.

By the time he'd tested all the positions through ten o'clock,

Reuben's eyes were bleary from staring, his entire body ached from the tension, and his hand was cramped from squeezing the watch too tightly. He hated to stop with only two positions left to try, but he desperately needed a break.

Returning the watch and key to their box, Reuben flopped over onto his back. Despite the mounting disappointments, he still felt strangely confident that he was right about the watch's secret, and he wondered what might be hidden inside it. He closed his eyes and imagined a tiny velvet pouch stuffed with diamonds. Or rubies. Something small but precious. Something he could sell. His dream of riches wasn't over, he thought, not by a long shot.

He woke to the sound of someone at the apartment door. A muffled thump, the scrape of a key. Reuben sat up with a gasp. He hadn't meant to fall asleep. What time was it? How long had he slept? His eyes shot to the alarm clock. Almost six. But it couldn't be his mom at the door—she had to work in Ashton that evening. And yet there was no mistaking the familiar squeak of the lock turning.

Reuben leaped up, snatched the wooden box, and shoved it under his bed. He was groggy, disoriented, wondering if he should hide. He was still trying to decide, watching with dread through his bedroom doorway, when the apartment door swung open.

"Hey, kid, guess who's home?" called a familiar voice, and Reuben almost collapsed with relief.

His mom stepped in, closing the door with her foot. She had her purse slung over one shoulder, a larger handbag with her change of clothes in it over the other, and grocery sacks in both hands. She turned and saw him gaping at her. "Oh, hey! Change of plans. I'm off tonight." She cocked her head to the side. "Reuben? Are you okay? Hello?"

Reuben snapped to and rushed to help her. Her forehead was

beaded with sweat. She thanked him as he carried the grocery sacks into the kitchen. "Whew," she breathed, letting her purse and handbag drop to the floor. She kicked her shoes off to complete the pile. "Were you wondering why I didn't call from the market?"

"Sorry, no, I just woke up," he said, hurrying back to lock the door. "I guess I fell asleep. I mean, I know I did—I just didn't mean to." He shook his head. He still felt rattled from waking up in such a fright.

"I'm sure you needed it," said his mom, with a tired smile. As usual, she looked as if she could use a long nap herself. "Well, I was afraid you'd worry when you didn't hear from me, but I was rushing to make the first bus. Otherwise it would've been another half hour." She beckoned him over for a hug. "I got asked to trade shifts. I'll have to work Saturday, but it's nice for tonight, anyway, right?" She kissed his head and walked into the kitchen.

"Sure," said Reuben, after a pause; he tried not to sound disappointed, but it had just occurred to him that now he was going to have to put off testing the watch.

His mom, washing her hands, looked over her shoulder at him. "'Sure'? That's it? What, did you have big plans?"

"Plans?" Reuben repeated, and almost winced. His tone sounded guilty even to him.

His mom stopped scrubbing and narrowed her eyes at him. "Is something going on?"

Reuben struggled to recover. She was about to start grilling him. "Of course not," he ventured desperately—and then he had it. He lowered his eyes. "I mean yes. Yes. Sorry, Mom, but, well, I was going to throw a huge party."

She stared at him for several seconds, her expression blank. "A party," she said at last, shaking her head. "And you weren't going to invite your mother. I should have known." She went back to washing her hands. "I'd say you were in hot water, but we still don't seem to have any."

They were having omelets for dinner. Eggs were on sale, his mom said as Reuben helped put away the groceries, and she hadn't felt up to facing one more fish today. Reuben responded agreeably as she talked, trying to do a better job of masking his impatience. He was thinking about the watch, however, only half listening, and was surprised when she suddenly grabbed his hands. Evidently, she had just asked him a question.

"Did you put ointment on these today?" his mom demanded again. She was inspecting the scrapes on his arms.

"Oh yeah." Reuben shrugged. "I was going to."

She placed her hands on his cheeks and drew their faces together. "Put. Ointment. On. Your. Scrapes."

Reuben crossed his eyes. "Yes. Ma'am. I. Will."

"I'm going to jump in the shower," his mom said. "Meet you back here in fifteen minutes."

Fifteen minutes! Reuben found the tube of ointment and went into his room, casually closing the door behind him. Then in a mad scramble he got out the watch, set it to eleven o'clock, wound it up, and placed it on his pillow. Slathering ointment up and down his arms, he stared at the watch as it sat there so beautifully, doing absolutely nothing.

Reuben clenched his teeth. Through the thin walls he could hear the squeak of the shower faucets and his mom yelping something about the cold water. Her shower would be very short. He looked at the watch, the alarm clock, the watch again. Now the water was going off. He wiped his ointment-greasy fingers carefully on the inside of his shirt. A few more minutes. Nothing. He sighed and hid everything away again. Only one setting left to try, and it had to be the one! But it would have to wait.

Reuben set the table as his mom made the omelets. They did their usual tiny-kitchen dance, bumping each other with their hips and accusing each other, with pretend irritation, of hogging the space. But all the while Reuben's mind was on the watch.

"Guess what I got called at work today?" his mom said.

"Employee of the year."

"I can understand why you'd think that. But no, this is something I don't like to be called. I'll give you a hint: it rhymes with 'monkey.'"

Reuben scratched his head. "Gunky?"

She rolled her eyes at him. "Fine, sure. I got called gunky. Because of all the gunk on me, I guess."

"I told you that you shouldn't go crawling through all that gunk," Reuben admonished.

"And *I* told *you* that I didn't have a choice," his mom said, scowling. "If I don't crawl through the gunk, how am I supposed to get to the goop?"

She was being pretty funny, but Reuben was still finding it amazingly difficult to concentrate.

After dinner his mom glanced at the clock and said that an old movie was about to come on. "Looks straight-up silly," she said, "but it might be fun. What do you think? Movie or dream house?"

Reuben's scalp tingled. Just like that, he had his opportunity! "Do we have popcorn?" he asked, knowing that they did. "If we do, I vote movie."

His mom nodded, stifling a yawn. "We do indeed. I was hoping you'd say that."

"Do you care if I miss the start, though?" Reuben asked. "I kind of want to finish a book I'm reading. I only have a few pages left." It was a thin excuse but plausible. He usually did have a book going.

His mom patted his cheek. "Go read. I'll fill you in."

Reuben retreated to his room and closed the door. He found a library book he'd already finished, opened it to the last chapter, and laid it on his bed. Beyond the door he could hear his mom switching on the television, then moving about the kitchen, pouring popcorn kernels into a pot. He knew he should wait until she went to bed. But it was the last test. He had to know.

He got out the watch and key. From the television came the muffled sounds of movie dialogue; he heard his mom groaning at some feeble joke. He set the watch to twelve o'clock. "Midnight," he whispered, and felt a shudder run through him. He had a sudden conviction that he ought to have tried the twelve o'clock setting first. Wasn't midnight always the magical hour?

Then he had to laugh at himself. What was he expecting, anyway? Certainly not magic. It wasn't as if he believed in fairy tales. Besides, he was thinking of twelve o'clock as midnight, but of course it could also be noon. Nonetheless, it was with a sense of powerful expectation that Reuben wound the watch.

Moment of truth, he thought, easing the key out of its winding position.

And everything went black.

POWER and PRICE

Reuben yelped. That was the sound he made—a yelp, like that of a dog being kicked. Which was exactly how he felt, as if he'd been kicked, hard, in the gut. He thought he might throw up. He closed his eyes and opened them again and still saw nothing but darkness. He squeezed them tightly, opened them again. Nothing. His skin burned with panic.

His mom knocked on the door. "Reuben? Are you okay?"

Reuben looked toward the door but saw nothing. He opened his mouth to answer but found himself speechless with horror. The door opened. His mom's voice said, "Reuben? Reuben?"

Then, to Reuben's even greater shock, her voice retreated. He heard her walking to the bathroom calling his name, then into her bedroom. He couldn't make sense of it, was still in too much of a panic to think. His thoughts were a terrifying jumble. It took him several seconds to remember the watch in his hand. The watch! He flung it down onto the bed as if it were a burning coal.

The instant he did so, he could see again. His relief was so powerful that tears started to his eyes. He bent forward, covering his face with his hands, trying not to weep. For some sliver of awareness in him understood that he needed to protect this terrible secret, to keep it from his mom at all costs.

"Reuben?" His mom was in the living room again. She sounded half-concerned, half-suspicious. Not alarmed, though. He had hidden from her too many times for her to be truly alarmed. "I swear, if you jump out and scare me, I'm going to scream. You know you hate it when I scream."

Reuben tossed a pillow over the watch, which he dared not touch, and in a faltering voice he called out, "In here." If he'd been thinking clearly, he would have waited until he'd composed himself, but he was too shaken up. All he knew was that he desperately wanted his mom to come back.

When she appeared in the doorway, he threw his arms around her, burying his face against her chest. She held him tightly. "Oh, honey, what's the matter? Are you okay? What happened?"

Reuben shook his head, not looking up. He had no idea what to say.

"I heard you cry out—I thought you'd seen a rat or something. Where were you? I looked in here and didn't see you."

"You did?" Reuben said, utterly confused. But of course she had. He'd heard her.

"Well, I just poked my head in, but you weren't on your bed."

For a moment Reuben felt as if his brain were out of focus. Then, suddenly, realization thundered inside his head. It crashed and hammered and pounded like a violent storm: *She couldn't see you! She couldn't see you! She couldn't see you!*

"I was...under it," he muttered, trying, despite the crazy tumult in his mind, to think of an excuse. "I was...getting my book out from under it and then I thought I saw something—or, well, I thought I heard something, and then I looked over and thought I saw a person in my closet...."

"You poor thing. Did you bang your head?" his mom asked, gently feeling the crown of his skull for a bump.

"No, I'm fine. I just panicked, I guess. It was...only my jacket."

His mom rubbed his back soothingly. "Believe me, I've had my mind play tricks like that plenty of times. It's no fun, I know. Scary stuff." There was not a hint of doubt in her voice, only sympathy.

"I'm okay now." Reuben looked up and managed a smile. "I'm fine. Really. I just need a minute."

She kissed his forehead. "You're pretty good, kid. This time you scared me without even trying."

"Sorry," Reuben said again.

"You should be," she said, and winked. "Just come out when you're ready, okay?"

He closed the door behind her. Then, as quietly as he could, he locked it. He stood with his hand on the doorknob, his mind still whirling. *She hadn't seen him.* She had looked at his bed and hadn't seen him sitting right there. He turned to look at the bed, to see what she had seen—what she *hadn't* seen. It was impossible. But it had happened.

He stood there, perfectly still, trying to think of what to do. His heartbeat was galloping. He had an idea and ran to his closet. Once again he pulled out the box of toys. A few years earlier his mom had given him a toy digital camera for Christmas. He had loved it at the time, though he was pretty sure it was a factory reject she'd gotten on deep discount. It took terrible photos, and you couldn't print them or anything, only look at them on a miniature screen. But it would serve his purpose now.

In a moment Reuben had the camera out. Was there any chance the batteries weren't dead? He pressed the pale green power button. The camera emitted a barely audible whine. The little display screen flickered on. Yes!

Reuben went to the bed and uncovered the watch. A chill of dread ran through him, but he ignored it. He had to know. He held the camera out at arm's length, pointing it back at himself. Then he took a deep breath and reached for the watch. At the last instant, he closed his eyes—he wasn't sure why. Perhaps he felt it would be less frightening if he didn't actually experience that first moment of blindness. But even with his eyes closed, as soon as his fingers touched the watch, Reuben sensed the light beyond his eyelids being extinguished. The imperfect darkness was made perfect. He shuddered and snapped the picture.

He opened his eyes onto blackness, then let go of the watch. Instantly the room rematerialized around him, as if he'd thrown a switch.

"Wow," he whispered.

And then again, "*Wow!*"

Bracing himself, Reuben turned the camera around and looked at the display screen. There was his bed. There was his closet door. A little fuzzy, both of them, but clearly there.

Reuben, however, was clearly *not*.

He quickly got used to the blindness. Again and again he grabbed the watch, snapped a picture, let go of the watch, checked the display screen. He soon learned that if he held the camera and the watch too close together, the picture would be totally black. If he held the watch out away from him with one hand, though, and extended the camera in the opposite direction with his other hand, the display revealed pictures of his lamplit room. And in those pictures, Reuben was never there. He was so amazed by this, so enthralled, that he forgot everything else and just kept taking picture after picture until, out of the blue, the watch abruptly stopped working.

It happened as he was lying back on his bed (despite his excitement, he felt incredibly tired now), staring blindly up toward the camera in his hand and squeezing the watch in his other, his arm flung out to the side. He was just about to click another photograph when the light returned and the camera and his hand appeared before him—as did the ceiling, the light fixture, the whole room. With an effort, Reuben sat up. He blinked at the watch, still in his hand. He held it to his ear. The ticking had stopped.

His mind, as if slogging through mud, came very slowly to understand. Fifteen minutes. You had to wind the watch up, and then you got fifteen minutes of invisibility. Reuben set the watch and the camera down and rubbed his eyes. Then he dropped his arms and simply sat for a while, gazing at nothing. He felt the way he did some mornings when he was not yet fully awake. The morning stares, his mom called it. Zoning out.

Eventually the sound of his mom's laughter brought him out of it. He remembered, as if from a long time ago, that he was supposed to be joining her to watch the movie. Rousing himself, Reuben put the watch away. He yawned, closed the closet door, then leaned against it a moment. He could probably fall asleep right there. He forced himself to shove away from the door and go out into the living room.

His mom sat on the sofa, watching the movie. She had changed into her pajamas. She took one glance at him and said, "You look so tired, Reuben. I don't know why I didn't notice before. Did you not sleep well last night?"

"Maybe not," Reuben mumbled, sinking onto the sofa beside her.

"Here," she said, passing him the popcorn bowl. "You need to take it easy." She nodded toward the little television screen. "Evidently, this guy wants to adopt an elephant. No doubt hijinks will ensue."

Reuben got comfortable in his corner of the sofa. "No doubt."

Within seconds he was half-asleep. He was aware of his mom groaning at the feebler jokes and chuckling at the better ones for a while, then falling silent, which probably meant she had glanced over and seen his eyes closed. Before long he was completely out.

He woke up to the blaring orchestral music that always seemed to play at the end of old movies, and, sure enough, the credits were showing. The bowl of popcorn remained untouched. He looked at his mom and saw that she was blinking away a stunned expression. So she had fallen asleep, too.

She saw Reuben looking at her. "That was really good," she mumbled. She yawned.

Reuben nodded. "It might be my favorite movie ever." He yawned, too.

They smiled, hugged each other good night, and went to their rooms.

Reuben closed the door behind him and went straight to his closet. He almost expected to find nothing there. It would make a lot more sense to discover that he had dreamed the whole thing.

But the watch was just where he'd left it, waiting for him.

Reuben woke the next morning to the sounds of his mom getting ready in the bathroom. The groaning of old pipes behind the thin walls, the splash of water in the sink. He opened his eyes. He'd left his lamp on. He had no memory of falling asleep. In fact...

He sat up in alarm. The watch was in his hand. The toy camera lay on the bed nearby. He remembered winding the watch again and starting to take more pictures. After that, though—nothing. Reuben pressed the camera's display button to look at the last few pictures he'd taken. They were all more or less the same: his lamplit pillow, very blurry. He remembered noticing that extra blurriness, as if the camera had begun to feel just as bleary-eyed as he did. But then what? He must have fallen asleep right in the middle of what he was doing. Unbelievable. What if his mom had come in to check on him with the watch in plain sight?

The thought of it propelled him out of bed to put the watch away at once. Yesterday had surely been the longest, most exhausting day of his life, but even so, he should have been more careful. Reuben closed the closet door, shook his head, and was just turning away when the knowledge of what the watch could do—of what *he* could do—suddenly hit him again full force, as if for the first time.

I can turn invisible! he thought. *Invisible!*

He laughed and leaped up as high as he could, trying to touch the ceiling. His fingers still came a foot short, but so what?

"So what!" he cried exultantly. He jumped again, just because he felt like it. Then he flung open his door and went to the kitchen—he felt absolutely ravenous—where he flung the cabinet doors open, too. Wow, he could not *wait* to eat.

"Well, look at you," his mom said when she emerged from the bathroom. Reuben was spooning great heaps of cereal into his mouth and munching greedily, like a wild beast. "You seem a thousand times better this morning. How do you feel?"

"Great!" Reuben said, and gulped down half his glass of orange juice. (It was his second glass.) He gasped with satisfaction and clapped the glass down on the table. "I guess I just needed some rest. How are you?" He shook more cereal into his bowl.

She was watching him with amusement. "You'd think I was starving you, poor child. I'm fine, thank you. Kind of dreading

He sat up in alarm. The watch was in his hand.

the long day, but tomorrow's Saturday, right? We'll at least have the morning together."

"Soundzh good," Reuben said cheerfully, tilting his head back to speak through a huge mouthful of cereal.

Since today was a day that she had to go straight from one job to the other, his mom packed herself some sandwiches and a change of clothes, then went through her usual ritual of naming all the things in the cupboards, fridge, and freezer that Reuben could eat for supper. ("Got it, Mom," he said repeatedly.) Then, also as usual, she made him promise to be home when she called to check on him at the end of her first shift, encouraged him to talk to other kids at the community center, and so on and so forth until Reuben felt ready to explode. Normally, he didn't mind the speeches so much. Today all he could think about was getting her out the door.

Finally, with a hug and a kiss and a dash to the elevator, she was off to catch her bus. It was 7:03 AM, and Reuben had the whole day to himself. He shivered with expectation. By 7:04 he was already winding the watch.

If he wanted to try out his invisibility in public—for what good was being invisible alone?—Reuben needed to make sure he understood it properly. And so for the next hour he conducted experiments, taking photos of himself around the apartment, in different degrees of light and shadow, with the camera held at varying distances from the watch. By the time the camera batteries died, he had learned a few important things.

First of all, even with the cheap display on the camera, he could see that the invisibility was not entirely perfect. Wherever his figure should have appeared in the images, there was a slight haziness in the air, like the heat shimmer rising from summer pavement. It was easily overlooked, though, and almost impossible to detect in shadow. Reuben would do his best to keep to the shadows.

He also discovered that the invisibility did not conform to

his shape. Instead, it emanated outward from the watch in all directions, encompassing everything within its range, which extended just a few feet. The watch, he reflected, was like a tiny golden planet surrounded by a magical atmosphere, inside of which no object or creature could be seen from the outside. Nor could anything *inside* the atmosphere see *out*, which was why Reuben had to hold the camera far away from the watch—beyond its atmosphere—in order to successfully take a picture. When the camera was invisible, it was blind, just like him. That seemed to be the rule: blindness was the price of invisibility.

Reuben's final realization came when he found himself yawning, sluggish and bleary-eyed, despite having awakened, quite refreshed, only an hour before. How could he already be so tired again? All he'd done since then…He slapped his forehead. The watch. Of course. For whatever reason, turning invisible took its toll on you. Indeed, he was so drowsy he scarcely made the connection before collapsing onto the sofa.

At last, having napped away his fatigue and demolished another bowl of cereal (for he'd grown hungry again, too), Reuben prepared to venture out. He just needed a way to carry the watch in secret. A quick search through his closet produced a hooded sweatshirt with oversized front pockets. He had never liked this sweatshirt—its zipper was permanently snagged at the chest, and its orangey-brown color and big pockets made him look like a kangaroo, he thought. But it suited his purposes now, and Reuben wriggled into it eagerly, as if it were his favorite.

He studied himself in the mirror, making sure he was ready. Tennis shoes: check. Shorts: check. Sweatshirt: check. Secret watch of invisibility…

Reuben thrust his hands into his sweatshirt pockets and grinned.

Check.

Following Directions

Reuben stood by the storage room window, waiting for the cat. He was beginning to feel annoyed, as if they'd agreed to meet here and the cat was late. He had thought it best, this first time, to practice on a creature who couldn't call the police if something went wrong. But he'd been down here almost an hour and was losing patience.

From his long familiarity with the storage room, Reuben already knew by heart how many steps would carry him to the nearby stack of boxes or to the bureau-sized fuse panel, and what angles he would take to reach them. As he passed the time there now, it occurred to him that to be mobile while invisible—to be able to move freely without bumping into furniture—he should make a habit of memorizing such things anytime he entered any room, anywhere.

That was good thinking, he told himself, then went back to being crushingly bored. He stared out the window, trying by force of will to make the cat appear.

The watch was in his hand, fully wound and open, with the key inserted all the way to its bow. He had only to back it out of its winding position to vanish. If he saw the cat stalking down the alley, he would do just that. And if the cat came into the room and started eating, Reuben would have passed his first test. He wondered if he should reappear while the cat was still there, or if surprising it like that would run it off for good, thus ruining the building manager's chances of befriending it.

Just as he was wondering this, though, it was Reuben who got taken by surprise. With no warning whatsoever—no approaching footsteps or other sounds of movement—he suddenly heard the doorknob turning. And even that was so quiet he almost didn't hear it. His eyes shot to the door, which was already slowly swinging open.

Reuben crouched down, tugging at the watch key. The room went black.

Trembling, he listened. For a moment there was only silence. Then, from the doorway, a melancholy sigh. Of course. It was the building manager, come to see if her cat had dropped in. She'd approached stealthily to avoid spooking it. Now she was leaving again, the door closing behind her. A brief fading of hurried footsteps. Silence.

Reuben reappeared, still crouching and still trembling. He stared at the door, then turned to stare at the bowls of cat food and water, the open window, the entire storage room, which the building manager had perceived to be vacant.

He shook his head. She had looked right *through* him.

He knew this was what invisibility was all about. But something about the encounter was weirdly unsettling. It was as if he wasn't real, he realized. Present, but not real.

An emptiness.

A ghost.

Reuben's next stop was the Lower Downs library branch. There were never many people there, which made it a perfect spot to practice. Until he got the hang of the watch, the fewer potential witnesses the better.

The branch was not a brightly lit, modern sort of library, but an old one, musty and dim, with battered card catalogs arranged around the front desk so that the librarian—a brusque, curly-haired man in glasses who never made eye contact—could ensure that they were kept in order. Reuben had always loved it. When he wasn't checking out books, he would find open spaces on the shelves through which he could peek into adjacent aisles. Pretending to browse, he would shadow library patrons, making note of the books they selected, searching for secret messages in the ones they paged through but returned to the shelves. He liked to imagine that their choice in reading material was a clue in some urgent mystery it was his duty to solve.

Today, though, Reuben made a quick pass through all the library sections, looking for the most deserted. Among the aisles of the history section there wasn't a soul. With eager anticipation, he squeezed the bow of the winding key in his pocket. Then he cast a final glance around, pulled out on the key, and vanished.

Blind now, Reuben found himself suddenly attuned to all the various library sounds: the buzz of a failing fluorescent light, the distant rattle and thunk of books being shelved from a cart. He moved carefully, slowly, down the aisle. To ensure that his whole body was within the watch's range, he walked in an exaggerated crouch. (If he'd been visible, he would have looked exactly like a tiptoeing thief in a cartoon.) After a dozen paces, he pushed the key back into the winding position. The bookshelves reappeared on either side of him. He had estimated that a dozen steps would take him to the far end of the aisle, and he'd been pretty close—he was only one giant step short. He'd also done a decent job of keeping to the middle, having veered only slightly to his left.

Reuben felt his confidence surging. He was already good at this.

With more passes up and down the aisle, he developed a better sense of the length of his crouch-stride. He concentrated on keeping his steps consistent, to make them reliable measures of distance. He found that by focusing on his destination, then holding it fixed in his mind, he could walk almost straight to it. The main difficulty was keeping his balance. He was never in danger of falling, but he was surprised to find how disorienting it could be to walk in total blackness (not to mention doing so while stooping down).

Still, he rapidly improved, and before long Reuben moved over to the next aisle for the sake of variety. Up and down he walked in blindness, picking points on the shelves to aim for—that enormous green book, that multivolume set with purple spines—and reappearing next to them. He imagined it was like swimming underwater, surfacing periodically to get his bearings and a breath of air. He'd seen people do such things in movies.

When he had perhaps a minute left on the watch (he'd become adept at gauging the time), Reuben decided to try walking backward. After all, backing up might sometime prove critical. He went very slowly, for it turned out to be much trickier, and stopped after only eight steps, feeling uncertain of their length and his direction. He reached out his left hand, and sure enough, his fingertips touched the spine of a book sooner than they ought to have. He was slightly off track.

He pushed in on the key, and the bookshelves materialized. So, too, did the curly-haired librarian, scanning the shelves at the end of the aisle. He must have just rounded the corner. Reuben quickly straightened up out of his conspicuous crouching stance, and as he did so, the librarian, suddenly aware of movement in his peripheral vision, glanced in Reuben's direction.

To judge from the man's reaction, he might have spotted a rhinoceros charging down the aisle. He recoiled violently, flinging his arms out for balance and knocking a book from the shelves. Reuben was so startled by this that he jumped back and almost fell down himself. Their wide eyes met. The man, straightening his glasses, blushed a deep shade of crimson. He turned and hurried from the aisle. A second later he reappeared, snatched up the fallen book, and hurried off again.

Reuben felt an impulse to go after the librarian and apologize for scaring him. But that would make no sense. The man must believe he'd simply failed to notice Reuben coming along the aisle, for although it had *seemed* as if a boy had appeared out of nowhere, obviously that couldn't be the case. Anyway, the librarian was clearly humiliated by his overreaction. He wouldn't care to discuss it.

Reuben, composing himself, found that he was grinning from ear to ear. He thought about the night before, when he'd told his mom that he thought he'd seen someone in his closet, and she had responded with such understanding and familiarity. "Believe me," she'd said, "I've had my mind play tricks like that plenty of times."

It was occurring to Reuben that people, especially adults, are rather quick to dismiss small mysteries, to assume that they have simply misunderstood or failed to observe something, and to go on about their business. And that for this reason a boy like himself, with a watch like this, could get away with any amount of mischief, if only he was bold enough.

ℯ𝓮⌒

By the time his mom called after her shift at the market, Reuben had successfully performed a number of mischievous acts. His favorite had been at the community center, where he had invisibly stage-whispered the name of a boy he knew from school (Miles Chang, who was pretty nice, actually) from several different locations, suppressing his giggles every time Miles, who was trying to play a game of Ping-Pong with a friend, banged down his paddle and called out, "Who keeps saying my name? Are you doing that? Well, did you not hear someone say my name? Am I going crazy?"

Later Reuben had eavesdropped invisibly on Officer Warren as he talked on a pay phone (something about a meeting and therefore boring), then eavesdropped invisibly on the complaint line in the lobby of his building (the top-floor residents all had squirrels in their ceilings—that was more interesting). He had also taken three short, drooling naps and consumed half a dozen peanut butter and jelly sandwiches. It was amazing how being invisible took it out of you.

"How's your day been?" his mom asked on the phone. He heard her take a bite of her dinner sandwich. He knew that as soon as they hung up, she would dash off to catch her bus to Ashton.

"Not bad," Reuben said. He was turning the watch this way and that under the kitchen light, admiring the way it gleamed. "Just the usual stuff."

"Did you talk to any kids at the community center?"

Reuben almost laughed. For once he could answer honestly. "Yeah, I talked to Miles Chang."

"The nice one?" She was speaking with her mouth full. "His dad's the teacher you like?"

Reuben detected the hopefulness in her tone. Now he felt guilty. "That's him," he said, and quickly changed the subject.

As soon as he'd hung up, Reuben left the apartment again. He spent half the evening roaming the building, knocking on doors and listening to residents express their bafflement when they found no one in the hall. It was hilarious and perfectly thrilling. He might have gone on for hours if he hadn't felt so wrecked with exhaustion. As it was, he barely managed to get the watch put away before falling into bed. He didn't even brush his teeth.

The next morning, for the first time he could remember, Reuben woke up wishing his mom had to work. He felt rested now and eager to use the watch again. Instead he had to apply himself to a slew of Saturday-morning chores, then sit through an hour of designing dream houses with his mom—an activity that, under the circumstances, required a supreme effort of patience and offered none of the usual satisfactions. His mom did make him a hearty omelet, though, using up the last of the sale eggs. And though he'd had to feign his cheerfulness all morning, he felt so joyous when she left for work in the afternoon, his goodbye hug was genuinely affectionate and enthusiastic. His mom went out with a puzzled smile, and Reuben flew to his closet.

For the rest of that Saturday, and indeed for the entirety of the next few days, Reuben could think about almost nothing except his newfound ability. He went to bed at night exhausted, thinking about the watch, and he woke up in the morning excited, still thinking about it. He spent every waking hour practicing, testing the limits of his skills and all the time improving them.

More than once he thought of Mrs. Genevieve. Wouldn't she be amazed if she knew what the watch could do? Reuben rather wished he could go and show her. But having the power of invisibility was the sort of secret you kept from absolutely everyone if you could. It was the secret of a lifetime.

Reuben had grown used to feeling different from other kids. He hadn't liked it, but he'd made the best of it. Now, all of a sudden, he was not just different—he was special. This was an entirely new and wonderful thing to feel, and he had no intention of spoiling it. The more adept he became with the watch, the more special he felt, and as a result he worked harder at mastering it than he'd ever worked at anything in his life.

Reuben's skills improved so rapidly, in fact, that when on Tuesday afternoon he spied the Directions turning down an alley behind the neighborhood hardware store, he abandoned his long habit of observing the men from a safe distance. Instead, quickening his pace to catch up, he followed them.

Almost at once he realized his mistake. He had figured the Directions were taking a shortcut to the next street, when in fact they were just taking a break and evidently didn't care to do so in public view. They stopped not far into the alley and now, as well as he could make out, were simply standing around or leaning against walls. One was lighting a cigar. That would be Righty. The sight of Righty smoking cigars was familiar to Reuben, who could actually hear him puffing on it now to get it going. Its acrid, sweet smoke drifted over him in the alley. That's how close he was.

Reuben wanted to scream at himself. He'd been following hard on the men's heels, counting on their heavier footsteps to mask the sound of his own. Now he was much too close, and they were so watchful by habit he was afraid to make any movement. Would they notice a strange irregularity in the alley floor? Or spot a hazy patch in the air, like a faint shimmer of fumes with no apparent source? Had he been lucky enough to stop moving in one of the alley's shadier spots? In the darkness of his invisibility, Reuben had no idea.

Instead, quickening his pace to catch up, he followed them.

Lefty sighed. "It's like having two jobs." He seemed to be taking up the thread of an ongoing conversation. "Like the Lower Downs isn't enough? We don't even *know* that other neighborhood."

"You've already said that," said Frontman in his familiar drawl. "Fact, you've said it about a million times. We get it. And we all agree. Complaining doesn't help anything."

"It does me," Lefty said. "It makes me feel better."

"It's temporary," said Righty, speaking around his cigar.

"That means it isn't forever," said Lookback in his reedy voice.

"I *know* what 'temporary' means. And I don't care. It's still exhausting. We have to do our usual thing here, then hustle over there and knock on doors all evening? It's too much."

"You don't even have a family," said Lookback. "What are you going to do, anyway? Watch TV all evening? I've got a wife and kids. I've got a puppy, for crying out loud. A sweet little thing, too—you should see how he wriggles around. So cute! But do you hear me complaining? No."

"Well, it makes me feel better," said Lefty again.

"You ought to feel pretty good by now, then," said Frontman. "You ought to feel wonderful."

"It's not like we're the only ones having to do it," said Righty, and Reuben heard him snipping off the lit end of his cigar with a little pair of scissors. He never smoked an entire cigar at once. "It's everybody. Like Mr. Faug says, we all do what we're told, even him. It isn't easy for anybody."

"So you think we're like this big happy team?" Lefty scoffed. "We're all in it together?"

"Let me ask you," Frontman interjected. "Do you want to *not* be in it? You want to tell Mr. Faug that you're out? You want him to tell the boss that you were just too tired to do it anymore? Be my guest. It was nice knowing you."

100

"Yeah," Righty added in a low voice, "I hear The Smoke loves it when people quit. I hear he's very forgiving."

"Hey, I'm just *complaining*," Lefty said. "I'm not saying I want out. I'm not stupid."

"Prove it," Lookback muttered.

Ignoring him, Lefty changed his tone and said, "But say, did you really mean that? That it was nice knowing me? Because seriously, sometimes I can't tell—"

"Oh, for crying out loud," Frontman said with a sigh. "Let's get going."

Reuben heard them gather themselves and start to walk again. They had turned around. They were coming back up the alley. He was directly in their path. He sidestepped once, then twice, then held still. Righty passed so close to him that Reuben could smell his sweetly smoky breath.

He listened to them go, then backed himself up against a wall and reappeared. "Okay," he said, trying to calm himself. "Okay, you're good. You're fine." He wiped his sweaty palms on his sweatshirt. "Just don't do that again. Stop being stupid." He shook his head and exhaled with relief.

And suddenly Reuben found himself smiling. He had spied on the Directions themselves, had heard them talking business when they thought they were alone. Now, *that* was something to be proud of! He was surely the only one who had ever done that. Imagine what else he could do!

He wondered what they had been talking about, though. Why did The Smoke have them going around some other neighborhood? And not just them but "everybody," which he assumed meant all the other Directions in New Umbra. The thought of all those men moving in their strange formations up and down the sidewalks, knocking on people's doors for reasons unknown to him, filled Reuben with misgiving. He'd never heard of such a thing before.

At length he let it go. Whatever was happening, it was happening elsewhere. And ever since he'd discovered the secret of his miraculous watch, Reuben had found it impossible to think of anything else, much less worry about it. So it was in a cheerful, unworried frame of mind that he went home that afternoon, unaware of how precious his mood was—as all fine things are precious when they are coming to an end.

THE EDGE OF THE PRECIPICE

His mom had the evening off, so Reuben made sure to be home in time to put away the watch and key before she arrived. As he tucked them gently inside their elegant box, he took a moment to admire them and to reflect that these last several days had been the best of his life. And there were more to come, he thought. So many more.

Before he closed the box, Reuben's eyes lingered on the inscription, as they sometimes did, and once again he found himself wondering about P. William Light. How long had *he* owned the watch? And how had the watch passed from Light to its next owner, and then to its next, and so on—and what had become of them all? Reuben wondered how many people had known the watch's secret. It was quite possible, even likely, that a person could treasure the watch for its rarity and beauty without ever being aware of its secret power. He liked to think that it took a special kind of person to discover the hidden truth.

From the apartment doorway came the sound of jingling keys, and with a little sigh he put the box away and closed his closet door.

Preoccupied as he was, it took Reuben a while to realize that something was the matter with his mom. Not until she'd shuffled into the kitchen and begun frying fish for their dinner did he suddenly notice how tired she looked. Exhausted, in fact. He could see it in her slumped posture, the untidiness of her ponytail, the darkness under her eyes. That was when it hit him that she hadn't made a joke of any kind since—well, he wasn't sure when. Yesterday, maybe, or even the day before.

At once the lightness of mood in which Reuben had been skipping obliviously along transformed into something else. It was like the cave-ins he'd seen in old westerns about mining towns—in a matter of seconds, everything was dark. And he was buried under a mountain of guilt. His mom had sensed a change in him, he thought, had noticed how he was always eager to be alone. Naturally, she was feeling quite hurt, and probably lonely, too. Reuben wanted to pinch himself. He was all she had. He needed to do better.

"Hey, I've been thinking," he ventured, taking a seat at the kitchen table. "What if we had the mansion built on the water— I mean literally *on the water*, with support beams or whatnot to keep it from sinking—and every room on the bottom story had glass floors? And they'd all have submarine hatches you could climb up through, so you could swim from room to room if you wanted."

He saw his mom nod thoughtfully as if considering the idea.

Then she flipped the fish with her spatula. For the first time Reuben could ever remember, she made no reply.

"Mom? What's wrong?"

That was all it took. His mom turned off the stove, shifted the pan to a different burner, and came to sit down across from him. She looked absolutely miserable.

"The thing is," she said quietly, "prices are up. People are buying less." She cleared her throat and scowled at the tabletop.

Her words and her manner were so confusing that Reuben felt a prickle of alarm. "What are you talking about?"

His mom placed her palms flat on the table, took a deep breath, then looked up to meet Reuben's eye and let it all out in a gush. She was being let go at the market. They needed a smaller staff, at least for the time being. She lacked seniority there, and besides that her employer had sniffed out the fact that she'd recently applied for a different job, and was none too pleased about it. The Friday of next week would be her last day.

As his mom talked, Reuben's first reaction was one of relief. He was just glad her unhappiness wasn't his fault after all. Then what she was saying really sank in, and his stomach sank along with it. Her troubling words from last week returned to him: *behind on the rent.* The discovery of the watch's incredible secret had temporarily swept them to the back of his mind.

"Are we going to have to move again?" he asked.

"Maybe?" His mom shrugged noncommittally. "It depends on whether I can find another job that pays as much as I make at the market."

Reuben could tell that she was forcing herself not to look away. She was meeting his eye, but it took a real effort. "You don't think you can, do you?"

She looked at him. She shook her head. "There's nothing out there," she said in a strange voice. Her throat was tight. She was trying not to cry.

Reuben reached for her hand. "Mom, it'll be okay. There's always another way, right? That's what you're always saying."

"Yes, and I'm very wise," she said, trying to sound smug. But her voice cracked, and she shut her eyes tightly and tears rolled out from under her closed lids. "This place of ours," she said in her choked voice, "it's rough around the edges, I know. It's no great shakes, right? But, Reuben, we're not far off from something really hard, and I didn't want that for you."

Reuben knew what she meant. In his rambles around the neighborhood he had seen some pretty terrible places. Places he couldn't believe people had to live in, and yet they did. For there was no place lower down than the Lower Downs to go. You just sank to the bottom, and the bottom was awful.

"It's going to be okay," he said. "No matter what."

His mom still had her eyes closed. She nodded vigorously and squeezed his hand. Then she wiped the tears from her face and looked at him with shining eyes. "Yes," she said firmly. She nodded again. "Yes, that's right."

"I'll say one thing," Reuben said, testing the air. "They'd better not try to kick us out."

"No way," said his mom. "We'll cling to their legs."

Reuben thought for a moment. "We may have to rob a bank, you know. We should get some masks."

"Masks are expensive, honey," his mom said, and Reuben felt a wave of relief. She was getting back to herself. "We can make our own. We'll use brown paper bags. We can cut out eyeholes."

"We should paint scary faces on them. To show that we mean business."

"That's smart thinking. We don't want them to try any funny stuff."

So went their conversation throughout dinner, his mom feeling better now that she was no longer keeping a big secret from him. Reuben knew that she was still seriously worried, though, and so was he. Partly about where they would have to live, but mostly about her. She must always have been keeping one anxious eye on the precipice, he thought, always afraid that one day they would stumble and fall off. He had simply been too young to realize it.

Before he went to sleep that night, Reuben sat for a long time with the watch in his hands. He had found it himself. Against the odds he had found it, and he had figured out its secret. He could turn invisible. Surely this wasn't all for nothing, he thought. Surely with this miraculous watch he could work a miracle himself.

The next morning Reuben wandered all around the neighborhood, deep in thought. He kept out of sight, as usual, but he wasn't using the watch. He wanted to remain alert and clearheaded. He was trying to think of what to do. He wasn't getting anywhere, unfortunately. His mind, like his feet, kept circling around, sticking to the same paths, and inevitably it always returned to the joke he'd made about robbing a bank.

He suspected that with the watch in hand and a certain amount of planning, he could pull it off. But it was one thing to indulge in silly daydreams about robbing a bank and quite another—quite a frightening thing—to imagine actually doing it. Anyway, though he had to admit he was not exactly the most shining example of proper behavior, Reuben had no interest in becoming a real criminal.

Still, his mind kept going back to the idea, and so he kept getting nowhere. The morning became one long exercise in frustration. He went up to the community center roof, where he lay on his back and stared at the sky, which was weirdly striped with the white vapor trails of jet airplanes. Reuben imagined the bars of a jail cell, the stripes of a prisoner's uniform. He got up and headed home for lunch.

Not far from the hardware store, he saw the Directions emerge from a neighboring business and amble in his direction. It was Wednesday. Reuben was already ducking into an alley to avoid their attention when he noticed Officer Warren coming out of the hardware store. That made no sense. Officer Warren knew the Directions' routines as well as Reuben did, probably even better, so why would he risk bumping into them? Police officers always avoided the Directions as much as possible. They did it to avoid humiliation, for not even they dared to oppose the Counselor's men. Yet here stood Officer Warren, and it was clearly no accident. He stood under the awning, his thumbs hooked in his belt, gazing down the street. Waiting.

Reuben surveyed the empty street. He slipped his hand into his sweatshirt pocket and vanished. Moving carefully, his heart racing, he made his way to a sidewalk trash can near the hardware store entrance and crouched behind it. Something in the trash can smelled horrible. He pinched his nostrils closed and waited. He wasn't worried about anyone coming by and stumbling over him, not on this stretch of street at lunchtime on a Wednesday. It wasn't just the police who avoided the Directions. Everybody did.

A couple of minutes passed as Reuben breathed through his mouth. He could still kind of smell whatever it was. He wondered if a raccoon had crawled into the trash can and died there.

Finally he heard the footsteps and the voices of the Directions. The men approached, slowed, stopped. Their voices died away. Reuben imagined their looks of surprise to see Officer Warren.

"Afternoon, gentlemen," he heard the young police officer say. "How are you all doing?"

Frontman replied tersely, forgoing his usual drawl. "We're working, that's how we're doing. Can we help you with something, Officer?" It wasn't a real question. It was an expression of irritation.

"Actually," said Officer Warren, "I was hoping that you could. I've just been inside, speaking with Mr. Carver. I'm sure you know he isn't in the best of health. What you might not know is how bad he's struggling lately. He can barely keep the doors open. He's living on beans and water."

"Everybody's got their problems," muttered Lefty.

"That's true, that's true," said Officer Warren. "But I was just wondering if you all might give Mr. Carver a break this week. I'm worried about him. It can hardly make a difference to your employer, but it will make a great deal of difference to Mr. Carver."

"I'm amazed," said Frontman. "You actually want me to say that to Mr. Faug? And what do you suppose Mr. Faug will say to *his* boss?"

There was a silence. Then Officer Warren said, quietly, "Nobody has to say anything, do they? It isn't much money, we both know that. It would be easy to overlook it."

"No, it would *not* be easy," snarled Frontman. "You have no idea what you're talking about. If we made an exception for Mr. Carver, we'd have to make exceptions for the whole neighborhood, and we're not going to do that, understand? We're not sticking our necks out, we're not taking any chances, we're not making exceptions. Do you intend to pay Mr. Carver's share yourself? If not, you need to stand aside. Now."

Another silence.

Reuben heard the flick of a lighter, the faint popping sound of Righty puffing on his cigar to get it going. The lighter snapped shut, and Righty said, "I don't think he heard you."

"Sure doesn't look like it," said Lookback.

Reuben desperately wanted to reappear and peek around the trash can. But there were almost certainly several sets of eyes peering out windows right now. As quickly as he dared, he retraced his steps to the alley, listening with all his might.

"You know what's curious to me?" Frontman was saying. "It's curious to me that someone like you, Officer Warren, someone who gets on the subway every week, going off to different neighborhoods and having private meetings with unknown persons—you know, the sort of unusual activity that very much draws the attention of our employer—it's curious to me that someone like *that* would want to make things even worse for himself by doing what you're doing at this moment."

"He looks surprised," Lefty said. "Now, why would he be surprised?"

Reuben had reached the alley. Out of view of the street, he reappeared, then scurried forward to watch around the corner.

"I don't think he looks surprised," said Righty. "I think he looks angry."

"I don't care how he looks," said Lookback. "I'm tired of standing here in the street."

"That's right," said Frontman. "We are very interested in your private life, Officer Warren, and we intend to ask you some questions about it. Now, do you wish to discuss this here on the street, or shall we make an appointment to discuss it later, in private?"

Another silence. Reuben shouted in his head, trying to will Officer Warren away. He was afraid of what was going to happen to him.

"Stand," Frontman growled, "*aside*."

Officer Warren stood rigidly under the awning, glaring at the Directions. The men were exchanging annoyed and uncertain glances. Then, just when it seemed that something had to happen, something did: Mr. Carver's voice called out from within the hardware store. Reuben couldn't make out the words—perhaps something about the day being too hot for standing around outside—but what the old hardware store owner said out loud didn't really matter. Everyone knew what he meant. *Let them come in,* he was saying. *Let them come. Don't get yourself hurt over me. I'll be all right.*

Finally, slowly, Officer Warren stepped to the side. He continued to glare at the other men. His eyes passed from face to face. Frontman only smirked, but both Lefty and Righty looked extremely uncomfortable under the police officer's gaze. Righty dropped his cigar and ground it with his heel as if he hated it. Lefty was visibly squirming, tugging at his shirt collar, pulling up on his pants. Lookback was steadily ignoring Officer Warren, just looking straight ahead as if the policeman weren't standing right there glaring. After a beat, Frontman sauntered into the store, and the others followed.

For a few moments Officer Warren remained under the awning, clenching and unclenching his fists, looking disgusted, angry, and upset. Then, with a heavy tread, he walked away. He didn't look back.

ⲉⲗ

Reuben, furious, stalked back to his apartment building. His anger was giving him a new idea to consider. It was probably even worse than the bank-robbing idea, he knew, but far more satisfying to contemplate.

He was wondering what the Directions did with all those envelopes of money. He knew that the men went to the subway station every Friday morning, and based on years of rumor and hearsay, he'd deduced that this was when they made their weekly visit to the Counselor's mansion to deliver the money and their reports, and to receive payment for their efforts. This meant that by every Thursday evening, they must have gathered their entire week's worth of collections from around the Lower Downs. What if Reuben followed them and figured out where they stashed the money?

He relished the idea of making those men report to the Counselor that they'd lost the money. He imagined the Counselor (Reuben pictured him as a tall, formidable, exquisitely dressed man) coldly informing the Directions that they could expect a visit from his employer, who would be most displeased. Oh, how they would quake in their boots at the thought of The Smoke coming for them, and how it would serve them right!

But by the time Reuben had eaten lunch, it had occurred to him that the money he stole from the Directions would have come from people like Mr. Carver, or the young apartment building manager, or the friendly baker he had liked so much. It was also true that he had no idea what The Smoke might actually do to the men. He remembered Lookback mentioning his wife, his kids, his puppy. Reuben hated Lookback, but did he really want anything bad to happen to the man's family?

He grunted with irritation. Why couldn't anything be simple? he thought as he headed out again. Why couldn't he just steal from the bad guys and not worry about it? He was squeezing out through the storage room window when it hit him.

The large reward.

Mrs. Genevieve had warned him against calling that phone number in the classified ads. The advertiser was clearly eccentric and probably rich, and given the strange circumstances surrounding the watch, she'd suspected that such a person was not to be trusted. This was exactly what Reuben hoped. For if the advertiser meant to pull off a double cross, then Reuben would have no qualms about turning the tables. Did he not have a tremendous advantage over anyone intending such treachery? Of course he did. He could turn invisible!

His mind flashed from idea to idea: meeting places, secret arrangements, sacred agreements. Briefcases filled with money. Sneaky entrances and exits. With a sudden, thrilling thumping in his chest, Reuben realized that he could do it. He really could. He'd be robbing a robber, thwarting a thief.

That was the only way to go about it, really, for the thought of actually handing over the watch was no longer tolerable to Reuben. Not since he'd discovered what he could do with it. Accepting money for the watch would be like accepting a golden egg in exchange for a goose that laid such eggs every day. No, the surest path to fortune was to *use* the watch, not give it up.

Reuben scurried down the back alley, feeling bolder by the moment. The first thing to do was to find out who this mysterious advertiser actually was. Then he could do some serious spying. He wouldn't agree to meet until he knew everything he needed to know. What he needed right now was to understand the situation better. He needed information. He needed to call that number.

Reuben's feet were ahead of his mind. He'd been hurrying along all this time, and he arrived at the library just as he arrived at his decision. The library had everything he needed. Taking the front steps two at a time, he went straight to the magazines-and-newspapers section. Mrs. Genevieve had said the advertisement appeared "in all the papers," so Reuben just snatched up the first local newspaper he found on the rack. He spread it out on a table and flipped to the classified ads. Sure enough, there was the ad, with its perfect description of the watch, its mention of a large reward—and the telephone number.

Reuben dug into his pocket for change.

A battered old pay phone hung in the library foyer. Reuben stood before it, taking deep breaths, struggling against his usual reluctance. He counted to three, dropped his coins into the slot, and punched in the number before he could lose his nerve.

He'd already worked out what he was going to say—a version of the same uncle story he'd used before. *We're not sure*, he'd say, *but we think my uncle might have found the watch you're looking for. Would you like to take a look at it?* He would ask for a name and an address, and he would see what else he could get the person to tell him. Especially the amount of the award, but also any other information that might help him form a plan. He would ask question after question. The fact that he was only a kid was in his favor. Grown-ups weren't worried about kids posing threats to them.

The phone on the other end of the line began to ring. Twice, three times, half a dozen times. After the tenth ring, Reuben checked the number on the scrap of paper he'd written it on. He was sure he'd gotten it right. After a few more rings, he decided to hang up and try again. But just as he reached to replace the receiver in its cradle, he heard a tinny voice. He brought the receiver back to his ear.

"Hello?" he said, his voice quavering a bit.

The person on the other end was breathing hard, as if having run upstairs to answer the phone. After a short pause, Reuben said hello again. A man's voice, still breathless, said, "Yes?"

There was a fit of coughing. Reuben waited politely for it to subside, then said, "Hi, I'm calling to inquire about the newspaper ad. About the watch? We think my—"

The man's voice broke in. "Do you still have it?"

Confused, Reuben said, "The ad? No. I, um, wrote the number down. I..." He trailed off, wondering if he had misunderstood.

"The watch," said the man, his voice every bit as breathless as it had been before. "Do you still have the watch?"

Reuben's stomach flopped. "Oh, no! It isn't my watch. I don't have it personally, myself. I mean, we're not even sure it's the same—"

"You're the boy," said the man. "With the uncle. Do you still have the watch? What is your name?"

114

Reuben began to shake. He swallowed dryly. He opened his mouth to speak, but no words came out. The receiver had grown slippery in his hand.

"Don't be afraid," said the man, his voice oily now, and the result was that Reuben became very afraid indeed. "Don't be afraid. Just tell me who you are, and we can discuss the reward. You'd like a nice reward, wouldn't you? Tell me, do you still have the watch? You do, don't you?"

"I'm sorry, there's been a mistake," Reuben said, his voice scarcely above a whisper. His heartbeat boomed in his ears. "I don't have it. My—my friends put me up to calling. I'm sorry. I have to go."

"DO YOU STILL HAVE IT!" the man screamed, his voice cracking wildly.

Reuben slammed the receiver into its cradle and burst out of the library doors at full speed. He ran all the way home, through the lobby, up flight after flight of stairs, never stopping until he had locked the apartment door behind him. Even then, he felt as if the man were in the room with him, still screaming.

"Oh no," he panted, his chest heaving. "Oh no, oh no."

For Reuben understood now that he had gotten himself into something enormous, something terrible. How could he have been so foolish? An ancient watch that could turn you invisible? There must be people who would stop at nothing to get it. Dangerous, wicked people. Reuben had no doubt that he'd just spoken to one, had in fact called him right up on the telephone.

And he had thought himself so clever.

REUBEN'S

DILEMMA

Reuben had fallen into an entirely different life. A dangerous one. Yesterday's ideas of fun suddenly seemed babyish and ridiculous, and today's grandiose plans of outwitting devious watch collectors seemed positively absurd. What had he been thinking? What had he done?

But I'm just a kid, he thought, and he kept thinking it, as if somehow it could change what had just happened. *I'm just a kid! I'm just a kid!*

He had a powerful impulse to call his mom, to be comforted, to ask for help. Twice he even picked up the phone. But what would he say? He would have to tell the whole story—the secrets he'd been keeping, the lies he'd told her, the risks he'd taken—which was awful enough. But it would also terrify her. That something bad might happen to him was her greatest fear.

Reuben paced the apartment. Who could help him, then? Officer Warren? No, too risky. The Directions were already keeping an especially close eye on him—Frontman had just said so. Whom else did he trust?

There was only one answer, and it came to him quickly. Mrs. Genevieve. Yes. He knew he could trust the watchmaker. Yet he couldn't just call her. To help him, she would need to know all the facts, the most important of which he'd never be able to convince her of over the phone. She would have to see it for herself.

The mere thought of venturing outside now was unnerving, and far worse to return to Middleton. Reuben stared at the apartment door for a full minute, gathering himself. Then in a violent rush he unlocked the door, wrenched it open, and flew.

By the time the train pulled into the Brighton Street station, Reuben was sweating in his hooded sweatshirt as if he'd run all the way there. Inside its right front pocket his clammy fingers squeezed the key, ready to tug on it if necessary. He followed the small crowd of disembarked passengers up the steps from the platform, out of the station, and into the sunlight.

The first thing he saw was a group of Directions across the street. They were not the same ones he had seen walking past that sad little park. These men he'd never seen before. They were obviously Directions, though, four men standing on the sidewalk in a loose diamond shape. The one in front was questioning a middle-aged couple; one of the flankers was jotting down notes. Reuben attached himself to a group of bickering teenagers (who didn't notice him at all), walked with them a few paces, then peeled off down an alley. He broke into a run.

A minute later he was alone on an empty side street.

A minute after that, he was nowhere to be seen.

So began Reuben's stealthy journey to Mrs. Genevieve's shop. He moved fast, almost at a trot, his ears attuned to the sounds of the street. Whenever possible, he trailed a finger along walls and fence railings to help keep his path straight. Every now and then he reappeared briefly in the shadows of a cross alley or an empty doorway, got his bearings, scanned the sidewalk ahead for obstacles, and vanished again. Occasionally a vehicle went by on the street, which caused him no end of distress—he kept expecting to hear a screech of brakes, a door flying open, an angry voice shouting out. Once, he was given a shock by a sudden voice beside him, only to realize that he was passing an open window. A woman was talking on the telephone.

"Hello?" she called out, interrupting herself.

Reuben froze in midstep, one foot suspended in the air.

"No, no, I can hear you," the woman said, her voice even closer now. She had thrust her head out the window. "I thought I heard somebody gasp. Yes, *gasp*. How should I know why? I think it must have been a cat. Oh yes, you're very funny—a gasping cat." Her voice faded as she moved away from the window.

Eventually he came to Mrs. Genevieve's block. He circled it twice, peeking out from alleys and then disappearing again. The block was fairly deserted. Few pedestrians, no Directions. From an alley across the street, Reuben watched the front of Mrs. Genevieve's shop. He strained his eyes, trying to see through her display window, but the dazzle of reflected sunlight prevented him. He waited several minutes. No one entered or exited.

Reuben scanned the sidewalks once more. Empty. He took a deep breath, fixed the nearest parking meter in his mind's eye, and vanished. The parking meter, which he found with his outstretched hand, alerted him to the curb. He stepped down carefully, then hurried across the street. He had estimated that it was ten crouch-steps wide, but on his eighth step he hit the far curb and stumbled, banging his knee. Somehow he kept quiet and held on to the watch. Regaining his feet, he crept forward until his fingers touched the glass of Mrs. Genevieve's display window.

Reuben listened. No voices, not even a murmur. He readied himself. To get a glimpse inside the shop, he would have to reappear for a second or two—a very risky couple of seconds if anyone besides Mrs. Genevieve was in there. This time he was smart, though. He remembered how bright the sun was, remembered the dazzle, and so with his free hand he shielded his eyes and pressed his nose right up against the window. He pulled out on the key.

The watchmaker sat at her counter, writing in a ledger, teacup close at hand. She was alone.

Reuben's relieved exhalation fogged the glass.

At the sight of him darting in through her doorway, Mrs. Genevieve seemed to wilt. "Oh no," she said, shaking her head. "Oh, you foolish boy. You've come back." But despite her apparent displeasure, she lost no time going over to lock the door, briefly laying a hand on his shoulder as she passed.

Reuben had never felt more grateful for a simple, gentle touch. Tears sprang to his eyes, and he said nothing for fear his voice would break.

Hanging on the back of Mrs. Genevieve's shop door was a clock-shaped sign that read *Check your watch—we'll be back soon!* The sign's clock hands could be adjusted to indicate when the shop would reopen. Mrs. Genevieve set the time for an hour later and flipped the sign around to be visible from outside.

"Quickly," she said, shooing Reuben toward the door behind the counter. "We must go into my rooms."

Soon he was sitting on Mrs. Genevieve's miniature sofa, hands in his sweatshirt pockets, looking up at the watchmaker with pleading eyes. He wanted somehow for her to have a solution to his dilemma, but as he tried to explain what had happened, she only stood before him, holding her teacup over a saucer, shaking her head.

"Why did you not tell me this?" she asked the instant he stopped speaking. "That you went first to these other places? That you showed these others the clock watch?"

Reuben shrugged miserably. "I didn't think about it. I realize now how stupid that was, but I honestly didn't. It didn't occur to me that it would matter."

"It matters," Mrs. Genevieve said curtly. "Very much, it matters. The four men—the Directions—they returned that very afternoon, do you know? They wished to hear if a boy had visited me. From others in the neighborhood they had heard reports of you and this watch, so naturally they thought to ask me about it as well. You may guess what I told them."

"Thanks," Reuben mumbled.

"And now," Mrs. Genevieve went on in her angry tone, "because this monstrous individual, this 'Smoke' is aware that a boy like you was seen with the watch, the neighborhood has lived in dread, for all of his Directions, from everywhere in New Umbra, have come every day to knock on the doors of every home and business, asking about this boy. About *you*, Reuben. I alone know whom they seek. Think of all the parents in Middleton who do not know the truth, who fear to discover that it is their own child The Smoke wishes to find."

Reuben stared morosely at his feet. It seemed impossible that he could have caused such a thing. Worse, he knew that Middleton was only the beginning. Once it became clear that he was nowhere to be found in this neighborhood, the Directions would be sent into other neighborhoods, one by one, terrifying every parent of a boy who looked anything like him, until at last, inevitably, the search would extend to the Lower Downs. It was only a matter of time.

"And as if you did not find this to be enough trouble," Mrs. Genevieve was saying, still in her clipped and angry tone, "you ignore my advice and call this number in the paper! Has it occurred to you that this awful man, the one on the telephone, had perhaps heard only a rumor of this search under way in Middleton? That perhaps he *believed* it was only a rumor? But no, you called him—a boy called him—and now he is convinced of the truth. Now he, too, will be searching for you, whoever he is."

Reuben closed his eyes. In her anger, Mrs. Genevieve was clearly trying to make him feel as bad as possible. After all, the man on the phone was probably certain of the truth before Reuben called him. But there was no point in arguing, and anyway, Mrs. Genevieve was right about the most important thing—he would now have this mysterious man looking for him, and Reuben didn't even know what he looked like.

"Why have you come back?" Mrs. Genevieve demanded, and Reuben opened his eyes again. It was remarkable to him that she could give such an angry lecture while standing perfectly still, holding her teacup. When his mom got angry, her hands were all over the place—in the air, in her hair, everywhere. Not Mrs. Genevieve. Her anger was all in her eyes and her tone.

"Perhaps," Mrs. Genevieve continued, "you wish now for me to speak with the Directions, to request a reward on your behalf? Surely you must see that I am no longer in a position to do so. They will find it strange that you did not approach me on the day you approached the others, only to do so now. They will suspect that I was not truthful with them. Do you understand?"

"I wouldn't ask you to do that!" said Reuben, a little hurt. "I—I really just hoped you could help me understand what's going on. So that I could—so that I'll know what to do."

The watchmaker furrowed her brow. "What do you mean by this, 'what to do'? What is there to do but return to one of these other shops and give them the watch? You may try again to sell it

It was remarkable to him that she could give such an angry lecture while standing perfectly still, holding her teacup.

if you wish—this I leave to you—but in any case you must leave the watch and go away as quickly as possible. You are only a boy."

"It isn't that simple," Reuben said. "There's something—very special about the watch. I figured out what it does. I know its secret."

Mrs. Genevieve had been about to take a sip of her tea. She looked sharply at him over the rim of her teacup. "And so? What is this secret?"

Reuben hesitated. He had been bursting to tell her—it had been his plan all along. Mrs. Genevieve was already in on part of the secret, if not quite the most incredible part. But now that the moment was at hand, he felt strangely reluctant.

"Well?" Mrs. Genevieve looked exasperated. "Do you intend to share this information?"

Reuben swallowed hard and forced himself to nod. He had to tell her. "I'm afraid you won't believe me, though, Mrs. Genevieve."

The watchmaker clicked her teeth impatiently.

"Right. Okay. Here goes." Reuben took a deep breath. "The watch can make you turn invisible."

Mrs. Genevieve stared at him. She seemed to be waiting for him to tell her he was joking, then get on with the real explanation. He could insist for hours and she would never believe him. And why should she? Reuben would have thought it impossible, too.

"Here, I'll show you," he said, and took the watch from his sweatshirt pocket.

Mrs. Genevieve flinched at the sight of it. "You have it in your *pocket*? Can you truly be so reckless as this? This rare and beautiful clock watch, and you—"

Reuben pulled out on the key. The room went black.

He waited for her cry of surprise. Instead he heard a tinkling sound, as if something had shattered on the carpet—the teacup and saucer, he realized—followed in the next instant by a heavy, tumbling thump that could only be Mrs. Genevieve herself.

Reuben hurriedly pushed the key back in.

The watchmaker had fainted dead away.

⁊

It was fortunate that Mrs. Genevieve had collapsed forward rather than backward. Her head struck the sofa cushion on its way to the floor, breaking her fall and sparing her a nasty bump. She regained consciousness almost immediately, sat up very slowly with Reuben's help, and though she told him she felt as if she'd been hit by a train, she appeared to be more or less intact. After a few sips of brandy that Reuben, per her instructions, fetched from a cabinet and poured into a small glass, she rose unsteadily to the sofa, where she sat gazing into her drink as Reuben (also per her instructions) cleaned up the mess on her floor.

"But how can this be?" she said, not for the first time. "How am I to believe this?"

"It does take some getting used to," Reuben said, wiping his brow. He was having trouble with the broom and dustpan. "You don't have a vacuum cleaner, do you? It's kind of tough to sweep a carpet."

Mrs. Genevieve seemed not to hear his question. "But how can it work?" She looked up from her glass. "What happens to you when you disappear? What do you feel?"

Reuben shrugged. "I feel normal. Well, I go *blind*, but I feel normal."

"You go blind," Mrs. Genevieve repeated, mumbling the words. "You go blind."

"It was scary the first few times," said Reuben. "But nothing bad seems to happen. I mean, my eyes seem to be okay.

Whatever's happening—the magic or whatever—it doesn't hurt me. I think it's just the price you have to pay."

Emerging from her dazed-seeming ruminations, the watchmaker set her glass on the little side table. She clasped her fingers over one knee and regarded Reuben thoughtfully. "You use the word *magic*," she said slowly, "but I believe this seems like magic only because we do not understand it. So let us try to understand, yes?"

Reuben nodded and sat down in an upholstered chair across from her. It hadn't occurred to him that he might actually learn how the watch worked. He had been much too absorbed in what it could *do*.

"The secret must lie in the metal," Mrs. Genevieve mused after a pause. "This brilliant watchmaker was no doubt an alchemist as well. In his time, most men of genius were. Do you know this word, *alchemy*? The attempt to transform common metals into gold? Perhaps the watchmaker created this unusual metal by accident, and in the course of his experiment he discovered its incredible power."

"It seems crazy that a metal could have special powers, though," Reuben said.

"Crazy?" Mrs. Genevieve frowned. "But a great many metals have 'special powers,' Reuben. Some are toxic, some radioactive. For heaven's sake, think of magnets!" She fell silent a moment, pursing her lips. "Yet how does one control this power? This is a wonder to me."

"Do you want me to show you again?" Reuben asked, taking the watch from his pocket.

"Yes, please do," said Mrs. Genevieve, reaching for her glasses. She squinted at him with focused attention. "And explain to me everything as you do so. First you wind it...."

Reuben pointed out that there was no need to wind the watch again, as he had allowed it to unwind for only a few seconds. "So you can spread the fifteen minutes out—a minute here, another minute there, if you see what I mean." Mrs. Genevieve nodded. "And then you just back the key up out of the winding position like this."

Reuben disappeared, and Mrs. Genevieve gasped. He reappeared to find her gaping and half-risen from her seat. She blinked and slowly settled back onto the sofa cushion. "As you say, this will take some getting used to," she said in a thin voice. "Please give me a moment."

After a few more demonstrations, Mrs. Genevieve had begun to get used to it. She had stopped gasping each time, at any rate. And she had begun to develop a theory. "You say that it makes you very tired?"

"Supertired," Reuben said. "Something about being invisible just takes it right out of you."

Mrs. Genevieve shook her head. "But why should it be so exhausting? Unless..." Her hands flew to her mouth. "Of course! We have been thinking of the watch spring as the source of power. Naturally, this is the case with normal watches. But this device, to do its work, requires far more energy than such a spring can produce. It is you, Reuben. *You* power the watch! It takes energy from *you*!"

Reuben screwed up his face. "What?"

"You say your skin must be in contact with the metal, yes? Please consider, you are not magically transformed, are you? No, instead a field is generated—a field of invisibility that emanates from this watch. A human being possesses enormous energy, Reuben. This watch uses you like a battery!"

Mrs. Genevieve was clearly pleased with her idea, but Reuben wasn't at all. It felt like being told he had a parasite—a tapeworm or a leech. With a disgusted feeling, he set the watch down on the carpet and wiped his hands on his sweatshirt. Evidently, he had more to get used to than he'd realized.

Mrs. Genevieve was tapping her teeth with the tips of her well-manicured fingernails, thinking. "The winding is for your own protection," she said presently. "Yes."

"Protection?" Reuben grimaced. The watchmaker was troubling him more and more with every word she uttered.

"This is what I think," she said. "*If* the spring is wound, and *if* the key is in the proper position, and *if* you touch the metal with your skin, then a sort of circuit is completed, and the watch is energized. It does its job. But when the spring is unwound, the circuit is broken, and the watch no longer receives energy. Yes, I think it very likely that I am right. The power is mystifying, but the concept is simple." Mrs. Genevieve contemplated the watch on the carpet, considering her idea. She went back to tapping at her teeth.

"You didn't say why it's for my own protection," Reuben pointed out. "The winding."

Mrs. Genevieve lifted her gaze toward him. "Surely you can see for yourself, Reuben, what would happen if this watch continued to take energy from you indefinitely. If, say, you grew weak and lay down and fell asleep but continued to hold this watch in your hands? It would continue to do its job. You would continue to be its battery."

Reuben's mind flashed to the batteries in his toy camera. An icy shiver ran through him. "You mean, it would drain me completely, until I was...?"

Mrs. Genevieve looked at him steadily. "Yes, child. Until you were dead."

Reuben crossed his arms tightly over his chest. He drew his feet up under the chair, away from the watch. Such a dark possibility had never occurred to him. After a long silence, during which both he and the watchmaker gazed soberly at the watch, he asked, "Why do you think it makes me blind when I use it? Do you think it's hurting me, and I just don't know it?"

"Perhaps," Mrs. Genevieve said slowly, "but I think not. This blindness I do not believe does you harm. It can be explained simply enough. When the metal of the watch is energized, it generates a field that bends light around it. If you are within this field—in this place where light cannot reach your eyes—then naturally you cannot see, for vision requires light. Simple, yes?"

"I suppose so," Reuben said uncertainly. Mrs. Genevieve made it all sound like science, but he didn't wholly understand it. Still, having even this general sense of how the watch worked helped him get over his revulsion. It was not a creepy, evil thing; it was just an extremely clever device—and a beautiful one at that. Carefully he picked it up and returned it to his sweatshirt pocket.

Mrs. Genevieve took another sip of brandy. She cradled the glass in her lap and gazed without focus in the direction of the shop, as if she could see through the walls and out into the city, where all the trouble was. Reuben felt a stirring of hope. Perhaps she was about to solve his dilemma as readily as she had explained the workings of the watch.

"Of course," Mrs. Genevieve said presently, "I see now why it is not so simple to hand over this watch. You fear that others are aware of its secret. And that they wouldn't wish anyone else to know it. Perhaps because of this you fear that they will do you harm."

Reuben nodded.

"You are not foolish to wonder this. However, I believe you could proceed in such a way as to avoid problems. First you set the clock watch to a different time, and then you give it up to one of these shop owners. You admit that you found it—perhaps you even tell the truth about *where* you found it—and that this non-sense about your uncle was a lie. Then you go home, Reuben, and forget about all of this. It is doubtful anyone will suspect that you discovered the clock watch's secret, which, as we know, is not so easy to do. I will point out again: you are only a boy. You will not be considered a threat. The Directions will stop trying to find you. They will leave you alone."

Reuben thought about this awhile. Mrs. Genevieve was probably right, he knew.

And yet.

He looked at the watchmaker doubtfully. "So I should just hand it over to The Smoke. That's what you really think I should do?"

Mrs. Genevieve attempted another sip of brandy, only to find her glass empty. An irritated expression passed over her face, and she set the glass onto the side table again. It occurred to Reuben that she was stalling, searching for the right answer. Her eyes were deeply troubled. At length she said, "It is true that much evil might be done with this watch."

"That's what I was thinking, too," Reuben muttered. Even if he hadn't wanted to keep the watch, hadn't needed it to help his mom, could he ever live with himself if he let it fall into the hands of The Smoke? The Smoke, of all people!

Mrs. Genevieve sighed. "I wish, as I have so often wished, that one might call upon the police."

"Yeah," Reuben said, and that was the end of their discussion about New Umbra's police. They knew perfectly well that the police couldn't help them. Indeed, speaking with the police would only bring this dilemma to a swift and unpleasant conclusion. Everyone knew that both the police commissioner and the mayor took regular meetings with the Counselor. They kept the city running, but they were not in charge, and neither of them wanted to cross the one who was. Nobody did.

"Do you have a family, child?" Mrs. Genevieve asked, studying him.

From the moment he met her, Reuben had been wondering when she would ask that question. He had planned not to answer it, to give out as little information about himself as possible, but he found now that he wanted to tell her the truth. "My mom," he said simply. "It's just my mom and me."

Mrs. Genevieve nodded, looking more and more unhappy. Still anxious, still worried, but also strangely sad. "I think perhaps the best thing for this beautiful but terrible clock watch," she murmured, "would be to fling it into the ocean."

Reuben leaped to his feet. "But how could I do that?" he cried, his voice rising. "As long as they think I still have the watch, I'm in trouble! Even if I did throw it in the ocean, they wouldn't believe me!"

They regarded each other, Mrs. Genevieve sitting still as a statue, Reuben's chest heaving as if he'd been running for his life. Neither one said what they both were thinking, which was that it might well be worse for Reuben if The Smoke *did* believe such a thing. For if The Smoke suspected that Reuben had purposely gotten rid of the watch to keep it out of his hands—this elusive prize he'd sought for so many years—then there would surely be a retribution.

This is what happens to boys who cross The Smoke. And this is what happens to their families.

Reuben looked away from Mrs. Genevieve. He didn't like seeing his own fears reflected in her eyes. It made them worse somehow. He turned and went to the shop door.

"Where are you going?" Mrs. Genevieve asked, startled.

"I have to go home," Reuben said. His hand was on the doorknob. He felt afraid to go out, yet he couldn't stay.

"Reuben!" Mrs. Genevieve said sharply.

He flinched and looked back. Her blue eyes glistened with tears.

"You must be careful," she said, looking quite stern as she tried to keep her face composed. "More careful than you have been. These Directions—they are all over the neighborhood.

Four here, four there, always looking. So many eyes, Reuben, and all of them looking for a boy like you."

For a moment Reuben made no reply. She'd said nothing he didn't already know. And yet he still felt grateful to her, in ways he couldn't properly express. At last he said, "Thanks for your help, Mrs. Genevieve. And thanks—um, thanks for caring, I guess. Yeah." He nodded. That felt right. "Thanks for caring." For only now was he realizing how much it meant to him that the number of people who worried about him—the number of people in all the world—had expanded from one to two. Somehow it felt like more than that.

The watchmaker had risen from the sofa but only stood there, regarding him with a look of helplessness. She looked as though she needed comforting herself.

"It's going to be okay," Reuben said. And with that, he flung open the door and ran out.

LOOKING FOR LIGHT

Locking the apartment door behind him, Reuben stumbled to his room and dropped the watch onto his bed. He was exhausted, sweating, faint with hunger. He'd used the watch too much with too little rest, the result of feeling pursued. From now on he needed to plan ahead better, for that feeling wasn't going to go away, he knew. He struggled out of his sweatshirt as if from a straitjacket and let it fall to the floor. He stood there a moment, panting from the effort.

He should tell his mom everything. He knew that he should. He even *wanted* to tell her. But then what?

Reuben staggered into the kitchen, took a TV dinner from

the freezer, and fumbled it into the microwave. With bleary eyes he watched it go round and round on the revolving glass tray. If he told his mom the truth, she would make him give up the watch. Her child in danger? No question. But he would still be in danger, he was sure of it, and so would she. The Smoke would want his secret protected. The Smoke would take no chances.

Reuben peeled off the TV dinner's plastic covering and watched the steam escape. *Escape*, he thought. That was what he needed. New Umbra had suddenly become a nightmare. The Directions were looking for him. The man on the phone was looking for him. The Smoke himself was probably out looking for him. Yes, he and his mom needed to get out of the city, but where would they go? With what? They had no money, no family. And how could Reuben convince his mom of anything without telling her the whole truth?

He didn't have the answers. He didn't think he even knew all the questions. It amazed him that earlier on this very day, he had been trying to figure out a way to get money so that they could *stay*. Now he needed to accomplish the exact opposite, and it seemed infinitely harder.

The dinner, a bland potpie, was still half-frozen in the middle. Reuben ate it anyway, too hungry and tired to care. He sat hunched at the kitchen table, thinking. The watch had gotten him into this mess, and now he needed it to get him out again. But what was he missing? If his mom was right, if there was always another way, then there had to be something he hadn't considered yet. So what was it?

He tried to think of the things he didn't know. How did others know about the watch, for instance? How did they find out about it? He was tormented by the awareness that The Smoke knew things he didn't. The same with the man on the phone. If Reuben knew what *they* did, maybe his path would seem clearer. Maybe he could set them against each other somehow. Cause a commotion and slip away for good. *He* was the one with the watch, after all. He had power; he just needed more information.

But that was the problem. How could he find it? Where to even start? Reuben groaned and put his head down on his arms. What was he missing? What had he overlooked?

He was still asking himself these questions when he fell asleep. And half an hour later, he woke up with the answer.

It had happened to Reuben before; maybe it happened to every-body. Important things would emerge while he slept, remain floating on the surface of his thoughts when he woke. *P. William Light.*

The name was a clue to a mystery he'd never tried to solve. Sure, he'd spent hours wondering about this man to whom the watch had once belonged, but he'd never tried to actually find anything out. All of a sudden P. William Light was an ally, a friend from the past. Maybe he had something to tell Reuben, some advice to give.

And maybe, Reuben thought as he jumped up from the table, he was grasping at straws because he was desperate. But what else was he supposed to do?

He went to his closet and unbundled the wooden box. One of the antiques dealers had told him that it was perhaps a century old, and very well made. Its custom design and magnificent con-tents suggested that its owner had been wealthy, possibly a figure of some importance. At the time, Reuben hadn't found the box itself of much interest. But now questions began to form.

Why hadn't P. William Light included an address in the inscription? If the watch were mislaid and then found again, how would the finder locate the owner? Reuben scoured the box in case he'd missed something. Nothing. Had Light been important enough to assume that everyone knew him? If so, maybe Reuben could find out something about him. That would be a start, anyway.

He glanced at the alarm clock. The library closed in an hour. Outside, storm clouds had gathered. Thunder rumbled in the distance. A few fat drops of rain began to fall. Reuben didn't mind. An impending storm was a good excuse to pull up his sweatshirt hood, the better to hide his face, and to hurry along the sidewalk without drawing attention.

In the library foyer Reuben walked past the phone with a shudder. He couldn't bear to look at it. Had it really been only a few hours since he'd fed coins into it with such confident expectation? That had been in his old life. The life before that voice in his ear.

The library had always seemed rather dim to Reuben, but now, in contrast to the threatening darkness outside, it seemed brilliantly bright. It also appeared to be completely empty. He went straight to the reference section and began flipping through encyclopedias. He found entries on a few different men named "William Light"—an Australian military man, a rodeo star (who went by "Billy"), a crooked politician—but none whose first initial was *P*. He checked a biographical dictionary. Nothing. He closed the heavy book with a frustrated thump of the cover. He was going to have to face the librarian.

Reuben approached the desk warily. The librarian hated conversation. He always made Reuben nervous with his brusque talk and the way he avoided eye contact. And now Reuben had embarrassed him by startling him among the bookshelves last week. He felt sure the man would resent having to help him. Still, Reuben summoned his nerve and made his request as politely as he could.

" 'P. William Light'?" the librarian repeated gruffly, looking above Reuben's head. His eyes shifted back and forth behind his glasses as if he were watching an insect flying around. "Who was he?"

"That's what I'm trying to find out," Reuben explained. "I

think he might have been someone important, probably around a hundred years ago."

Now the librarian was looking down at his desk. His eyebrows were so bushy they overhung the rims of his glasses; it made his glasses appear to have eyelashes. "Indexes," he said, and rose from his chair.

Half an hour later the desk was covered with binders, directories, and other assorted volumes. The librarian had gone through them one by one as Reuben stood anxiously watching, shifting his weight from foot to foot. The man had spoken not a single word, which, over the course of a half hour, created a remarkably awkward tension. From time to time Reuben glanced around. They remained the only two people in the library.

The librarian drew his finger down rows and rows of words, page after page. After the first few minutes, Reuben had stopped trying to figure out what sorts of indexes he was checking. None had produced results. But now the man paused, marking a place with his finger, and looked up in the direction of Reuben's arm. "You're looking for a person? Not a place?"

Reuben flinched. The sudden gruff questions were as unnerving as the silence. "That's right," he said quickly. "P. William Light." The librarian grunted, licked his finger, and flipped the page. Reuben looked away in despair.

At last the librarian closed a binder, shook his head, and muttered something indecipherable. Perhaps he thought this sufficiently communicative. Not until he rose from his desk and began putting his materials away did Reuben realize that the librarian had found nothing, that the search was over. The disappointment caught in his throat like a stone. After a moment he managed to mumble his thanks to the man, who did not reply, and drifted away scowling. Never had he met anyone so reluctant to speak unless absolutely necessary.

At the library door Reuben hesitated, looking out at the

still-dark afternoon. There was a haze of drizzle in the air, fuzzing the outlines of everything on the street. Something had occurred to him. He turned and walked back to the librarian's desk.

"Excuse me," he said. The man turned from a shelf, his arms full of binders, and looked expectantly at Reuben's shoulder. "Why did you ask if I might be looking for a place instead of a person?"

The librarian cleared his throat. "Because there's a place called Point William—a town about fifty miles up the coast—and the lighthouse there is called the Point William Light. There's a newspaper story about it. We have it on microfiche." He turned and went back to shelving his materials.

Reuben blinked. P. William Light. *Point* William Light. *Property of Point William Light.*

Minutes later, at Reuben's request, the librarian had set him up at a dusty microfiche machine and scrolled to the pertinent story. Reuben stared at the screen. There it was. Point William, a small town with nothing to distinguish it except for its historic lighthouse—known as the Point William Light—and the fact that the lighthouse had always been kept by members of the same family, generation after generation, all the way back to its earliest days. It was the town's local paper that had done the story, focusing on a squabble about property ownership.

Reuben had been reading for approximately one minute when the librarian announced that the library was closing.

"Okay," Reuben said, trying hurriedly to finish the article.

The librarian flipped a switch. The screen went dark. "We're closing," he repeated, and returned to his desk.

Reuben pushed his chair back, his eyes still fixed pointlessly on the screen. He had read enough, though, and his mind was churning. Property of Point William Light. The same family for generations. If he was right—if that *P* stood for *Point*—then the descendants of a person who had once possessed the watch were still living in Point William. They were the lighthouse keepers.

Reuben felt himself shudder, whether from excitement or anxiety he couldn't have said. He had solved one mystery only to fall into another. What did the watch have to do with those people? Did they have any claim to it? What might they tell him? Was there any way they might *help* him?

And the most pressing question of all: What was he going to tell his mom?

For Reuben knew, without even considering it, that he had to go to Point William. He would find answers there. He'd known it the instant he learned the truth about the inscription. A voice in his head—his own voice, but somehow smarter and more confident than him—had said it plainly.

Follow the light.

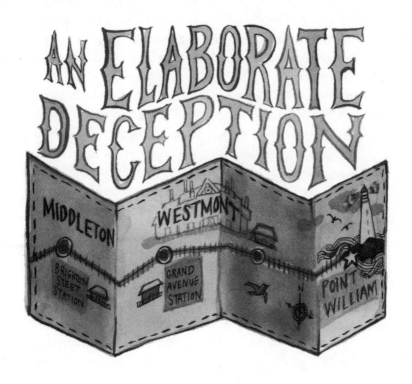

AN ELABORATE DECEPTION

In the end, it was surprisingly easy.

"I'm glad you want to go," his mom said. She'd been home perhaps twenty seconds when Reuben hit her with his story. "You know that, right? I'm just a little taken aback. You've never been on a sleepover before. Miles Chang? The nice one?"

Reuben shrugged. "Yeah, he just came up to me at the community center. He said his dad can pick me up Friday morning and bring me back Sunday afternoon."

He was making it so easy for her: the nice kid, with the nice teacher for a dad; the offer of a ride so she wouldn't have to worry about getting him there; the chance for her son to finally make a friend. And yet his mom chewed her lip a long time, as if in deep inner debate about the matter, and Reuben had to pretend not to be seriously worried about her decision. He didn't have a backup plan.

"What if they want to take you to a movie?" she wondered aloud. "Or go out for dinner? You'd need money."

So *that* was her hesitation, the fact that they were desperately broke. "Oh, don't worry about that!" Reuben groped for what to say. "They probably won't. I mean, I'm sure they won't, and anyway I have a few dollars—"

His mom shushed him. "No, you keep your money. I have a little I can give you. Oh, don't look so surprised! Maybe I can't pay the rent, but I can certainly fund my son's first sleepover…."

Yes, it was all surprisingly easy. Reuben felt enormously relieved. And enormously guilty.

After they'd said good night, Reuben went to his room and counted the money she'd given him, along with the small amount he'd saved himself. It ought to be enough to pay for a train ticket, he thought. If not, well, he *could* turn invisible, after all.

As he put the money away, he noticed that his hands were trembling. He thought he knew why. That conversation with his mom had been the last big obstacle. Now that he'd gotten through it, the matter was settled. He was going. By this time on Friday, he'd be in another town, a place he'd never been, and he'd be entirely on his own. He would have to keep his mom convinced that he was at a sleepover. He would have to observe and deal with strangers. He had to try to learn something incredibly important—and potentially dangerous—without getting discovered himself.

He was becoming, in other words, an actual spy.

ﾟ

Friday morning Reuben lay in bed, listening to his mom bustle about the apartment. It was almost time. He'd been awake for over an hour, but he was waiting until the last possible minute. The less discussion the better.

When his mom had come home from work the night before, Reuben had pretended to be asleep. He'd heard the soft thunks of her shoes as she kicked them off, heard her sigh with relief as she dropped her bag beside them. Then she had slipped quietly into his room and sat on the edge of his bed. And there she had remained, just sitting, for what seemed like ages. Was she hoping he'd wake up and talk to her? Or was she just looking at him, thinking troubled or tender things? Just being a mom?

At last she had risen, pulled the covers up around his shoulders, and kissed him very gently on the forehead. Reuben had felt a knot in his throat, and it took everything in him not to open his eyes and speak to her. Afterward he had lain awake for a long time, staring into darkness.

It was time. His mom had to leave now or she'd be late for work. Reuben rolled out of bed and walked into the living room, making a show of yawning and rubbing his eyes. His mom was putting her bags over her shoulders. She set them down again and gave him a big squeeze.

"You have fun," she ordered, and reminded him of his promise to call her each night.

"I will," Reuben said. "You have fun, too."

His mom rolled her eyes. "Oh, I'll have a grand time, I'm sure." She kissed him and went out.

Reuben locked the door behind her and went to his bedroom closet. In case his mom checked his backpack, he hadn't put the wooden box in yet. Now he took it from its hiding place, still in its bundle, and wrapped it up in his windbreaker, which he stuffed deep inside the backpack. The watch and key he would keep in his sweatshirt pocket, ready to use.

Queasy with nerves, he forced himself to eat breakfast. He might need every ounce of energy. He took the fastest shower of his life, for it made him very ill at ease not to have the watch on him at all times, and as soon as he'd dried off, he made sure the watch was fully wound and set precisely to twelve o'clock. He had developed an abiding dread of the hour hand getting nudged out of position unbeknownst to him. He had nightmares of finding himself in a dangerous situation, discovering too late that the time wasn't properly set.

But the watch was fully wound; the hour hand was in precise position. He was ready.

Reuben got dressed, shouldered the backpack, and went out.

Yesterday he had spent the better part of an hour studying subway maps and train schedules, making sure of his route. To his dismay, however, he arrived at the Lower Downs subway station to discover that the line he needed was closed due to track repair.

The morning was unseasonably cool, but standing before the faded map on the station wall, jostled by early commuters who seemed to resent his backpack, Reuben started to sweat. He had to get to the Grand Avenue station, the city's central terminal, where he could purchase a train ticket to Point William. The route he'd planned would have been very straightforward. But now, because of the closed line, he had to take a more complicated one that involved changing trains twice—and the first change would be at the Brighton Street station.

Reuben studied the map intently, hoping he was wrong. But no, any other route would take him halfway around the city, a longer trip by far, and he might miss the train to Point William. There wouldn't be another until evening, and arriving in a strange town after dark was too daunting, too scary even to contemplate. And so Reuben memorized the new route, bought his ticket, and headed warily down to the platform.

It was rush hour. The Lower Downs subway commuters stood shoulder to shoulder in their work clothes, carrying their secondhand briefcases and purses and satchels, smelling of harsh soap, cheap aftershave, cheap lotions and perfumes. Some stared sleepily ahead; one or two were reading. Reuben squeezed in among the masses, and when the train came, he squeezed through its doors along with all the others.

Only after he was on the train did he notice the Directions in his car. Frontman and the others, on their way to the Counselor's mansion, where they would deliver their reports and their envelopes, receive their wages, and no doubt discuss the boy they'd been seeking without success in Middleton. They stood near the doors, hanging on to straps. They were the only passengers not pressed against anyone—people were giving them room. The four men chatted idly with one another, but even on the subway train they kept up their habit of surveying the area around them. Reuben, peeking out through a tangle of adult arms and shoulders, would be hard to spot. And yet.

He was supposed to get off at the Brighton Street station. What if they saw him, a boy fitting the description of the one they sought, disembarking in precisely the neighborhood they had been searching? Inside his sweatshirt pocket, Reuben's fingers squeezed the watch key.

Don't fiddle with it! he scolded himself. Did he want to accidentally vanish in the middle of all these people? A young boy disappearing into thin air would cause a panic. It would certainly get the Directions' attention. And where would he escape to? The car was so jam-packed he could scarcely move.

Reuben quickly tried to calculate a different plan. Nothing worked. He could skip the Brighton Street station, but to no good purpose—the next few stations were also in Middleton. The one after that was in Westmont, but *that* was the neighborhood in which the Counselor's mansion was located, and he dared not risk getting off at the same stop as the Directions. Besides, most of the commuters worked in Middleton and would

*Only after he was on the train did
he notice the Directions in his car.*

be getting off soon. What if he found himself alone in the car with the Directions?

Brighton Street was the next stop. Reuben slowly moved his hands up the straps of his backpack, as if adjusting them. Then, just as slowly, like an extremely sleepy person who can barely bring himself to tie his shoes or rise from his seat, he took hold of the hood on his sweatshirt and eased it up and over his head. Slowly, slowly, he brought his hands back down to his sides. He slipped one hand into the pocket with the watch.

The train stopped, and the doors slid open. Reuben lowered his head and angled it slightly away from the Directions. He synchronized his step with that of the woman who'd been standing next to him, letting her shield him from view, but she was only moving to take a vacated seat, and so he instantly adjusted, matching his stride to that of the nearest man pressing toward the doors. Out on the platform he slipped behind a pillar and waited, listening. He had tuned himself to the Directions' voices, though he couldn't make out their words. If he noted a tone of exclamation or puzzlement...

He heard no such thing, and as the train pulled out of the station, he edged around the pillar to keep out of sight. The commuters streamed up the steps toward Brighton Street, leaving the platform mostly empty. Reuben leaned against the pillar. He hadn't even used the watch, but already he felt worn out from the tension.

He withdrew the watch from his pocket and checked the setting. Still at twelve o'clock. He tucked it away again and proceeded, anxiously, to wait. Middleton, of course, was the last place that he wanted to be. He even thought he noticed some of the people on the platform looking askance at him. The Directions had probably already knocked on their doors, asking about a boy who met Reuben's description. Or maybe he was imagining their sidelong glances. Maybe it wasn't necessary to hide his face.

He hid his face regardless.

Ten minutes later Reuben greeted, with tremendous relief, the telltale wind that precedes approaching subway trains. It came blowing out of the tunnel, smelling of burned rubber and grease, followed by the train's light suddenly piercing the gloom. Then came the train itself, squealing along the tracks. It was fairly crowded, and Reuben scanned the passing windows for the ideal car. Spotting a group of kids, he tracked the car down the platform and jostled his way aboard.

Judging from their matching T-shirts, the kids were part of a church group, accompanied by a couple of frazzled-looking adults. Reuben got in among them as if he belonged. By some miracle there was even an open seat, and after a split-second battle with embarrassment, he dropped into it and fixed his eyes on the floor. He sensed one or two of the kids giving him looks of surprise and annoyance. They quickly forgot him, though. They were all talking over one another, loud and boisterous.

The train lurched and began to move. Furtively Reuben checked his watch—still properly set. He put it away. He was perched a bit uncomfortably on the edge of his seat; his backpack took up most of the room, but the subway car was too crowded for him to take the pack off. He leaned back against it, trying to settle in as best he could. The train would make several stops, passing through Westmont and a few other neighborhoods before he needed to get off again. The kids around him were being obnoxious, teasing one another, vying for attention, repeatedly being shushed by their exasperated group leaders. Reuben was grateful for them; they were his camouflage. He let his eyes roam around the train car.

Beyond the church group were the usual throng of work commuters (it was still rush hour), one or two families, and a teenager clinging to a pole, wearing a dilapidated set of earphones. Reuben's eyes drifted to the opposite end of the car: more commuters, as well as a few other isolated passengers whose purpose or destination he couldn't guess from their manner. Among these, in the far corner of the car, with a satchel and some papers in his lap, sat an oddly fierce-looking man with hunched shoulders. There was something in the fixed concentration of the man's gaze, an air about him of coiled tension, that made him seem very much like a cat that had just spotted a mouse.

For a moment Reuben wondered what the man was staring at so intently. And then, in the next moment, he stopped breathing, for he had just realized that the object of the man's gaze was himself.

He wanted to be wrong, but he knew that he wasn't. There was no mistaking it.

Reuben was the mouse.

THE STARING STRANGER

Reuben jerked in his seat as if he'd been shocked, and quickly looked away. But the image was burned into his mind. The man had been sitting with a pencil in his hand, the satchel lying flat in his lap, a folded bundle of papers half-hidden beneath it. A casual observer might have thought the man was simply deep in thought, gazing out across the car without actually seeing anything. But he hadn't been gazing at nothing. He'd been staring at Reuben.

Maybe it's nothing, Reuben told himself, trying to believe it. His heart was racing. *Calm down. You're being paranoid.* He snuck another glance.

The man was still staring at him. And that was definitely the word for it: *staring*. Not a casual or absent gaze, but a look of searching intensity. Their eyes met, and Reuben looked away again, a sour, acid taste rising in his throat.

You took the watch out, he thought. *He saw you get on by yourself, and he was watching you, and he saw you glance at the watch.* Reuben swallowed hard. He needed to be calm, try to think clearly. He had been careful, hadn't he? Bending over the open watch, shielding it with a cupped hand? It was almost impossible for the man to have seen it from all the way across the car. But then why was he staring at Reuben? Who was he?

Reuben pretended not to be unnerved. Let the man think himself mistaken; let him come to the conclusion that this boy with the backpack was just a member of the church group, just a random kid with nothing to hide. He allowed his eyes to drift casually in the man's direction, not looking directly at the man, but near enough to take in his appearance. The man wore a very old dark blue suit that seemed too tight for him, bunching around his hunched shoulders, while the knot in his brown tie seemed entirely too large—it looked like a bread roll held in place by his chin. His brown-and-gray hair looked greasy even from a distance, possibly slicked with hair oil, and was combed across a large pale bald spot in the center of his head. His eyebrows were gray and owlish and gave the man a ferocious aspect. Or perhaps that was simply the effect of his glare, the horrible glare that Reuben was pretending not to notice.

The train pulled into a station. Passengers moved toward the doors; a few seats opened up. The man rose, clutching his belongings awkwardly against his belly, and moved to a seat near the middle of the car. He was now much closer to Reuben, and Reuben felt thoroughly sick.

He told himself that the man might just be strange. There were plenty of strange people in this city. What was that folded bundle of papers under his satchel? It looked like a map, covered with scribblings. Yes, it was, a map of the city. Maybe the man was a tourist. A very weird tourist. Maybe Reuben reminded him of a boy he knew, a nephew or grandson. Maybe he thought Reuben *was* a boy he knew, and was just waiting for Reuben to recognize him and say hello.

Reuben told himself these things, but he didn't believe any of them.

The train made more stops. More people got off and on. Sometimes passengers obscured the man from Reuben's view; sometimes Reuben was conscious of his unwavering gaze from across the car. Several times Reuben, in his nervousness, came close to peeking at the watch without thinking about it. Exactly the opposite of what he needed to do, which was to look normal, as if he belonged to this group of kids, and keep the watch hidden at all costs.

Reuben was so preoccupied by the creepy stranger, so intent on trying to act as if he didn't notice the man's stare, that he almost missed his stop. He had lost track of the stations along the line, and the conductor's loudspeaker announcements were always unintelligible, so he had no idea where he was until the children around him began gathering themselves to disembark. Reuben looked up, startled into focus—and felt a warm rush of relief. This was his stop, too! He could get off with the church group!

When the doors opened, he thrust himself among the other kids, ignoring their skeptical and annoyed looks, and stayed with them as their group leaders herded them out onto the platform and up the stairs. He hoped they would be changing trains, just as he was. But it soon became clear that this was their last stop, and Reuben was forced to separate from them. He glanced around the crowded station. No sign of the stranger. Maybe he hadn't even gotten off the train.

Reuben latched onto a family headed for his platform. It was a young couple with three young children, one of whom was carrying a balloon. Reuben followed them so closely that the balloon kept bumping him in the face. The kids noticed him and gave him curious looks, but their parents were concentrating on keeping them close in the crowd, making sure they were all holding hands. Yes, they were indeed catching the same train. Reuben would stick to them like glue, pretending to be an older brother.

Waiting on the crowded platform, he began to calm down. He still hadn't seen the stranger, and the more he considered, the more he thought that he probably wouldn't. Most likely the man had simply been odd, and Reuben simply paranoid.

The train came, and Reuben followed his adopted family aboard. Again the car was crowded, but a couple of men gave up their seats for the mother and her youngest child, who had begun to cry about something. Reuben stayed close to the father and the other two children, holding on to the same pole. Once again he had a balloon in his face. He began to think the child was doing it on purpose. Well, it was only a few stops to the Grand Avenue station. He could put up with it for that long.

At the last stop before Grand Avenue, the family got off, along with several other passengers. The balloon trailed away. Turning slightly—very slightly, for the car was still crowded and his backpack limited his movement—Reuben looked around for another potential family. Mostly he was surrounded by sleepy-looking grown-ups without children. There was also a very old couple, each cradling a tiny dog, and a construction crew wearing dusty coveralls. Reuben shifted the other way and craned his neck.

Seated in the far corner was a man in a very old, ill-fitting blue suit.

Reuben gasped and looked away, as if by looking away he could make the man not be real. It might still be a coincidence. It really might be. The Grand Avenue station was the city's busiest terminal. Lots of people would be headed there this morning. Lots of people would have needed to change trains, just as Reuben had. This strange man, too. It was just a coincidence that he'd gotten on the same car.

The train pulled into the Grand Avenue station. The doors opened. Reuben, watching the man out of the corner of his eye, stepped out onto the platform with a dozen other passengers. The man exited the car through the other door. Reuben froze. People pushed past him, muttering. Some were disembarking, others boarding. Reuben had lost sight of the man in the crowd, but he was taking no chances. He jumped back onto the train and grabbed the nearest pole.

As the doors were closing, a pale hand with yellowish, badly bitten fingernails grabbed the pole a few inches above his own. Reuben looked up into the eyes of the stranger. The man must have been right behind him. His staring brown eyes were bloodshot. He was a small man, or rather an average-sized man whose hunched shoulders made him seem shorter than he was. Nonetheless, he towered over Reuben.

"What are the odds?" the man murmured. His breath smelled powerfully of mint. "I keep seeing you on the same trains. Did you get off at the wrong stop, too? Funny, isn't it? How easily one grows confused among these crowds." His mouth moved as if he were trying to smile but not quite managing it. He was being cagey now, trying not to seem menacing. His voice was eerily familiar, like something from a scary radio program.

Reuben's tongue felt dry and strange in his mouth; it might have been a leather strap. His scalp tingled. He had to get away, and he didn't know how. He tried to put the pole between himself and the stranger, but the car was too crowded for him to move far.

"You aren't lost, are you?" the man said, knitting his brows together into an expression of concern, a simple change of aspect that nonetheless made him seem almost handsome. Perhaps he actually had been handsome once. "Do you need help?"

Reuben shook his head, avoiding the man's gaze. His mind bounced around crazily, searching every corner for an answer. He was dimly aware that a few of the adults nearby were casting sidelong glances at him and the stranger, having heard what the man said. Then his awareness of this fact crystallized, and Reuben felt a rush of hope, because of course that was his answer: other adults.

The train was pulling into the next station. Reuben grabbed the arm of a woman near him. "Please!" he cried, looking up into her startled face. "This stranger is following me! He's been following me all morning! Please help!"

For a second the woman looked annoyed at being grabbed. Then, as Reuben's words sank in, she scowled at the stranger, whose bloodshot eyes grew very wide. Other people were turning toward them. Suddenly there erupted a great commotion of inquiring and angry voices. Reuben saw the men from the construction crew pushing through the crowded car.

"What did he say?"

"The kid says this guy is following him!"

"Which kid? Which guy?"

The doors opened, and Reuben yelled, "Please stop him! Please stop him! Help me!" He bent double and bulled his way forward, pushing as hard as he could, squeezing through the rising tumult and out the door. He looked back to see the grown-ups pushing and pulling, seeming to grab hold of one another at random, calling out in louder and louder voices. The stranger was lost among them.

Reuben kept moving, his ears attuned to the excited cries behind him.

"I have him!"

He bent double and bulled his way forward,
pushing as hard as he could, squeezing through
the rising tumult and out the door.

"Was the boy telling the truth? Hey, kid!"

"What the hey? Where'd he go?"

More cries of "Where is he?" and "Where'd he go?" followed Reuben to the stairs.

Anywhere but here, he thought. That's where he was going.

He flew up the steps as fast as he could, running awkwardly because of his backpack and because he had one hand in his sweatshirt pocket, clutching the watch. Out on the busy street he asked a hot dog vendor the way to the Grand Avenue station. He set off at a gallop, already out of breath.

Every few steps Reuben glanced over his shoulder. No sign of the stranger. After a couple of blocks he slowed to a fast walk, gasping, his side aching. Finally he arrived at the Grand Avenue station.

Normally, Reuben, who had never traveled anywhere outside the city, would have found an out-of-the-way corner in which to stand quietly, reading signs and watching other travelers until he figured out what to do. But a glance at the huge clock suspended above the gallery told him he hadn't a minute to lose. He approached a young woman reading a train schedule, and she directed him to the right ticket counter. There was a long line.

In a state of agitated confusion, Reuben waited. He had too many things to think about all at once. Checking the clock, checking the street entrances for a sign of the stranger, checking his progress in line. He had no thought of anything else. And then, all of a sudden, he was at the counter, paying for his ticket; then racing to the platform, from which his train was about to depart; then sliding into an empty seat—sweating, gasping, and frazzled—just as the train heaved forward.

The old man across from Reuben gave him a sleepy glance and closed his eyes again. Reuben took off his backpack with relief, dropping it onto the floor between his feet. Still panting and terribly thirsty, he watched out the window as the train left the station, passed through a final subway tunnel, and emerged into open air. It rattled along the tracks through a neighborhood Reuben had never seen, veering toward the coast. His thoughts were still wildly scattered, flying out in every direction like birds startled from a tree.

Not until he had caught his breath, cooled down, and handed over his ticket did those birds begin to settle back onto their branches. The train had passed into a new neighborhood now, and would soon leave that one behind as well. And Reuben knew that, for the moment, he was safe. Safe from the Directions, safe from the stranger.

He also understood—not with any sudden burst of realization, but rather a gradual awareness of something he'd known right away—why the stranger's voice had sounded familiar. He had heard it on the library pay phone. He was sure of it. And now that he'd met the voice's owner, he was at a loss for what to think. The man, with his outdated suit and stooped shoulders, did not seem powerful, and yet, at the same time, he seemed dangerous—more dangerous by far than the Directions ever had.

And Reuben had something the man desperately wanted, and now the man knew what he looked like.

Reuben shuddered and stared out the window, straining for a glimpse of the distant ocean. He needed to see it, needed to know that he truly had left the city behind. And soon he did see it—a light, glittery blue, bright and promising, and Reuben felt his shoulders relax ever so slightly. He realized how badly he'd needed this, needed a chance to figure some things out without constantly worrying about being identified. No wonder he'd leaped at the idea of going to Point William. Yes, he'd wanted answers, but he had also wanted out of New Umbra.

He kept staring at the ocean in the distance, that broad sparkling of blue. Even now, his mom was icing down fish at the market in Riverside—a job she hated, but hated even more to lose. Her head was full of worries, and it was only going to get worse. Reuben was going to fix that, though. He'd be going back for her, and the next time he left New Umbra, he'd be leaving for good.

He was practicing his escape.

PART II

THE MEYER LEGACY

A Riddle and a Ruse

By the time the conductor announced Point William as the next stop, Reuben had long since finished writing one letter to Mrs. Genevieve—a rambling, anxious one—only to crumple it up and write a substantially different letter, a shorter, calmer one that reflected the improvement in his outlook. For the long train ride from the city had done much to dispel his feelings of anxiety and gloom. With every little town station that Reuben had passed through, with every glimpse of the sparkling ocean in the distance, he had felt an increased sense of confidence, even optimism.

Reuben read over the letter one last time. It informed the

watchmaker of his destination and purpose and asked that she contact his mother should he not return to New Umbra. He had every expectation, he wrote, of a short, safe trip and a timely return. But accidents do happen, and seeing as how his mom believed him to be staying with a friend in the city, when in fact he was in a town fifty miles to the north, he thought it important that someone he trusted know the truth of his whereabouts. If Mrs. Genevieve hadn't heard from him by the time she received this letter, would she please call his mom at the following number? He thanked her in advance, thanked her again for all she'd done to help him, and promised to visit her as soon as it was safe to do so.

Satisfied, Reuben sealed the letter inside the stamped and addressed envelope he'd brought with him. If he mailed it today, it should arrive in New Umbra on Monday, or Tuesday at the latest. He hoped it would prove unnecessary. He hoped he would be back at home Sunday evening, armed with answers. It was possible, wasn't it? He stood and pulled on his backpack. Clutching the letter in one hand, he quickly returned the other to his sweatshirt pocket, to the reassuring touch of the hidden watch. Yes, anything was possible.

At the Point William station Reuben disembarked into the sunshine of a beautiful morning. He took in a deep breath of pleasant seaside air, glanced around, and walked across the platform to study a display map of the town. There wasn't much to study. He was minutes from the town square, minutes from the shore, minutes from everywhere, really. Rounding the station house, he shielded his eyes against the sun and looked seaward. There it was, rising above the rooftops of the town—the dark green lantern dome of the lighthouse.

Reuben deposited his letter in the station mailbox, checked his watch, and set out walking.

Point William, he discovered, was a storybook town. Its

residents enjoyed charming green parks; ample sidewalks lit by decorative lampposts and shaded by old trees; views of the bay from its boardwalks and high streets—and, from almost any spot in town, at least a glimpse of its picturesque lighthouse. A hundred feet tall, built of gleaming whitewashed stone, the lighthouse stood within shouting distance of the mainland, on an oblong grassy island just large enough to accommodate the keeper's house, a small stone oil house, and the lighthouse tower itself.

Moored to a pier on the island was a blue rowboat that at present hardly needed mooring, for the tide had almost entirely receded. The little boat floated in mere inches of water and soon would be resting on mud.

Reuben gazed out at the island, wondering how to proceed. It hadn't occurred to him that he wouldn't be able to approach the lighthouse on foot. He sat cross-legged at the edge of the nearest mainland dock, considering the problem. He'd been at it for some minutes when a figure emerged from the keeper's two-story white clapboard house and walked—or, rather, skipped—across the grass toward the oil house, a squat stone building partly obscured by small, gnarled evergreens. The figure appeared to be a young girl in a bright red hat. She glanced briefly in Reuben's direction but did not seem to notice him sitting motionless on the dock. She ducked into the oil house.

Reuben waited to see if she would reappear. Seagulls dipped in and out of his view, uttering their forlorn cries. A few had begun to splash down into the rapidly diminishing water between his dock and the island, snatching up tidal snacks. On the island nothing moved. Reuben rose and hurried back to the bustling town square, which on his way down from the train station he had naturally avoided.

He found what he wanted in the first place he tried, an old-fashioned general store doing a brisk business. Its friendly proprietor, a stout middle-aged man with curly red hair, greeted him with a look of curiosity—no doubt he knew all the children in town and wondered at the appearance of a stranger—but fortunately he asked no questions, and soon Reuben was back at the dock.

There were several such docks dotting the coastline, and farther to the north was a long boardwalk fronted by snack stands, a T-shirt and sundry shop, a bait shop, and a seafood restaurant or two. Some children roamed the boardwalk, and there were pedestrians moving about the streets between his dock and the town square. But no one was close enough to see what Reuben was up to. He sat down on the weathered planks, yanked off his sneakers, and poked his feet into the knee-high muck boots he'd bought. The sneakers he stuffed into his backpack.

Reuben climbed down a ladder into the smelly black mud uncovered by the outgoing tide. He sank up to the middle of his shins. Okay, he thought, he could do this. With effort he took a couple of backward steps through the sucking, clinging mud, into the shadows beneath the dock. He got out the watch, made sure it was fully wound, and stared across the mudflats toward the island. There was still no one in sight, but if he reappeared too soon, anyone watching from the windows of the keeper's house or the lighthouse tower could easily spot him.

He had fifteen minutes to make it across that expanse of mud. Reuben concentrated on the island's little dock. He would shoot for that, try to reach the shadows beneath it before his time ran out.

"You can do this," he told himself again, this time whispering it aloud. And pulling the winding key into position, he vanished and set out blindly across the mud.

He had taken two steps when one of his feet came halfway out of its boot and he almost fell face-first. Worse, in his flailing to keep himself upright, he almost let go of the watch, which would have been flung off into the mud and quite possibly lost. The thought upset him so much he had to take a minute to calm down. He slipped the watch back into his right sweatshirt pocket, keeping his hand firmly wrapped about it; and in that way, with only one hand free to help him maintain balance, Reuben pushed ahead.

The crossing was much more difficult than he had expected it to be. The hardest part was keeping his feet inside the boots, which stubbornly resisted every step. He was tempted to abandon them—to go back to the dock, remove his socks and roll up his pants, and proceed with bare feet. But all that would take time, and there was no guarantee that someone wouldn't happen along at any moment, ruining his chances. Besides, who knew what broken glass or jagged, rusty tin cans lay hidden in that mud? So Reuben pressed on with the boots.

The boots weren't the only problem, though. He was beset by gnats or some other kind of tiny insects that clearly were not fooled by his invisibility. There was nothing he could do about them, either. Waving them away with his hand was fruitless— they came right back—and so he was forced to endure them crawling on his face and neck. He exhaled violently every few seconds to keep them out of his nostrils.

On he plodded, his boots making loud sucking, slopping sounds he had no way of hiding. But Reuben's labored footsteps were only a minor part of the many noises out on the mudflats— there were also the constant cries of seagulls and other birds; the occasional flickering sounds of tiny, stranded fish; the minute skitter of crabs startled out of his path. The sound of all this wildlife about him was unnerving to the point of distraction, and when fifteen minutes were almost up and he had yet to reach solid ground, Reuben began to worry that he'd veered off course and would reappear in some unpredictable spot, out in the wide open for anyone to see.

Then, with perhaps a minute of invisibility left, he felt the ground rise steeply before him and grow firm and rocky. He had reached the island. Using the edge of the mud as a guide, he moved quickly to the north and soon bumped up against the gunwale of the grounded rowboat. He worked his way around it just as his time ran out, reappearing suddenly but safely, hidden among the pilings under the dock.

There was no one around. After a moment's casting about, Reuben found a reasonably dry bit of rocky shoreline, not quite under the dock but still in its shadow. With both hands free now, he indulged his pent-up annoyance by furiously swatting at gnats for several seconds before falling back onto the shore, exhausted. The gnats returned, but in fewer numbers, and meanwhile he had composed himself and pulled off his stinking, slimy boots. He took a water bottle from his backpack and drank it dry.

Now that he was out of all that mud, Reuben detected, intermingled with the salty sea air, the smell of something cooking. Something rich, savory, delicious—he picked up only scattered whiffs of it, but that was enough to make his stomach growl. He gulped down a cereal bar and was immediately thirsty again. At least he was restored enough to get back to the business at hand. He yanked on his sneakers, hid his boots under the dock, and then crouched in the shadows, winding his watch.

Soon enough he would be making his presence known. To get any answers about the watch, he would have to ask questions— he couldn't just sneak around, he knew. But Reuben wanted to observe for a while first. He wanted to be certain of what he was getting into.

There still seemed to be no signs of life on the island. Now that the tide was fully out, he saw that the seaward part of the island was fringed with a great jumble of granite boulders and slabs that looked as if they'd be fun to climb around on. The higher ones were drying out in the sun, their dark gray lightening by the minute; the lower ones were crusted with barnacles and periwinkles. He looked at the keeper's house, which stood at the base of the looming lighthouse tower. Its sun-dazzled windows were impenetrable.

The little stone oil house, perhaps twenty paces from where Reuben crouched, had no windows at all. The stunted trees grown up around it would provide decent cover, he thought—some of their branches drooped all the way to the ground, forming a screen of evergreen needles. He vanished, moving quickly up the gentle grassy slope until his extended free hand caught hold of an evergreen branch. He ducked beneath it and reappeared. No sooner had he done so than he heard the girl leaving the oil house—she was talking to herself. Peering around the corner, he saw her go back inside the keeper's house.

Reuben didn't even pause to listen. The oil house was empty; otherwise the girl wouldn't have been talking to herself. Now was his chance to look around in there. He vanished, rounded the corner, and found his way in through an open doorway.

As it turned out, there wasn't much to see in the oil house, and Reuben felt a bit foolish—he'd hoped for something exciting, though he couldn't have said what. The walls were covered with hanging tools and supply shelves, and in the far corner stood a rusted oil drum, atop which was perched a handmade doll. Another doll lay on a blanket on the floor. Clearly, the girl had been playing. The only furniture was a heavy wooden bench, on top of which, sitting in a ring of condensation, was an almost-full glass of iced lemonade.

Reuben's eyes lingered on the glass, first because he was so thirsty, and then because of a dawning realization. She must be coming right back! Even as he thought it, he heard a distant screen door bang closed.

For an instant Reuben stood frozen—he hadn't prepared for this possibility—but then his instinct to hide took over. He ran to the oil drum, which came almost to his shoulders, and heaved himself up. His knees and toes bumped against it with small, hollow booms. He grimaced, hoping the girl couldn't hear. Grabbing the doll to keep it from falling, Reuben squeezed down into the narrow corner behind the drum, his backpack scraping stone.

In the distance he heard the girl calling out an apology— something about the screen door slamming. He had a few seconds. He reached up to adjust the doll, making sure he'd left it in its original position. It was only a rag doll, yet someone had gone to a lot of trouble on it, carefully stitching its stern face with life-like features and adorning it with hand-sewn clothes. It appeared to be a woman wearing a man's hat, a knee-length traveler's cloak, and tall boots. Also, the doll's stitched leather belt supported a holster. Reuben knew it was a holster because embroidered onto the doll's right hand, very distinctly, was a pistol.

What in the world kind of doll was *that*? he wondered as he wriggled out of his backpack and sat on it. There was just enough room in the corner to huddle like that, with his back to the wall and his knees pressed against the drum. Quickly he checked the setting on his watch. He wouldn't use it unless he had to. He needed to preserve his strength.

The girl entered the oil house humming. Reuben heard the rattle of ice in her glass; the humming stopped as she took a sip. He was so thirsty the thought of that cold lemonade made him feel desperate. He almost gave himself up to beg for a drink. But popping out from behind the oil drum was not exactly the best way to introduce himself. He was going to have to wait.

The girl had begun to talk in different voices. Apparently, she was diving right back into her doll play.

"But how did you get up there, Penelope?" she said huskily. A male voice.

"I climbed, silly! What do you think?" A woman's voice. Lighthearted but strong.

"But how? How did you even get across the water?"

"I swam!"

"You swam all the way over there?"

"Of course!"

And so on. The doll characters, who evidently were brother and sister, continued to speak to each other, and Reuben heard the girl rustling around the oil house, enacting some drama with the brother. After a minute she suddenly rushed toward the oil drum—he heard the rapid patter of her shoes—and she came so quickly that he flinched, thinking she'd spotted him, and pulled out on the winding key. Then she was standing at the oil drum, moving her doll around on top of it, saying things that Reuben couldn't register for all the blood rushing in his ears.

She was still talking in her made-up voices, though. That meant that she hadn't seen him. Reuben allowed himself to breathe. Presently she moved away from the drum again, and he reappeared, listening.

The scene the girl was acting out with her dolls sounded dramatic, but Reuben wasn't concentrating on the story—he was concentrating on the girl. She seemed full of spirit, and the remarks that she had her dolls make to each other were rather witty, he thought. More than once, in fact, he almost chuckled. He liked this girl, and as a consequence he was feeling encouraged. If he was going to talk with someone in this family of lighthouse keepers, a likable child was infinitely preferable to some unknown adult. He just needed to think of how to introduce himself and what to say. Assuming he ever got out from behind this drum.

Such were Reuben's musings when, several minutes into the doll drama, the story's tone shifted to one of even greater urgency, and the girl began to recite a sort of chant:

"Scarcely seen at low tide,
Never seen at high,
Only from the watery side,
Never from the dry.
Always bring your tools, mate,
And keep your lanterns low.
The rights are all for fools, mate,
The lefts for those who know.
So go ye at the low tide,
And never at the high.
Above the X, *below the* Y,
Get in and out—or die!"

It was a curious sort of poem, to be sure. Reuben wondered if the girl had read it in a book. Listening intently to what the dolls had to say about it, he got the impression that the brother and sister were supposed to have made it up when they were children—apparently to help them remember something. The sister made the brother repeat it, and this time Reuben paid even closer attention. It sounded like a pirate riddle; that part about the *X* made him think of a treasure map.

In the distance, a screen door banged closed. Reuben heard a woman's muted voice calling out in disapproval, but there was no reply from the culprit who had let the door slam. The girl fell silent. Grass-muffled footsteps approached the oil house door.

"What's up, redbird," said a young man's voice. It was a lazy voice, drawling and half-mumbling. Though his greeting was a question, the tone fell at the end, like a statement—and a statement of weary resignation at that. The words were breathed out in a sort of sigh.

"Mom hates it when you let the screen door slam," said the girl.

"So why'd you do it?"

Scarcely seen at low tide,
Never seen at high,
Only from the watery side,
Never from the dry.
Always bring your tools, mate,
And keep your lanterns low.
The rights are all for fools, mate,
The lefts for those who know.
So go ye at the low tide,
And never at the high.
Above the X, below the Y,
Get in and out—or die!

It sounded like a pirate riddle; that part about
the X made him think of a treasure map.

"*I* didn't *mean* to!" the girl protested.

"Well, who says *I* did?"

"You could have said you were sorry." The young man made no reply to this, and the girl let the matter drop. "So..." She seemed to be searching for something to say. "Are you working at the marina tonight?"

"I doubt it. They haven't called."

"Well, what's up? Do you want me to sit on your back while you do push-ups? You could try to beat your record."

"Maybe later," said the young man, who was surely the girl's brother. His voice had been coming from the doorway (Reuben had pictured him leaning against the jamb), but now he closed the door behind him and crossed the room, walking in the direction of the oil drum. Reuben vanished. There was a shuffling sound, then a hollow boom, and once again Reuben, heart in his throat, thought he'd been spotted. But no, the young man had merely heaved himself up onto the oil drum to sit.

"There's a bench, you know," the girl said.

"Is that what that is. I wondered."

"You never like to do what people expect you to do," the girl said.

"No, that's your department. Ten years old and already the most Meyer-like of all the Meyers." He shifted his position on the drum. "Besides, you expected me to come talk to you, didn't you?"

Now it was the girl's turn to be silent. After a pause her brother said, "So are you going to tell me what happened at this sleepover thing? It was your first one, right?"

There was another pause, and then: "Just the usual stuff."

"They teased you."

"Not everyone," the girl said. She spoke so softly Reuben could barely hear her. "It's okay. A couple of them are just mean." She sniffed, then sniffed again, and Reuben realized she was crying.

174

The young man dropped down from the oil drum and went over to her. He said something in a voice so low that Reuben couldn't make it out. After a moment the girl mumbled a reply, and her brother snorted and said, "You see? That's what I'm talking about. Smart aleck." There was a rattle of ice, then an exaggerated slurping sound. "Ah! That's some good lemonade. Believe I'll just finish it off...What? No? Oh, what a look! Very nasty. Obviously, you've been practicing."

Again the girl muttered something that made the young man snicker, and the exchanges continued like this until Reuben heard the girl laugh, too.

"That's more like it," her brother said. "All right, I'll let you get back to old Penelope. What's she gotten herself into this time, anyway?"

"Trouble," the girl replied, "what else?"

"That's good. I hope she keeps it up."

The door opened, and the young man's footsteps retreated. The girl did not return to her doll play, however, but rose and went to the door. Reuben had a feeling she was watching her brother go. He willed her to go after him. He was so parched that his thirst was all he could think about.

Fortunately, after a miserable few moments, he heard the girl give a little sigh and go out. He waited, listening, then straightened to peek over the top of the oil drum. He was alone—the distant creak of the screen door confirmed it—and the lemonade glass was still there on the bench. In his haste to get over the oil drum, Reuben nearly fell on his head. The glass was almost empty, and what little liquid remained was less lemonade than ice water, but that was fine by Reuben. He gulped it down, then crunched the last few ice cubes until his mouth ached from the cold.

He felt sure the girl would be coming back. The dolls were gone, but she'd left the blanket and the lemonade glass. Reuben wound his watch, considering the best way to reveal himself. If he handled it wrong, the girl might run and fetch her brother, and he didn't want to talk to any grown-ups yet. The thought filled him with dread.

He went to stand lookout near the doorway. If anyone else came, he would disappear. He watched the keeper's house, trying to think of what to say.

Hi, my name's Reuben. Do you happen to know anything about a watch that turns people invisible? And can you tell me how The Smoke knows about it? And do you know who else might know about it? See, I need to know what I'm up against so I can figure out how to sneak my mom out of the city, which happens to be swarming with these guys called the Directions, who are all looking for me. No, I can't just tell her. She'd make me give up the watch, but then we'd still be in danger, I'm sure of it. It's kind of complicated....

Reuben groaned and rubbed his head. This wasn't going to be easy. Especially because he couldn't tell the truth. Not all of it, anyway, or even half. He had to protect his secret. So what was he going to say?

He was still groping for an answer when the screen door opened and the girl skipped out into the sunlight. She remembered the door just in time to fling one foot out behind her and catch it before it banged. Then she resumed her skipping— evidently, she wasn't one to wallow in bad moods. As she drew close enough for Reuben to get a good look at her, he saw that she was not wearing a bright red hat after all, but rather had a startling, wiry mass of red hair that shot up and out from her scalp like a volcanic eruption. It bounced all around her head as she skipped. She wore sandals and a light blue summer dress and was carrying the dolls, one in each hand.

Reuben backed away from the door. He supposed there was no way he could avoid frightening her, and sure enough, when she skipped through the doorway and saw him standing there, she gave a little shriek, dropping her dolls and leaping back, with her hands covering her mouth.

"Sorry!" he cried, holding his palms out apologetically. "Sorry, I didn't mean to scare you."

The girl stared at him a moment, bug-eyed. Then she burst out with the brightest laugh Reuben had ever heard. She clapped her hands against her chest and doubled over. When she straightened, tears of laughter shone in her eyes. "Well, you did," she said, comically fanning her eyes with both hands. "Whew! You scared the dickens out of me! Who are you?" Her eyes (which were green as grass) darted around the oil house, as if searching for an answer. "And how did you even get here?"

Her eyes settled on his face again. Now that she was over her initial shock, she seemed merely baffled. She had a round face that was completely covered with freckles, as if she'd gotten a suntan through a screen, and her top two front teeth stuck out ever so slightly from her curious smile. She didn't look at all as Reuben had expected, but now that he'd seen her, her appearance seemed to fit her voice. He couldn't have explained why.

"So...do you know any other words?" she asked him. "Or was that it?"

"Sorry," Reuben began, and the girl gave him a wry look. "I mean, yes, of course I do." He felt the return of his shyness and had to push through it. "I'm in town visiting someone. I wondered if I could see the lighthouse."

"Did you look up?" the girl said, jerking her thumb over her shoulder, in the direction of the lighthouse tower. "It's that big white thing with the green top." She saw Reuben's uncertain expression and quickly said, "Oh, I'm just teasing! Sorry, I don't mean to be rude." Scooping up her dolls with one hand, she extended her other. "I'm Penny Meyer."

Reuben told her his first name, and they shook hands. He noticed that she was holding her dolls behind her back and trying to seem casual about it. That was funny, he thought. She had to know that he'd seen them. Maybe she was hoping he'd forget. Or at least not be impolite enough to mention them. He wanted to tell her not to worry, that if he wasn't too old to play secret spy games, she wasn't too old to play with dolls. But of course he couldn't say that, and he felt his tongue freeze up again, and said nothing.

"Let's start over," said Penny, sitting down on the bench. "You didn't tell me how you got here. The tide's out!" Her eyes flicked to his shoes (checking them for mud, Reuben realized) and back to his face. "Are you a wizard or something?"

"No broom. Just boots. I left them down by the dock."

"Aha!" Penny said, as if she understood, yet she still looked puzzled.

"Muck boots," Reuben explained. "I walked through the mud in them."

"Oh, I know, I know. I'm just wondering how it is that no one saw you coming."

Reuben felt his cheeks grow hot. He shrugged. "No one was outside."

"Maybe not," said Penny, "but Luke is up in the watch room, and…" She frowned and shook her head. "Well, whatever! Obviously you're here, and I'll take your word for it that you didn't fly. So who are you visiting? I know pretty much everyone in town. No one mentioned any Reuben coming to visit. A boy with a sandwich name? I believe I'd have remembered that. Not that it's a bad name! I like it." And as if to prove she meant it, she said it again: "Reuben." She nodded with approval. "Anyway, who are you visiting?"

Reuben took his gamble. "You."

"Me?" Penny said, drawing her head back as if avoiding a slap. She searched his face. "You aren't joking?"

Reuben swallowed and locked eyes with her. "No, I really

178

have come to see you. Or someone here, anyway—someone at Point William Light. But it's you I'd like to talk to about it. I found something...something very old and unusual. And I figured something out about it that led me here, to you. I know that sounds strange, and maybe it's hard to believe, but it's true. I'm in a really serious situation, and I need to know if you can tell me..." He trailed off, not only because he wasn't exactly sure how to continue but also, and more significantly, because Penny's eyes were growing wider and wider with every word.

There was a short silence, as if Reuben's words were taking a while to reach her, and then Penny let out a squeal. She leaped to her feet, once again dropping her dolls—flinging them, rather, in opposite directions—and clasping her hands together in front of her with a look of unbridled astonishment. Her green eyes seemed huge. Her mouth hung open. Staring at Reuben, she moved her lips once or twice before finally managing to speak. And when she did, what she said astonished Reuben in turn:

"So it's *me*, then," Penny said, in an awed tone. "I'm the one. And *you*. You're the one to ask. After all these years! After more than a *century*, Reuben!" She grabbed him by the arms and looked wonderingly into his eyes. "After all this time—it's *us*."

The Tale of

Penelope

For a few seconds they stared at each other. Reuben had never dreamed of such a dramatic response. He was trying to think of what to say when Penny abruptly released him, whirling toward the door and crying, "I have to tell the others!"

Reuben lunged forward. "No, please!" he hissed, grabbing her hand. She turned back in surprise. "Just you," he said with an imploring look. "For now, anyway. Just you, okay?"

And so it was that Penny remained in the oil house and agreed, after considerable pleading on Reuben's part, to tell him what was going on. Or, rather, she started to tell him; then she changed her mind. Then she changed it again. And then again.

She was so reluctant, she said (when Reuben at last looked ready to die from exasperation), because the story she had to tell him was the family's most closely guarded secret. She and her brothers were strictly forbidden to reveal it to anyone. Indeed, she said, the story never *had* been revealed to anyone outside the family. Never. Not to anyone.

And yet, although Penny was reluctant, she was not *entirely* reluctant. In truth she was bursting to tell him and only resisted doing so because of the family rules. Eventually she persuaded herself that Reuben wasn't just anyone—he was, in fact, the key to everything, was actually a *part* of the secret himself. Besides, he was hardly a threat. He was only a boy, and a trustworthy one at that.

"You *are* trustworthy, right?" Penny asked.

Reuben, with more conviction than he actually felt, assured her that he was.

"Okay," she said. "I'll tell you. But you have to swear that you'll never tell another soul without my permission."

Reuben swore that he would not.

And so, at last, Penny told him the story.

The lighthouse at Point William, according to Penny, was almost as old as the country itself. And from the very beginning, the keepers of the Point William Light had been Meyers. The protection of ships in dark and inclement weather was a critically important job, one that must never go unfilled or be entrusted to the hands of a negligent keeper. At the Point William Light such an unthinkable circumstance had never occurred, for there was always a Meyer ready to be passed the torch.

Every generation of Meyers had proved well suited to the sacred duty of keeping the light. They had without exception been constant, reliable, unfailing in their duties. *Though the governor flounder,* a local saying went, *and the president flail, a Meyer will always float.*

So highly regarded was the Meyer family as an institution of solid, honest folk, sound of judgment and steady of course, that when one day there came along a Meyer who was unpredictable, unconventional, reckless, and daring, no one in Point William—or indeed, anywhere—knew what to make of her.

(*Her?* Reuben thought. And then, with a thrill of recognition: *Penelope!*)

Was it not inevitable? Generation after generation of children bound to that island, to their family's sacred task, watching generation after generation of ships pass in the night? Ships bearing exotic cargo from faraway countries; ships laden with unfamiliar spices so pungent and in such quantities that they prickled noses even from across the water; ships clamorous with strange animals whose cackling and growls reached the ears of the land-bound children and sent goose bumps down their backs? And above all, ships worked by sailors, and carrying passengers, who had journeyed across the ocean from places unknown and who to places unknown would return? All those children, all those years, all those ships! Why should it have been surprising that at least one child would grow up yearning to see the world?

Such a one was Penelope Meyer. To put it plainly, as she herself would have done, Penelope was an adventuress. By the age of twelve she was teaching her beloved younger brother, Jack, all manner of surprising things, such as how to steal honey from beehives and pies from windowsills, how to build campfires in the rain, how to tie knots so complicated that no one could untie them but her. At thirteen she built her own raft. When it proved unseaworthy and sank a mile offshore, she swam back, wrung out her clothes, and announced her plan to build a better one.

"I know what I did wrong," she said to Jack when he begged

her not to try it again (for Jack adored his sister and preferred that she not drown). "I won't make the same mistake twice!"

Nor did she—then or ever. Bold enough to take chances, smart enough to learn from her failures, Penelope Meyer grew into a young woman who wore trousers instead of skirts, rode horses and sailed boats (both of which, as often as not, were borrowed without their owners' precise knowledge), and seemed every bit as likely to punch a man as to curtsy to him. Her parents loved her but could do nothing with her. Her brother could never keep her in check, though she let him bind her wounds and listen to her tales. And when at age seventeen she stowed away on a ship bound for Gibraltar (Jack found her note two days later), no one in Point William was surprised.

In the years that followed, Jack received letters from so many different ports in so many countries, he found it difficult to keep track of them all. The map he'd hung on the wall of his room positively bristled with pushpins.

Two years after she left for Gibraltar, Penelope returned to Point William to visit her family. She sailed into port on a clipper ship, sunburned, tall, and slim, red hair flying out from beneath a sailor's cap. For presents she had brought her mother a beautiful silk kimono; for her father, a stuffed marsupial. Her parents received their gifts with appropriate exclamations of wonder, though no doubt what they cherished most was their daughter's assurance that she had plenty of money and a great many friends almost as loyal as Jack, and was never in harm's way.

As soon as she and Jack were alone, however, she showed him where a snake had bitten her just above the knee ("Painful but not deadly," she assured him when he paled) and for a keepsake gave him a scarred and misshapen bullet—one that clearly had been fired from a gun and later extracted from whatever (or whomever?) it had struck. Jack solemnly accepted the gift but urged her not to tell him the story behind it unless she intended to catch him when he fainted.

Penelope, laughing, agreed that she had better not.

The time between Penelope's return visits to Point William grew longer with every departure. After the first one she was away for three years; after the next, it was five. She returned each time bearing more gifts, more stories, more scars. Always, when seeing his beloved sister off again, Jack would wonder whether this was the last time he would see her carefree smile and wave. From her letters, and even more from the tales she had told him in private, he knew it was rather a miracle that she had ever returned at all.

And indeed there came a time when Penelope's visits were cherished memories only. For some years she had continued to write to Jack—but then one year her letters turned cryptic and strange. She had partnered up, Jack knew, with a kind of scholar-adventurer whose deep learning and ambitious nature had led him to many a rare discovery and who as a consequence was growing quite rich. ("He has such books, Jack, as you wouldn't believe, and manuscripts and scrolls older than mountains. He knows things no one else knows or ever will. I trust him not at all, for reasons I won't trouble you with, but I can only admire his brilliance and bravado, and have hopes he will lead me into fortune. I feel sure he will, if only I keep my wits about me—and my hand on my holster.")

It was not the first letter of Penelope's to have spoken of shadowy acquaintances or partners, but it was the last. Jack received a few more letters that year, but they no longer made reference to anything or anyone specific, and he got the unpleasant impression that Penelope was writing only to let him know that she was still alive. Later, when the letters stopped altogether, Jack wondered if she might also have been writing in order to feel closer to someone she loved and trusted, however far away he might be.

Time passed, as time must. For many years Jack was too pre-occupied with thoughts of Penelope, and later with helping his aged parents, to think much about himself. He was, moreover, rather a shy man, and it was not until he was in middle age and living alone on the island that fortune smiled on Jack Meyer. The town doctor's daughter, a sparkling young woman beloved by every young man in town, fell in love with—of all people!— the lighthouse keeper, and insisted that he propose to her.

Jack, who was just as bedazzled as anyone by the lovely April Jones, nonetheless argued that he was too old for her, that she might one day come to regret marrying him. But April argued right back, with far greater force, and Jack was compelled to give in and be happy.

Point William breathed a collective sigh of relief. Everyone had been wondering what would happen when Jack Meyer grew old and died. Who would keep the light if not a Meyer? Fortune had smiled not only on Jack, therefore, but on the whole town.

Sure enough, Jack and April soon had a baby boy, and the year following the baby's arrival was the happiest that Jack had known since childhood. He went about his duties whistling; and from the mainland shore and the decks of passing vessels, the lighthouse keeper was often seen on the island rocking the baby in his arms or laughing and swinging him about. He also doted on April, who, true to form, made a point of out-doting him in return.

So it was that when Jack entered his dark study late one autumn evening in search of reading glasses and found the window open, with a cold breeze billowing the curtains into the room, he was, at that moment, the most contented and carefree he had ever been— or, after that moment, ever would be again.

Whistling to himself (quietly, for the baby was asleep in the adjacent room), puzzled but untroubled, Jack set his lamp on the desk, leaned out the window and drew the shutters closed, and then closed the window itself. Only then, as he turned back to face the room, did he become aware that he was not alone.

In the corner behind the door stood a man.

Jack was so used to keeping quiet for the baby's sake, even his alarmed exclamation came out in a whisper. The man wore a long traveling cloak and an ancient-looking hat that shadowed his face.

"Hello, Jack," the man said, in a voice so familiar that Jack's fright instantly turned to bewilderment. The man removed his hat, simultaneously unshading his face and uncovering his head to reveal a jumble of curling red hair streaked with white, and Jack saw then that the face smiling at him now was not the face of a man at all.

*Jack saw then that the face smiling at him now
was not the face of a man at all.*

The Tale of Penelope (Continued)

Don't look so surprised," said his sister. "It's only been twenty years." She crossed the distance between them with three brisk strides and threw her arms around Jack.

It took him a few moments to recover from his shock. "Penelope!" he whispered at last. "You're alive!"

Penelope drew back, swatting him roughly on the shoulder. "Why, of course I'm alive, Jack," she said, looking offended. "You know I'd have told you if I wasn't!" Then she laughed and kissed his cheek.

They stood for a time regarding each other in silence. Penelope, her brother noted, stood as straight as ever, but gone was the fair complexion of her youth. Her skin was blotchy now and etched with wrinkles, like a coffee-stained parchment that had been crumpled up and then smoothed out again. She had dark circles under her eyes, which had grown heavy-lidded, and one of her earlobes was noticeably disfigured, suggesting a long-ago encounter with fang or blade. There was a seriousness, even a gravity, about her that had been absent before. She looked as strong as ever, perhaps even stronger, but she also looked... What was it? Jack wondered.

Haunted. Shadowed. To avoid betraying these feelings to his sister, Jack lowered his gaze and saw that her knee-high boots were splotched with black mud.

"I waited for the tide to go out," Penelope said, which made no sense. Jack thought he must have misunderstood her. "I did my best to scrape most of the mud off. I don't wish to make an enemy of your wife."

Jack started and looked up. "My wife! April! Good God, you've never even met her!" He chuckled. "She always says I couldn't surprise her if I tried, but I believe this will do the trick. She's just gone to bed, so let me fetch her and you can tell us everything. I'm tempted to get Jack junior out of his crib— but no, we'll just peek in at him, and in the morning you can... Penelope, what is it?"

His sister's expression had darkened. "You have a baby?"

"Of course. Well, he won't be a baby for much longer, I suppose. He's already over a year old. Why, what's the matter?"

Penelope was shaking her head. "This changes things," she muttered. "I shouldn't have come. I almost didn't. But I wanted to see you, and...well, Jack, you're the only person I trust. The only person in all the world."

Jack stared at his sister, instantly serious. "Let me fetch April," he said gravely. "Then you can explain everything."

"I can't explain everything—"

"Then you'll explain what you can." Jack came back almost at once with his young wife, who embraced Penelope as if she were her own beloved sister.

"Please be comfortable," April said, after they had exchanged greetings. "Jack, you must take her cloak and hat and bring her a blanket...."

Soon they were all sitting around the great room fireplace with cups of tea, and Penelope had been given a plate of hot beans and bread—which was all, she insisted, that she had the stomach for tonight. Her boots were off; her cloak and hat had been hung up; a blanket lay across her legs. She would have presented a picture of tranquil domesticity had it not been for the gleaming revolver on the table beside her chair. The pistol had been revealed when she handed Jack her cloak, and with apologies to April (whose eyes had gone wide at the sight of it), she'd removed it from its holster to be more comfortable.

"There's no need to apologize," April said, quickly recovering. And though for the rest of the evening Jack's eyes were repeatedly drawn to the gun, April herself made a point of never glancing at it again, as if it were no more out of place on her table than a lace doily would have been.

As Penelope ate her simple meal, she listened to Jack and April's account of all the happenings in Point William since her last visit so many years before. Then, gesturing for them to remain seated, she rose and slipped her revolver back into its holster. In silence they watched her step to the window, draw back the curtain an inch to peer out, and let it fall closed again. From a deep pocket inside her loose-fitting trousers, she withdrew something neither Jack nor April could see, for she subtly shifted her body to shield it from view. After the merest glimpse, she returned it to her pocket. Jack had the impression she'd been checking the time, though why she would do that so slyly, he had no idea. Still, he might have thought no more about it had she

191

not repeated the curious gesture several times over the rest of the night.

"I don't know if you'll remember, Jack," she said, returning to stand by the fire, "or if you even received any of my last letters, but I fell in with a man named Bartholomew.... Yes? You remember him? I believe I mentioned him just twice before I thought better of putting his name down in writing. It was the sort of thing he might kill a person for if ever he should find out. Very dangerous fellow, Bartholomew. Very dangerous. The only man I've ever truly feared. I knew within five minutes of meeting him that he was more intelligent than anyone I'd ever known, including myself. And I have no small opinion of myself, Jack, as you know. Still, I believed I could handle Bartholomew if only I was careful."

"You thought he would lead you into fortune," said Jack, now holding April's hand tightly in his own.

"And he did. A very dark fortune. Years and years of treachery, of wicked people lurking behind every corner, in every shadow, behind every door. People who wanted the same thing Bartholomew wanted—and who, when at last he was within reach of it, would stop at nothing to claim it for themselves. In the end, he proved cleverer than the lot of them. He was so clever, in fact, that when the time came for him to kill *me*, I knew exactly what he had in mind, yet could think of no way to avoid it. *That*, I can tell you, is a nasty feeling."

"You knew he was going to kill you?" April whispered, scarcely daring to speak the words.

"Yes. I had known for a long, long time that such a day would come—a day when I no longer seemed of use to him, when he would consider my continued existence a threat. I knew too much about his secrets, you see, and he wouldn't risk my telling anyone."

"Why didn't you try to escape," Jack asked, "before that time came?"

Penelope shook her head. "By then the dangers were too various, the ground too uncertain. Bartholomew's shadow, no matter how frightening, was the safest place to hide. Oh, believe me, almost from the beginning I'd been looking for the right chance to get away—but no chance ever came. Then it was too late, and I knew I had come to the end."

Penelope stood with her back to the comforting fire, her hands clasped behind her. But her mind, her memory, was thousands of miles away. Jack and April could see it in her eyes.

"What spared you?" April asked at last.

Slowly, Penelope's eyes seemed to clear. Looking at the two of them, she half smiled and waved a hand. "Luck. Pure and simple luck. On the night before he was to spring his final trap, and in so doing come into possession of the precious thing he had sought for so many years, Bartholomew was bitten by a spider. A terrible sort. He grew delirious, and soon lay shivering and helpless on the floor. I thought the bite might kill him. Certainly, I could have, and I'm sorry to admit that I was tempted. Instead I took from him what I needed to escape, and leaving him to his fate, I fled."

"But he survived," Jack said. "Bartholomew." He uttered the name in a tone of contempt.

Penelope nodded. "I managed to slip through the hands of his enemies, who wanted what I had taken from him. But later I learned that Bartholomew still lived and was on my trail. And what I must tell you now is painful, but I can't avoid saying it: for all these many years, in every corner of the world, he has pursued me, and he continues to do so even now."

April gasped. Jack shot to his feet. "What?" he cried. "Even here?" With an angry look at his sister, he ran to the door and checked the bolt, and was crossing the room—going to check the back door as well—when Penelope intercepted him.

"Not here, Jack, not tonight, I swear!" she said, holding him by the arms in a powerful grip. "You have to believe me. I know where he is tonight—he's in the city—and he has no way of knowing I've come." She looked pleadingly at April. "You must forgive me, both of you. I didn't know you had a child! I've taken every precaution imaginable, but if I'd known you had a baby, I wouldn't have dared to come even then."

"Why did you peek out the window?" Jack demanded. "If you're so sure this monster is in the city, why are you so anxious?"

"Habit, brother," Penelope said, still clutching his arms. "Constant watchfulness has kept me alive, but it's also a curse. I'm always wary. I'm never…anything…but *wary*." These last words she spoke slowly, with a great heaviness, and as she released his arms with hands visibly trembling, Jack for a moment wondered if she hadn't actually said *weary*. For just then his sister looked like the most exhausted person he'd ever seen.

"How do you know that Bartholomew is in the city?" he asked.

"Because, Jack. There's more to it than I've told you. I'm not just being hunted by Bartholomew." She looked him squarely in the eye so that he would see the truth in her words. "I am also hunting *him*."

Jack blinked in confusion. "I don't understand."

"Of course not, because what I'm saying sounds like madness. My life is no longer about me, Jack. It's about putting an end to a wickedness that has survived in this world for centuries. I'm in a position to do it, and until the day I die, I must do everything I can to succeed."

"Why have you come, Penelope?" asked April, and turning toward her, they saw with some surprise that the baby was in her arms. She had flown to his crib at the first mention of danger and now cradled him protectively as he slept on, undisturbed.

194

"I came," Penelope said reluctantly, "because I may *not* succeed before I die. I came because I wanted to influence what may happen after that."

There followed a pause, during which Jack and April exchanged glances. Whatever anger they had felt toward Penelope was dissipating, leaving only a state of tense anxiety and a desperate desire to understand.

"I'll make more tea," said April, handing the baby to Jack. "Then you can tell us the rest."

In the end, however, though Penelope would tell them more, she would also leave much unanswered. It was to keep them safe, she said. No one would know about this visit to Point William Light—never had she been more careful to disguise her movements and cover her tracks—but it could be found out that she had connections here. If Bartholomew ever came seeking answers, Jack and his family would be protected by their ignorance.

"But how could he tell we don't know anything?" Jack asked. "Wouldn't he think we were just keeping your secrets?"

"It's his own secrets he's worried about," said Penelope, "the ones that he knows I share. And he'd be able to discover easily enough that you don't know them. He'd also see that you can't help him locate me. Bartholomew has ways of finding things out that you can't imagine. I'm sorry, I don't wish to frighten you. On the contrary, I'm telling you that it wouldn't suit his purpose to harm you. Pain leaves its own trail, and he knows as well as I what sort of dangerous game the two of us are playing. No, as long as I keep you in the dark about certain things, you'll be safe.

"There are some things, though," Penelope continued, "that I must tell you—and ask of you. Jack, you've never told anyone about the secret place, have you?"

"A secret place?" April repeated, turning from the bassinet, which Jack had brought into the room for the baby. She peered questioningly at Jack and Penelope, who stood facing each other before the fire. "What secret place?"

Penelope smiled. "I hope you won't blame my poor brother for keeping secrets, April. When we were children, our parents made us promise never to tell a soul about this place, only because it was dangerous and they feared someone would come to harm. I'll bet Jack has wanted to tell you, but after keeping that promise all his life, he's found it difficult to break."

Jack's face had reddened. He was visibly uncomfortable. "She has me pegged," he muttered to April.

"Jack Meyer!" said his wife, setting her hands on her hips. "I'd never have imagined you were keeping a secret from me. Is there anything else?" Her tone was sharp, but she didn't seem truly indignant. In fact, she seemed impressed.

Now Jack looked relieved. "Nothing else, April. I promise."

"There, that's settled," Penelope said. "We all know that Jack is as good as his word. And because I'm sure it still makes him uncomfortable to break the promise himself, I'll tell you what it is, April. There are some old smuggler or pirate tunnels nearby, tunnels that flood whenever the tide comes in—that's what makes them so dangerous. They've been there for ages."

"We had a special way of remembering how to find the entrance," Jack put in, "a sort of verse that our grandfather taught us. We never knew if he made it up or if it had been handed down for generations, perhaps even learned from one of the pirates themselves! That's what I liked to believe as a boy, anyway. Papa took us into the tunnels once, just to show us, then forbade us ever to go into them again. And of course we had to promise not to tell anyone about them. He said they were haunted by children who had drowned in them. 'Those tunnels are already full of ghosts,' he said. 'Let's not make it any more crowded down there.' "

"Who knows if anyone ever actually drowned?" Penelope

said. "That might have been something he said just to scare us into keeping our promises."

April shook her head wonderingly. "So you never went back, and you never spoke of them again? You Meyers—so steady, even as children!"

"Well," Jack said, "Penelope and I talked about it all the time, but only between ourselves. It's true we never went back, though."

Penelope snorted softly. "*You* never did, Jack, but do you really think I didn't?"

Jack gaped at her, then broke into a grin. "Honestly, I don't know why I'm surprised. Of course you did. Probably dozens of times."

"Hundreds, more like," Penelope said. "Mostly to see if I could get away with it. But to the point, Jack, you're sure you could still find the entrance if you needed to?"

"Of course! I couldn't forget if I tried."

"Good. Because tonight I hid something extremely important down there—but you must never retrieve it."

"I don't understand," Jack said. "Why are you telling us, then?"

"When I leave here," Penelope explained, "I'll be going into the city, where I intend to arrange it so that if something should happen to me, and if the right sort of person comes to possess... No, let me say it another way. If Bartholomew outmaneuvers me, in the city or elsewhere, you needn't worry that he'll ever come here—he won't need to, for he'll have what he desires. Of course, I don't intend to let that happen. I'd die ten times over first!

"But still, someone else may contact you one day, offering to return something to you. If that happens, then it will most likely be a good person, and therefore someone you may decide to take into your confidence. You must decide for yourself, though. The Meyers have always been excellent judges of character. Only if the person seems trustworthy and good—only if you are absolutely certain that you haven't been approached by a spy—only then should you risk venturing into the secret place. What I've hidden there will help you do what must be done.

"If, however, you have any suspicions whatsoever about the person's good nature—if, for instance, a reward is demanded, or the person seeks information in exchange for returning what's been found—in any such case you must claim ignorance, offer no help, and by no means go to recover what I've hidden. Never assume that you can do so unobserved. Let my secrets remain secrets, for uncovering them may only put you in danger and lead to greater wickedness."

When Penelope had concluded this troubling speech, April was left aghast. "But what about you? How would we help you?"

Penelope tossed the dregs of her tea into the fireplace, sending up a hiss and a thick plume of smoke. "If someone comes to you," she said, "then I'm beyond help. Dead, most likely—I'm sorry to be so blunt—though I suppose it's possible that I'll grow too old, or otherwise incapable of finishing the task I've set myself, in which case I may feel compelled to pass it on to another. I have yet to find anyone I'd trust to do the job, but I may yet. I'll know it if I do—I'm no poor judge of character myself. But even if that happens, I will need to disappear. For your sake and my own, I can never return here after tonight. You'll never hear from me again."

"Oh, Penelope!" April cried, and Jack stared at his sister with anguished eyes.

"I'm sorry," Penelope said quietly. "That's just the plain truth of it." Then she brightened and said, "But remember, that's only if I *don't* succeed—which naturally I mean to do! And if I do, then you can be sure that I will take the first train back here to Point William. And I will insist on a party."

Jack laughed, and with tears in his eyes he embraced his

sister, squeezing her tightly. "The world has never seen the likes of you, Penelope. You know that, don't you?"

"I should hope not!" Penelope said, also laughing, her own eyes now just as bright. "And it never shall again, I daresay!"

Soon after that, Penelope slipped away into the night, never to be seen again by the brother who loved her. Jack had begged her to stay longer, but she said she could not. Before she left, however, she pointed out that in the light of day, after she'd gone, he might come to doubt her words.

"But who is the best judge of character in this town?" she asked. "It's you, Jack, and everyone knows it, including yourself. And *you* know I'm telling the truth, don't you? You can tell."

"Yes," said Jack. "Yes, I can tell."

"Then remember this moment, and never doubt the truth you know."

There was one last thing that Penelope asked of Jack that night, and it was the most significant of them all. Taking his hands in her own, which were more callused and scarred than an old fisherman's, she looked into his eyes. "Please believe me when I tell you, brother, that this trouble I'm caught up in—it's bigger than I am. It's bigger than the both of us. And it may well outlive us both. There's a centuries-long history of wickedness and woe that we may help bring to a close. We have to make sure that if I fail—if I die or disappear, and if..." Here she faltered, her voice trembling ever so slightly, and Jack stiffened, suddenly understanding.

With a glance at April, in whose arms their baby son still slept, he muttered, "And if I die, if something happens to *me*..."

Penelope nodded gravely. "Our arrangement, what we've agreed upon tonight, must live on, waiting for its opportunity. I'll do everything I can to make it so that another person—and thus another chance to put an end to this evil—may come here one day. But if that day comes after you and I have gone..."

"Then there needs to be a Meyer who is ready for it," Jack said.

"Yes," Penelope said. "And a good one at that."

They looked at each other for a long moment. The most important moment they'd ever shared in life.

"You can count on me," Jack said.

"I always have," said Penelope, and went away forever.

The Keepers' Secret

When Penny fell silent at last, Reuben sat motionless for some time before he became aware that she was looking at him, waiting for a response. He blinked exaggeratedly, as if coming awake. For though his eyes had been open, though he'd been looking straight at Penny, he had stopped seeing her. Even now, the characters from her story resisted yielding the stage in his mind to the present one—the actual one, the space in which he lived and breathed—so that for a few moments longer it continued to feel as if Penny and Reuben were ghosts in that long-ago great room. Then the scene shifted, and it was Penelope and Jack who were ghosts in the oil house. And then it was just Penny and Reuben, alone.

"You," Reuben said thickly, "are an amazing storyteller."

Penny clasped her hands together, beaming. "You think so?"

"I lost track of where I was. How did you do that?"

Penny laughed. "Oh, the Meyers have been great storytellers for ages now! We've had to be. None of this could be written down, obviously, but it's been so important to remember—the story's been passed down from generation to generation, told again and again. We all learn it once we're old enough to be trusted with the secret. I just heard it for the first time last year. Amazing, isn't it?"

"That's an understatement," said Reuben. "I hardly know what to say. You memorized all those details?"

"Oh yes! Of course, I tell it in my own style, tweaking the dialogue and details and such. Everybody does that. But the most important parts have always stayed exactly the same. That's what being a Meyer has meant ever since that night: not just being trustworthy, which was already established, but being a great storyteller." Penny smacked her lips. "Is there anything left in that glass? I feel like I have a mouth full of feathers."

As Penny let the few remaining drops of water trickle into her mouth, Reuben reminded himself to proceed with caution. His mind had begun to draw connections that made him so excited he feared he would reveal too much. That phrase of Penelope's from the story—*lead me into fortune*—followed by the revelation that Penelope had hidden something "extremely important" in the smugglers' tunnels that would help whoever retrieved it; these things, together with the pirate riddle he'd overheard Penny chanting, had led Reuben to a single, thrilling conclusion.

Treasure.

It was clear that the watch had once belonged to Penelope

(Reuben hadn't the least doubt that this was what Penelope had kept stealing glances at that long-ago night), and she had used it to acquire a fortune, something that would aid in her battle against Bartholomew—or, rather, in the event of her death, that would aid Jack and whatever trustworthy stranger returned her watch to Point William. Someone like Reuben. He felt a twinge of guilt when he thought of that word, *trustworthy*. But was it not for someone like him that Penelope had left the treasure behind? Bartholomew was long gone. What mattered now was that his mom needed him, and to help her he needed money.

Reuben watched Penny put down the glass, her green eyes twinkling with excitement, and felt another pang of guilt. He wouldn't take all of it, he decided. He would take just enough to help, and the rest he would leave for the Meyers. They wouldn't even know the difference. They were going to be rich.

Penny was smiling eagerly at him, anticipating more questions. Reuben tried to focus. He might have the watch, but he seemed to be the only one in the dark. "So your family has been passing down that story ever since it happened," he said. "When was that? How long has it been?"

Penny leaned forward. "That baby, Jack junior? He was my great-great-great-grandfather. Jack and April told him the story when he was about my age, and then years later they told it to *his* son—their grandson—and so on down the line. April actually lived long enough to tell it to her great-great-grandson! Can you believe it? She was almost a hundred by then and couldn't walk anymore, but my grandfather told me she was sharp as a pin."

"Your grandfather knew April," Reuben said, trying to wrap his mind around the idea of so many generations.

"He was about my age when she died," Penny said. "We didn't get so lucky with Grandpa. He passed away last year, just a few weeks after he told me the story. It's always been the tradition for the oldest Meyer alive to tell the story to you the first time. That way, even with so many generations, you're still only one or two people away from that night with April and Jack and Penelope."

"It's incredible," Reuben said, and then: "I'm sorry about your grandpa."

Penny looked down. "Thanks," she muttered. "We all miss him."

Reuben, who had no memory of his own grandparents, or even of his father, did not know what else to say. He sat in uncomfortable silence, bursting with questions—the most important of which he needed to be crafty in asking.

"Well," said Penny at length, "we really do need to tell my family that you've come. But first, do you suppose you could tell me what it is that you've found?" She was perking up again; clearly, she hoped to be the first to know.

"Sure," Reuben said, and he made as if to get up. Then he hesitated. "Oh, but before I forget—you left something out of your story, and it's eating at me. What was the special way that Penelope and Jack had of remembering where the secret place is? It surprised me that April didn't ask."

Penny stared at him, her smile frozen, though her eyes had changed. "You...you noticed that? Well, of course you did. Who wouldn't be curious, right?" She cleared her throat. "The truth is, Reuben, I left that part out on purpose. Because, you know, I'm sworn to secrecy about it myself."

"But you told me everything else!"

"Most of it, I suppose I did, yes." Penny abruptly covered her face with her hands, as if she was afraid to look at him.

"So why not tell me the rest of it?" Reuben pressed. "What's the harm?"

Penny peeked out over the tops of her fingers. "Surely you see the difference between telling you an old story and giving away the exact location of a secret place. You can understand that, can't you?"

"Well, if you won't trust me with that," Reuben said peevishly, "then I'm not sure I want to show you what I found." But seeing Penny's hurt look, he softened. He might just have to figure out the location of the smugglers' tunnels on his own. "Sorry, you're right. I do understand. Anyway, you've earned a look at the thing. But can I have something to drink first? I'm parched."

While Penny ran to fetch more lemonade, Reuben took the bundle from his backpack and considered what to do. He was going to have to talk with the grown-ups now, and his stomach lurched at the thought. He'd almost begun to hope that he could avoid it.

Reuben went to the door and peeked out. He felt sure that Penny had told him the truth, that her family was trustworthy. They might even want to help him, might even share the treasure willingly. But what if they didn't? And worse, what if they insisted on taking the watch? They might believe they had some claim to it, since for a time it had belonged to Penelope. But Reuben didn't think the Meyer family had any more right to it than he had. After all, how had Penelope come to possess it herself? Lawfully? He doubted that laws of ownership could pertain to something like the watch. Whoever possessed it was the owner, and that was that. Reuben was now the owner, and he meant to keep it that way.

Penny came back with a half-full pitcher of lemonade, and the two of them took turns pouring and gulping and gasping with satisfaction. At last, his thirst slaked, Reuben opened up the bundle. He set the wooden box on the blanket between them. "There you go," he said. "This is what brought me here."

Penny opened the box and gazed reverently at the inscription. She shook her head in wonder. "So that's how she made sure."

"I guess she figured the safest bet was to name the place and not the person," said Reuben. "In case all of this outlived her and Jack, like you said. She was really thinking long-term."

"So was Jack," said Penny, not taking her eyes from the box. "He didn't know what her plan would be, so he did what he could. Ever since that night, there's always been a Jack Meyer at Point William Light." She traced a finger over the inscription. "Every firstborn son for generations has been named Jack."

"And every firstborn daughter has been named Penelope," said Reuben, a bit startled. He had just guessed Penny's full name and felt amazingly stupid for not having realized it sooner.

She smiled. "Of course. Because what if this inscription had said something like *Property of Penelope Meyer, Point William*? Jack didn't know what sort of instructions or clues she might put out in the world, so he did the one thing he could think of to help. He tried to do his part."

"It took me a while to figure out what the inscription meant," Reuben admitted. "I thought P. William Light was a person."

"Ha!" Penny cried. "That never would have occurred to me. I suppose if you aren't from around here, you wouldn't know, would you? Plus, back in Penelope's time this lighthouse was much better known—it was much more important then. May I pick this up?" At a nod from Reuben she lifted the box and studied it from different angles. "There were fewer towns back then, too," she went on. "Between Point William and the city was basically nothing but farmland and villages. Penelope couldn't have guessed how much less significant this place would become over time."

She looked questioningly at Reuben. "Is this all?" she asked, trying to keep her voice light. "Just this empty box?"

"I have some information about what was inside it," Reuben hedged. "I was hoping that coming here would help me figure some things out..." He trailed off, faltering under Penny's intense gaze.

She was reading his face, her eyes slightly squinted. After a moment she twisted her mouth to one side and looked away. "Just so you know," she said after a pause, "that's not going to fly around here."

"What isn't?" Reuben said.

"Lying." Penny looked frankly at him now. "You can't trick a Meyer, Reuben. It runs in the family. Jack was the best judge of character Penelope had ever known, remember? Well, he made sure his son was the same, and his daughter after that. Every Meyer for a century has been taught how to read people, how to see them for what they are. In our house, it's like learning how to hold your spoon. It's just taken for granted."

Reuben blushed fiercely. "Really?" he said, stalling for words.

"It's true," Penny said matter-of-factly. She shrugged. "We could probably make a fortune playing poker—if we gambled, that is, which we don't—because we could always see through a bluff. That's what my brother Luke says, anyway."

"Luke?" Reuben asked, seizing on the chance to change the subject. "Not Jack?"

"Jack's my oldest brother. Then there's Luke, and then me." Penny studied Reuben's face again and said, "Okay, I can see that you're not going to tell me anything else right now, so let's not waste time." She jumped up, still holding the box.

"Wait, what?" Reuben said, scrambling to his feet.

Penny was already at the door. "It's time to tell the others," she said, and ran out before he could stop her.

There was no help for it now. Reuben took a moment to gather his courage. He checked the watch, tucked it away again, and went out. He caught up with Penny at the screen door, which she was holding open for him.

"After you," she said. "I want to make sure it doesn't bang."

(Reuben had to stop himself from saying, "I know.")

Inside the keeper's house, Reuben was almost overcome by

the delicious smell he had scented on the wind earlier. His stomach growled so loudly that Penny cocked an eyebrow and said, "Obviously, we need to feed you. There's a pot of cullen skink on the stove. I'll get you some shortly."

"What's cullen skink?" Reuben asked, looking nervously around. They stood in a large great room with a dining table at one end, a fireplace and sitting area at the other. *The* fireplace, he realized—the one he had imagined during Penny's story. In fact, the entire room was much as he had pictured it, only brighter, airier, with open windows and floral-printed curtains fluttering in the sea breeze. Trying to settle his mind, he took in the well-swept wooden floors, the thoroughly dusted shelves, the walls covered with framed photographs, maps, and drawings of all sizes.

"Cullen skink?" Penny was saying. "It's only the best thing ever! It's a kind of fish stew. It's Scottish. Penelope"—she lowered her voice, her eyes darting toward an open doorway—"Penelope mentioned liking it in one of her letters, so Jack learned how to make it. A Scottish sea captain's wife told him. We have a recipe book full of dishes from around the world, things that Penelope wrote about and Jack learned to cook. For him, it was a way of feeling closer to her across the oceans. For all the Meyers since then, it's been a way of feeling close to both of them—across the years."

"You're kind of blowing my mind," Reuben said.

Penny laughed. "Come on," she said, grabbing his arm.

She led him down a hallway, past a staircase and several open doors—a bedroom, a study (*the* study, Reuben thought), more bedrooms. Reuben noted the placement of furniture and counted his steps, trying to commit all of it to memory. It would be tricky to navigate invisibly, but he might have to.

"I always know where to find Mom after lunch," Penny said. "She sneaks off with a book. She's a teacher, so she only gets to read during the summer—that's her little joke." They veered into a cozy nook with a bay window facing the sea. Sure enough, a slender woman in a sky-blue sundress sat near the window, so engrossed in a book she didn't seem to notice them. Penny cleared her throat dramatically. "Mom!"

Mrs. Meyer started and looked up. At the sight of Reuben, she smiled, her brow wrinkling slightly in puzzlement. "Well, hello! Who's this? And—my word, Penny, if you aren't excited about something! Look at your eyes flashing! What is it?"

"This is Reuben," Penny said. Reuben shyly lifted a hand in greeting. "And you're not going to believe why he's here."

Mrs. Meyer marked her place in the book and set it aside. Clasping her hands in her lap, she nodded good-naturedly. "Go on. Try me. Have you come proposing marriage, Reuben? I have to say, you seem awfully young. But I suppose—"

"This belonged to Aunt Penelope!" Penny blurted out, holding up the box. "Reuben's the one, Mom. He's the *one*."

"I don't..." Mrs. Meyer cocked her head to the side, still smiling, as if trying to perceive the joke. "What do you mean, Penny? Which one? One what?" Even as she spoke, however, her expression was changing, turning more serious—in fact, growing quite stern. "Penelope Meyer!" she cried suddenly, in a shocked and disapproving tone. She glanced at Reuben, then back at her daughter. "Do you mean to tell me that you told this boy—what, for the sake of a joke? I'm astonished. I am"—she shook her head, gaping at her daughter, clearly appalled—"I am so, so..."

Penny stepped forward and opened the box. "Read the inscription, Mom."

It took Mrs. Meyer a moment to wrest her eyes from Penny's earnest face. Then it took her a moment to absorb the inscription. Then, abruptly, she stood up, snatching the box from her daughter and drawing it closer to her eyes. She stared at it so intently she seemed to be trying to see right through it.

"My God," Mrs. Meyer said, and her eyes went to Reuben, who nodded. She looked back at the inscription. "My God," she repeated. "It's finally happened."

By the time Reuben finished his second bowl of cullen skink, Penny's mother had telephoned every Meyer in Point William. There were, evidently, a few who had grown up in the keeper's house and knew about Penelope and Jack but now lived in town—Meyers who had chosen not to keep the light but nonetheless kept the secret. In addition to these were the men and women who had married them and been entrusted with the Meyer family secret. And Mrs. Meyer's first phone call had been to Penny's father, who, it seemed, had a job in town, so all told there would soon be more than half a dozen adults slopping across the mudflats to the island, for of course no one could bear to wait for the tide.

When at last everyone had been called, Mrs. Meyer turned to Penny. "I'm going to send your brothers across to help the great-aunts. I'll tell Jack. Will you fetch Luke? The intercom is on the fritz again." She squeezed her daughter's shoulder, smiled uncertainly at Reuben (she did not know yet what to make of this boy showing up on his own, out of nowhere), and went out.

Penny turned to Reuben. "Want to go up with me? Luke's in the tower."

Reuben nodded, hurriedly scraping the last of the soup from his bowl.

"I hope you like stairs," Penny said.

"I don't mind them," Reuben said, but he soon would.

Out the back door and across a strip of grass, the two children entered the lighthouse tower through a metal door so heavy Penny needed both hands to pull it open. Right away they started to climb. The cast-iron steps spiraled up and up around the interior of the tower's stone cylinder, with a narrow metal landing every twenty steps; and though Reuben, peering up through the open space in the middle of the spiral, could see that there was an end to the steps, it wasn't long before he felt as if they must ascend all the way into the sky. As much as he loved to climb, he had a belly full of stew, and these stairs were unusually steep. His face burned, and to his embarrassment his breathing grew noticeably ragged.

Penny, meanwhile, climbed lightly and easily ahead of him as if gravity did not apply to her. "You get used to it," she said sympathetically. "I pop up and down these steps about a hundred times a day. Dad installed an intercom system, but it's always shorting out, what with the damp and the mice, and even when it's working, you can hardly make out what the person's saying on the other end. It's easier just to run messages up in person."

"If you say so," Reuben panted. "Why does your"—he panted—"dad have a job in town? Isn't he"—pant—"the lighthouse keeper?"

"Well, officially, yes, but really our whole family has the job. Though, to tell you the truth, it isn't much of a job anymore. By the time I was born, just about every lighthouse in the country was automated. Ours is, too, now, but there's been a ton of wrangling with the Coast Guard and the local government and my family—a big legal mess about who actually owns the place and who should be in charge of maintaining it."

Penny was backing up the stairs now so that she could face Reuben as she spoke. He got the sense that she had slowed down for his sake. Still embarrassed, but grateful nonetheless, he made a weak gesture and a spouting noise to indicate that she should keep talking.

"There's been a controversy about it my whole life," Penny said. "A few people in town think it isn't fair that it's always Meyers who get to live here—I guess the government paid for the house and owns the land, or thinks it does, and it's traditionally paid the keeper's salary, but that was supposed to have changed with automation...."

Penny tossed her hair with an air of exasperation. "I don't know—it's all very confusing. But at least *you* can understand, right? Of course we couldn't leave! How could we? We had to stay here because of Penelope and Jack! And we couldn't tell a soul about it! So the Meyers have made a few enemies, fighting for the right to stay on. It's only nasty people who've made a fuss, though, nobody you'd care to be friends with, anyway."

Reuben nodded, panting, to show he understood. That must be the reason for the teasing Penny had endured at the sleepover.

"We made a kind of settlement in the end," Penny said, "but the whole business has been awfully unpleasant, as you might imagine. They even did a story about it in the paper that wasn't at all nice."

The story he'd read on microfiche, Reuben realized. Or tried to read.

"There've been lots of times," Penny was saying, "when Mom and Dad have wanted to just give up and move out. And believe me, until I learned about the secret, I wanted them to! I wanted to have a normal life, like the other kids in town."

Reuben, pausing with his hands on his knees, nodded again. "I'll bet," he panted, "I'd have felt the same."

"Old Jack made a sacred promise, though," Penelope said in a reverent voice. "And the Meyers have always kept it. Can you imagine being the one to break it? What a horrible thought! Oh, there've been plenty of arguments about it over the years, but in the end everyone always agrees that Jack and Penelope were trying to do something extremely important and that we must all do right by them. Well, *almost* everyone agrees—my brother Jack hates the whole business. But that's just Jack. So are you ready to go on up? Or should I just skip ahead while you rest? I kind of need to hurry."

"Sorry," Reuben said, straightening again. He was curious about this rebellious brother of hers, but he had neither the breath nor the time to ask about him. "Yes, I'm ready."

One more curve of the spiral brought them to an open doorway. A small room stood before them, its walls lined with maps and equipment, its windows revealing open space and a glimpse of the ocean horizon. "This is the watch room," said Penny, hurrying inside. "But looks like Luke is up in the dome." She scrambled up the iron rungs of a nearby ladder, which led through an opening in the ceiling.

Reuben followed her up into a brilliant world of sunshine and glass. The lantern dome was composed mostly of windows, and its interior was almost entirely occupied by the enormous lamp apparatus (an imposing system of prisms and lenses, rather than the simple giant bulb that Reuben had imagined). Everywhere he looked, light danced and sparkled; it was like being inside a diamond.

"We've come a long way since the days of kerosene," Penny said, noting his look of surprise.

Luke emerged from the other side of the lamp—a wiry, redheaded teenager, so sweat-soaked he looked as though he'd gone swimming in his clothes. "What's the excitement?" he asked when he saw Penny's expression. He looked wonderingly at Reuben. "And where did *he* come from?"

In an excited rush of words, Penny told Luke what was happening. Her brother's expression, skeptical at first, rapidly shifted to one of delight. When he understood that he was needed below, he wasted no time with follow-up questions but only laughed and said, "Well, what do you know! So today's the day? Amazing!"

He pumped Reuben's hand and gave him a wink, tousled Penny's already tousled hair, and scampered down the ladder. "Pull the drapes, will you, Pen?" he called up. They heard him laugh once more as he hurried down the steps.

Penny went about the lantern dome, lowering canvas drapes over the windows. "He was cleaning the glass," she explained. "We generally keep these covered during the day; otherwise it gets so hot it can damage the prisms."

This came as no surprise to Reuben, who was sweltering in his sweatshirt. Yet despite the heat, Penny was painfully, maddeningly thorough, making sure she had done her job exactly right, and by the time they descended into the watch room again, Reuben felt ready to faint.

"Here, let's go onto the gallery," Penny said, opening a door to the outside. Reuben followed her out onto a railed walkway that ringed the tower. It was blessedly cool on the gallery, and the view was spectacular, with the ocean stretching away far below them on one side, and on the other side the town laid out like a three-dimensional map, its grid of streets and tiny-looking buildings all, from this height, plainly apparent.

Wind was whipping Penny's red hair every which way about her head, so that from down below she must look like a strange animation of flames. She produced a sailor's cap from somewhere and tucked at least a portion of her hair beneath it. "Look!" she cried over the wind in their ears. "There's my dad and my uncle!" She pointed out two minuscule figures hurrying side by side across the town square. Reuben could just distinguish the two redheaded men—like walking matchsticks—among the other pedestrians.

Several members of the Meyer family had already begun to assemble on the mainland dock, and trudging across the mudflats to meet them now was Penny's brother Luke, followed at a slower pace and considerable distance by another young man, wearing blue jeans and a T-shirt, who must be Jack.

After a few moments Reuben noticed that Penny had stopped watching her family. Instead she stood peering for a long spell in one direction, then again in another, and still again in another, until finally he asked what she was looking for.

Penny glanced at him. "You're sure you weren't followed here, right?"

"Pretty sure," Reuben answered, and shifted uncomfortably. He knew he hadn't been followed, didn't he? But just thinking about the possibility unnerved him, made him feel less confident.

"We aren't as vigilant these days as they used to be," Penny said, still gazing out over the town. "But we do keep an eye out for anything unusual. *Anyone* unusual, I suppose I should say."

"Someone like Bartholomew," Reuben said.

Penny turned to look at him. "It's funny, I know he has to be long gone, just like Penelope. But it's definitely Bartholomew I'm thinking of when it's my turn to watch. It keeps me on my toes, I can tell you. If it had been *me* up here when you came across the mud, you can be sure—well, that isn't fair. Luke keeps a good lookout himself. Everyone takes breaks now and then, and he had work to do in the dome."

Penny wasn't just trying to be fair, Reuben suspected. She was trying to convince herself that it was a fluke that he'd arrived here unnoticed. She didn't want to think it could happen twice.

He returned his gaze to the scene at the mainland dock. Getting the elderly Meyers down the ladder into the mud was taking some time, with the younger men helping from above and below, guiding feet onto rungs and offering steady hands. When at last they were all down, the women produced brightly colored parasols to shade themselves from the sun, while the older men lowered the brims of their hats. Then the eldest Meyers each took the arm of a younger one, and thus began the strangest procession Reuben had ever seen: three generations of the same family slopping, slowly and painstakingly, across the stinking black mudflats, with the gaily printed parasols wavering overhead, and seabirds swooping and diving and skittering all about them in search of tidbits.

It was a sight to see, at once comical and grave, and Reuben watched with a curious feeling of reverence. As the minutes passed, however, and the procession drew nearer the island, his feeling shifted to a mounting dread. A confrontation was coming, one from which he could not run or hide but must face head-on, and the thought of it made him queasy. More than that, he realized unhappily—he was in fact quite nauseated, and with a sudden sense of panic, he moved away from Penny to spare her, then stuck his head through the railing, sick.

STRENGTH AND STEALTH

The two children lingered on the gallery, giving Reuben time to recover. Penny had fetched him a clean cloth and a bottle of water from a cooler in the watch room ("Probably too many stairs and too much cullen skink," she said brightly), and after resting awhile with his back against the tower wall, he was starting to feel better. He wasn't some wicked person like Bartholomew, he reminded himself. He was just a kid in danger—a kid whose *mom* was in danger—because of something he'd found. And he needed to do what he could to get them out of hot water. He had to make sure he could do that.

When Reuben looked at things this way, his path seemed simple enough. But it was not going to be an easy one.

Inside the watch room, a squawking, crackling sound erupted. Penny went inside, listened intently with her ear against a wall-mounted speaker, then pressed a button and said, "What?" More squawking and crackles. Penny shook her head and pressed the button again. "I can't understand you! We'll just come down. I repeat: we're coming down!" There was a final brief squawk, like a hiccup, and Penny turned to Reuben, now standing in the doorway. "I'm sure that's what they're telling us to do. Are you ready?"

Reuben's stomach clenched again, but he was no longer sick, only anxious. He nodded.

They were met in the kitchen by the same friendly man who had sold Reuben muck boots at the general store. He turned out to be Penny's father. He appeared markedly more stern than he had been behind the counter, and Reuben saw Penny lower her gaze. Mr. Meyer drew her into a hug, and he gave Reuben an assessing look as he patted his daughter's back. With another gesture, he bade them both sit down at the kitchen table. Outside in the great room voices clamored, but here in the kitchen no one had spoken yet.

Mr. Meyer regarded them with his arms crossed. Penny looked down at the table, but Reuben forced himself to hold Mr. Meyer's gaze. It was extremely uncomfortable, yet he felt it important to show strength from the outset.

"You aren't in trouble, Penny," her father said at last. "You're very young, and what's done is done, and of course this has taken all of us by surprise. No one was expecting someone as young as Reuben here. No one ever imagined it was you who'd be approached, and no one here blames you. Even so, I will remind you that sometimes you may believe you've thought something through—and perhaps you have—but your parents, who have been around thirty-odd years longer than you have, may well know something about a situation that you do not. Does that make sense?"

"Sorry, Dad," Penny whispered. Reuben saw that her lip was trembling. She looked positively tormented.

"Hush now," Mr. Meyer said gently, laying a hand on her shoulder. "You're a good girl, Penny. I can't remember the last time we had to correct you for *anything*—"

"Last March," Penny mumbled, and her father laughed.

"You see? Over a year!" Mr. Meyer lifted her chin and smiled at her until she couldn't help smiling back. "Now then, Reuben," he said, extending his hand. "Nice to see you again, and welcome to our home."

"Again?" Penny said.

"Reuben bought some boots from me earlier," Mr. Meyer said. "Little did I know he was headed this way. What a day! I'm sure this all feels rather remarkable to you, too, Reuben. What do you say we go in there and get this business sorted out?"

Reuben swallowed hard and nodded.

In the great room they found the rest of the Meyer family seated around the long dining table. The tumult of voices fell away, and all eyes turned to Reuben, who shoved his hands inside his sweatshirt pockets so that no one could see them trembling. At the far end of the table, an old man was holding the wooden box, which Reuben had left in the house. No doubt they had been passing it around, taking turns inspecting it. Except perhaps for one of them, a young man of about twenty with close-cropped red hair who stood by the cold fireplace, apart from the others. His expression was sullen, but he was paying close attention. That had to be Jack, Reuben thought.

"Everyone, may I introduce you to Reuben?" Mr. Meyer said. "I'm sorry, Reuben, I don't know your last name."

"That's okay," Reuben said, forcing himself to speak up. "Just

Reuben is fine." All around the table eyebrows shot up. "Very nice to meet you all," he added quickly, hoping to seem less impertinent.

Extra chairs had been brought in, but though Penny and Mr. Meyer took seats at the table, Reuben remained standing. He felt instinctively that he must remain on the outside of their group. Knowing what he knew about them, he couldn't help feeling a strange respect for the entire family. But to be a boy in a room full of adults is to be fairly powerless, and Reuben needed to assert himself however he could.

"Well," said Penny's mother, after another awkward pause, "as you can see, Reuben, everyone's been having a look at this remarkable box. We're all very impressed. Won't you tell us where you found it? And where you've come from?"

Reuben's face felt very hot. "I'm sorry, Mrs. Meyer, but to be honest, I don't feel ready to do that yet."

"I beg your pardon?" Mrs. Meyer said, taken aback. From all around the table came the sound of indignant gasps and mutters.

"Everyone, calm down," Mr. Meyer said, looking from face to face. "Let's just calm down."

"The boy's right!" barked the old man at the end of the table. With quivering hands, he set the box down. "Why should he start telling us things about himself? He doesn't know us yet, does he? Sure, he's heard the story—but it's just a story to him, isn't it? Maybe he has good reasons to be careful himself."

"Uncle William has a point," said Mrs. Meyer. "Reuben, I'm sorry. I didn't mean to put you on the spot. I assumed you *wanted* to tell us—well, whatever it is that you know."

"It's okay," said Reuben. "I...I probably will. I just need to be sure of some things first. Like I told Penny, I'm in a bit of a serious situation." He glanced at Penny, who was watching him intently. "Penny told me the story, but she left some parts out—she was being careful, like she was supposed to be. If you

*In the great room they found the rest of the
Meyer family seated around the long dining table.*

all could tell me *everything*, though, it might help me figure out what to do."

"You're asking a lot, young man," said one of the great-aunts. Her hair, done up in a tight bun, must once have been red but was now mostly white with red streaks. "You've presented us with an empty box. Yet you seem to expect that this will be enough to garner our trust."

Reuben tried to keep his voice steady. He was having trouble catching his breath. "Well, what I *can* tell you right now is that I know what was inside the box, and I can promise you that it's very important. I understand why Penelope was being so careful about it. She was right to be. And I'm trying to be very careful about it, too."

Some of the Meyers looked annoyed, but most looked impressed, and there followed a disconcerting outburst of half-whispered exchanges. They all knew he was hedging, Reuben deduced, but they also knew he was telling the truth.

Penny's father cleared his throat, and glancing around the table, he said, "At the very least, I think we can agree that young Reuben here has proved he has mettle. We can all see how hard it must be for him to stand up like this before an entire family of strangers."

There was a general nodding of heads. Mr. Meyer looked back at Reuben. "I'm sure we all want to help you, son, not least because this secret has driven our family crazy for generations"—this remark garnered some muttering and chuckles—"but it's a serious matter, and we'll need to discuss it before proceeding. Will you give us some time to speak privately? Perhaps Penny could show you around—"

"But I want to stay for the discussion!" Penny exclaimed, looking horrified at the thought of being excluded.

"If you don't mind," Reuben cut in quickly, "I think I'd rather just lie down for a while." He started to say that he had a headache, but remembering how easily the Meyers sniffed out falsehoods, he cut himself off. The fewer words the better.

"Of course," said Mrs. Meyer. "You've been traveling. You must be tired. Penny will show you to the guest bedroom. If you need anything, she'll be just across the hall from you, in her room. Penny, please close the door behind you as you go."

With a pained look, Penny stood up. "Come on, Reuben," she said, sighing, with a lack of politeness that Reuben actually found touching, for it made him feel as if they'd been friends a long time. He followed her across the room, making as he did so a final, concentrated study of his surroundings: the dining table, the sideboard, the fireplace sitting area with its armchairs and overstuffed sofa.

Yes, he thought, he could do this. It would be his best chance.

At the hall door Reuben turned and looked back at the table. "Thank you," he said simply. He glanced at the kitchen doorway, gauging distances and angles. Only a glance, for all eyes were upon him—he felt especially scrutinized by Jack, looking at him sidelong—and then he followed Penny into the hall.

"I can't believe they're sending me below," Penny mumbled when she'd closed the door.

"Sending you where?" asked Ruben, suddenly confused.

"What? Oh, that's just a nautical expression," Penny said. "I mean I can't believe they're not letting me discuss the important stuff." And indeed she looked very downcast.

"Sorry, Penny. I wish they would have let you," Reuben said, and he meant it, mostly because it would have made things easier for him. He felt sure she'd been excluded because her parents wanted her to keep an eye on him, and that they'd tell her so later. But the funk she was in did suit his purposes—she was distracted by what she was missing, was focused much more on that than on Reuben.

"Thanks," Penny mumbled, and she led him down the long

hallway to the guest bedroom. It was simply appointed, with a double bed, a small desk and chair, and a wardrobe. Sunlight shone softly through a curtained window. "Okay, I guess just let me know if you need anything," she said, "or if, you know, you change your mind and want to tell me what was in the box...." She looked at him hopefully, but Reuben only gave her an apologetic smile, and wrinkling her nose with frustration, she turned and went into her room.

Reuben closed the door as if he were in no great hurry. Then, moving fast, he took out his watch, made sure it was wound and set properly, and shoved it back into his pocket. He inspected the door—it was quite old, with a latch apparatus that couldn't be locked without a key. Tearing a scrap of paper from a notepad on the desk, Reuben wadded it into a marble-sized ball and stuffed it into the keyhole. Then he took the wooden desk chair and wedged its back beneath the doorknob. He couldn't have Penny looking in on him.

Leaping onto the bed, he reached behind the curtains and unlocked the window. The screen behind the glass had a warped frame that squealed when he raised it. He froze, listening for Penny. Nothing happened. The screen was only halfway up, but Reuben was able to wriggle through the narrow gap and drop down behind the shrubberies lining the wall. Keeping behind the shrubberies and below the windows, he headed around the back of the keeper's house, where there was no longer any cover and the lighthouse tower loomed overhead.

Reuben reached into his sweatshirt pocket and vanished.

The back entrance was a plain wooden door with no screen, and Reuben remembered (for he had been paying close attention) that Penny had lifted up on the knob when she opened it, to prevent it from sticking. He did the same, his heart thumping madly, and swung the door partly open. He waited, listening, then slipped inside. The back door led into an anteroom just off the kitchen. He could hear the murmur of voices from the great room, but only a murmur. He crept through the anteroom, his shoulder brushing against jackets hung on wall hooks, then stepped through the open doorway into the kitchen. The smell of cullen skink was powerful here; his stomach churned. He saw, in his mind's eye, the stove to his left, the counter and refrigerator to his right, the small table straight ahead. The doorway into the great room stood just beyond the table. He moved forward, careful not to let the rubber soles of his shoes squeak on the linoleum, and crouched near the open doorway. He could almost make out the words being spoken around the dining table. But only almost.

You have to do it, Reuben told himself. So do it.

He stepped through the doorway into the great room. There was no break in the conversation, no exclamation of surprise from the direction of the fireplace. Reuben stole across the open space, found the sofa exactly where he thought he would, and got down behind it. He reached through the fabric drape hanging from the bottom of the sofa's frame and felt around. There was nothing beneath the sofa, and just enough room. He lay on his back, his head turned toward the room, and squeezed himself into the narrow space beneath it. An extremely tight fit—the sofa springs pressed down against him through thin fabric. If anyone decided to move to the sofa, Reuben was in for a lot of pain.

For now, though, he was in the perfect hiding place. With a practiced twitch of the winding key, he regained his sight. Yes, he was completely hidden from view, and his left eye was positioned exactly at the half-inch gap between the floor and the fabric drape. Across the room, Reuben could see the feet of everyone sitting at the dining table—a motley assortment of stockings and socks and bare feet, for in their excitement none of the visitors from shore had bothered to put on shoes after removing their muck boots. He swiveled his eyes toward the fireplace. Yes, there were Jack's dirty sneakers. Everyone was accounted for. Now he could concentrate on what was being said.

"—got here without being seen, though?" one of the older women was saying. "Was no one in the watch room?"

"That's my fault, Aunt Caroline. I was working up in the dome. Thought I was keeping a decent lookout, but I guess not."

"It doesn't matter how he got here," said one of the men. "What matters is if he was followed. Do we even know for certain that he's alone?"

Penny's father said, "I spoke with Carmichael at the station. Reuben was the only person to get off the train. We haven't seen any other strangers in town, so I think we've established that it's just him."

"For now," said a woman's voice.

"Point taken, Aunt Penelope. Let's all keep an eye out the windows for any strangers near the dock. I'm not sure what more we can do until we know what we're dealing with."

"One thing we do know," said Penny's mother. "We're dealing with a child on his own. Where is his family? Where did he come from? How is it he's traveling by himself? It was all I could do not to reach out and hug him to me."

"Give the kid some credit," said a low, drawling voice from very close by. "He's looking out for himself, isn't he?"

"What was that? Speak up, son! We don't all have young ears."

"He said that Reuben seems self-reliant, Uncle William," Mr. Meyer said loudly. "And I agree with Jack in the sense that we don't want to underestimate him. But I also agree with Rebekah that we are now responsible for him. He said he was in a serious situation. We can't let him leave here alone. We have to keep him safe."

On this point everyone voiced agreement. Reuben was touched.

He had never had so many people express concern for him (and if ever he had deserved concern, it was certainly now). But it would do him no good. He couldn't let the Meyers keep him here. He had to go back for his mom.

The conversation moved around for a while, sometimes focusing on how to find out what Reuben knew about the box's contents, and other times on how best to help him when he was so reluctant to share information. Finally, and rather forcefully, one of the great-aunts declared that the answer was obvious—they simply must retrieve whatever the original Penelope had hidden in the secret place.

Reuben concentrated all the harder now, straining to register every word.

"What are the odds," the great-aunt said, "that after all these many decades there is still some Bartholomew-type prowling about? I, for one, would give almost anything to know what's behind all of this, and we now have a legitimate opportunity. I think it's safe enough; I think we risk little. Let the Jacks fetch crowbars and flashlights and go down there, and let us see once and for all what this has all been about!"

There was scattered applause and suppressed cheering. Reuben could sense the mood shifting at the table. Excitement and relief were winning the argument.

"But do we share what we find with the boy?" someone asked. "Without first learning from him what he knows?"

"Perhaps what we find would help us to decide," said Mr. Meyer.

"Well, we can't go now," said Penny's brother Luke. "The tide's started to come in. The next low tide isn't until three in the morning. Do we want to plan for then?"

"It's true we'd have the benefit of darkness," said Mr. Meyer. "No one could see us from the shore. Oh, but wait—"

"Right," said another voice. Then all at once the others burst out saying "Oh yes, the storm!" and "It'll be such a nasty blow" and "Couldn't ask for a fouler night" and other such things, and everyone agreed that they had better wait until the following day, when the skies would be clear.

No one was more in tune with the weather, Reuben realized, than a family of lighthouse keepers. And perhaps their foreboding should have been more contagious, but where the Meyers saw a need for caution, Reuben saw an opportunity. They had said enough to reveal that the smugglers' tunnels were right here on the island.

And so, bad weather or not, tonight was the night he would make his move.

THE MYSTERY OF JACK

When Mr. Meyer knocked on the guest room door, Reuben opened it, rubbing his eyes and yawning. No doubt he looked so genuinely weary that Mr. Meyer thought it pointless to ask if he felt rested after his nap. "You look wrecked, son," he observed instead. "Are you feeling all right?"

Reuben forced himself to focus. "I'm fine, thank you. Just tired."

The fact was that in his efforts to return to the guest room, he had been forced to use the watch not once but twice, and each time for the full duration of its winding. The Meyers had caught him off guard with how abruptly they adjourned their meeting and scooted back their chairs, and Reuben had spent a harrowing half hour getting out of the house and then back to the guest room window, with Meyers young and old wandering around, indoors and out, seemingly at random.

"Well, perhaps you'll sleep better tonight," said Mr. Meyer, turning to include Penny, who had just emerged from her room. "The family hasn't quite agreed on what information to share with you, I'm afraid, and will probably take the weekend making that decision. In the meantime we'd like you to stay as our guest. Maybe when you get to know us better, you'll feel more comfortable sharing, as well."

"Thank you for having me," said Reuben, careful to keep his expression neutral. "I think I can stay a night or two. Would it be possible for me to make a private phone call, though?"

This request was met with an uncomfortable pause, and Reuben realized that he wouldn't be allowed anywhere near a phone without revealing whom he intended to call. Mr. Meyer clearly felt the need to be careful himself.

"I have to check in with my mom," Reuben admitted. "So she won't worry." He looked Mr. Meyer directly in the eye. In this instance, anyway, he was telling the truth.

"That's good of you," said Mr. Meyer, after studying him a moment, "and honestly, I'm glad to hear it. I'm relieved to know you have a family. Even better, the fact that you feel compelled to call your mother will put some of our more nervous Nellies at ease. It's very Meyer-like of you, you see." He gave Reuben a cheerful wink, and to Penny he said, "How about you help me clear everyone out? This will take some doing."

The telephone in the kitchen, evidently, was the only one in the house, and Reuben's request for privacy caused a great deal of disruption and took a remarkably long time to accomplish. Sitting awkwardly in the kitchen, nibbling on a plain cracker (for his stomach was still unsettled, but his hunger had returned), Reuben listened as Penny and her father chased down all the Meyers wandering in and out of the house, upstairs and down, explaining repeatedly why everyone needed to clear out. Finally, amid a fair amount of grumbling and confusion—and a hostile glare from Jack as he passed through the kitchen—Penny and her father managed to get all the Meyers ushered outside.

"Sorry for all the trouble," Reuben said, blushing, when Penny came to announce this. He was mortified to have caused such a commotion.

"Are you kidding?" Penny replied with her bright laugh. Her freckled cheeks were flushed and glistening with perspiration. "It isn't every day I get to order them around. That was fun!" She wished him well with his phone call—pausing for yet another wondering look at this mysterious new friend of hers—then bounced out of the kitchen humming, her fine mood having returned.

Reuben watched her go, wishing he felt half as carefree as she seemed to. What a relief it would be to feel no worry, no guilt, no expectation of danger to come. He looked with dread at the clock over the counter. His mom would have just gotten home from the market. Time to act quickly, no matter how much he wanted to put it off.

"Reuben?" That was how she answered the phone, and Reuben was instantly on guard. Her anxiety and expectation seemed to reach through the line and squeeze his throat. Why was she so worried?

"Hi, Mom!" Reuben said, forcing the words out. His chirpy tone sounded false to his own ears, but he had to press on. "Just checking in, as promised."

Her sigh of relief sounded like interference on the line. "Oh, honey, thank you. Everything going okay?"

"Everything's great, Mom. I'm having fun. You can stop worrying."

"I'm glad to hear you say that," his mom replied. Then she added, "You're sure?"

Reuben realized now that she wasn't just worried. She was worried about something specific. "Mom, what's the matter?"

There was a pause. "I'm sorry," she said. "I wasn't going to bother you with this over the phone, but I think maybe it's too important to wait. I just spoke with Mrs. Peterson from across the hall. She said those men came around today—you know who I mean."

Reuben felt ice in his belly. The Directions. His mom always referred to them as "those men" if she had to mention them at all. The Directions were just about the only thing his mom never joked about. With an effort he kept his tone even. "Of course I know. What do you mean they came around?"

"Mrs. Peterson said they're going all over the neighborhood— not just the local ones, evidently, but scads of them from all over the city. They started showing up around lunchtime. They're asking about a boy who fits your description. Well, they said they think he's nine or ten, but since you're small for your age, I thought they might mean you."

Reuben's pulse sounded like kettledrums in his ears. He could barely hear his mother's voice. So The Smoke knew. Somehow he'd figured out Reuben was from the Lower Downs. Why else would the Directions suddenly be searching there? Reuben tried to remain calm, yet when he spoke, his voice sounded distant to his own ears, as if someone else were speaking. "Why would they be asking about me?"

"A boy *like* you," his mom said. "I was hoping it wasn't *actually* you. They say this boy found something that doesn't belong to him. They want him to hand it over so they can return it to its owner. They say he won't be in any trouble, they know that boys will be boys—that's what Mrs. Peterson said. It's just that this thing is important, so they need to get it back. A skinny brown-haired boy, that's who they're looking for."

Reuben's temples throbbed. His face was burning and slick with sweat. Yet somehow he managed to keep his voice steady. "Mom, there's tons of skinny brown-haired boys in the Lower Downs. And I'm eleven."

"I know. Of course. But—"

"Mom. Whatever it is, I don't have it. I'd have to be crazy to keep something if I knew they wanted it, wouldn't I?" Reuben asked. And at that moment he did feel crazy. Completely insane.

"Oh, Reuben, that's what I thought!" his mom said with another gusting sigh of relief. "But you're sure, though? You're absolutely sure? This sounds pretty serious, kid."

"I'm sure, Mom," Reuben said. "Whoever they're looking for, it isn't me."

Long after they had hung up, Reuben sat at the kitchen table, his head in his hands. The ticking of the ominous clock in his mind had suddenly accelerated. He'd counted on more time to figure things out, to decide what to say to his mom, to get them both out of the city. But now the Directions were going door-to-door in the Lower Downs? What if they came by again when his mom was home? What if they asked for a picture of him? All they had to do was show it to one of those Brighton Street employees to confirm that Reuben was the one they sought.

His eyes swiveled toward the phone. He could call her back right now, tell her the truth, tell her where he was, and that's all it would take—she'd be on the next train to Point William. But what if the Directions suspected the truth already? What if they were secretly following her?

Reuben squeezed his head and let out an anguished sound, half growl and half howl. He felt frightened, and he felt angry, and at the moment he could hardly distinguish between the two feelings.

"Reuben?" Penny poked her head in through the kitchen doorway. "Sorry, Dad sent me to check on you, and it didn't sound like you were talking anymore, but then I heard you—you know, kind of scream a little there. Are you okay?"

He looked up at her as if he didn't know her. He shook his head, trying to clear it.

"No?" Penny stepped inside, looking concerned. "Can I help you? What can I do?"

"No, no, I'm fine." Reuben climbed shakily to his feet. "It's just—things are complicated. I'm fine, though. Thanks, Penny."

"You don't have to thank me," she said, and to Reuben's astonishment she came over and hugged him. "We're in this together now, right? And whatever it is, it's going to be okay." She drew back to give him a reassuring smile.

Reuben managed a weak smile in return. He nodded.

"I'd better tell the others you're off the phone," Penny said. "The tide's back in, and Luke's going to row some aunts and uncles over to the mainland. But most of them left their shoes in the house!" She chuckled and turned to go.

"People are leaving?" Reuben asked, confused.

"Only to get pajamas and toothbrushes," Penny said from the doorway. "They'll all be back for dinner. Believe me, no one wants to miss any of this!"

Reuben looked bleakly after her. *Great*, he thought. *Perfect*.

Of course the Meyers were excited to find out what had been hidden in the smugglers' tunnels all this time. Some of them surely thought the same thing he did, that a chest full of gold pieces or jewels was down there, just sitting there across the generations, tantalizingly untouched. At least in this respect they might not be disappointed, since Reuben intended to leave most of the treasure for them. But naturally they were also dying to know the *reasons* for everything—to understand why they had done what they'd done for all these generations. And in this respect they were going to be seriously let down.

Yes, tomorrow morning there would be a lot of disappointed people on this island. Disappointed and angry. Maybe someday, Reuben thought, he could write a letter explaining everything. Maybe they would understand. Maybe they would even forgive him.

As the world outside grew dark and the blustery winds of the approaching storm caused the stunted evergreens to sway and shimmy, Reuben sat in the open doorway of the oil house. *Let the Jacks fetch crowbars and flashlights.* The phrase had stuck in his head. He had a flashlight in his backpack, and he'd seen crowbars among the tools in the oil house. All he needed now was for time to pass. Time was in absolutely no hurry to oblige him, though. Three o'clock in the morning seemed ages away.

Aware that he was probably being watched, Reuben avoided glancing toward the granite boulders on the seaward side of the island—*the watery side*—and kept his eyes on the troubled sky. The Meyers mustn't suspect he had any notion of where to find the entrance to the smugglers' tunnels. He went back over some of the words he'd heard Penny chanting in the oil house:

> *Scarcely seen at low tide,*
> *Never seen at high,*
> *Only from the watery side,*
> *Never from the dry.*
> *Always bring your tools, mate,*
> *And keep your lanterns low.*

Reuben hated to think how Penny would feel if she knew she'd given away the secret. Horrified. Mortified. Positively ill. What had Jack called her? *The most Meyer-like of all the Meyers.* It was a good thing she'd never find out. She was going to be unhappy enough as it was—the thought made Reuben feel ill himself. Penny was possibly the nicest person he'd ever met. Her whole family was nice, for that matter, with Jack being the lone exception.

Dining with the Meyers had been awkward, to say the least,

235

yet almost everyone had taken extra care to make Reuben feel welcome. In high spirits, they'd told funny stories, and teased one another good-naturedly, and urged second helpings on Reuben. No doubt by private agreement they had resisted asking him any probing questions, treating him instead as if he were just one of Penny's friends. The nicer they all were, however, the worse Reuben felt, and Jack's penetrating stares continued to unnerve him. By the time dessert was served, he couldn't bear another minute. Politely declining, Reuben had excused himself.

"You can't help it," he muttered to himself now. He ripped up a few blades of grass near his feet and let the wind carry them off. "It doesn't matter that you like them, so stop thinking about it."

Penny appeared at the screen door of the keeper's house. She pushed it open with a foot—she was carrying a bowl in each hand—and with the same foot eased it closed behind her. She was pretty nimble, Reuben reflected, and as she walked across the grass toward him, his mind played a strange trick: it conjured an image of Penny climbing up a drainpipe. Reuben thought he knew why. He would have liked to have Penny as his friend before now, in his other life, would have liked her company on those lonely days among the alleys of the Lower Downs.

"I brought you some berries and cream," Penny said. "It was obvious to everyone that you wanted some."

"Right. I forgot. Meyers always know." He accepted the bowl and spoon that Penny held out to him. "Thanks." He spooned a bite of sliced strawberries and whipped cream into his mouth. It was so delicious he instantly wished he had more than just one bowl.

Penny sat down next to him. "Good, isn't it? We have a cousin with a berry farm. She always gives us the best. And the whipped cream comes from a dairy not far from here."

"So this isn't a Penelope dish?"

Penny laughed and tossed her hair back over her shoulders. "You must be from the city if you think this dessert is exotic. No,

Penelope never wrote about berries and cream, but I'll bet she ate plenty of it growing up here."

"She did if she had any sense," Reuben said with his mouth full.

Penny lifted a spoonful to her mouth, then paused and looked at him sidelong. "So are you? From the city?"

Reuben looked out at the waves tossing in the bay. He took another bite.

"Come on." Penny nudged him with her elbow. "One thing. Surely you can tell me one thing."

Reuben felt another pang of longing. He wanted to tell her everything, he realized. Not just one thing, but everything. He was tired of carrying the burden of all his secrets alone. But telling Penny would be disastrous. She would have to tell her family, and they would surely intervene. They would want the watch. And so he bit his lip and continued to look away.

"You *want* to tell me," Penny teased. "I can tell! So why don't you?"

Reuben almost blurted it out: *My mom's in danger, okay? Or she will be soon, anyway, and it's because of something I—something . . . well, I didn't mean to do anything bad. But now I'm stuck. I have to get her out of there, but we have nothing. . . .*

He sighed. He couldn't say any of it. One thing would only lead to another, and it would all come tumbling out, and that would be that. He glanced at Penny, who was searching his face with a troubled expression, and quickly looked away again. "I promise I'll explain everything eventually," he said, and felt better even as he said it. Yes, when all of this was over, he would definitely write that letter. He looked back at her. "I promise, okay?"

Penny twisted her mouth to one side. "Fine," she said. "I guess I'll have to accept that. I *will* hold you to it, you know."

The screen door banged, and both of them started. Jack had just stormed out of the keeper's house and was marching down toward the pier. He was clenching and unclenching his fists, and even from this distance Reuben could see the muscles working in his arms. He looked as though he wanted to rip something apart and had both the strength and the ferocity to do just that.

"What's the matter?" Penny called out, waving her spoon at Jack. She seemed completely unperturbed by her brother's evident anger.

"The boat's come loose," Jack snapped, with a hostile glance at Reuben. "Luke can't tie a knot to save his life."

The children rose and went around the oil house to watch as Jack threw off his shoes and waded into the surging water. The rowboat hadn't drifted far and was trailing its mooring line. Jack snatched it and dragged the boat back to shore. With forceful, jerking motions, he set about securing it to the pier.

"I don't think Jack likes me," Reuben said quietly as they watched.

Penny laughed. "Don't let that bother you," she said. "Jack doesn't like anyone."

"He seems to like *you* well enough," Reuben ventured, remembering how Penny and Jack had interacted in private, though of course he dared not mention that.

Penny shrugged. "That's different, I guess. Kid sisters get special status. That's what Jack says, anyway."

Jack was fastening a tarp over the boat now. He paused to wipe water from his eyes and then from his head. His red hair was cropped so close to the scalp that, from this distance, it seemed little more than a coating of brick dust. Reuben wouldn't have been surprised to learn that Jack had shaved it off in a fit of anger.

"What's he so mad about?" he muttered.

"Oh, he always finds something," Penny began in a light tone, but then she trailed off. Jack had finished his task and was looking up at the sky, across which dark clouds were flowing swiftly, like an invading fleet.

"Usually he takes it out on a punching bag," she continued, more seriously now. "He got teased growing up, you know, because of the way our family is. And then he had to watch Luke get teased, too. When it started happening to me, he just lost it. That was the last straw."

Reuben considered this new information. "I guess that makes sense," he said. "I'm sure I'd be mad, too, if I got teased like that."

"It isn't just the teasing," Penny said. "I think he resents our family for seeming so weird to other people, and he hates other people for thinking we're weird—because he knows that we're just trying to do what's right."

"You don't seem weird to me," Reuben said.

Penny shot him a grateful look. "Well, we kind of are, though. Compared to a lot of families, anyway. I mean, sure, the Meyers have a reputation for being the most upstanding citizens in town, but it goes too far for most people's tastes. Nobody in our family ever drinks a drop of wine; nobody ever lies or cheats; everybody eats properly, exercises, pitches in wherever we're needed. The list goes on. But *you* understand, Reuben. We have to be this way—we have to be clearheaded people, good judges of character, reliable and steady. Because of that original promise, because of the secret! It's our duty!"

Reuben shook his head in wonder. It hadn't really sunk in until now—the trial it had been for the Meyer family to do what they had done, the burden they had borne all these years. It was incredible, but in a way it was awful, too. "What do you mean," he asked, "when you say Jack 'lost it'?"

Penny looked at him soberly. "Let's just say nobody would tease him now. Nobody would want to be Jack's enemy." She sighed. "Of course, no one would want to be his friend, either."

"You seem worried about him," Reuben said.

"Of course I'm worried about him."

Jack had left the pier and was stalking back up to the keeper's house. He glanced over at them as he passed. "Thanks for the help, you two."

Penny laughed her bright laugh. "You're welcome! We watched as hard as we could!"

Jack disappeared into the house, letting the screen door bang behind him.

"He shows his love in so many ways," Penny said, and now Reuben laughed, too—he couldn't help it. He licked his spoon clean and dropped it into his empty bowl.

They were quiet for a while. The wind had grown steady and strong. Waves crashed against the island rocks.

At length, in a soft voice, Penny offered a final point on the subject of her brother. "Jack is kind of a mystery to the rest of us. He does love us, though. He's mad, but he loves us. That much I know." She gazed out at the churning waters with a look of such wistfulness that Reuben felt an urge to hug her, to tell her that Jack would be all right—that everyone would be all right. He could sense how worried she was. But he only nodded and, like her, looked out to sea. The waves were getting bigger, crashing with greater force against the rocks. Reuben could feel the occasional tingle of sea spray even where he sat.

It was a perfect night for feeling the way he felt: guilty, conflicted, afraid. In the course of a single day Penny had become his friend—and not just any friend, but the best kind, the kind you want to share your secrets with. He kept thinking about what she'd said to him in the kitchen. *We're in this together now, right?*

Reuben tried not to think about how she was going to feel tomorrow, when she found that he'd gone. The thought of her reaction made him so miserable that, in a way, it was a relief to know that after tonight he wouldn't have to see her again.

But only in a way. In every other way, it felt like the loss of a lifetime.

The Rabbit Trap

At exactly three in the morning, Reuben woke with a gasp, thinking, *Low tide!* He was never supposed to have fallen asleep in the first place. Thunder rumbled outside. Wind and rain rattled the windows. He looked around, disoriented. He was on the sofa. The other Meyers were spending the night and had been given the guest rooms—as well as Penny's room, which meant that Penny was sleeping in the great room, too. Now he remembered. She lay on a pallet of blankets near the fireplace. In the near darkness, Reuben spied her sleeping form.

Evidently, his fatigue had been too much for him. He'd been lying on the sofa, fresh from a warm bath, listening to the murmur of Mr. and Mrs. Meyer talking in the kitchen. Penny had already fallen asleep, her red hair spreading out from her head in all directions, so abundant that it covered her pillow. She was sleeping with her mouth open, her two front teeth plainly visible. There had been a lamp on then. Her parents must have turned it off when they went to bed.

Reuben peered at the luminescent dial of the mantel clock. It confirmed the time, which somehow he'd already known. Perhaps he'd been counting the minutes in his sleep. He drew back the blanket, eased off the sofa. He took his sneakers from the floor and crept into the kitchen, where a light had been left on over the stove. From his pocket he withdrew the note that he had written earlier and set it on the table. *Be back soon*, it read. He had intentionally left the meaning unclear. He only hoped to put off a search until after he'd caught the morning train.

In the anteroom off the kitchen, he took down the darkest of several raincoats, a navy-blue one that was only a couple of sizes too big. He put it on, transferring the watch to one of the raincoat's deep pockets. Then, with his sneakers tucked inside the raincoat and his socks stuffed into them, he slipped out the back door.

Rain pelted him even under the eaves of the house. The wind blew it into his face. High overhead a beam of light flashed into the darkness. Two quick strokes, followed by a pause, then a third stroke. Another pause, and the pattern repeated. The light was so brilliant it must be visible for miles. Yet it was designed to penetrate the darkness over the stormy sea, not the ground beneath it, and Reuben gazed up at it from a near-total darkness. He was taking no chances, though. When he had rounded the corner and gotten a fix on the oil house door, he vanished completely.

Barefoot, he crossed the wet grass at a fast walk. He had, of course, memorized the distance, and when he slowed and stretched out his hands, he found the door just where he'd expected it to be. Inside with the door closed it was quiet. Reuben pulled out on the winding key, but there was virtually no change in the darkness. He found his way to the oil drum and the backpack he'd left hidden behind it, along with his muck boots, which he'd brought up from beneath the pier after dinner. His searching fingers unzipped the pack and probed its contents until they came upon the familiar form of a flashlight. Reuben turned it on long enough to fetch a crowbar, then switched it off again. He was used to darkness now.

Storing his sneakers inside the backpack—he would want dry feet later—Reuben put on the boots and tightened the raincoat around him. Then he vanished and went out again into the crashing storm.

It took him mere seconds to make his way to the base of the lighthouse tower, but several minutes to go from there to the northern shore of the island. Traversing the close-packed granite boulders would have been challenging enough without the added difficulty of fierce wind and whipping rain—and blindness made it virtually impossible. At last Reuben was compelled to reappear and trust in the darkness to hide him. He even had to resort to the flashlight, flicking it on for a few moments at a time to be sure of his path. (The regular bursts of lightning were no help, for they appeared only as orange or yellow patches in the sky, swallowed up in an infinite blackness of thunderclouds.)

Laboriously he picked his way over the slippery rocks, often losing his footing, repeatedly wiping water from his eyes. Finally he reached the end of the island, where the granite yielded to a skin of seawater swirling over mud.

Scarcely seen at low tide, never seen at high, Reuben thought, wiping his eyes again. Here, just where the rocks met the receded water, was where he must search. He switched on the flashlight—there was no help for it—and passed its beam over the granite forms bordering the water. *Above the* X, *below the* Y. His eyes darted this way and that. He had hoped the signs would be obvious. They were not. He forced himself to become more methodical. Choosing a nearby boulder with a distinctive jagged edge, he began to scour the lowermost slabs to the right of it, one by one.

Each of the nearest three boulders seemed promising at first glance—each bore formations of barnacles and seaweed that looked, to Reuben, very much like *X*s. But barnacles and seaweed would not have been counted upon, and he knew it. The fact that he wanted to see an *X* so badly meant that he was going to see *X*s everywhere. *Calm down*, he told himself. *This may take a while.*

And then, on the very next boulder, he found an *X* chiseled into the stone.

Reuben nearly whooped with amazement. The *X* was about the size of his hand. It wouldn't have been noticeable from even a few paces off. But there was no doubt that it had been etched with a chisel, the grooves not large but deep, and lined with green-and-brown slime.

Now, he thought excitedly. *Below the* Y.

Above the marked boulder were at least six or seven more before the island's bank leveled off to flatter terrain. Reuben was sure he would find the *Y* chiseled into one of the lowest ones, since these were most likely to be hidden underwater when the tide was in. His search produced nothing, though, and he found himself searching the higher ones with mounting frustration. Nothing. He returned to the one marked with an *X*. What was he missing? Had the *Y* been painted instead of etched, then washed away by decades of surf? Should he simply start attempting to pry up every boulder above the one with the *X*? Time was precious.

He studied the boulders with his flashlight, trying to determine which one might be the most easily moved. They all seemed dauntingly massive. And one of them, two boulders up, was not nearly round enough to get rolling downhill, which was probably his only hope for moving any of them. It was more rectangular in shape, and branched at the top.

Like a *Y.*

Reuben was furious with himself for not noticing it sooner, but only for a second—then he was thrilled, shouting in his head with excitement and scrambling over the middlemost boulder, looking for a good place to get leverage with the crowbar.

As it happened, there was not just a good place but a perfect one. A slot had been chiseled into the base of the boulder's uphill side. Reuben shoved the end of the crowbar into the slot. It went in almost halfway, then stopped and would go no farther. Its midpoint braced against a rock footing, the crowbar stuck out like the raised end of a seesaw.

Reuben, without thinking, wiped his wet hands on the raincoat as if it could possibly dry them. He grabbed the raised end of the crowbar and shoved downward on it with all his might. With a great sucking sound, the boulder levered upward, revealing a foot-high gap. Globs of mud dripped and plopped from the raised edges. He couldn't believe how easily the boulder had come up. Then he saw that its interior had been almost entirely chiseled out, revealing that what had appeared to be solid rock was, in actuality, a roughly hewn dome. That hollowness made the boulder far lighter than it would have been otherwise.

The dome of rock was very heavy nonetheless, and Reuben's grip was weakening. Looking around for something to keep the dome propped open, he discovered a groove chiseled into the rocks near his feet, just inches below the lowered end of the crowbar. Putting all his weight onto the crowbar, he pressed the end down into the groove, where it caught and held, locked into place by the weight of the boulder. The raised rock dome and the crowbar now resembled a gigantic version of a homemade rabbit trap, the kind a child would make, with a box propped up by a twig.

Reuben shined the flashlight into the gap. A narrow stone chute slanted downward about the length of his body, then appeared to level off. Beyond that he could see nothing. He didn't give himself time to think about it. He thrust his feet into the gap, then his legs, then let himself slide all the way in, his back pressed against the wet, flat stone.

At the bottom of the slope Reuben found himself shining his light down a long stone tunnel. Here and there water dripped from cracks in the ceiling, which was high enough for him to stand up straight. Those long-ago smugglers would almost certainly have needed to crouch, though. And they would have needed to know their way around, for the tunnel, at its far end, branched into two.

The rights are all for fools, mate, the lefts for those who know.

With echoing, splashing footsteps, Reuben hurried down the tunnel and turned to his left. The next tunnel was shorter, and it, too, branched in different directions at its end. Reuben again turned to his left. And then, not long after that, turned left again. He counted his steps and counted the turns, but really, getting back out should be simple: he would just need to turn right at every branch instead of left.

But where was he going? And how far might these tunnels stretch? Did they pass beneath the island, beneath the mud, all the way to the mainland? Or no, all these lefts should actually take him seaward, shouldn't they? Reuben felt rather turned around. He paused. All about him, the sound of dripping water echoed off the stone walls and ceiling. The crashing of the storm seemed far away, a memory. He steadied himself, reminded himself that he knew the way back. Purely from habit, he took the watch from inside his raincoat pocket and checked it. Then he pressed on. Surely the tunnels couldn't go much farther.

And indeed, around the very next turn he came to a dead end. A stone wall rose up before him. The ceiling rose, too; Reuben shined his flashlight up as if from the bottom of a well. Iron rungs had been set into the wall—irregularly and not very generously, it seemed, for some had daunting gaps between them. Aiming his flashlight into the gloom above the highest rung, fifteen or twenty feet above him, Reuben saw an opening in the wall, like the entrance to an alcove.

He was close. He could feel it. In his mind's eye he could almost see it—an ancient chest at the back of the alcove, brimming with gold pieces, the answer to everything. Reuben could fill his pockets. In minutes he'd be gone.

This is really happening, he thought, his heart thumping wildly. *You've almost done it!*

The first rung broke away as soon as Reuben put his weight on it. His boot splashed down into ankle-deep water. The iron had been completely rusted through. He stood in a puddle, looking down at the broken rung—and also at bits of other rungs that had fallen from their places over the years. *No no no,* he thought, frowning. He was too close. He shined the flashlight at the wall again.

The next rung looked to be slightly less rusted. Or maybe he just wanted to believe that. Still, he had to yank his left foot awkwardly high just to get purchase on it. The rung wobbled in the wall, yet Reuben had no choice but to trust it. Shoving off with his right foot, then immediately pressing with his left, he lurched upward and caught hold of the next rung, which from the ground had been impossible to reach. He nearly dropped his flashlight in the process, but he managed to hold on. So did the rungs, though just barely. They wiggled in the wall like loose teeth.

Reuben shoved the narrow plastic end of the flashlight into his mouth, clamped his teeth down on it—and suddenly all the

Aiming his flashlight into the gloom above the highest rung, fifteen or twenty feet above him, Reuben saw an opening in the wall, like the entrance to an alcove.

experience of his boyhood took over. He was an expert climber, an old hand at negotiating tricky spots. The walls on either side of him were close enough to be of use whenever a rung was missing: here he found a toehold in the stone, there a handhold, and there again he braced the sole of his boot against a side wall and shoved himself higher. And when—as happened twice—one of the rungs broke loose and fell with a jangling splash down below, Reuben didn't panic or drop his flashlight or even pause to look down, but fluidly shifted his weight and continued to climb. He felt a familiar calmness brought on by concentration. His one discomfort was the flashlight in his mouth. His jaws ached, and it was difficult to swallow; in fact, he was drooling. It felt very much like being at the dentist.

Soon, though, he was at the topmost rung, letting the flashlight drop from his mouth onto the floor of the alcove (for it was indeed an alcove, only a few yards deep) and reaching for an iron stake driven into the rock, probably for that very purpose. A good thing, too, for no sooner had he grasped the stake than the topmost rung, which he still held tightly in his other hand, broke free from the wall. Reuben tossed it down next to the flashlight and hauled himself up. He swallowed a few times, just because he could. He felt an urge to rinse and spit.

Taking up the flashlight, he shined it at the rear wall of the alcove. No chest. There was, however, a dark metal hatch built into the wall. Reuben was reminded of the submarine hatches he'd envisioned in the floors of his dream house. He'd never actually seen a hatch in real life, but this one looked much as he would have imagined. The problem was that it was closed and, worse, secured in its iron frame by a thick, rusty chain and a padlock fatter than his fist.

Still, he was so close. Reuben quickly walked forward on his knees (the ceiling in the alcove was low) and examined the padlock. It looked ridiculously old, and bigger than any lock he'd ever seen. It was spotted with black and green and was, in places, badly rusted. He yanked on it. The chain rattled; the lock held firm.

He pursed his lips, thinking.

The chain. A chain was only as good as its weakest link, right? Reuben began inspecting the heavy links of this one. Some appeared as sound as the day they were forged, but most were rusty. One of them was badly so—in fact, more rust than solid metal.

Now the phrase *Always bring your tools, mate* sounded mockingly in Reuben's mind. A second crowbar would have come in handy right now. Did he dare return to the oil house? How soon would the tide start coming in again? He glanced around anxiously for something else he could use. His eyes fell on the broken iron rung.

Reuben crawled back, snatched it up, and returned to the chain. He began to hammer the rusted link. *Clank. Clank. Clank.* He misfired, scraped his knuckles on the stone floor, put them to his mouth and tasted blood. Ignoring the throb of pain, he went back to hammering. *Clank. Clank. Clank.* He was a character from Greek myth. A blacksmith in the bowels of the earth.

Clank. Clank. Clank.

The link gave. Not much, but his flashlight verified a significant crack. He could see all the way through it, a narrow yet undeniable gap in the metal. Reuben excitedly positioned this broken spot against the metal of the adjoining link, then took hold of the chain and pulled on it with all his strength, trying to force the gap wider. He rested, then pulled again. The link stretched a centimeter. He yanked at the chain viciously now, again and again, each time positioning the gap in the link to receive the brunt of his force. The gap widened a little more. A dozen more yanks, and Reuben suddenly lurched over backward. He'd done it. The link had broken free. He got up onto his knees, breathing hard, dripping with sweat inside the raincoat.

"I can't believe it," he whispered.

For here he was, pulling the broken chain loose, its enormous padlock no longer an obstacle. He checked his watch, tucked it away again. He grabbed the hatch's simple handle and pulled. The heavy round door resisted a moment, then yielded with a shuddering groan, swinging wide open.

THE HUNTERS IN THE NIGHT

Reuben passed through the opening like a mouse into its hole. The hatch gave onto a cramped stone chamber, scarcely half as wide or as deep as his bedroom at home, with a ceiling low enough that even he was forced to stoop. It was as damp as the tunnels had been, its walls spotted with fungus and lichen. Near the back wall a chunk of masonry and rock lay where it had fallen from the ceiling. Reuben shined his flashlight around. The only thing in the chamber seemed to be himself.

He turned and inspected the wall surrounding the hatch. Again nothing. Yet his hopes were not dashed nor even diminished. He felt a confidence now, a certainty. He was the first to have entered this chamber since Penelope had locked the hatch behind her more than a century earlier. In Reuben's mind, she had without a doubt left treasure here, and without a doubt he would find it. There would be a hidden lever, a stone to pry up, something. He searched the walls again, more carefully this time. Then he shined his light up at the hole in the ceiling. He saw damp earth and stone, a beaded spiderweb, and nothing more.

Reuben turned his flashlight onto the fallen chunk of ceiling. It was about the size of a manhole cover and a good foot thick. He kicked at the rubble around it and found something brown and pulpy—a rotten stick of some kind. Whatever that was, it hadn't been part of the ceiling; it had been on the floor. He shook his head in disbelief. What were the odds? Of all places for the ceiling to give way, it had to be directly over the only thing in the chamber?

If it had been a chest, it was a small one, and more or less crushed now. Reuben set his flashlight onto the floor, its beam directed at the chunk of stone and masonry. He got his fingers under the chunk's jagged edge and heaved upward. A brilliant orange centipede appeared in the light, flashed over the end of Reuben's boot, and wriggled away into the darkness. Reuben's yelp of alarm sounded strange in the confines of the chamber. Flattened, somehow, like calling out from under a bed.

He got the chunk up onto its end and was ready to flip it over when it buckled into several pieces. Piece by piece he tossed aside the rubble, careful now where he put his fingers, always on the lookout for crawling things. There was a lot of rotten wood that appeared once to have had a specific form—a flat piece and three or four slender pieces. Not a chest. A stool, he decided, or a small table. And what Penelope had left resting on top of it was now mixed up with its remains and the ceiling rubble. A few sweeps of his hand and Reuben had uncovered it.

It was a slender metal box, about the size of a book. Once gray, it was mostly black and green now, with patches of red rust. Reuben looked at it dubiously. Could it be full of jewels? It made no sound when he shook it, and now, finally, his heart began to sink. It was occurring to him that perhaps the reason he'd felt so convinced, so absolutely certain that Penelope had left treasure behind, was that he so desperately *needed* it to be treasure.

"Oh, please," he whispered. "Please be *something*."

The box was unlocked, but its clasps had long since rusted shut. Reuben took up a stone and broke them open. The lid remained stuck tight even so, and broke off completely when he tried to force it. Inside the box was a leather pouch much like the one in which Reuben had found the clock watch. The leather was stiff and unyielding; it gave off a strangely fishy odor. The pouch's single clasp was rusty but still functional, and soon Reuben drew out a thin sheaf of warped, mold-spotted papers. He felt around inside the pouch to be sure. Empty. The papers were everything.

Reuben squeezed his eyes closed, fighting back sudden tears. *This* was what had been hidden down here all this time—a handful of old papers? He wanted to scream, wanted to tear the papers to shreds. He had banked everything on the expectation of treasure, and now he had a handful of *papers*? He took a deep breath, then another, and then another.

They must be important, he reminded himself when he began to feel steadier. *They must be valuable*. Reuben opened his eyes, and now he saw that he was holding a letter from Penelope. Her last one.

Okay, he thought, his excitement quickly returning. *Maybe she gives directions. Maybe she'll tell me where to go*. Flashlight in one hand, ages-old letter in the other, Reuben began to read. The letter was written in a strong, sure hand, with a general disregard for margins, its words often crowded up against the edges of the page. It read:

My dear brother, if you are reading this, then I have failed in the task which I have appointed myself. Yet it is possible that you or another will prevail, and it is in this hope that I write you now. What I set down here you may find hard to believe, but you will soon have proof of my words, if you have not already seen it for yourself.

Jack, you know I possess something which the vile Bartholomew desperately desires. Believe me when I tell you that he has worked harder and longer than the most diligent laborer, has studied far more than any priest, and has lied, bribed, stolen, and even killed—oh yes, and more than once, brother—in his feverish quest to claim it for himself. Reading these words, you may wonder at such mania for the clever little clock that has now—in the hands, I hope, of a good and decent soul—found its way back to you. For it is possible that neither of you has discovered the clock's secret.

Reuben had arrived at the end of the first page. Carefully he peeled it off the stack, the paper taking with it some of the ink from the following page. The words were still mostly legible, though, and anyway he already knew the secrets that Penelope, in meticulous detail, revealed there. He moved quickly on to the third page, where he was brought up short by the first line.

Such a wondrous thing, and yet so wicked.

Reuben frowned. He had not expected this.

A long history of evildoing traces to the origins of this clock watch, this beautiful object that rests with such apparent innocence, even as I write, in the pocket of my cloak. It is important, Jack, that you know at least a part of that history.

Early on in our acquaintance, Bartholomew related to me (and later he showed me in a centuries-old book written in Italian, and another in English) a legend of a brilliant inventor. His patrons were two noblemen of fabulous wealth, brothers whose riches were almost as unequaled as the inventor's genius. Each ruled a small kingdom, and each was as vain as only the richest of lords and dukes can become. For these brothers the inventor created many extravagant contraptions whose workings never failed to mystify the guests of their royal courts, a distinction which pleased the brothers immensely. Yet the men were exceedingly jealous of each other, always arguing about who possessed the greatest invention and always pressing the inventor to create something superior to what had come before.

Not daring to show preference for either brother, the inventor wisely chose to live beyond the borders of either kingdom. Nonetheless, one day the brothers' spies learned that the inventor had discovered a quantity of an unusual metal that possessed seemingly magical properties, and that with it he was performing private experiments. Together the noblemen confronted the inventor, insisting—on pain of death—that he reveal his secrets. When he told them what he might do, given time and freedom from other cares, the brothers agreed that he must make for them the device he had described.

For many years after, the inventor wanted for nothing but his freedom. He lived in comfort, but always under guard and always knowing that his life's greatest work was destined to be delivered, against his will, into the hands of these men. Yet he persisted, his brilliance won the day, and the time came when each of the brothers was presented—in secret, as they desired—his own exquisite clock watch.

Reuben found that the flashlight beam wouldn't hold steady on the page. His hands were trembling. *Two* watches? There were *two*?

The legends, Jack, tell nothing of blindness, but I believe the inventor used it to his advantage. For the story goes that even as the brothers disappeared, so too did the inventor. He was never seen again. Some say the brothers had him killed, for he was the only one besides them who knew their secret.

Reuben felt his skin break out in goose bumps. Penelope's words described exactly his greatest fear—that even if he gave his watch to The Smoke, he and his mom would still be in danger. The papers in his hand were shaking too much to read now. He laid them on the floor and bent over them to continue.

My own belief is that a man of such genius surely anticipated what the brothers would do, and planned all along to make his escape. I like to think he made his way to a distant land and lived out his life in peace.

That's what I'm *trying to do*, Reuben thought, feeling as if Penelope were writing directly to him. And as if she could hear him, he begged her to tell him how.

Now, brother, we arrive at the reason I'm telling you of the legends. Yes, there were two clock watches made, but that's not the whole of it. Out of spite for being forced to do the brothers' wishes, the inventor enacted a form of revenge in advance. He let it be known that if either man possessed <u>both</u> devices, something extraordinary would happen. He left behind a manuscript when he fled (the various translations are all remarkably faithful to one another), upon which was written the following words:

The possessor of both shall know no fear of death;
Though time may pass, he shall feel it not,
Nor feel aught pain or loss with any breath
He draws; nay, who holds these both shall have no mortal care,
Until such time as he lose possession, which God grant he will,
For it is not fitting that any man,
Be he low and wicked, or a good man or great,
Exist for long in such abnormal state.

You can see for yourself, Jack, what these words suggest. The metal from which the clock watches were made possessed even more astounding properties than the brothers had realized. The inventor, like all great minds of the time, was known to practice alchemy, which (as perhaps you know) was the attempt to transform common metals into gold, or in some cases into something even more precious—a substance that offers eternal youth. In this unique metal, evidently, he had met with success.

He must have predicted the effects of these last words. At once the brothers turned suspicious and mistrustful of each other. Though each swore never to steal the other's clock watch, each feared the other's treachery. The darkness between them grew, and the inevitable outcome was war between their two kingdoms. By war's end, both kingdoms were ravaged, and both brothers dead.

From that time on, the clock watches have remained in the province of rumor and legend. It is believed that certain vicious rulers rose to power after possessing one of them. Some legendary assassins and thieves, too, are thought to have used the clock watches to achieve their wicked ends. And it is also understood, Jack, that whoever possesses one

259

of the devices is always in search of its twin—partly in the hope of attaining eternal youth, but still more out of the terrible fear that another, more cunning person will emerge from the shadows to claim the second device for his own, at whatever bloody cost.

In other words, dear Jack, since the creation of the twin clock watches, there have always been twin hunters in the night. And now I am one of them, and Bartholomew is the other.

Reuben shuddered and looked over his shoulder, though he knew he was alone. He tried to steady and soften his breath, for just the sound of it in that strange chamber was giving him the creeps. This must be what Penelope had felt like, he thought, every minute of every hour of every day, for years and years.

The letter continued on its final page:

And yet I believe there is a chance to put an end to it all. Who can say if I am the first to hatch a plan to destroy the clock watches? But I aim to be the last, brother. In this secret contest I have one advantage: Bartholomew wishes to possess both devices (and God help this world if he does), whereas I seek only to destroy them, and need not proceed with the same degree of caution to protect them.

Here you enter the story, Jack. You may wonder why I did not destroy at least the one clock watch in my possession. My answer is that I believe it offers us our best chance, not only because it confers invisibility to its possessor, but also because one who grows familiar with the use of it will better

understand the habits and limitations of the one who car-
ries its twin. In other words, a skilled hunter has the great-
est chance of outfoxing another.

But who will be this hunter whose aim is to deprive not only
another but also himself of such power? It must be a per-
son of great character. Though I esteem your character more
highly than anyone's, Jack, I don't believe you have the dispo-
sition to be a hunter—nor would I ever wish such a path
for you. No, I only leave my life's mission to you, trusting you
to find the right person to finish it. I pray that you will, and
that you will live a long and happy life.

No sooner had Reuben finished the letter than he started over and read it again. He wanted to have missed something, but he knew he hadn't. There was no treasure. What Penelope had revealed about the watch's secret he already knew, and what she revealed about its twin only filled him with fear.

Or not *only*, he realized. There was fear, certainly, but there was also something else.

Reuben wiped his brow and sat on the floor of the chamber, staring at the letter in the beam of his flashlight. It had not offered the help he was seeking. And yet. Ideas lurked among the shadows in his mind. He could almost see them. Not only a greater understanding but a kind of help. Not the answer he'd looked for, but an answer nonetheless. What was it? Reuben squeezed his eyes closed, trying to sort his thoughts.

There was something about Bartholomew that seemed familiar. Why? And that line about vicious rulers coming into power with the help of a clock watch—why did *that* seem familiar? And why...?

The answers sprang out at him without warning, like a

jack-in-the-box, and with a gasp Reuben opened his eyes. Two revelations had struck him in quick succession. Each startled him—in fact, positively jolted him. But he knew them both to be true.

The first was that The Smoke had the other watch.

The second—shocking to Reuben even though it emerged from his own mind—was that he intended to steal it.

THE GHOSTS OF OTHER CHILDREN

Reuben sat in the chamber, trying to absorb what he'd discovered and what he meant to do. He had no idea how he was going to accomplish it. The one thing he felt sure about was that he had to try.

For he would never persuade his mom to flee the city now. She'd struggled too long to risk something like that, not without money, not when she could simply hand the watch over to The Smoke, believing that would be the end of it. In her mind it would be the least risky choice, the best way to protect Reuben. But she would be wrong, Reuben thought, and *he* needed to protect *her*.

So he would turn the tables on The Smoke. It never would have occurred to him if not for Penelope's letter, but all those rumors of The Smoke being some mysterious, all-seeing specter—what else could be behind them if not a clock watch like Reuben's? Whoever he was, The Smoke was simply a man who could turn invisible, who used that secret power to his advantage. If Reuben used his own watch to steal The Smoke's, he would be taking away not only that power but also all the authority that came with it.

Yes, he thought, growing excited, he would expose The Smoke as a fraud, and the Counselor and the Directions would rebel, and the search for Reuben and the watch would be called off. He and his mom would be safe. Maybe they wouldn't have any money, but he would still have his watch—it would still be his secret—and with the watch, given time, he could find a way to make money. With the watch he could do anything.

Like taking down the lord of New Umbra, Reuben thought, marveling at his own idea. Why not? From a distance the plan seemed simple enough. The trouble was only in the details. He would have to figure those out as he went along.

Reuben returned his attention to the letter, wishing he could copy it down. He didn't intend to take it with him—he would leave it here for the Meyers. They deserved an explanation, and this would be his way of giving them one. That is, Penelope would do the explaining for him. Reuben himself would already be gone, beyond any attempt to stop him.

He wanted to memorize the whole letter, but he lacked Penny's extraordinary gift for recalling and recounting words. After spending several frustrating minutes on the first paragraph alone, he was compelled to adjust his goal, focusing instead on the letter's most important part—the words attributed to the genius inventor, words that Penelope herself had memorized long ago.

Immortality was a concept Reuben could scarcely get his mind around, and perhaps for that reason it didn't hold any particular appeal for him. Or perhaps he was simply too young, for he knew that the idea was wildly attractive to adults. History was full of people searching for a fountain of youth, wasn't it? To someone like The Smoke—someone who obviously relished his power—the prospect must be irresistible. He could rule New Umbra forever. Reuben figured he'd better understand the legend inside and out, because he felt sure that The Smoke did.

And so he studied the words, concentrating with all his might, and only when he felt sure he had them by heart did he let his eyes leave the page. The moment he did so, a sort of spell was broken, and Reuben was struck with misgiving.

How long, exactly, had he been sitting here? He tried to guess the time spent searching for the tunnel entrance, the time spent in the tunnels, the time he'd spent absorbed in the letter and its surprising revelations—and discovered that he really had no idea. His mind had been overwhelmed by too many things, and he'd lost track.

Even as he thought this, Reuben was hurriedly bundling the letter up again, replacing it in its box. Surely it hadn't been too long. Surely he was fine. Out of habit he checked the watch— only to be certain that it was ready for use, but he was struck by the irony nonetheless: here was the most ingeniously designed clock in history, but it could not tell him the hour.

Reuben ducked out through the open hatch. At once he sensed a change in the tunnel acoustics. On his knees at the edge of the alcove, he shined his flashlight down. The puddle seemed to have expanded; the entire floor was covered with water. The tide must be coming back in.

He needed to get out of there *now*.

Clamping the flashlight between his teeth and taking a firm grip on the iron stake, Reuben got onto his belly and wriggled backward, searching with his foot for the highest rung. He knew it was only a few feet below him, but it seemed much farther. At last his boot came down upon it, and he prepared for the trickiest part. He had to let go of the iron stake; the very thought made him sweat inside his raincoat. Amazing how much more difficult it was to descend than to climb up. That topmost rung—the one that had broken away—would have made a tremendous difference. As it was, Reuben would have to cling to the alcove edge, like hanging on to the edge of a cliff. There was nothing to get a grip on.

There was also no other choice. And so, mustering his nerve, Reuben released the iron stake and pressed his hands hard against the floor of the alcove. For a moment he was perched like that, in an awkward position so familiar that his mind flashed back to when he was younger, climbing down from the kitchen counter, readying himself to drop the last foot or so. The boy in that memory seemed like one from another lifetime. And yet in some ways he hadn't changed at all. Years later, and Reuben was still climbing to high places, trying to get his hands on things he wanted.

He had much of his weight on the rung now, his chest and hands supporting the rest as he stretched downward with his other foot. The flashlight in his mouth bumped against the alcove edge, and so he craned his neck all the way back, the beam wavering and jerking on the ceiling above him. He strained, searching in vain for the next rung, and as his hands were tiring, he began to wonder whether he should risk reaching down with one of them. If he could just get a grip on the rung that his foot rested upon—

Suddenly, though, that rung was no longer there. It had broken loose with a tiny pinging sound, the sound of a distant game of horseshoes, and yet to Reuben it seemed the most dreadful sound he'd ever heard. He felt his knee bang against the wall, felt the toes of his boots sliding down the stone, felt the entire weight of his body pulling on his hands, which could not hold on. He cried out as his hands ripped free from the alcove edge. His boots scraped stone, came down hard on the next rung, which likewise broke free, and then he was plummeting through space.

He plunged into water. His feet struck the floor of the tunnel hard enough to hurt, and his teeth clacked together painfully, but if the water had been only as deep as he'd *thought* it was, he would surely have broken bones. Instead it was deep enough to break his fall—waist-deep, in fact. So deep that he had no time to recover from his fright and experience relief, for he had only fallen from one danger into another. He would never have guessed that the tide could fill the tunnels so quickly. He wouldn't have thought it possible. Now he was deep in the tunnels, and the water was still rising.

All of this occurred to Reuben in the space of a moment and in almost total darkness. The flashlight, which had fallen from his mouth when he cried out, was somewhere nearby, still shining weakly underwater. There was a very faint glow in the water around his boots, which were now entirely filled with water themselves. He tried to move—he needed to locate the flashlight—but it was as if anvils had been strapped to his feet. He could scarcely budge them.

Awkwardly, with one hand clinging to a rung in the wall and the other held high overhead, he struggled to free his feet from the boots. Only after he'd succeeded and felt his bare feet on the stone floor (the boots had claimed his socks)—only then did Reuben realize why he'd been holding his hand up in the air. Without thinking, he had snatched the watch from his raincoat pocket and was holding it high to keep it clear of the water. He continued to do so as he turned this way and that in search of the flashlight.

In a moment he'd spotted it, already sunk to the stone floor a few paces away.

And in the next moment, the light went out.

All was black. As black as it ever was when he vanished. Reuben heard his own breathing, loud and desperate, as if he'd been running for miles. "No," he whispered, "no, no, no!" He splashed over to where he had seen the flashlight and felt for it with his feet. He found it almost at once and, holding his breath, stooped down for it, just managing with the other hand to keep the watch out of the water. He came up, shook the flashlight, switched it off and on again. Nothing. He tried again and again, with no results, and with an anguished shout, he flung the flashlight out into the darkness, heard it crack against a wall and plop into the water. Instantly he regretted it, was tortured by the wish to try the switch one more time, tortured by the thought that it might have worked. Now there was absolutely no hope for light.

He considered climbing up those iron rungs again, high enough to escape the rising water. Then he rejected the idea, doubting his chances of reaching the alcove a second time, not trusting the rungs, and at any rate recoiling from the prospect— if by some miracle he did make it up—of spending hours there in total darkness. No. He had to get out. He just needed to keep his head. He was used to navigating through darkness, he reminded himself, and he knew the way back out.

"Keep your head," he whispered fiercely. "Keep your head, keep your head."

And so Reuben set out, trudging through water, holding the watch aloft with one hand and finding his way along the wall with the other. The water was cold, he noticed now, and his movement made splashing echoes in the tunnel. His memory of the centipede haunted him as his fingers traced the stone wall, with its many crevices and holes in which others might be lurking. He imagined, too, creatures in the water with him, swimming things and slithering things he could not see.

"Keep your head," he growled, more loudly this time, but the note of panic in his voice upset him so much that he clamped his mouth shut and said nothing more. He told himself to focus on the wall. The wall was his way out, and he must think of nothing else.

He turned right at the first corner. Ages later, it seemed, he came to the next corner and turned right again. He remembered how many steps he'd taken along each stretch of tunnel on the way down here, and they didn't line up with those he was taking now. That must be because he was moving through water this time, Reuben thought, and doing so altered his stride. It made sense, yet doubt assailed him. Could he have overlooked a branch on the way in, a side tunnel that he had walked right past, only to have taken it blindly now?

He slowed, then stopped. No, he had to trust his memory, had to trust his earlier self. Panic would get him killed. It would drown him like the children in Penny's story, the ones Penelope and Jack's papa had warned them about to keep them out of the tunnels.

The water was at Reuben's chest, the blackness unrelenting. He wished he had not thought of those drowned children. Gone now were all thoughts of slithering and creeping things, replaced by the far more horrible thought of those children drowning, and of himself drowning just like them. *The wall*, he thought desperately. *Concentrate on the wall.*

At the next corner he turned right again, and then it happened. The new stretch of tunnel was narrower, the water markedly higher; it was as if Reuben had stepped out of a sluggish backwater and into a lively brook. He felt the water suddenly at his chin, and in a rush of alarm he jerked his raised hand even higher, straightening his arm completely above his head, and banged his already bruised knuckles against the low tunnel ceiling. He almost dropped the watch, in fact probably *would* have dropped it had he not instinctively secured it with his other hand. But in doing so he lost contact with the all-important wall. Realizing this, Reuben felt himself panicking and lunged back to find it.

He missed.

He must have missed it only by inches, his searching fingers shooting past the corner into open water, but in such darkness inches were enough. He stumbled, his face went underwater, and he contorted wildly to keep the watch clear. When he regained his footing, Reuben had no idea which direction he was facing.

And now, finally, panic overtook him. He could no longer think clearly enough to tell himself to calm down. Indeed, he could hardly think at all. Like anyone in a true panic, Reuben lost his grip on reason. He found himself up against a wall, not knowing which one it was or where it would lead him, and he followed it a few paces before deciding it was the wrong one, the wrong way, and turned back. He could not have said why. Soon he was floundering left and right, back and forth, from one wall to another to still another...or they might all have been the same wall, he might have been stepping away and turning back again and again, for every time his hand lost contact with the stone, he felt as if he'd lost contact with *all* things and was caught up in a nightmare of water and darkness and screams.

For Reuben was certainly screaming now. He screamed for help, and he screamed in terror of drowning, and then he screamed because in his utter panicked confusion he imagined his own screams to be those of the drowned children—not of their ghosts but of the children themselves, as if they were still drowning and Reuben were down here in this blackness drowning right along with them.

Then the water began to choke him when he opened his mouth, and his screams gave way to violent coughing and spitting jets of cold salt water, until something in him took over and made him be silent. He pressed himself up against a wall, lifting his chin as high as he could to keep the water out, and though he already stood in total darkness, Reuben squeezed his eyes tightly closed, as if bracing for a deadly blow. He was no longer flailing about in panic, but he remained in a state of terrified confusion. He knew that he had stopped screaming, but he could still hear the screams of the other children. They were screaming the same thing, over and over and over.

Then, with a shock, Reuben realized that what they were screaming was his name. He opened his eyes and looked all around him, horrified, somehow expecting to see their own horrified faces come looming up at him out of the darkness like pale sea creatures rising from the bottom of the ocean.

Reuben! they shrieked. *Reuben! Reuben!*

Reuben, aghast, spotted one of them, or the ghost of one of them, a smudge of light at the end of a long, dark tunnel. He stared at it, paralyzed with fear, mesmerized by the sight of it. It wobbled and flickered—a life, he thought, about to be extinguished. It sought his company.

"Reuben!"

The truth shocked him even more than his nightmare vision had. Reuben listened and stared. His wildly scattered thoughts came galloping back, corralling themselves into a more rational place.

"Reuben!"

Not drowning children. Not a nightmare.

Penny.

INTO THE DARK

Outside, the storm thrashed on, but inside the oil house, with the door closed, there was something almost like silence. At least it felt like silence to the two children who had just struggled through the torrents of rain and wind, with waves crashing around them as they picked their way over slippery submerged boulders—the water ankle-deep, then suddenly thigh-deep, then ankle-deep again, constantly shifting and sucking at their legs, repeatedly knocking them to their knees. Through it all, Penny had somehow managed to maintain a grip on her storm lantern, and Reuben on his precious watch, until at last they were stumbling across wet grass and, by unspoken agreement, headed for the oil house. Now they sat huddled in the soft light of the lantern, shivering from the cold seawater and, in Reuben's case, from the not-yet-faded terror of drowning.

Penny's mass of red hair was plastered against her head, her face, the collar of her raincoat. It looked like a strange variety of red seaweed. "'Be back soon'?" she muttered at length.

Reuben was staring at the lantern, still feeling as if he dared not look away. But Penny's words roused him from his trance. His eyes went to her face, her own eyes reflecting the lantern light. Her expression was serious, even angry.

"You saved my life," Reuben said in a monotone. His brain felt dulled somehow; his words came out with great difficulty. "I dropped my flashlight. It was totally black down there, I was lost, and I thought I was going to drown. The water was up to here." Slowly, as if he were still moving through water, he raised his hand up to his mouth. He let it drop into his lap.

Penny's expression softened. In fact, she looked so concerned for him now that Reuben was reminded of his mom, and that did it—he began to cry. He covered his face. He felt Penny lay her hand on his arm. After a minute he stopped and wiped at his eyes. He took a few deep breaths and felt steadier.

"Sorry," he said.

"No," Penny said. "It must have been the most awful thing. I can't imagine."

Reuben nodded. "Well. Thanks."

They fell silent once more. Their shivering was slowly beginning to subside. After a while Penny took her hand from his arm and wrapped her arms around her knees again. She rested her chin on one knee. "What did you find down there, Reuben?"

Reuben made himself answer. "A letter. From Penelope. It explains everything."

"May I read it?"

They picked their way over slippery submerged boulders—the water ankle-deep, then suddenly thigh-deep, then ankle-deep again, constantly shifting and sucking at their legs, repeatedly knocking them to their knees.

"I left it down there so that you—all of you—could find it later. It's in a dry place, or dry enough, anyway."

Penny was looking intently at him. "And that's all? Nothing else?"

Reuben shook his head.

"You're telling the truth," she said after a moment, but she didn't seem any less troubled. "So that thing you had in your hand outside—that little metal compass thing you were trying not to get wet—you already had it with you. That's what was in Penelope's box, isn't it? Where is it now, in your pocket?"

Reuben looked away. "I can't tell you."

"I saved your life!" Penny snapped. "You said so yourself! And it doesn't even belong to you!"

Reuben, flinching at her tone, thought for some time before he replied. "Okay," he said, looking back at her. "Okay, I'll tell you, because you're right, I do owe you. And it's not just that—I actually really want to. Honestly, I do. But..." He screwed up his face, doubtful of what he wanted to say next.

"But what?"

"But you're wrong about its not belonging to me," Reuben said in a rush. "It belongs to me every bit as much as it belonged to Penelope."

Penny's mouth fell open. She closed it again very deliberately, her eyes narrowed, and her face suddenly expressed such indignant anger that the flames in her eyes seemed to come not from reflected lantern light but from the furious girl herself, as if she were a mad sorceress. Yet she said nothing, and as she and Reuben stared at each other with eyes locked (he forced himself not to avoid her terrible gaze), her expression slowly transformed from one of outrage to something more like irritated seriousness, until she seemed more like the Penny he thought he knew.

"You think you're telling the truth," she said with a shake

of her head. "I'll bet I can guess how you have it figured. You're thinking it wasn't really Penelope's to begin with. You're thinking it's finders keepers with this thing."

"Something like that," Reuben said mildly.

"But then it *did* belong to her," Penny insisted. "And she specifically wanted it to be returned to Jack—or at least to our family!"

"Not exactly," Reuben countered, with an apologetic look. "She wanted Jack involved, yes, because she wanted him to help her complete her mission if she couldn't do it herself. Or for some other Meyer to do it if Jack wasn't still around. That much I agree with. And the box, obviously—Penelope had it custom-made, so obviously it should be returned to your family, and I brought it back, didn't I? But the watch is different. You'll see what I mean once you've read the letter. She wanted—"

"So it's a watch," Penny interrupted.

Reuben frowned. He hadn't meant to reveal that. He hadn't had a chance to decide what secrets to keep and what to share.

"May I see it?" Penny asked, though from her tone it was clear that this was less a request than a demand. "Surely I deserve to. I've done nothing but help you since you got here."

The thought of showing someone else the watch made Reuben itchy all over. With the exception of Mrs. Genevieve, it had been his secret from the beginning, and his alone. But Penny was right. She did deserve to see it.

"First," he said slowly, "you have to promise you won't try to take it from me. And you have to promise you won't run inside and tell anyone about it. They're all going to find out about it soon enough."

Penny regarded him warily. She hesitated long enough that Reuben began to worry that he'd just put an idea into her head.

"You have to promise," he repeated, "or there's no way you're going to see it. I can't risk it, Penny."

Penny narrowed her eyes at him. But after another moment's consideration, she promised.

Reuben withdrew the open clock watch from his raincoat pocket. For the flicker of an instant his mind played a trick on him, transforming it into the image of a screaming cartoon face, the winding key sticking out from the center like a petrified tongue. He blinked, and the disturbing vision was gone. He found himself shivering even more. Reading Penelope's letter had done something to him, he realized. He was more aware than ever of the watch's wicked potential.

But it was also a thing of beauty, a fact confirmed by Penny's gasp of admiration. She bent over it, studying it. Reuben could tell she wanted to hold it but wouldn't ask him, rightly guessing what his answer would be.

"It's lovely," she whispered. All traces of irritation were gone from her face now. She looked up at him with wide eyes. "But what's its secret? Why is it so important?"

"I'll show you," Reuben said, surprising himself. Having gone this far, he realized he wanted to tell Penny everything. In fact, he was bursting to tell her. Rising quickly, he fetched a cloth from his backpack and wiped the surface of the watch until it was completely dry. With the key snugly inserted and no seams in the metal, he didn't think water could have gotten inside; but its previous owners had clearly taken pains to protect the watch from the elements, and Reuben was following their lead.

Soon he was ready. He gave Penny a firm look. "Don't scream. Nothing bad is going to happen, I promise. I'm just going to disappear. But it can be upsetting to see it happen, so you need to brace yourself."

"Wait!" Penny said, looking panicky. "You're going to *disappear*?"

"Only for a minute," Reuben said. "Can you handle it?"

Penny stared at him, then slowly nodded.

"Don't scream," he repeated, with another warning look. "I mean it. Now here goes." He pulled out on the winding key. Everything vanished, and in the darkness he heard Penny's strangled cry, followed by a smacking sound as she clapped her hands over her mouth. He reappeared. At the sight of her astonished face, he couldn't help smiling.

"You disappeared!" Penny hissed, hands still over her mouth.

"I told you I was going to."

"Yes, but—you *disappeared*! Reuben, you—"

"Disappeared," Reuben said, grinning. "I know."

When Penny had calmed down, Reuben vanished for her again, and then a third time. Then he wound the watch and slipped it back into his pocket. He grew serious. "Listen, Penny. There's a man—a very bad man..." He hesitated, unsure now how much he should reveal.

Penny stiffened. "Who are you talking about?" Her features were suddenly strained with anxiety. "Do you mean someone like Bartholomew?"

"Maybe. Maybe not quite so bad. Maybe worse. I can tell you he's very powerful, though."

"What about him?" Penny whispered. "Is he following you?"

"Not here," said Reuben. "But he's definitely looking for me. Back home, where I come from. He wants the watch."

"Oh, Reuben." Penny sounded sick.

"Yeah."

"And your mom?"

Reuben shook his head. "She doesn't know. If she did, she'd tell me to give him the watch—to protect me—and I can't do that."

"No," Penny agreed, after considering a moment. "No, not if he's as bad as you say. But why didn't you just destroy it? Then he could never get it!"

"I thought about it. But I don't believe a man like him would just leave me and my mom alone after that. I was hoping to find another way." Reuben took a deep breath, let it out, and looked at her soberly. "And thanks to Penelope, I've found one. I know what to do."

Penny blinked. "I'm confused. Is this about the letter? Would you please tell me what's going on?"

Reuben started to speak, then checked himself, remembering that if he revealed too much, he could lose the watch. He had to be careful. "If I tell you," he said, "you can't tell your family about any of this until I say it's okay. No matter what. If you do, I'm going to disappear, and you'll never see me again."

"Reuben!" Penny gasped.

"Sorry, but that's the only way I can tell you. Promise me that, and I promise you that when the time is right, you can tell them everything. That's the deal, Penny. It has to be."

Penny clearly saw that he meant what he said; she was also clearly torn. If she agreed to the deal, she had to keep a secret from her family. If she didn't, her family would never learn what the secret even *was*. She covered her face with her hands.

"Okay," she whispered after a long pause. She lowered her hands just enough to reveal her earnest green eyes. "Okay, I promise."

And so Reuben told her everything. First he told her what Penelope's letter said, and then about finding the watch, about the difficult circumstances he and his mom were in, about the horrible strange man on the pay phone and the train. And finally he explained to her about The Smoke.

"The whole city," Reuben said. "He's got the whole city under his thumb. He has the other watch. It's the only thing that makes sense. Nobody's ever seen him. He's got someone called the Counselor who handles all his business for him. And these men, the Directions, they do all his dirty work because they're scared. You wouldn't believe the rumors about him—he's a ghost, he's a monster, he's any bad thing you can think of. Nobody knows exactly what, but everybody's afraid of him."

"Because he can turn invisible," said Penny, with a look of revulsion, "because he can do terrible things and never be seen."

Reuben nodded.

"That's disgusting," Penny said. "I *hate* this man!"

Reuben laughed, surprising himself. "Well, yeah, so do I. So does everybody. But guess what? I'm going to stop him. I think I'm the one to do it. Like Penelope, except—well, I'm a kid, right? So it's even better. He won't be expecting a kid to try anything like that."

Penny stared at him, aghast. "Stop him? You? *That's* your plan?"

Her response was not exactly encouraging, but Reuben held firm. "Why not? He's only powerful because he has the other watch, and I can use my own watch to take it away! So that's what I'm going to do."

Penny shook her head. "But why would you risk—?" She cut herself off, looking at him with sudden understanding. "Your mom."

"Right," Reuben said. "If it were just me, no. I wouldn't even go back there. But if I don't stop the search as soon as possible, they're going to figure out who I am, and that means her, too. As long as The Smoke is in power, she's in danger."

Penny looked ill. "I can't believe this. I really can't—it's so terrible! You really think you can stop him?"

"I really do," Reuben said, wishing he felt as certain as he sounded. "There's no way the Counselor and the Directions will follow his orders anymore, not if they realize he's just a man. Believe me, I've heard some of them complaining. If I steal the watch and expose him, the whole thing will fall apart."

"I don't know," said Penny, nervously rubbing her hands together. "I don't know, Reuben. Like you said, we're just kids."

Reuben hesitated—he hadn't said anything about *her* being

a kid—then pressed on, feeling a powerful need to defend his plan. For the sake of his own confidence, he desperately wanted Penny to agree with him. "Hey, it was Penelope who gave me the idea, remember? And isn't this exactly what she wanted? It's what she risked everything for, what she dedicated her life to doing. And I can do it, Penny. I can finish it!"

"You think I don't know what Penelope wanted?" Penny snapped, scowling.

Reuben drew back, stung. *She doesn't think I can do it*, he thought, and he felt his fragile confidence beginning to break. He looked down, his eyes settling on his feet. They were bruised and scratched, and very much a small boy's feet. The sight of them discouraged him even more.

"Well, I'm sorry," he said thickly. "I don't have any choice. I have to go. I have to try."

Penny made a soft, anguished sound, as if she'd just received terrible news. She reached over and took his hand. Confused, Reuben let her hold it. He felt both grateful and embarrassed. He turned his eyes to the lantern again, but he knew she was looking at him.

When at last he brought himself to look at Penny's face, Reuben saw that her expression had changed to one of admiration, which embarrassed him further. Worse, he could tell that she was going to accept his plan, which meant that soon he would have to leave her and go out into the night alone, which not only made him sad but also scared him. He looked away again.

"You should let my family help," Penny said. "You don't have to do this alone."

"You know as well as I do that they won't let *me* do it at all. I like your family, Penny, but this is mine to do." Reuben felt his throat tighten as if, once again, he might cry. He squeezed her hand and moved to stand up, but Penny wouldn't let go. He sat back and looked at her.

"Fine," she said. "It's yours to do. But I'm coming with you."

"What?" Reuben's heart leaped. The very thought of her coming along made him feel a hundred times lighter. But surely he had misunderstood. "Do you mean to the train station, or...?"

Penny rolled her eyes. "Why do you think I snapped at you, Reuben? I'm scared! But how could I possibly not go with you? How could I not help you? Am I supposed to just sit here while you go and try to stop that man all by yourself? When Penelope gave her *life* to put an end to all this? When my family has kept her secret for generations, just so something could be done about it?"

Reuben was taken aback by Penny's vehemence, but of course it made sense. He'd made her promise not to tell her family, and so the only way she could help him would be to go along herself. She felt compelled by her duty. *The most Meyer-like of all the Meyers.*

"You don't have to do that," he began, trying to muster a tone of conviction.

Penny interrupted him. "I don't know if you're just trying to be gallant or what," she said. "I can tell that you want me to come. We're partners now, Reuben. Might as well shake on it."

They regarded each other, both smiling nervously now. After a moment Reuben nodded, and they awkwardly shook the hands they were already holding, which made them laugh.

"I'm glad that's settled," Penny said. "Also, I feel like throwing up."

"You kind of get used to that," Reuben said.

They lost no time. Reuben put on his socks and shoes while Penny stole back into the house for supplies. She soon returned, carrying a school backpack and wiping at her eyes. Reuben gave her a questioning look.

"They're going to be so upset," Penny said, her voice

cracking. "I left them a note telling them not to worry, but..."
She shook her head and sniffed.

Reuben nodded. He knew how she felt.

"Well, enough of that, right?" Penny gave him a tight smile and gestured toward the door.

They went out together. The crossing to the mainland was less difficult than Reuben had expected. Though the rain still fell, the wind had died down; the storm was passing, and though the deep water was choppy, it wasn't terribly so. They sat side by side, each with an oar, and, pulling hard, finding their rhythm, they battered through the little waves at an encouraging pace. Soon they had tied the boat to the mainland dock and were making their way through the quiet town.

They were headed for the train station. Reuben knew from the schedule that there was an early-morning train. When Penny had pointed out that the stationmaster knew her, Reuben replied that they would be sneaking aboard. They had to avoid leaving a trail.

"You mean ride without *paying*?" Penny had asked, sounding quite offended.

"You can buy a ticket when this is all over, if it makes you feel better."

"I most certainly *will*!"

There was no movement in the town, no sounds other than the steady patter of rain, the gurgle of rainwater in the drainpipes, the occasional distant rumble of fading thunder. They kept to the shadows, making use of the streetlights without passing directly beneath them. They stopped at every corner, gripping each other's elbows, looking in all directions before hurrying across the street.

At one such corner, not far off the square, Reuben glanced behind them. It was only a matter of habit now—he no longer half expected to see anyone.

And yet this time he did.

A few blocks back, a figure darted from beneath a streetlight into an alley between buildings. Reuben made a guttural noise, as if he'd been punched in the belly.

"What?" Penny gasped, wrenching around to look at him.

He grabbed her hand. "Run!"

They ran two blocks as fast as they could go. Then Reuben pulled her into an alley. "We're being followed," he panted, peering around the corner of the building.

"Are you sure?" Penny whispered, clutching at his raincoat. "You really saw someone?" Her hands were shaking.

Reuben was scared, too. All he wanted to do was hide. "Remember, I can make us vanish if I have to. The important thing will be to keep quiet. We'll squat down and hold our breath. You'll need to get right up against me, as close as you can. Okay, Penny?"

"Okay," Penny breathed. "Does it—does it hurt at all?"

"Hurt? No," Reuben said, then remembered that he'd kept the blindness a secret. He hadn't wanted to reveal any weaknesses, not even to Penny. There was no help for it now, though. "It doesn't hurt, but you won't be able to see."

"It makes you *blind*?" Penny hissed. Reuben felt his raincoat tighten around his chest and shoulders and understood that she was fiercely clutching the back of it with both hands.

He turned his head to meet her eyes, which were very wide. "You have to trust me, Penny. It's scary, but that's all. Okay?"

Penny's face was taut with fear. Nonetheless, after only a brief hesitation she nodded. "Okay," she whispered. "Okay."

Reuben turned back. He listened and stared, his eyes tracing the string of rain-fuzzed streetlights into the distance. Only his face was exposed around the corner of the building, yet he could not help feeling that someone even better hidden was out there peering at him. He kept perfectly still. The rain fell on pavement and rooftop, on parked cars and rubber trash bins. Otherwise there was nothing—until suddenly there was. The shadowed doorway of a house released part of its darkness into the lesser darkness of the rainy street. The figure stood on the sidewalk just over a block away. Reuben thought he could make out the movements of the head turning left and right. Searching for them.

Abruptly the figure began to move. Some decision had been made. Their pursuer began to run in their direction. Not a sprint, but a deliberate, quick-paced run. Covering ground.

Reuben drew back into the alley, his skin prickling horribly, and turned to Penny. He gave a nod, and together they squatted down, huddling close. Reuben's hand was already in his raincoat pocket, already on the winding key. They vanished.

The footsteps reached their alley and slowed. Then stopped. Penny was gripping Reuben's free hand so tightly it hurt. Her nails dug into his palm. There was a crackle of street grit as the person shifted. Then rainy silence again. Reuben imagined the eyes searching the alley. A shuffle, a scraping sound, and the footsteps started up again. They were oddly light and percussive, like tiny slaps, and faded rapidly as the person moved on.

Reuben pushed in on the key. Penny's face appeared before him, her eyes squeezed tightly shut. "Here we go," he whispered, rising. He stepped across the alley to the opposite building and peered around it in the direction of the footsteps. Penny hurried up behind him.

"Who is it?" she whispered, her mouth at his ear.

"I can't tell. A man, I think. He's really running now. He's turning at the next corner."

"We're not far from the station," Penny said. "Should we risk it?"

Somewhere in the distance, a car door closed. An engine started up. There was nothing particularly menacing about either sound, except for the question behind them: who was getting into a car, in the rain, in the wee hours of the morning?

They looked at each other with anxious eyes.

"That's him," Reuben whispered, and Penny nodded.

They stayed where they were, listening. But rain and distance played tricks on their ears. Neither could tell from which direction the sounds had come, nor could they trace the path of the car as it moved through the town, its gears shifting as it picked up speed. The only thing they knew for certain was that the car was not coming closer. Slowly, they began to relax. The engine sound faded. Soon there was only the rain again.

"What is going on?" Reuben whispered, not expecting an answer.

"Please let's go," Penny said, a response as good as any.

Minutes later they were at the edge of the train station parking lot, crouching behind a hedge. On the far side of the lot stood the station house, its windows glowing. In the lot was parked a single old van, which Penny said belonged to the stationmaster. It was the sort with a flat front—this much Reuben could make out, but the rainy darkness made its features difficult to discern. For some reason it reminded him of a sphinx.

"How long until the train?" Reuben whispered. Penny was wearing a watch that actually worked as a watch.

"Less than an hour. We should hide near the platform. It won't stop for long. Some dockworkers from Tucker get off every morning, but that's it."

The hedge, which was formidably prickly, ran all the way around to the back side of the station. They would have to walk across the wide-open parking lot. But there was no one around, and—a lucky stroke—the lot's only streetlamp was broken. They would have the cover of darkness.

Hand in hand they moved out from behind the hedge. Reuben kept his other hand in his raincoat pocket. They walked quickly, anxious to get across the lot and hidden away behind the station house. As they passed beneath the streetlamp, a crackle sounded beneath their feet. Broken glass. Someone had put the lamp out with a rock, Reuben thought. And at first the thought did not alarm him, for he was thinking of mischievous boys.

But then a different possibility occurred to him, and he felt suddenly cold. What if someone had broken the lamp precisely because he wanted this parking lot to be dark? And no sooner had Reuben thought this than he heard Penny suck in her breath. He turned and saw that she was staring at something off to their left.

Reuben followed her gaze. Next to the stationmaster's van, on the side opposite the lot entrance, so that they hadn't been able to see it before, was parked a second car. And even as they looked—even as they realized that they'd been outsmarted—the car's headlights flared on, illuminating their shocked and frightened faces, blinding them completely to whatever was coming next.

AN UNEXPECTED ALLIANCE

Reuben pushed in on the winding key. Everything went black. He wrapped his arms around Penny and tried to pull her back toward the hedge. But Penny resisted; she seemed rooted to the spot. "Come on!" he hissed. "Penny, come *on!*"

"Hey!" shouted another voice, loud but muffled, as if coming from inside a box. The car door opened and the voice shouted again, sharper and clearer this time. It was a man's voice, charged with alarm. "*Penny!* Oh my—where are you, Penny? What happened? *Penny!*"

"It's okay!" Penny pulled free of Reuben's grasp. He heard her running toward the voice. Still frightened and uncertain, he scurried sideways until he imagined he was out of the headlights' glare. He crouched in his private darkness, listening.

The man's voice was at once shocked and relieved. "What in the—what's going on, Penny? Holy—" (It was Jack's voice. Reuben recognized it now.) "Are you okay? You just disappeared! I can't believe that just happened! It did happen, didn't it? You disappeared—just like that! Or am I crazy?"

"No, you aren't crazy," said Penny's voice, surprisingly assured. "But quick, Jack, you have to tell us. Were you the one following us through town? Because if it wasn't—"

"What? Yeah, it was me. Who else would it be? But, Penny, where's the kid? What happened to him? Oh man, I think I need to sit down. I can't believe this."

"Reuben!" Penny's voice called. "It's okay. It's just Jack."

Reuben said nothing.

"Is he gone?" Jack asked.

"I don't think so. It's—well, it's hard to explain. But, Jack, we really need to know for sure that you were the only one following us. Did you drive here just now? In this car?"

"What are you talking about? Of course I did. You just saw me get out of it." He sounded worried. "Are you really okay? How many fingers am I holding up, redbird?"

"Yes, yes, I'm *fine*. Three fingers. But, Jack, I didn't know you had a car! Since when?"

"Since a while ago," said Jack, his voice still very uneasy. "Alex Ling lets me keep it in his garage."

"But why didn't you tell me!"

"Penny, for crying out loud, forget the car. I just saw you disappear and reappear—right there in my headlights. Like something from a bad dream. *Am* I dreaming?"

"I know, it's amazing, isn't it?" said Penny with a little laugh. "Did you hear that, Reuben? It was Jack the whole time. But how did you know to come here, Jack?"

"Wild guess. He came by train. I figured he'd be leaving by train, too. The question is what you're doing here with him. And where *is* he, anyway? Hey, kid, are you out there or not?" Jack's voice, though calmer now, was tinged with anger.

"Reuben?" Penny called. For the first time, she sounded concerned that he might actually be gone.

"I'm here," Reuben said.

Jack sucked in his breath, clearly startled. "Was that him? Where is he?"

"He's invisible," Penny said simply.

"You have got to be kidding me. I can't believe this is happening."

"Reuben," Penny called out, "won't you please come back? So that we can see you?"

"Not just yet," Reuben said. "He has to promise."

"What's he talking about?" Jack demanded. "Promise what?"

"Right," Penny said. "Of course, I see. Jack, you have to promise that you won't try to take anything from him or try to stop him."

"And why should I do that? When I don't even know what he's up to? He made you *disappear*, Penny. Is that even safe?"

"Please, Jack. You have to trust him. I trust him, and I know more than you do about all this. He's trying to do the right thing, trying to do what Penelope and Jack would have wanted."

"You're joking, right? Him?"

"Well, gee, I don't know, Jack," Penny said. "Do you know any other invisible people around here? Yes—*him*. Now promise."

There was a long pause, during which Reuben felt sure Jack was trying to make him out in the darkness. It occurred to him that Jack might charge in the direction of his voice, hoping to catch him by surprise and nab him. Moving in his habitual crouch, the rain obscuring his already quiet movements, Reuben took up a new position several paces to his left.

"Fine," Jack said tersely. "Whatever. Hey, kid, I promise I won't try to rob you, stop you, or otherwise do you bodily harm. Okay? Now show yourself, why don't you?"

"I don't think so," Reuben said. He heard Jack make another startled sound and curse under his breath. There was a shuffle of feet as brother and sister turned instinctively toward his voice.

"He's moving around out there and we can't even see him," Jack muttered. "This is some creepy business. I don't like it."

"Reuben, what's the matter? He promised." Penny sounded worried now. "Won't you please come out?"

"You have to promise *her*," Reuben said. "Not me. Promise Penny." His words were met with a brief silence. He imagined the brother and sister looking at each other. He crept to a different spot, just in case.

"Well?" Penny asked. Reuben thought he detected a hint of amusement in her voice. Amusement and perhaps a little pride.

Jack grunted. Then, after another pause, he said, "Yeah, okay, redbird. I promise you." More loudly he said, "Did you catch that, you spooky little kid? I promised her. We're all good here."

Reuben reappeared. This time he was able to enjoy the look of shock on Jack's face. Penny looked startled, too, even though she'd known what to expect. Then she broke into a smile, and to Reuben's surprise she ran over and hugged him, as if she truly had been afraid he was gone for good.

"This is crazy," Jack said, shaking his head.

"You don't know the half of it," Penny said.

"What say you start filling me in, then?" Jack was studying their faces. He heaved himself up onto the hood of his car, a battered little black sedan, and braced his feet on the bumper. Bare feet, Reuben noticed. That explained the light slapping quality of the footsteps they'd heard. And his clothes were soaking wet—he wore no raincoat. Of course, to follow them, he must have swum to the mainland from the island. He would have had to. They had taken the rowboat.

Penny looked at Reuben. "Can we tell him? We might as well, right? He can help us."

"Don't get ahead of yourself, ladybug," said Jack. "Start with the telling."

Reuben shrugged. "You're the storyteller, Penny."

"Oh, goody, a story," Jack said. "I hope it's scary."

℮⌒

By the time Penny had told Jack everything, he was up and pacing, his eyes intent on her face. Every now and then he would shoot a fierce glance at Reuben, who would have been utterly unnerved by the intensity of these glances if he hadn't detected behind them a grudging respect. Reuben sensed that Jack's opinion of him had risen considerably when he'd insisted Jack make his promise to Penny. That an unknown little boy could so quickly figure out the key to his heart had surely impressed him. And the tale Penny told (which made Reuben sound far braver than he actually felt) could only have reinforced Jack's opinion of him.

Reuben and Penny were sitting on the car's bumper now. Jack had switched off the headlights, and there was just enough light from the station house and from a streetlamp beyond the hedge for them to make out one another's faces in the gloom. All their expressions were serious. It was still raining softly, but the children in their raincoats and Jack in his intensity paid no attention. They might have been gathered around a fireplace, for all they seemed to care.

"So this guy—what did you call him?"

"The Smoke."

"The Smoke. He's used a watch like yours to make the city into his own private kingdom."

"Right. The Counselor handles all his business for him, and

the Directions bring him money from every neighborhood. And he has them always searching for any sign of the other watch."

Jack scowled. "But is this guy a hundred years old or what? How long has this been going on?"

"As long as anyone can remember. At least that's what my mom told me once."

"He wouldn't have to be that old," Penny pointed out. "There could have been someone before him, and The Smoke knocked him out of power."

"You mean knocked him out of life," Jack said.

Penny shuddered. "Maybe."

Jack looked down at Reuben, his hands on his hips. "This is a dangerous guy, kid. You're really going after his watch? You're going to waltz right into the dragon's lair?"

Reuben felt a shiver at Jack's words. "I don't like it," he said quietly. "But yes."

Jack nodded. His lips were drawn tight. He squinted up into the sky. The rain had softened to a fine drizzle. There was a break now in the clouds to the north, revealing a patch of stars. To the south, where the city lay, all was darkness.

"Fine," Jack said, and cuffed Reuben's head so hard it made his ears ring. "I'll take you." He moved toward the rear of the car.

"Jack!" Penny cried reproachfully.

"That *hurt*!" Reuben said, his eyes stinging.

"Sorry," Jack said, opening the trunk. "I meant it in a good way. Now turn your heads, little ones, because I'm very delicate and shy." He began peeling off his wet clothes.

Penny looked apologetically at Reuben, who was clutching his head. "Jack," she said uncertainly, "did you just say you're going to take us?"

"Why not? Let's get this all over with—that's my thinking."

"Are you going to be naked?" said Reuben coldly. He felt

resentful and confused about the cuff and wondered if they were being toyed with. "Because if so I think I'd rather walk."

"Lucky for you I keep extra clothes in the car," said Jack, leaning out from behind the trunk. Sure enough, he was already pulling on a dry T-shirt, tugging it down over his muscular torso. "Also some money."

"You do?" Penny asked, sounding extremely puzzled. "First I find out you have a car, and now you're telling me you keep supplies in it?" She let out an uneasy chuckle. "What, were you planning a getaway?"

Jack gave her a long look and then a somewhat rueful smile. "Only every day, redbird. Only every single day." He withdrew again, digging around in his trunk.

"Oh," Penny said in a small voice. And then, her voice faltering: "Oh, Jack. I should've realized. You've always wanted so badly to leave, but you never did. You could have, but you didn't. You stayed because…because…"

"Now, don't go ascribing intentions," Jack interrupted, slamming the trunk closed. He stepped into full view, now wearing dry blue jeans and combat boots, and jingled his keys. "Point is, we're leaving. So get in the car, you two. Backseat."

He tossed Penny a towel, then climbed behind the steering wheel and started the engine. Its rumble was like the sound of earthquakes in movies. Deep, palpable vibrations you could feel in your feet. The sound was surprising. The car looked unremarkable from the outside, just a plain old black sedan in seemingly poor repair—but it clearly had a souped-up engine.

"Penny," Reuben murmured, catching her by the arm. "Is he telling the truth? You're sure?"

Penny wiped at her eyes. She nodded. "It's good, right?"

"I don't know what to think. You're upset."

"Oh, never mind that. That's about something else. We'll be much safer with Jack along."

Her brother gunned the engine, its seismic rumble revving to a lion's roar.

"Much safer," Reuben muttered. "Right." But Jack was revving the engine so loudly now that Penny didn't hear him.

They took off their backpacks and got into the backseat, stuffing the bags into the floorboard space. Pulling the door closed felt to Reuben like making some sort of final decision, and he sat for a moment gripping the handle. Then he slammed the door shut.

Jack looked at him in the rearview mirror. "Hey," he said, speaking up to be heard over the engine, "how did you manage to get the hatch open, anyway? That was one beast of a padlock on the chain."

Reuben started to reply. "I broke through one of the—wait, how did you know about that?" He hadn't mentioned the lock and chain at all, only that there had been a hatch.

"Jack Meyer!" Penny exclaimed. She lowered the towel she'd been using to dry her face. "You've been into the tunnels?"

Her brother glanced back at her with raised eyebrows, as if to express amazement that she might ever have thought otherwise.

Penny rolled her eyes. "Right. Of course you have. I'm surprised you didn't go ahead and break through the hatch yourself."

"Don't think I wasn't tempted. But I do have my limits, you know."

"You could have fooled me," Penny remarked.

"Well, it's true I don't always know what they are," Jack admitted. He switched on the headlights and glanced back again. "You both buckled in?"

Penny and Reuben hurriedly fastened their seat belts. "Okay," Penny said, "we're—"

The tires squealed like maniacal pigs, there was a smell of burned rubber, and the car bolted forward with a surge that slammed their heads back against the seat. Jack wrenched the wheel, throwing Penny up against Reuben—his mouth was suddenly full of her hair—and then they were out on the road, and this time it was Reuben being thrown up against Penny, who was trying to protest to her brother but whose words kept getting cut off with little involuntary shrieks of alarm. Then the car straightened out, and Reuben, clutching at the back of the seat in front of him, craned his neck to see out the windshield. Before he could figure out where in town they were, they were out of town altogether.

Jack let out a bark of laughter, and Reuben wonderingly studied his expression in the rearview mirror. He was smiling—the first truly joyful smile Reuben had seen on his face—and despite the noise of the engine, Reuben could just hear him muttering to himself.

"Invisible? The kid can turn *invisible*? Well, no wonder, Aunt Penelope! No wonder you thought it was such a big deal!" Jack shifted gears, and the car, already flying, lurched forward even faster. He banged the steering wheel with his fist.

"Finally!" he cried, and Penny and Reuben jumped in their seats and looked at each other. The relief in Jack's voice seemed somehow bigger than him, as if he'd been waiting for something to happen not only for his whole life but for the duration of all the generations that had come before it.

"Finally," Jack cried, "here we go!"

PART III

HOME
AND NOT
HOME

MRS. GENEVIEVE'S INSTRUCTIONS

Jack Meyer's black sedan—the decrepit-looking little car whose engine and driver were not at all what Reuben had at first supposed—ripped like a rocket through the night. Reuben had stopped counting the seconds between mile markers; the results were too alarming. In fact, for the same reason, he had stopped trying to look out the rain-streaked windows altogether. It seemed as if they were driving through a storm, but whenever Jack slowed to take a hairpin curve in the road, the rain softened, only to batter the windshield again as he accelerated. It was the speed of the car making the raindrops hit so hard.

"So the man on the phone," Jack was saying, speaking up to

be heard over the noise of the engine and the rain. "You're sure he was the same man you saw on the train? You're an expert on voices?"

"I don't have to be," Reuben replied. "If it had happened to you, you'd know."

"It didn't 'happen to you.' *You* called the number, right? The guy didn't call you."

Penny said, "That isn't what he meant, Jack, and you know it."

"So you wouldn't have called the number?" Reuben challenged. "If it had been you?"

Jack glanced at him in the rearview mirror. "Oh, I would have called the number. And in fact, I think we should call it again and find out what this guy knows. How does he know about the watch? Does he have any idea there are two of them? Does he know that The Smoke has one? We need some information here."

"I don't think that man would tell us anything," Reuben said. "Even if he did, I wouldn't trust a word of it. He seemed— unstable. Not quite right. Everything about him scared me."

"He scares me, too, and I didn't even see him," Penny said. "Just your description of him is going to give me nightmares, I can tell."

"You two realize that it's all scary people from here on out, right?" Jack downshifted to take a curve. "We don't deal with the scary people, we don't get anywhere."

The children were quiet for a minute, thinking about scary people. The windshield wipers rocked back and forth. To Reuben they seemed to be saying *Don't. Go. Don't. Go. Don't. Go.*

Penny broke the silence. "If The Smoke knows everything about everything, as you say, then he surely knows about this man on the phone. How could he not? After all these years, all those newspaper advertisements? So why does he leave the man alone? Why doesn't The Smoke consider him a threat?"

"Maybe because he *isn't* a threat," Jack said. "The Smoke isn't worried about some crazy little guy in an old suit, spending all his money on classifieds. Come to think of it, The Smoke probably uses him. Keeps tabs on him. If the guy ever gets on the trail of the other watch, The Smoke will find out about it."

"So we definitely *shouldn't* contact him," Penny reflected. "It might tip off The Smoke."

"Or maybe we should contact him, give him false information, use it to our advantage. We can't sit around waiting for The Smoke to figure things out. The kid says we have to act fast, right?"

"His name is Reuben," Penny reminded her brother. "And he's sitting right here."

Reuben gave her an appreciative look. "Jack's right, though. We need to find The Smoke right away. That means going to the man closest to him."

"You mean Cassius Faug," Penny said. "The one they call the Counselor."

Reuben nodded.

"And what do we say to this Counselor?" Jack wanted to know.

"That's the part we need to work on," Reuben said.

"Better work away, then," Jack said. "We'll be hitting New Umbra by dawn."

They tore on through the rainy night, their velocity rendering farm fields into backyard gardens, towns into villages. They had the road almost entirely to themselves. The few vehicles they encountered streaked past like shooting stars, nothing more than the headlights themselves, no time to discern the hurtling forms behind them. Only as they approached the outskirts of the city and traffic increased did Jack slow down at all, though if he was aware of the speed limit he gave no sign, swerving around the early-morning delivery trucks and work vehicles with subtle twitches of the wheel. He weaved through them with such alarming swiftness that they seemed not to be moving— just a scattering of vehicles parked at random on the highway leading into the city.

One expects, with a large city, to be dazzled by its galaxies of artificial lights. The thousands upon thousands of lit windows in the skyscrapers, of traffic lights and streetlamps, of neon signs glowing in street after street. New Umbra, however, did not dazzle. It loomed. A mountainous darkness whose meager sprinkling of streetlights and illuminated office windows seemed only to emphasize the darkness itself. A deeply unnerving darkness.

Reuben, who for most of the drive had hardly given a thought to his damp clothes, suddenly found them exceedingly uncomfortable. His seat made loud squeaking sounds when he shifted around in it, though, and he forced himself to be still.

They rolled past a sign announcing the city limits. Jack eased up on the accelerator, and at a less conspicuous speed they entered a district of warehouses, train tracks, factories. Smokestacks sent up dark clouds of vapor and smoke. The sky was turning gray. The rain had stopped. By the loading docks of a warehouse, Reuben saw a security guard folding up a tattered umbrella.

"Here we are, kid," Jack said. "Home, sweet home."

Seeing the city like this for the first time, from the backseat of a car in the early-morning darkness, approaching it from an unfamiliar direction, Reuben was struck by how alien it seemed to him. Was New Umbra really his home? It didn't feel like it. The city was just the place he'd been living his life. Home for him wasn't so much a place as a person. His mom. The two of them thinking up dream houses, sharing a doughnut in a bakery, making each other laugh. The city was just a grim backdrop to that.

"Are you okay?" Penny asked him.

"Yeah, I'm fine." He must have looked pained, thinking about his mom, unaware that Penny was watching him. "I'd better be, hadn't I?"

"Maybe since you're fine, you can tell me where I'm headed," Jack said.

"Not home," Reuben said.

They stopped to refuel at a gas station, where Penny and Reuben changed into dry clothes in the restrooms and Jack purchased a map. They all studied it together in the privacy of the car. Outside of the Lower Downs, Reuben didn't know his way around the city except by subway. Jack, it turned out, knew the streets much better than he did. This came as a great surprise to Penny, who didn't know that her brother had ever been there.

"Oh, a few times," Jack said, waving off her questions. "Not exactly happy ones. It isn't my favorite place in the world."

"It isn't anybody's favorite place in the world," Reuben said.

"Except The Smoke," said Jack. "That guy probably loves it to death."

Penny looked out the car window at the bleak city skyline. "I think that's just what he's done."

~

At dawn the streets and sidewalks of Middleton's retail district were mostly empty. Water still trickled in the street gutters from the night's rain. Here and there a lamp clicked on behind an upper-story apartment window, early risers getting their bleary start to the day. Like most of the street-level shop windows, Mrs. Genevieve's was dark.

Jack and Penny studied it from across the street. They looked in both directions. A couple of blocks away, a woman in a nurse's uniform was climbing into a noisy old car that had just pulled up to the curb.

*At dawn the streets and sidewalks of
Middleton's retail district were mostly empty.*

"Bad spark plug," Jack muttered.

The car drove away. There was no one else in sight. Walking slowly, they crossed the street and rang the bell. After a few seconds they rang it again, then again.

"You still with us, kid?" Jack said quietly.

"I'm here," Reuben said.

"She isn't answering."

"Give her a minute. She was probably in bed."

"Here she is," Penny said with relief in her voice.

Reuben felt relieved, too. Not only because they had nowhere else to go but also because he'd been having terrible misgivings about Mrs. Genevieve, worrying that The Smoke had discovered their connection. He actually smiled now to hear her irritated voice from behind the glass, telling Jack and Penny that the shop was closed.

"Please, Mrs. Genevieve," pleaded Penny. "It's an emergency."

"What? What did you say?"

"We have a rush job on a watch," Jack said dryly.

Mrs. Genevieve was already opening the door. She stepped aside to let them enter, then uttered a faint, confused sound as Reuben swept in behind them. Her mind must have produced some mundane explanation for the odd feeling she'd just experienced (which was only natural, for no one ever thinks an invisible person has just walked by), and she closed the door and locked it, saying, "What is this that you said? An emergency? Who are you? How is it that you know my name?"

"Are you alone, Mrs. Genevieve?" Penny asked. "No one else is here?"

"Why do you ask? What's wrong, child?"

"Please just answer that question," Jack said, but his voice was polite for a change. He sounded entirely different. "If you'll answer our question, we'll answer yours."

"Please, Mrs. Genevieve," said Penny.

"You keep saying my name, but I'm certain that I have never seen you before," said Mrs. Genevieve. There was a pause, and then: "Yes, I'm alone. And I think that you must be friends of Reuben."

"We are!" Penny said.

"Is he all right?" Mrs. Genevieve asked. "What has happened?"

"You can ask him yourself, ma'am," said Jack. "He's right here in the room with us."

Reuben heard Mrs. Genevieve gasp. "Reuben," she whispered, "is it true?"

"It's true," he said. He spoke softly, but even so, she gasped again.

"It makes one ill at one's stomach," Mrs. Genevieve said, "to hear you there but not see you. Let us go into my rooms, please."

Inside Mrs. Genevieve's sitting room with the door closed, Reuben reappeared. He saw the poor watchmaker flinch and put a hand to her cheek. She could probably never get used to such appearances and disappearances. She wore pale yellow pajamas, house slippers, and a lightweight robe of faded red. The wrinkled skin beneath her striking blue eyes was puffy and purplish, and her face seemed drawn. She looked exhausted and unhappy.

The sight of her evoked in Reuben an unexpected feeling of tenderness, as if they were lifelong friends, and he instinctively stepped forward to shake her hand or perhaps even hug her. But though Mrs. Genevieve nodded and shifted her weight toward him, as if welcoming his approach, she seemed too troubled and distracted to make any other gesture. Unable to check his own awkward momentum, Reuben ended up shaking her elbow. She looked at his hand on her arm and then into his eyes, and again she nodded, then shook her head. She seemed not to know how to feel.

Reuben was aware of Jack and Penny watching them uncertainly. He felt clumsy, as if he were putting on a show. He hated being the center of attention. His words came out unnaturally stiff and stagy. "Well, Mrs. Genevieve," he said, feeling that his smile was false though his emotion was genuine, "I'm very happy to see you, but you don't exactly seem overjoyed to see me."

His words seemed to take a moment to sink in. Then Mrs. Genevieve stopped shaking her head and composed herself with a frown. She locked her eyes on Reuben's. "This is because I am not overjoyed, Reuben. Why should I be overjoyed, knowing that you are in grave danger? If you called me from the other side of the world," she said, "perhaps then I would be—well, I would not say overjoyed, but relieved. And yet you are here, in my sitting room. You should not be."

"I couldn't go home, Mrs. Genevieve. They're searching my neighborhood now. They haven't figured out who I am yet—at least I don't think they have—but my friends and I need a place to stay. I told them you would help us."

Mrs. Genevieve looked at Penny, who returned her gaze with a wide-eyed, expectant expression, like an orphan in an old movie hoping to be chosen. The watchmaker then looked at Jack, whose expression was polite but inscrutable. She looked back at Reuben.

"I'll make tea," she said, and went to put the kettle on.

Reuben took his backpack into the bathroom, where he pulled out the damp brown sweatshirt and draped it over the radiator. He was so used to wearing it now, with the watch snugly tucked into its right front pocket, that he felt uneasy without it. For the moment he nested the watch lightly among the clothes in his backpack, which he left partly unzipped. He would keep it close.

Soon they were all sitting with cups and saucers balanced on their laps. Mrs. Genevieve had also brought out a modest dish of pastries. It might have been a cozy scene had it not been so tense. The watchmaker could not have seemed more uneasy, and her frown only deepened the more she learned. Reuben had deferred to Penny's storytelling, but Jack had reminded his sister that time was precious, and so her account was remarkably brief, reduced to its fundamental details: the Meyer family with their generations-old secret, the revelation of the existence of a second clock watch, and Reuben's realization about The Smoke.

Mrs. Genevieve rose and set her tea on the side table. She had yet to take even a sip. "But this is incredible, what you have told me! How can it be true?" She shook her head and added, as if arguing with herself, "Yet with my own eyes I have seen what this clock watch can do. And what you suggest does explain how this man holds such power without being seen. It is *because* he is never seen! I have always wondered."

"It makes sense, doesn't it?" Reuben said. "It's ridiculous what he's managed to do with that watch."

"But we're going to stop him!" Penny declared, raising her chin defiantly. "That's why we've come!"

Mrs. Genevieve was stunned. "Stop him? You?"

"Well, we sure didn't come to play tennis with him," Jack said, laughing. "We intend to take him down." He sipped from his cup, returned it delicately to its saucer, and smiled at Mrs. Genevieve as if to express appreciation for her fine tea. He seemed entirely at ease. With a look of alarm, Mrs. Genevieve turned to Reuben, who nodded resolutely and told her about their plan. Or tried to, anyway, for after only a few words they fell into an argument, with Mrs. Genevieve insisting that taking any kind of action against The Smoke was too dangerous, and Reuben countering that he and his mom were already in danger—that this was the best way to get them *out* of danger—and Penny energetically (and rather wordily) chiming in that she and her brother were compelled to uphold their family's sacred duty, were bound by legacy to fulfill a quest begun more than a century ago, were—

"But you're only children!" Mrs. Genevieve protested when Penny paused for breath.

"With respect, Mrs. Genevieve, I beg to differ." Jack, who had been listening politely all this time, rose to his feet and looked down at her, his hands set casually on his hips. With a private wink at Reuben, so subtle that Reuben almost missed it, Jack went on. "You're right about these two, but they aren't the ones who'll be sticking their necks out. That's my role, not theirs."

Mrs. Genevieve looked wonderingly up at him. So did Reuben. Since their arrival Jack's manner had changed so completely that Reuben felt as if he were looking at a new person altogether—a polite and supremely confident man, an impressive and likable stranger. With that one subtle wink, he had let Reuben know that he was fudging the truth to ease the watchmaker's fears; and with his words and his manner, he seemed likely to succeed.

Indeed, Mrs. Genevieve, after gazing up at Jack for several seconds, at last said, "You are very young." She seemed no longer to be arguing, only making an observation. A rueful observation, judging from her tone: what she really seemed to be saying was that it was terribly sad for a young man like Jack to be headed so soon to his grave.

"Young and full of dreams," Jack said with another wink, this time for her. "Don't worry about me, Mrs. Genevieve. Believe me, The Smoke may be bad news, but compared to a lifetime suffocating in Point William, dealing with him sounds downright pleasant."

Mrs. Genevieve almost smiled at this, or at any rate she looked less dour. Perhaps she was amused by Jack's bravado, perhaps relieved. Or perhaps she, too, had once dreamed of escaping the life she had. Perhaps she had such a dream even now. Who could say? Her life, Reuben realized, was more or less a mystery to him. He was just glad that she didn't seem ready to throw them out.

"How, exactly, do you propose to 'deal' with such a man?" asked Mrs. Genevieve.

"By taking his watch!" Penny said, and because she was not in the least used to lying, she continued, "Reuben says he—" Then she caught herself, blushing, and changed directions. "He thinks you can help us figure out how to find The Smoke—"

"By explaining where the Counselor lives," Reuben put in. "That's the obvious place to start."

"Exactly!" Penny said, excitedly tossing her hair (which, now that it was dry, had risen out and away from her scalp and looked quite exuberant again). "And after we've got The Smoke's watch, we'll expose him! Once people realize that he's been pulling a scam—that they don't have to be afraid of him—his whole operation will fall apart!"

Mrs. Genevieve turned her gaze from Penny to Jack, still standing over them with a jaunty posture. "And you truly believe you can do this?"

"I know a few tricks," Jack said with a smile. "But it's true I have to find him first, which means I need to pay a visit to the Counselor. So you do know where he lives?"

"Of course," said Mrs. Genevieve. "Everyone knows of this place. I am surprised Reuben does not."

"I know it's in Westmont, but not exactly where," said Reuben. "And of course I know plenty *about* it. It's supposed to be a gigantic mansion, right? With a wall and huge gates and a gang of Directions as guards—but all broken down and dark and creepy, like it's haunted."

Mrs. Genevieve shuddered. "Yes," she said with a look of distaste. "Yes, this is accurate."

Penny, quailing at Reuben's description of the Counselor's home, tugged two handfuls of hair down over her eyes, as if this might prevent her from seeing the place in her mind. But Jack only laughed and said, "I love it. Come on, redbird, would you rather the guy hung out in an office with filing cabinets and fluorescent lights? That's even more depressing. A creepy mansion's much better."

"You say this because you have not seen it," said Mrs. Genevieve with the same disagreeable look. "Regardless, one cannot simply 'pay a visit' to the Counselor, Jack. He does not receive uninvited guests. One must be summoned."

"We'll see about that. If you'll just tell me—" Jack began.

Penny interrupted him, looking out from behind her hair. "Wait, you've seen it yourself, Mrs. Genevieve?"

Mrs. Genevieve hesitated, then nodded. "I have seen this place, yes. Only yesterday I have seen it. I was summoned, you see."

"What!" Reuben cried. "Why?"

Mrs. Genevieve sat down again. She rubbed her eyes. She looked so tired. "The Counselor summoned many proprietors from here in Middleton," she said quietly. "He wished personally to question everyone about their encounters with you, Reuben. Or in my case, the lack of such an encounter. The Counselor told me that he found this very strange. By this he meant suspicious, I knew.

"I told him it was not so strange. My shop, after all, does not sit on Brighton Street, unlike the other places you visited. The Counselor seemed dissatisfied with my answer. His manner was very alarming. He gave me threatening instructions and sent me away."

"Instructions?" Jack said.

She looked at him bleakly. "He told me what I must do if Reuben ever did come to my shop."

Reuben's heart had begun to race; he wasn't sure why. "What's that, Mrs. Genevieve?"

"What do you suppose?" Mrs. Genevieve said, her face grim. "I was instructed to keep you here by whatever means necessary, secretly call his men, and detain you until they arrived."

A STILLNESS BEFORE THE STORM

Reuben's mouth went dry. Mrs. Genevieve had closed her eyes and was slowly shaking her head. She looked like someone trying to awaken from a bad dream. His eyes flashed to Penny and Jack. They looked like people who had just realized that their own bad dreams were about to come true.

Then Jack was on his feet. He grabbed Penny's hand and pulled her up, too. "Is there a back way out of this place, kid?"

"I—I don't think so." Reuben was watching Mrs. Genevieve, who had opened her eyes at the sound of sudden movement and seemed surprised by the expressions of high alarm on all their faces. But why would she be surprised? Reuben blurted out what he hoped was the truth: "She hasn't been stalling us, Jack. She would never do that."

Mrs. Genevieve's eyebrows shot up. "Is this what he suggests? That I have trapped you?" She looked indignantly at Jack, who was stepping briskly to the door into the shop. "A horrible thing!"

"So you were just making tea?" Jack pressed his ear to the door. "You didn't happen to put anything special in it? I noticed you didn't take a drink yourself."

"What is this you are saying?" Mrs. Genevieve cried, rising shakily to her feet.

"Everybody, calm down," Reuben said, trying to calm down himself.

Jack had opened the door a crack and was peering out into the shop. He took Penny's hand again and looked at Reuben. "We should go. Right now, Reuben."

It was the first time Jack had ever used his name. Disconcerted, Reuben stood up. He took a step toward Jack, then looked at Mrs. Genevieve, who was shaking her head. He felt frozen with confusion.

Mrs. Genevieve snatched her teacup from its saucer with such violence that tea slopped over the brim, running over her fingers and dripping onto the floor as she raised the cup to her mouth. Her eyes fixed on Jack's, she drank off the tea in three gulps and clapped the cup back down onto its saucer. Reuben would never have imagined she was capable of such reckless movement.

"That doesn't prove anything," Jack said. "For all we know you stirred something into our tea and not your own."

"Jack," Reuben protested, "why would she have told us if she really *did* it?"

"You know her, maybe, but I don't. Her motivations are beside the point. I'm keeping Penny safe. Are you coming or do I have to put you over my shoulder?"

"Jack," Penny said, pulling on her brother's hand. "Jack!" He glanced down at her, and Penny gave him a look that Reuben couldn't read. She pointed at Mrs. Genevieve. "Look at her, Jack. She didn't do it. Just think for a second and you'll realize it's true."

Jack frowned. His eyes darted to Mrs. Genevieve, who looked as if a stranger had shoved her for no reason. A stranger she'd been trying to help.

Jack's features slowly relaxed. He eased the door closed. "Right," he said, and sighed. "Okay. Mrs. Genevieve, I owe you an apology." He crossed the room to stand before her. "I'm sorry. I hope you'll understand."

They regarded each other, Jack's expression serious but mild, Mrs. Genevieve's one of barely suppressed emotion. She was trembling. They were looking directly into each other's eyes. After a few moments, she gave the slightest of nods. Jack took her by the arm.

"You should sit," he said gently. Mrs. Genevieve let him help her onto the sofa, his arm steadying her.

Somewhere in Reuben's tumult of emotions and jangled thoughts was a sense of renewed wonder at the change in Jack's manner.

Jack glanced over at Reuben. "I think you're safe to put that away for now, kid."

Reuben looked down at the watch in his hand. He'd snatched it from his backpack without thinking, had been holding it at the ready. His fingers still squeezed the winding key. Slowly he relaxed his grip and put the watch away again.

"One cannot decline the Counselor's summons," Mrs. Genevieve told them when she had calmed down. "I tried to do so, but his men took me by the arms and compelled me to go with them. It was..." She frowned and shook her head.

"It was awful for you," Penny said, finishing the watchmaker's sentence. "I'm so sorry."

"No kidding. Sounds like you've been through the wringer," said Jack, and Reuben nodded in agreement.

"To be put through a wringer," Mrs. Genevieve muttered, "would, I think, be better."

"And yet you've said nothing to them," Jack observed. He sounded impressed.

"Of course not!" Mrs. Genevieve said, and her blue eyes flashed. "How could I call myself a watchmaker otherwise? I treat clocks carefully and with respect, and they do their business elegantly. It should be the same with people! But these men, they intrude, they force others to do their bidding, they operate according to some secret design, at the whim of their secret leader. They are the opposite of everything I value!"

"So that's why you didn't want to give them the watch?" Penny asked. "Even though you were afraid?"

"It is one reason," Mrs. Genevieve said with a significant glance at Reuben, who felt his chest tighten. She had risked— was still risking—so much for his sake.

Jack asked her about the visit. He wanted to know about guards, the arrangement of the room, anything at all that Mrs. Genevieve could tell him. He didn't like surprises, he said; the more he knew, the better. (Which was true, but it was also true that Reuben had earlier explained to Jack and Penny what he would need to know.)

And so Mrs. Genevieve described how the Directions escorted her from the Counselor's limousine, up the steps and through the mansion's front doors, across a cavernous entranceway, and finally into an empty office, where she was told to wait. And so she did, sitting in an armchair opposite a desk, breathing slowly to calm herself, and fanning herself with a newspaper she took up from a side table. Jack asked her about the armchair, how big it was, whether it was the only one, and how many side tables there were.

A look of understanding appeared on Mrs. Genevieve's face. "I should have realized this sooner! You need such details because you intend to enter this room using the clock watch, which makes you blind."

"Possibly," said Jack in a casual tone. "It depends on how things develop. I just want to be prepared for anything." This was another half-truth told for Mrs. Genevieve's sake. Or half of a half-truth. The actual plan was for Jack to be admitted to the mansion on a pretense while Reuben accompanied him unseen. Reuben would need a place to stand or sit without being tripped over, naturally; and after Jack had made his exit, Reuben would remain behind as an invisible spy.

"This is very dangerous, what you suggest," Mrs. Genevieve murmured. "To be invisible for only fifteen minutes at a time— how do you handle this risk?"

Both Jack and Penny cast looks at Reuben, who, as it happened, had not told them about the watch's time limit yet, though he'd known he would have to eventually. Sheepish, he avoided their eyes. Why *hadn't* he mentioned it, anyway? Because it was a weakness, he thought. Was anyone ever in a hurry to reveal their weaknesses?

Jack, meanwhile, without missing a beat, shrugged off Mrs. Genevieve's concern and pressed her for more details. They all listened carefully as she described the room: a desk with an office chair for the Counselor and two armchairs for visitors, a side table for each armchair, an enormous empty fireplace to the left, and a cabinet against the wall, just to the right as she entered.

"Is there space beneath the cabinet?" Jack asked.

Mrs. Genevieve considered. "Yes, it is very large and stands high on its legs. Even a man of your size might crawl beneath it. One might even more easily crouch inside the fireplace, the largest I have seen. There is only the short iron fender to step over, not even as high as my knees."

She went on to relate how the Counselor finally entered through a second door and, without shaking hands or greeting her (she seemed particularly affronted by his lack of courtesy), sat down and began peppering her with questions. His men looked on silently, she said, one guarding each door, one standing against the wall to the right, and one before the fireplace.

"Appointed positions?" Jack said. "They weren't just standing here and there at random, I mean."

"No, no, this clearly was their routine. Just as they always walk and look in certain directions."

"Right, Reuben told us about that. I like that these guys are predictable, at least...."

It would have to be the cabinet, Reuben was thinking. He couldn't risk bumping into the man standing in front of the fireplace. That was all right. The cabinet sounded easy enough. It sounded almost perfect, in fact.

But only for fifteen minutes.

⃪⃩➦

"Fifteen minutes?" Penny hissed. "You only get fifteen minutes? And you're only telling us this now?"

The rumble of water filling the tub issued from beyond the bathroom door. Mrs. Genevieve, exhausted and shaken, had excused herself to take a warm bath. She would surely feel better afterward, she said, and could think more clearly.

Reuben was avoiding Penny's eyes, but he felt her scowling at him from the sofa.

"First you didn't tell me about the blindness," she said tersely. "You kept it a secret until you had no choice. And now this business with the time limit! What else are you keeping from us, Reuben?" She threw her arms out in exasperation. "We're supposed to be a team!"

Reuben shifted uneasily in his chair and looked over at her. He'd *wanted* to tell her everything, had wanted to from the very beginning, but he was so used to holding on to his secrets.... No, it was more than that. The clock watch made him feel powerful— for the first time in his life, he actually felt *special*—and revealing his vulnerabilities might take away from that feeling. That was the truth, he realized. But the thought of explaining this to Penny made him feel even *more* vulnerable, and all he managed to offer her was an apologetic shrug.

Penny's scowl only deepened at this meager response, and Reuben averted his eyes again.

He was surprised by how much her disappointment stung him. He'd always known that he was shy and, yes, a little bit sad, but he hadn't realized he was lonely. Being around Penny, even for such a short time, had made him realize what he'd been missing. He hadn't ever had a friend before, he thought. Not a real one.

Reuben tried again. The words came with great difficulty, as if he were dragging them up and out of himself, like an anchor from the ocean. "We *are* a team," he said, his voice husky and strange-sounding to his own ears. "Okay? We are. I'm sorry."

Penny raised her eyebrows. She looked at him steadily, clearly expecting more.

"And just so you know, I also get tired," Reuben said, clearing his throat nervously. "Using the watch wears me out. And that's it. Now I've told you everything. I'm sorry I didn't tell you all of it before."

Penny started to scowl again, then stopped and adopted an expression of concern, and finally uttered a little growl of frustration.

Jack, who had been roaming the room studying the pictures on the walls, looked over his shoulder at Reuben, then at Penny. He raised one eyebrow and looked away again. "Don't be mad at him, redbird. He was just being careful. Personally, I'm glad to know it. I wouldn't want to be walking into this situation with a kid who didn't take precautions. I'm not exactly excited about doing it with a kid who *does*."

Reuben closed his eyes. He felt queasy and wished he'd had something to eat other than sweet pastries. A simple slice of toast, for instance, warm and very lightly buttered. That's what his mom would have given him on a morning he felt sick to his stomach. He could just see the look of concern on her face, and it made him feel even worse. He opened his eyes. He needed not to think about her right now.

His mind returned to Mrs. Genevieve's account of her visit with the Counselor. He had a feeling that something was hiding in the details, something that either would be of use to him or—if he couldn't identify and make sense of it—would destroy his plan and deliver him right into the hands of The Smoke. Maybe he was just anxious, but he couldn't shake the feeling. He thought over what Mrs. Genevieve had told them about the meeting, about the questions she was asked and the Counselor's erratic behavior.

At one point, dissatisfied with the watchmaker's replies to his questions, the Counselor had abruptly taken his leave. With a glance at the clock on the wall—"a cuckoo clock, no less," Mrs. Genevieve had said—he'd risen from his chair and informed her that he needed to consult with his employer. In his first gesture of courtesy, he'd waved brusquely at the telephone on his desk and told her she could use it if she needed to. He would be making his own call on a separate line, he said, and would likely be some time in returning.

Mrs. Genevieve was left alone once more. She had no one to call, however, and nothing to do but anxiously wait. At length she rose and examined the cuckoo clock, which was an exquisite antique and no doubt worth a fortune but was covered with dust and cobwebs. "I had no chance to see the cuckoo itself," she'd said in a tone of real regret, "for the Counselor returned just before the hour, and I was quickly given my unpleasant instructions and dismissed."

Reuben found himself fixating on that unseen cuckoo. He had always been fascinated by cuckoo clocks. He'd never seen one in real life, only in cartoons. There was something so appealing about the thought of that little bird hidden away. The mystery of it. The tantalizing notion that you could see it if you were present at the right time. But even then you would get only a glance. The bird would hide away again.

As a very young boy, Reuben had actually wanted to *be* such a bird. He had daydreamed about it, imagining the hiding place that the bird called home. It was mysterious, yes, but cozy, safe. And the bird had an important purpose. Part of it was public— to announce the hour to the outside world—and part of it was private—to hide away and wait.

To hide away and wait was exactly what was going to be required of him now, Reuben thought. To hide away and wait, and then to spring into action. Jack, meanwhile, had gone to the sofa and sat down next to Penny. He put an arm over her shoulders. "You know you can't lie to save your life, right? Better just keep quiet about the kid's role in this. Mrs. Genevieve's going to be nervous enough. She obviously loves him, and she's afraid for herself, too. You're good at cheering people up, so just focus on that."

"I didn't know we were *going* to lie to her," Penny said defensively. She sighed. "But you're right, I'm terrible at it. I'll just try to talk about clocks, I guess. *They* certainly seem to make her happy." She lifted her eyes to Jack's. "You're sure I shouldn't go with you?"

"Not this time, ladybug," Jack said. "You'd be putting yourself in danger for no reason. Imagine explaining that to Mom and Dad."

Penny's face crumpled a little. She threw her arm across Jack's chest and leaned into him, letting her hair spill over her face. She was either crying or trying hard not to. "Mrs. Genevieve isn't the only one who's going to be worried, you know," she murmured from behind her hair. "What if they figure out what you're up to? Or what if you run into that creepy man from the train?"

Jack squeezed her. "I'm not worried about some weaselly guy in an outdated suit, Penny."

Mrs. Genevieve came into the room as Jack was speaking. She still looked tired, but a fresher sort of tired, with scrubbed cheeks and damp hair. She wore a blue summer sweater that made her eyes stand out even more than usual. "Who is this person you are speaking of?"

"The man I called—that number from the newspaper ad," Reuben told her. "He saw me on the train, on my way out of New Umbra. We had an...unpleasant encounter. He was as creepy in person as he sounded on the phone."

"And just now you are telling me this? Was he following you, this man?"

"No, it was just bad luck. We were on the same subway car, and I was nervous, and I checked my watch to make sure it was set right—kind of, you know, trying to hide it at the same time. I think he noticed."

Penny had shifted to look at Reuben, squinting in concentration. "That's something I've been wondering about. If he didn't actually see the watch, how would he know you had it?"

"Good question," Reuben said. "It's funny. It wasn't clear to me at the time; I just *knew*. But now I think he knew what I was doing because he used to do the same thing. I didn't say so earlier, Penny, but when you told me about Penelope, you mentioned that she kept sort of slyly checking her watch. Well, I knew what she was up to the moment you said it. It's like what she wrote in her letter—a person who has one of the clock watches will understand the habits of whoever has the other one. The way that man looked at me, the way he acted, it was obvious he knew what I had."

"Why does this get worse?" Mrs. Genevieve asked no one in particular. She was looking at the ceiling, shaking her head.

"Chances are we'll never see him," Jack said with a reassuring glance at Penny. "Like the kid said, it was a coincidence. And anyway, if the guy used to have one of these watches, that means he couldn't even hang on to his most valuable possession. Doesn't sound like much of a threat to me. Who loses something like that?"

"It might have been stolen from him," Penny said. "That's probably what always happens, don't you think? Some nasty person finds out about the watch, then does whatever it takes to get his hands on it."

"That isn't how *I* got it," Reuben pointed out. "I found it. Someone hid it and then never came back for it." He thought back to that morning, high up on the ledge, noticing the pouch strap. It would have been so easy to overlook. And everything would have been different then. Instead, he had tugged on that strap and pulled out his future.

"It was in a plastic bread sack," he reflected. "How long have those been around, anyway?"

"Forty or fifty years, perhaps," Mrs. Genevieve said after considering a moment. "Reuben, where is it that you found this watch?"

Reuben hesitated. The others looked at him expectantly. He saw Penny narrowing her eyes, daring him to be evasive again. "In the Lower Downs," he made himself say. "In an alley."

Mrs. Genevieve did not look surprised. Reuben wondered if

she had already suspected that he was from the Lower Downs. She knew he wasn't from her own neighborhood, at any rate, and had probably guessed that he was poorer than most.

"Do you know," Mrs. Genevieve said thoughtfully, "that I once lived in the Lower Downs myself? This is true!" she said in response to Reuben's surprised expression. "Long ago, after my husband died, and I was for a time very poor. It was some years before I was able to open my shop here. But I tell you this because I have remembered something.

"Everyone in the neighborhood knew about it," she went on. "A madman who ran screaming through the streets one day, running as if being pursued."

"I've heard about that!" Reuben exclaimed. "People still talk about it. You actually lived there when it happened?"

Mrs. Genevieve nodded. "He was thought a madman because he was so clearly alone. There was no one pursuing him, you understand. None, at least, that anyone could see. Until now I was like everyone else—it never occurred to me that he might actually *have* been pursued."

"The Smoke," Penny whispered, exchanging glances with Reuben and Jack.

The man had run in a crouch, Mrs. Genevieve explained, as if cowering from an expected blow, and was screaming at his unseen pursuer to leave him alone. "I don't have it! I don't have it! Leave me be!" He would disappear behind buildings, and everyone would think that he had gone for good, but then he would reappear, ranting and screaming as before. From one alley he emerged limping badly, which later led some of the older neighborhood children (hoping to scare the younger ones) to insist that he'd been bitten by an invisible dog, that it was this dog that had been chasing him.

"They tried to convince the little ones that the dog was still on the loose," Mrs. Genevieve recalled. "If you went down the wrong alley, they said, this invisible dog would bite you!"

He hurt his leg because he fell, Reuben was thinking. *He thought he was being hunted—and maybe he was, though maybe the fear just got to him. So he climbed up to that ledge and hid the watch, then fell on his way down....*

Eventually the police cornered the man and took him into custody, Mrs. Genevieve said. They were trying to help him, but he resisted, fighting furiously and hurting one of the officers, which made things worse for him. He began to deny crimes that no one had accused him of. His fingerprints were taken, and to everyone's surprise they matched those of a notorious cat burglar, a thief who had been stealing jewelry and money for years. The cat burglar had never been seen, not even glimpsed, despite the fact that many of the places he'd burglarized were well guarded. The man went to prison.

"He must have gotten out, then," Reuben said. "That's surely who I saw on the train."

Mrs. Genevieve wrinkled her brow. "I do not think so. That man died soon after going to prison. I heard at first that it was a heart attack, and later that he took his own life. I don't know which is the truth, but he most certainly died. Everyone knew of this."

"I did suggest the possibility," Jack said to Mrs. Genevieve, "that the man on the train was just a creepy weirdo who sounded like the guy on the phone. But the kid says no."

"It was absolutely the same person," Reuben said.

"Maybe the man on the train had the watch *first,*" suggested Penny. "Before the cat burglar did."

Reuben shot her a grateful look. "Yes! That would explain it. He had the watch when he was a young man—or maybe even a boy—but then he lost it, or the next guy, the cat burglar, stole it from him, and he's been looking for it ever since."

"Just like The Smoke," Jack said with a sharp nod. "Okay, here's what I think happened: The Smoke figures out the cat burglar is his twin hunter—to use Penelope's words—and starts hunting him. He comes close, too, maybe lots of times, and the cat burglar becomes a paranoid mess. He stops sleeping, never stays in one place, constantly looks over his shoulder, until finally he just snaps and gets himself arrested. He doesn't have the watch on him, but The Smoke knows that he had it before, which means the guy must have hidden it somewhere in the city. So The Smoke's been searching high and low for it ever since— just like this weird bird on the train."

Reuben and Penny were nodding. It made sense to them, too.

"Such a man as this one on the train," Mrs. Genevieve said darkly, "a man who has been obsessed for so long—he could be very dangerous as well. And now that he has seen you, Reuben, he will be searching for you."

"He can join the club," Jack said. "Who *isn't* looking for this kid now?"

"Jack!" Penny scolded. "This is serious. What if you do run into him?"

"Okay, take it easy, redbird," Jack said more soberly. "I'm not worried about this joker, but I'm not going to be careless, either. We'll be fine."

Mrs. Genevieve clicked her teeth together. "I do not like it! I do not like knowing of this man. All his life he looks for this watch? Does he do nothing else? Does he *care* for nothing else? Only this desire for power, this...this *ridiculous* belief that a thing which makes you seem like nothing actually makes you special? It is twisted, this thinking!"

Reuben, excusing himself, went into the bathroom.

He stood looking at himself in the mirror. His cheeks were as red as they felt. He splashed cold water on them. What was it he was feeling? Anger? Shame? He honestly couldn't tell. What

"Such a man as this one on the train,"
Mrs. Genevieve said darkly, "a man who has been
obsessed for so long—he could be very dangerous as well."

reason did he have to feel either? Fear, certainly—he did feel afraid. But it was about more than sneaking into the Counselor's mansion. He thought of that long-ago cat burglar running like a madman through the streets. And of the obsessed man on the train, of his voice on the phone. The years and years of advertisements in all the newspapers. Mrs. Genevieve was disturbed by the mere thought of such obsession.

And what disturbed Reuben, thinking of her words, was that although they made sense to him, so, too, did the story of the cat burglar. Likewise the man on the train. The danger of having the watch could so easily make you crazy. He already felt a little crazy himself. But the thought of having it and then *not* having it? That seemed even crazier. Jack had wondered who could lose such an incredible thing, but to Reuben the bigger mystery was this: who would willingly give such a thing up?

Reuben splashed more cold water on his face, dried off with a towel, and left the bathroom without looking in the mirror again.

"You're sure?" Jack was asking Mrs. Genevieve.

"I wish I were not," she replied. "But no, he will not interrupt his search for anything less."

"Makes sense," Jack said, nodding. "If he's this close to finding the watch after all these years. So he's got everybody on the case, from the lowliest thug to the Counselor himself. Full throttle. Okay, then." Something in his expression made him look like a boxer about to leave his corner. "Full throttle it is."

"I can't bear this," Penny said, covering her eyes, as if she were at that same imaginary boxing match and her brother about to be soundly beaten.

"What are you talking about?" Reuben asked. "What do you mean?"

Jack gave him a tight-lipped smile. "The Counselor isn't going to agree to meet with me unless I tell him I have information about the watch. That means playing all our cards at once. But it's going to be my only way in."

Our only way in, Reuben thought as he and Jack exchanged somber looks. They had hoped to be admitted on some other, safer pretense. Evidently, Mrs. Genevieve had just shot that notion down. As Jack said, it made sense. Reuben felt a little foolish for ever having thought otherwise.

"When will you go?" Penny asked quietly.

"The sooner the better," Jack said. He bent over his boots, tightening the laces with deft, sharp little motions of his fingers. "We need to get the show on the road. Mrs. Genevieve, you can give me directions and a phone number, right? I'll call ahead to arrange the meeting."

"Actually, I think you should rest first," Reuben said. "It's been a long night." He was thinking of what lay ahead, of how tired he already felt. He needed to gather his strength, to be more alert when the moment arrived.

Jack raised an eyebrow. "A nap? Really?"

"Really," said Reuben, giving him a significant look. "You hardly slept last night, and if you end up using the watch..."

Now Jack caught on. "Right," he said, and as if to prove Reuben's point, he yawned. "You and Penny could probably use a nap as well. Would that be fine with you, Mrs. Genevieve?"

"Of course," said Mrs. Genevieve, rising. "Penny, you may lie down in my bed. Reuben is small enough to fit on my sofa. As for you..." She turned to Jack, but he waved her off.

"No need to fuss about me. I'll take the floor. Believe me, I've slept on plenty of floors in my day, and not all of them nice and carpeted like yours."

"I will busy myself in the workshop, then," said Mrs. Genevieve, though she did bring Jack a folded blanket to use as a pillow. Jack thanked her and, lying with his feet against the shop door, either promptly fell asleep or promptly pretended to.

Whether Jack was asleep or not, Reuben had the distinct impression Penny's brother was standing guard.

As Mrs. Genevieve showed Penny to her bed, Reuben stretched out on the sofa, his back to the room. His eyes were wide open, staring at the fibers of the sofa cushion. He wondered if it had actually just been nerves making him want to put off the moment of their departure. Could he really sleep knowing that when he woke up it would be time to go?

He forced himself to close his eyes, and almost at once he felt his leg give an involuntary twitch. He was distantly aware of his breathing growing deeper, dreamily aware of his questions being answered. Could he sleep at such a time? Evidently, he could. Was he just trying to put off the dreaded moment? It hardly mattered. He was slipping away, already almost fully asleep, and whether he slept a few minutes or a few hours, his experience would be the same.

The time would pass in a heartbeat. He would open his eyes. He would still be afraid. And the moment would have come.

ENTER THE COUNSELOR

The neighborhood of Westmont, shortly after noon on a warm Saturday, was nothing like the Lower Downs would have been. No children shouting in the street, no one setting up tables to sell secondhand items on the corners, no loud music coming from apartment windows or car stereos. A mail carrier was quietly making his rounds, and there were a few people out walking their dogs, a few parents pushing strollers down to the neighborhood park, from which could be heard the screech of seesaws and swing sets. Beyond the park was a church, in whose parking lot a teenager was trying out tricks on a skateboard. Other than the playground equipment, though, and the telltale clatter and scrape of the skateboard, the neighborhood was weirdly silent. The well-off people of Westmont were doing more or less what one might expect, but they were keeping their voices down.

Jack drove slowly along the tree-lined streets. Slumped in the passenger seat, Reuben craned his neck to peer out. The windows of Jack's car were darkly tinted, and on such a bright day he couldn't easily be seen from outside, if at all. Still, he shrank even lower as the Counselor's residence loomed into view ahead of them. It occupied an entire block.

"He couldn't find anything bigger?" Jack said, wagging his head.

It had always seemed natural to Reuben that the Counselor lived in a mansion, for as The Smoke's representative, he was more important than the mayor and far more lavishly compensated. What had seemed strange were the accounts of the cracked windows and missing shingles, the broken shutters and overgrown gardens, the bats roosting in crumbling chimneys. It was supposed that the Counselor was an odd man who cared for nothing but his job, that his riches were wasted on him because he allowed himself no time to enjoy them. But as Jack drove slowly around the block, Reuben found himself wondering if the man actually *liked* his home the way it was. This was an unsettling thought.

The wall surrounding the property was made of old gray stone, and here and there Reuben saw broken places in it through which some intrepid small person might squeeze, but there always appeared to be rosebushes or similarly thorny plants on the other side. The wrought-iron palings atop the wall had pointed tips, like spears, and were tangled through with those same thorny plants. Trespassing onto the Counselor's property would seem to call for a great deal of bleeding.

Jack had come around to the front gate again. It was elegant but formidable, composed of wrought-iron bars and standing ten feet tall. The driveway was flanked by untrimmed topiaries that resembled only vaguely the animals they'd once been shaped to represent—lions and swans and giraffes grown grotesquely fat, shaggy, and distorted, as if by a vile sort of magic. At the end of the driveway, parked by the mansion's front steps, was a shiny black limousine.

"This is tricky," Jack mused, moving on. "If I drive in there, they'll close that gate behind us, and there's no such thing as a quick getaway if you have to open a gate." He steered back the way they had come, pulling to the curb when they drew near the park and the church. "Let me think a minute."

Reuben only nodded. He was starting to feel sick now. After they passed through the gate, there'd be no going back.

The plan was simple enough: Jack had already arranged the meeting. He would pretend to haggle with the Counselor about the reward, then exit as quickly as he could, leaving Reuben behind to eavesdrop and snoop. The Counselor would surely call The Smoke, and with any luck he would say something, or Reuben would find something, that would lead them to The Smoke's hideout. Afterward Reuben would simply sneak out again. But what sounded simple in theory would be complicated and scary in practice, and his nerves and stomach were urging him to turn back. He felt a need to go to the bathroom again, though he'd gone just before they left Mrs. Genevieve's shop.

That had been a tough parting, with Penny hugging them both and looking as frightened as Reuben felt. Mrs. Genevieve had hugged Reuben, too, which had almost made him cry. She had pleaded with him not to go along, but he'd insisted that Jack needed a lookout. "I'll be waiting in the car," he'd said. "So I can honk the horn if I see something fishy or if something goes wrong."

"Which it won't," Jack had put in.

"But what if someone sees you?" Mrs. Genevieve had protested.

"At that point he'll still have the watch with him," Jack assured her, expanding their lie with a smooth ease that no other Meyer could have managed. "If anything spooks the kid, he can vanish."

Mrs. Genevieve still hadn't liked it. But at least she hadn't barred the door.

"Okay, I know what we're going to do," Jack said now, and he grinned. "They're really going to hate me for it, too." He shifted in his seat, one arm draped casually over the steering wheel, and looked at Reuben. "I'll meet you in this park afterward, all right? I'll wait for you however long it takes."

"What if someone notices you?"

"Then I'll go away for a little while, but I'll definitely come back. If you don't see me at first, just hang tight. You're a kid, so you'll blend in there. Make sense?"

Reuben nodded. He took a deep breath. "Got it."

"And listen, if something goes wrong while we're in there—if they spot you somehow—just get out. Don't worry about anything else, just go. And forget about the park. The park is where we meet if everything goes well. If something goes wrong, you get out however you can, as fast as you can, and we'll meet up again later at Mrs. Genevieve's shop."

"But what about you?"

"I'll make trouble," Jack said. He winked. "Don't worry, it comes easy."

The thought of something going wrong made Reuben's stomach flop. He looked bleakly at Jack and said nothing.

Jack narrowed his eyes, studying him. "You still up for this? We don't have to do it, you know. We can try to figure something else out. It isn't too late."

Reuben shook his head. "No. I can do it." He hesitated. "I'm just scared."

To his surprise, Jack reached over and put a hand on top of his head. He looked Reuben in the eye. "That only proves you aren't stupid. The more important thing is that you're good at this. You really are. So don't panic, all right? Just keep your cool and remember that you're the expert."

"I am?"

Jack raised an eyebrow. "Aren't you the one who found the watch and figured out its secret? And then tracked our family down? And found the smugglers' tunnels? I still don't know how you managed *that*. So yeah, if anyone is the expert, kid, it's you." He tousled Reuben's hair. "Now, are you ready? We'd better get moving or we'll be late."

He's right, Reuben thought, a little wonderingly. *You're the expert.* And to his surprise, he did feel rather better. He nodded at Jack. "I'm ready."

"Let's do this," Jack said, and gunned his engine. He did a U-turn in the street and roared back toward the Counselor's mansion.

When they drew up to the gate, Reuben was crouched in the passenger seat, keeping out of sight, his watch at the ready.

"There are four guys at the gate now," Jack muttered for his benefit. "They must've seen us circling the block. And now they're swinging it open for me, how nice. Okay, time to disappear, kid—this one wants to talk to me."

Reuben vanished. He heard Jack suck in his breath.

"That is seriously mind-blowing," Jack murmured. He rolled down his window.

A voice said, "You the one who called from a pay phone?"

Jack laughed. "What do you think? Am I supposed to be impressed that you know it was a pay phone?"

"I don't care what you think," said the man, though he sounded annoyed. He probably wasn't used to being challenged. "Drive on up and park behind the limo."

"Roger that," Jack said. He rolled his window back up. "Hold on," he whispered.

The car surged forward, throwing Reuben against the back of the seat, then just as suddenly slammed to a stop. Reuben tumbled halfway into the floorboard. "Be quick," Jack hissed, throwing open his door and jumping out. Reuben scrambled after him, feeling his way with his free hand.

"You can't park there!" a man yelled. "We can't close the gate!"

"I won't be long," Jack said coolly, stepping forward to give Reuben room.

Reuben slipped out behind him, tapping his back to let him know he was clear. Jack closed the car door, and Reuben heard the jingle of keys as Jack thrust them into a pocket. Several angry footsteps were approaching.

"Go on ahead," Jack muttered, and Reuben headed up the drive.

"I told you to drive up and park behind the limo!"

"Yeah, sorry, I'm bad at parking," Jack replied. "Don't worry. I'll move it when I come back out."

"You'll move it *now!*" The man sounded both shocked and furious.

Reuben had reached the limousine. He felt his way around it, located the front steps, and climbed up to the mansion's broad portico. The doors lay straight ahead. Would they swing in or out? Front doors usually swung in, didn't they? In his nervousness he found he couldn't remember, couldn't think clearly.

You're the expert, Reuben reminded himself, and once again it helped. He felt for hinges, found none. Of course. The doors swung in. He got into position and waited.

Meanwhile Jack was saying, loudly but calmly, that he had ten minutes to tell the Counselor what he wanted to know. "A minute longer and the whole thing's off. Do you want me to tell him that you slowed me down?"

There was no verbal response to this, but Reuben heard Jack walking up the drive. He imagined the Directions looking at one another, irritated but stymied. A moment later he heard them coming up the drive, too. They were muttering among themselves, walking quickly as they tried to catch up.

"Do I just go right in?" Jack called, springing up the steps.

"Wait for us," one of the men said gruffly.

But Jack said, "Oh, here we go," and Reuben heard the door latch opening, followed by a squeak as the door swung inward. He darted forward and brushed past Jack. Stumbling slightly over the threshold, he caught himself and felt his way quickly to the side.

"Beautiful entranceway!" Jack was saying, coming in behind him. His voice rang out in what was evidently a large open space, just as Mrs. Genevieve had described it. "Marble floors and a chandelier? Very nice! And look at that grand staircase! Does no one ever use it anymore? And, wow, look at the ceiling! Such detail! Shame about that water damage, though. Has the Counselor considered—"

Hurried footsteps and a scuffle cut him off. Reuben heard shuffling, sliding noises, followed by a thump as Jack was thrown up against the wall. "You listen to me," a man growled. "You don't just barge in like that. Here's how it works: We're going to take you over to that door. You're going to go in there and sit down. No more funny stuff. Believe me, this is not the place for it. Mr. Faug doesn't like funny stuff. Now lift up your arms."

"What, are you going to tickle me? I thought you said no funny stuff."

"You worry me," the man said. "I've got enough to worry about. We're going to frisk you, make sure you're clean."

"Well, I hate to break it to you, but I haven't showered since yesterday."

"You worry me," the man said again. Reuben heard the patting, swishing sounds of hands feeling for weapons. "Okay, he's clean."

"Really?" Jack said. "Excellent. Lead the way."

Their footsteps clattered across the marble floor. Reuben crept along behind them. It was a long way to the door, he discovered. The entranceway alone was bigger than his whole apartment.

"After you," Jack said.

"Suddenly he's polite," one of the men muttered.

"Let's keep it that way," said another.

The door was opened. The men began filing inside. Reuben came up behind Jack and touched his back. "Yep," Jack said simply, as if to no one, but Reuben knew it was for him. They moved forward, Reuben's fingertips against Jack's back to guide him. Jack stopped just inside the doorway and rapped on something wooden to the right. "Nice cabinet," he said. "Is it an antique?"

Reuben got down onto the carpeted floor and crawled under the cabinet, which was very deep and very tall indeed. He scooted all the way back against the wall. There was enough room for him to sit on his heels with his head bowed. He felt a flicker of relief. At least for now he was out of the way, could simply be still and listen.

"Of course it's an antique," one of the men was saying. "You think Mr. Faug likes the new stuff? The junk they make these days?"

"I wouldn't know," Jack said. "I haven't met Mr. Faug yet. I hope I will soon. We're down to nine minutes now."

"He's on his way. Go sit down."

"Shall I close the door?"

"I'll get it. You sit down."

But Jack closed the door anyway, and Reuben heard two of the men sigh with frustration. There was movement in the room, the men taking up their positions as Jack took his seat. And all the while Jack chattered on, commenting on the nice mahogany desk, the enormous fireplace, the interestingly patterned carpet, the quaint old cuckoo clock. He was cultivating a personality, Reuben knew. He was now the sort of person who talked all the time, and therefore it wouldn't seem surprising when he said odd things—things intended for Reuben's benefit.

A door squeaked open. Someone entered the room coughing, and Jack fell silent. The coughing sounds traveled in the direction of the desk, or at least where Reuben imagined the desk to be. A chair groaned, and the coughs began to subside.

"Mr. Faug, I presume," Jack said. For the first time, he sounded uneasy. "That's a nasty cold you have there."

"Allergies," said a gruff, froggy voice. The Counselor blew his nose.

"It's a shame," Jack said, his tone lighter now. Whatever had unsettled him, he was quickly rallying. "I know I should mind my own business, but have you considered dusting? It might help. You have a nice place here, but honestly, it's like a dust museum."

"Who is this man?" the Counselor croaked. "What's his name?"

"He didn't have any ID on him, sir," said one of the Directions. His voice came from the fireplace.

"Wait, they were looking for ID?" Jack sounded indignant. "You might want to have a talk with them," he said, presumably to the Counselor. "They told me it was weapons. Also, they were kind of rude."

"You told me that time was of the essence," the Counselor croaked. "Yet you are wasting it with nonsense."

"It's true. I apologize. I'll get right to it. As I said on the phone, I'm in touch with someone who found the watch your boss is looking for. We'd like to claim the reward, but my contact is nervous. Powerful people scare him. So the idea is that you give me the reward now, and then I'll call you later with the location of the watch."

"Are you the boy's uncle?" the Counselor asked. He coughed again briefly.

"Not sure what boy you mean," Jack said, "but I assure you I'm nobody's uncle. It's possible that my contact is. I haven't asked him."

The Counselor cleared his throat violently. "Who is your contact? What's his name?"

"He's never told me his real name. We use code names. It's safer that way. Also, it's more fun."

There was a silence. Reuben was sweating. Why was Jack antagonizing the Counselor? Why not just be polite?

A faint crackling sound reached his ears. A plastic wrapper.

"Oh, good," said Jack, "that should help clear up your sinuses. I'd love one myself, actually. No? Was that your last one? You know, it's a little impolite—"

"Do you think that I've been impolite to you?" the Counselor interrupted. He made a smacking, sucking sound as he moved the cough drop or candy around in his mouth. He sounded more relaxed, which for some reason Reuben found more disturbing than when he'd sounded annoyed.

"Well, I wouldn't make a fuss about it," Jack said. "This is just business. Your boss gets something he wants, and my contact and I split the reward. Everybody's happy."

"No one is happy," the Counselor said. "You've given me no reason to believe that this contact of yours actually has the watch."

"He described it perfectly, though. I told you that on the phone."

The Counselor made another sucking sound. "Any number of people could have offered me the same description. It appears in newspaper advertisements every day. Or you might have spoken with a proprietor on Brighton Street, someone who's actually seen the watch."

"That's a good point," Jack said. "I hadn't thought of that."

"You've wasted my time. My employer will be most displeased."

"Hold on, hold on," Jack said. "Surely we can figure something out. I know my contact wouldn't lie to me. We've had deals before. He's always been reliable."

"Very well. Pick up that telephone and call him. Tell him to bring the watch here immediately. When I've confirmed that it's the one my employer seeks, you'll get your reward."

"There's a problem with that idea," Jack said. "I don't have his number. He always calls me. He's very skittish, this guy. But look, I see your point, so maybe we can compromise here. You could give me half the reward now and half after you claim the watch. That's fair, right? We each have to trust the other a little bit."

"I have no reason to trust you," said the Counselor, his froggy voice rising. "You've given me no name, you have no identification, and what you are telling me is no different from what a great many others could! You seem to have no idea of the situation you are in!"

Sweat was streaming down Reuben's face, trickling down his sides. Jack had botched it. Something horrible was about to happen, and not just to Jack. Reuben had only a few minutes before the watch ran out.

"Oh!" Jack cried, snapping his fingers. Though he must surely be aware of the threat in the Counselor's words, his tone gave no indication. "You know what? My contact did tell me something else about the watch. I don't know if it will be useful—in fact, I was afraid it might be a deal breaker—but under the circumstances I suppose I had better tell you." He cleared his throat. "The watch is kind of . . . broken."

The room was very still for a moment. Then the Counselor's chair creaked. He exhaled loudly through his nose. "What

"I have no reason to trust you," said
the Counselor, his froggy voice rising.

do you mean," he said—his voice so low that Reuben almost couldn't understand him—"when you say that it's broken?"

"I mean it doesn't keep time anymore. You can wind it up, but nothing happens. It just unwinds again. The hand doesn't move."

There was another silence. And then the Counselor began to laugh. It was a raspy, ugly, disconcerting laugh. Jack laughed, too, in a false and wooden way, obviously intended to express a good-humored confusion. He'd been brilliant, though. He'd said exactly enough. Reuben felt shaky with relief.

"Of course it doesn't keep time," the Counselor said. "The watch is a rare antique, not a functioning timepiece. My employer wants it nevertheless. He is a collector." He let out another raspy laugh. "I thought that you meant the watch had been damaged in some other way. I wouldn't care to deliver that news to my employer. But this—this is good." The chair creaked again. "Very well. I'll speak with him about your reward."

"Now?" Jack said. "But if I don't want to miss my rendezvous, I need to leave right away. Hasn't your boss already authorized the reward?"

"He'll wish to discuss the details of the arrangement. Your associate will have to wait."

"You don't know him. He's edgy. If I don't show up on time, he'll take off."

"Perhaps you should tell him that you might be late. Perhaps you will suddenly 'remember' that you have his telephone number after all." The Counselor coughed again. He was stepping toward the door through which he'd entered. Reuben could hear the Directions moving that way as well. "Regardless, I have my own call to make, on a different line. You'll wait here until I return."

Reuben silently begged Jack not to argue. He needed to wind his watch again—he didn't have much time. If the others left the room, he would have his chance.

"Looks like I don't have a choice," Jack said with a sigh. "Try to make it snappy, won't you?"

The door was already squeaking open. If the Counselor heard Jack, he didn't bother to reply. Reuben heard the men leaving the room—all but one, who lingered a moment in the doorway.

"Hey," the man said softly, as if not wishing to be heard by anyone but Jack, "you should be more careful. You're pushing it, and you don't want to do that. Believe me."

"Are you actually giving me a well-intentioned warning?"

But the man was already closing the door behind him.

"What do you know?" Jack said. "I think he actually was."

Reuben pushed in on the winding key and reappeared in a room he'd seen only in his imagination. He'd never done that before; the effect was strangely upsetting. In its general arrangement the room was much as he'd pictured it—the placement and size of the furniture, the distance between walls, the location of the fireplace—but all of the smaller details were different. The pattern in the carpet, the wallpaper, the color of the chairs and desk. Everything was where it should be, and yet it had all suddenly changed, as if by magic. Though he knew better, Reuben had the bizarre impression that he was hallucinating. It made him queasy.

He wound the watch, looking out from under the cabinet. Jack sat with his back to Reuben and would not be turning around to look at him. They had agreed never to assume they had true privacy. Reuben was strongly tempted to whisper, though. He felt so alone and so nervous. Even the simplest exchange of words might help calm his nerves.

But what if that door swung open unexpectedly? So many things could go wrong. Reuben held his tongue. He needed to focus on nothing but being ready to vanish again. The watch wound, he mopped his brow and shifted positions, sitting now with his legs crossed. He was already very tired. He wouldn't use the watch until the last possible moment.

From where he sat, Reuben couldn't see much of the opposite door. His view was blocked by Jack's chair and the Counselor's desk. And the cabinet was deep enough that if he stayed where he was, with his back against the wall, he wasn't likely to be spotted even if his watch ran out. That much was in his favor, anyway.

So keep calm, he thought, and he reminded himself once more of what Jack had said: *You're the expert.*

He wondered if The Smoke would actually authorize the Counselor to give Jack half the reward up front. He doubted it— and Jack certainly didn't expect it—but then again, what was a little money to The Smoke? The man was so close to getting his hands on that second watch, the object of his dreams; who knew what he would agree to? Reuben wished he could be eavesdropping on that phone conversation. The spying would be easier, he hoped, once Jack had left and the Counselor thought himself alone.

Jack got up from his chair. Cracking his knuckles, he went to stand near the wall opposite the fireplace. Reuben could see him only from the knees down. He was probably looking at the cuckoo clock.

"You're a very odd man, Mr. Faug," Jack murmured as if to himself.

Reuben was startled. They had agreed to take no chances.

"Very odd," Jack continued in his musing tone. "With your—"

He cut himself short, and Reuben was left straining to hear what hadn't been said. What had Jack been about to say? He clearly wanted to communicate something to Reuben, so why did he stop? Had he heard someone coming? Reuben listened intently. He didn't hear anything but the faint ticking of the cuckoo clock.

Jack grunted, the sort of grunt that suggested he thought he'd heard something, though evidently he hadn't. Or that perhaps he actually *did* hear something, but it wasn't what he thought it was. Regardless, he didn't finish whatever he'd started to say. Instead, he walked slowly over to the fireplace.

Suddenly Reuben felt the skin prickle on the back of his neck. He didn't know why, but he felt itchy all over, and his heart started beating faster. What was it? Why was he so frightened all of a sudden? His fingers squeezed the winding key. He held very still. Sweat stung his eyes and blurred his vision. Reuben tried to blink them clear.

That was when he heard the breathing.

Faint, so faint that he almost couldn't hear it. But it was right in front of him. Reuben felt bile rise in his throat. Now he understood. Now he knew what he had sensed. He was not the only unseen person in the room.

The Smoke was there, too.

Reuben's heart was hammering so loudly he felt sure The Smoke would hear it. His pulse surged in his ears. He could no longer hear the breathing. But he could smell sweat and leather, a musky scent of hair oil or lotion, a hint of wintergreen. The smells of a living, breathing man.

Did he know that Reuben was here? Could *he* smell the boy hiding under the cabinet?

Reuben wanted to cry out for help. He struggled to suppress the urge, held his breath. All he could think about was The Smoke not finding him, not getting him. *Don't get me*, he pleaded in his mind. *Don't get me please don't get me don't get me.*

He didn't make himself invisible. Even the infinitesimal sound of the winding key sliding into place might give him away. His chest burned from lack of air. He hadn't been prepared, hadn't gotten a good breath. He'd simply stopped breathing.

Jack grunted again, a sound of mild bafflement, and turned away from the fireplace. Reuben saw his legs moving toward the Counselor's desk. After two steps they seemed slightly clearer, as if Reuben's vision had abruptly sharpened, though in fact his eyes still stung, were still blurry with sweat. No other person would have noticed the subtle change, no one who didn't know what Reuben knew. He had been looking right through The Smoke.

Jack was moving about the room now—not purposefully, as if looking for something, but randomly, as if he were restless. He took a few steps and paused, took another few steps and paused. Reuben was staring hard at where he knew The Smoke had been crouching, so close that Reuben could almost have touched him. But he couldn't tell anymore, couldn't distinguish one area of blurriness from all the rest. He closed his eyes. He was going to have to breathe.

Don't get me.

In the dead-quiet room there came a sudden, preposterously loud eruption of noise—*Clang! Cuckoo!*—and Reuben gasped.

Jack gasped, too, whirling to face the clock on the wall. The little doors clacked shut, and all was silent again.

"For crying out loud," Jack said. He gave a soft chuckle. Laughing at his own reaction. He dropped into his chair again, drummed his fingers on the desk.

Oh, please don't have heard me, Reuben was thinking. His gasp had been small. It was possible that Jack's louder gasp had drowned it out. Maybe. It depended on where The Smoke was in the room now. And Reuben didn't know.

He sat still, breathing as quietly and as little as possible. His head throbbing. Every muscle tensed.

It took him a minute to notice that the odors in the air around him had dissipated. The Smoke had moved away. But to where? He couldn't have left the room. Neither of the doors had opened. Which meant, Reuben suddenly realized, that he must have been in the room the entire time. How had he managed that?

The fireplace. It had to be. He'd been crouching in the fireplace.

Jack seemed to have relaxed. He was still drumming his fingers, and now once again he mused aloud, "Yes, sir, Mr. Counselor, you are one odd bird. You and your peppermints and your ancient suit."

Reuben wanted to scream, *The Smoke is right here in the room with us, Jack! He's right here!*

Then, out of the depths of his alarm and confusion, an understanding began to surface. Why had Jack mentioned the mints? He'd already made a point of mentioning them before, when the Counselor was unwrapping one for himself. For some reason he'd wanted to be sure Reuben knew about them. The mints and the ancient suit. Jack thought these details would mean something to Reuben. And suddenly they did.

The Counselor was the man from the subway.

It seemed crazy, yet it was the only thing that made sense. Reuben had described him to Jack and Penny, everything from his suit and tie right down to his minty breath. No wonder Jack's carefree tone had faltered upon the Counselor's entrance. He must have known it the moment he laid eyes on the man. It had caught him off guard.

Reuben's mind, still furiously making connections, didn't stop with the Counselor and the man on the train, though. He had smelled The Smoke's breath. It was minty. And he'd smelled something else that he thought might be hair oil. The man on the train's hair had been slick with it.

The man on the train was the Counselor.

And the Counselor was The Smoke.

They were all the same man. There was only one man. And now Reuben was the only person in the world who knew it.

By the time the Counselor's voice could be heard on the other side of the door, Reuben had figured some things out. The Counselor—The Smoke—must have a secret way into this room. He left visitors alone here, trying to make them believe they had privacy. Then he crept back in, using the watch, and eavesdropped on them. He hoped that they would make a phone call or talk to themselves. If they did, he picked up information that he could use against them.

Nor was that all. For regardless of whether the unfortunate persons he'd summoned had revealed any secrets, in his guise as the Counselor he might come back in and say to them, "My employer tells me that you admire that cuckoo clock," sending chills down their spines, because not only had they indeed gone over to study the cuckoo clock in the Counselor's absence, but they had also experienced the profoundly unsettling feeling that another, unseen presence was in the room with them.

The stories about The Smoke as a phantom, a spectral creature, thrived for good reason.

Explanations were surging forward in Reuben's mind, crashing and crashing like waves on a beach. He'd been so terrified when he realized that The Smoke was in the room, he'd felt convinced that *he* was the reason for it. But the truth, obviously, was that The Smoke had been spying on Jack. And to do so invisibly meant to do so blindly, which meant that he must have been concentrating very hard on Jack's movements and on his own. He had no idea that Reuben was there, and so almost certainly he hadn't sensed Reuben hiding under the cabinet, hadn't noticed his tiny gasp.

Almost certainly. This was the hope that Reuben clung to as

the door squeaked open. He pulled out on the winding key and vanished, his heart pounding as hard as ever.

The Directions took up their positions. The Smoke, coughing, was settling into his chair again. Reuben understood now that the "allergies" were fabricated, part of the man's ruse. As the Counselor he portrayed himself as impossibly noisy—coughing, sniffing, clearing his throat—and then as The Smoke he crept back into the room in perfect silence. He must use that froggy voice only with his rare visitors. That was why Reuben hadn't recognized it.

At last the Counselor—The Smoke—cleared his throat and said, "I've been authorized to give you a reward, but not according to your arrangements. My men and I will accompany you to the rendezvous. Your associate will deliver the watch directly to me."

"That's out of the question," Jack replied. "For one thing, my contact won't have the watch with him. I'm to leave his share of the reward money in a certain location. After he's collected it, he'll contact me and tell me where the watch is hidden, and I will convey that information to you. He won't do it any other way."

"You said you were to meet him," said The Smoke. "You said that he would leave if you didn't arrive on time."

"I meant that he'd leave if I didn't deliver the money on time. We have a system."

"But he must be there to collect the money."

"He doesn't show his face until after I've gone. I've never laid eyes on him, to tell you the truth. Like I said, he's skittish. If you came with me and tried to speak to him, I guarantee you he'd just slip away. Good luck getting the watch if he does *that*. He won't trust me anymore. I'll never hear from him again."

"You needn't worry about that," The Smoke said. "I will give you the money, and you will deliver it to the specified location. It will seem obvious to your associate that you are alone. He'll suspect nothing."

"What do you mean it will 'seem obvious' that I'm alone?" Jack said. "Will I be alone or won't I?"

"Such questions are no longer your concern," The Smoke said.

"I have to look out for myself, don't I? So let me be clear. I'm not going anywhere with you."

The Smoke laughed his raspy laugh. "You seem to believe that you are controlling the situation, but you are not. So let *me* be clear, young man. In a few moments my men will escort you to my limousine. You will tell the driver the exact location of the rendezvous point, and we'll all ride there together."

"No disrespect, Mr. Faug, but you're crazy if you think I'd actually do that."

"And you are a fool," The Smoke snarled, "if you think you have a choice. Gentlemen!"

There was a sudden rush of movement. The Directions had converged on Jack's chair.

"Wait!" Jack cried. "Okay, okay! I'll do it. I'll take you there. But you have to let me drive my car—that's how he knows I've been there. He looks for my car. If he doesn't see it, he's not going to show up. I'm telling you the truth here. We can still work this out so everyone's happy!"

After a pause, The Smoke said, "Perhaps he's telling the truth. Morrison and Clark, you will accompany me in this man's car. Edwards, you and Quigley will follow us at a distance in the limousine."

"We have to ride separate?" one of the men said.

"You'll survive, Quigley," said The Smoke.

"I know, sir. I'm just not used to it, is all."

"This is great," Jack said. "Really great. I'm glad we're getting this worked out. The one problem is that if my contact sees someone in the car with me—"

"Your vehicle's windows are quite dark," The Smoke interrupted.

"Well, that's true," Jack admitted. "I hadn't thought of that. Funny, I didn't realize that you'd even seen my car."

"There are a great many things you don't realize. Now tell me, what is your rendezvous point?"

"Burlington Plaza," said Jack without hesitation. He must have been anticipating the question. "In the little park just to the side of it. I don't know if you know that neighborhood, but—"

"I know it," The Smoke said. "It's all the way across the city."

"Yeah, that's kind of why I was in a hurry. I hope you don't mind if I drive fast."

"Take him outside and wait," The Smoke said. "Do not let him near his car until I've joined you."

"Easy, easy," Jack said as the men hustled him out. "I'm fragile, boys. Don't forget the money, Mr. Faug!" The door closed behind them.

The Smoke picked up the phone. "I want every group to proceed at once to the neighborhood of Burlington. Yes, every group. Form a perimeter. Be prepared to act quickly upon further instructions." He slammed the phone down.

"Oh my goodness!" The Smoke said, and let out a ridiculous, childlike giggle. "Oh my dear!"

The opposite door of the office opened with its telltale squeak, and a moment later Reuben heard a similar squeak from another door somewhere beyond it. He pushed in on the winding key and reappeared.

The opposite door had been left open. Reuben crawled out from beneath the cabinet and went over to peer through the narrow crack on the door's hinged side. Beyond it was a simple parlor with four chairs and a coffee table. Across the parlor another door had been left wide open, revealing a long, dim hallway with wooden floors and candle sconces arrayed along the walls. A side table ran half the length of the hallway, bearing only a single decorative vase. At the near end of the table, The Smoke was kneeling with his back to Reuben, tying his shoe.

As Reuben watched, the man sprang up and, bizarrely, climbed onto the table. He moved silently along it, skirting the vase in the middle, briefly grabbing a candle sconce for balance. He made not a sound. His shoes must be specially padded, Reuben thought. At the end of the table The Smoke jumped down and opened an antique cabinet. He took out a briefcase—presumably full of money—and then something that looked like a tiny black baseball bat, which he slipped up the sleeve of his suit jacket. Closing the cabinet, he climbed back up onto the table.

Reuben vanished, retreating into the corner by the fireplace. He heard the first parlor door close, then the door into the office. The Smoke crossed the room, breathing heavily, and went out into the entranceway. Reuben listened. The front door of the mansion banged shut. Not long after, he heard the distant, familiar sound of Jack's souped-up engine roaring to life. A second car engine started up, less dramatically.

When their sounds began to fade, Reuben reappeared. He ran across the huge entranceway and peered through the dusty windows that flanked the front doors. Jack's car was already disappearing in the distance, followed by the limousine. The mansion gates were closed. There were no Directions in sight.

He was alone.

Reuben sank to his knees. He ran a hand through his hair, which was slick with sweat, and wiped his palm dry on his pants. He took a long, deep breath, released it slowly. After a minute he took from his pocket a large hunk of cheese wrapped in a napkin—it had been the quietest snack he could think of—and with still-trembling fingers, he began to eat. He was trying hard to think. So much had happened so quickly that his mind hadn't been able to keep up.

Jack, though, had definitely been thinking fast. The plan had been for him to leave on his own. He'd done his best under the circumstances—driving his own car, he might at least have some control, some way of escaping. And he was tricky, for sure, much trickier than Reuben would have guessed. But Jack didn't know about that little black club hidden up The Smoke's sleeve, and Reuben had no way to warn him.

Be careful, Jack.

Still, The Smoke was being careful, too, Reuben reminded himself. He didn't want to lose his best chance of getting the other watch. For the moment, Jack represented that chance, and this would be true as long as The Smoke continued to believe in the nonexistent contact. Jack just needed to play his cards right. What was it Penny had said? The Meyers would be incomparable poker players, if only they gambled. Well, Jack was gambling, all right. Reuben could only hope he was good enough.

He stood up again. His heartbeat had returned almost to normal. He was much calmer now. He wasn't nervous to be alone in The Smoke's big, empty mansion. It actually felt familiar. How many hours had he whiled away exploring abandoned buildings in the Lower Downs? More than he could count. And now he had the strange feeling that what he'd been doing—all those hours, in all those buildings—was practicing.

The more he thought about it, the more Reuben began to feel excited. He'd come here hoping to find some clue that would lead them to The Smoke. And what had happened? He'd figured out The Smoke's ruse! The most powerful, feared person in New Umbra was, after all, only a man with some secrets, a man playing tricks no one knew about. No one except Reuben. And Reuben, of all people, knew how to stop him.

❧

The giant fireplace had been swept perfectly clean. Not even the faintest crackle of grit sounded beneath his shoe as Reuben stepped over the fender onto its stone floor. He looked back out into the office with a certain grim appreciation. The doors squeaked, the chairs groaned, the cuckoo clock ticked. But the floor of the fireplace was pristine, and the floor of the office was carpeted. All so that The Smoke could better observe the movements of his unsuspecting visitors without being detected himself.

"Tricky," Reuben whispered. He moved into the shadowy recesses of the deep fireplace. In the back right corner he found a dark opening, tall and wide enough for a man turned sideways to pass through. Yet it had been impossible to see from beyond the fireplace fender; the darkness and the angle of the wall prevented it.

"*Very* tricky," Reuben muttered, and slipped through the opening into the narrow passage beyond.

A half-dozen steps took him to a heavy velvet curtain. In the darkness behind it he found a closed door. He thought a moment. Yes. The curtain was there to muffle the sound and to keep any possible light from entering the passageway when the door was opened. Reuben opened it now—in contrast to the others, its hinges were well oiled, and it swung open soundlessly—and stepped into the room beyond. This proved to be a small study, dimly lit by a high, dusty window with moth-eaten curtains.

Reuben's gaze passed quickly over the cluttered desk, the upholstered chair, the filing cabinet, the bookcase. It was the walls that his eyes were drawn to. They were covered from floor to ceiling with maps—and the maps themselves were marked, every square inch of them, with penciled notes. There was enough tiny writing on them to fill a book, maybe more than one. Reuben took a close look at the nearest one. It was a map of Westmont, this very neighborhood. The other maps turned out to be of neighborhoods, too.

When Reuben realized what it all meant, he found himself averting his gaze, unwilling to look at the maps anymore. It

It was the walls that his eyes were drawn to.

was staggering. The work of more years than Reuben had been alive. Every scribbled *no* or *Check the roof* or *Return by moonlight*, every heavily scrawled *X*, every *Try again in fair weather*, every penciled date and time, was the result of countless hours spent searching the streets and alleys of New Umbra. Hours that became days, which became weeks, then months, then years. Then decades.

The Smoke truly had spent his entire life looking for the other watch. Reuben could hardly bear to think about it.

He stepped to the desk, upon which were scattered several loose stacks of envelopes. The envelopes all bore postmarks from other cities. Several had been opened, their letters unfolded and spread out on the desk. Reuben bent over them, squinting in the meager light. He didn't turn on the desk lamp. He didn't want to touch anything if he could help it.

Skimming to the body of the first letter, he read:

> *As usual, Mr. Faug, I write to report that no watch of your description has appeared this season, nor even any rumor of such a watch among our city's dealers and collectors. As always, however, I will remain alert and vigilant, not to mention grateful for your generous compensations.*

The other letters were all the same. Reuben wondered how much money The Smoke had spent over the years in search of the other watch. Vast sums, no doubt. What a waste. The Smoke had guessed correctly that the watch had never left the city, and it was here that he had concentrated most of his efforts. But not all of them. The man was nothing if not thorough.

Yet he had failed to find the watch, and Reuben had found it instead. With a small smile, he reached into his sweatshirt pocket and gave the watch a gentle squeeze.

"Come on," he whispered, surprising himself, for he realized that he was speaking to the watch. As if it were a tiny pet in his pocket. Or a friend. It was a strange thing to have done, and yet Reuben felt he understood it. He and the watch shared a secret. They worked together. Was it any wonder that Reuben thought of it as a sort of partner?

"Well, maybe," he admitted, and then he had to admit that talking to himself wasn't much better. He resolved to stop doing both.

The study's other door opened onto the parlor that Reuben had glimpsed earlier. He recognized the four chairs and the coffee table. An antique lamp stood in the corner, its bulb still burning. To his left was the door that opened onto the hallway with the long table, to his right the office door through which he had spied on The Smoke. In the opposite wall was the half-open door of a little bathroom—which reminded Reuben, instantly and urgently, that he needed to go.

He went as fast as he could, then washed his hands and drank thirstily from the tap. He used a dingy hand towel to dry the sink, which had been dry to begin with, and hung the towel back exactly as it had been. He left the door half-open.

There wasn't much to see in the parlor. It was just a place where the Directions had to wait while their employer, unbeknownst to them, was slipping out the back door of his study, sneaking invisibly into the fireplace to begin his spying. Reuben glanced at the magazines on the table and wondered if the Directions got bored, or if working directly for The Smoke's eccentric representative kept them too nervous to feel anything else. Either way, it seemed like a bad job.

Reuben opened the door to the hallway and stood uncertainly on the threshold. Weak light flickered in the candle sconces, which held not actual wax candles but artificial ones with flame-shaped bulbs. He took a step into the hallway and stopped again. Why had The Smoke gotten up on the table? He studied the dark wooden floor. It looked sturdy enough, not rotted out anywhere, as far as he could tell.

Reuben climbed up onto the table. It didn't budge or sway as he would have expected it to, not even a little bit. He had climbed onto enough tables to find this odd. It must be secured to the floor or the wall, he thought. But why? He walked carefully, watching his feet. The wood beneath them was worn and scuffed, in distinct contrast with the table's dark outer edges. When he came to the vase, he saw that the worn wood veered around it, just as The Smoke had done.

That's when he understood. He was following a path, the result of hundreds, even thousands, of crossings. The Smoke *always* walked down the hallway on this table. That was why he'd made it so secure.

Reuben was instantly anxious about losing his balance. He might have been walking along that ledge high above the alley rather than on a waist-high table in a hallway. What was wrong with the floor? Did The Smoke just have some sort of phobia? Or would something truly bad happen if Reuben fell off the table?

He was treading carefully, with no need to grab a candle sconce for balance as The Smoke had done. The Smoke had been trotting along, in a hurry, yes, but also with the ease of long habit. Reuben peered at the candle sconce above the vase. It was made of dark iron and firmly screwed into the wall. He gave it a tug. Solid as a rock, like the table.

He moved on to the end of the table and got down exactly where The Smoke had. He knelt, facing back the way he'd come, and studied the floor closely. It seemed normal enough, with regularly spaced nails and dusty seams between the floorboards. He noticed that he had the watch out, holding it before him like a candle, as if it would give better light. In his nervousness he'd brought it out without thinking. He inched forward and pushed down on the floor with his left hand. It made a creaking sound, but nothing more.

He shuffled forward on his knees and tried again, pressing down with his left hand, gently at first, then with more pressure. Again nothing. Reuben felt the stirrings of relief. Maybe The Smoke really did have a phobia. Something about long stretches of floor, or of tables falling over on him as he walked past. Reuben reached out a little farther and pressed down again.

The floor shot away so easily beneath his hand, offering no resistance at all, it was as if he'd tried to balance himself on the surface of water. He plunged forward, his elbows scraping on the edge of where solid floor met nothingness. His belly and chest struck the floor, and with a cry of terror Reuben writhed backward, getting his elbows back up onto the floorboards beneath him just as he sensed something coming down from above.

Later he would understand that the trapdoor was a rectangular section of floor that revolved around a central point, like a waterwheel. But in that moment all he knew was that something a few feet ahead of him had reared up and was bearing down on him. He wormed backward fast enough to avoid getting clubbed on the head by the spinning planks. But his hands—his hands were still out in front of him, suspended over blackness, and the descending floorboards struck them both, hard, at the back of the wrists.

Reuben cried out again, this time in pain, and felt himself let go of the watch. He heard it strike metal and skitter downward with a scraping sound, passing along a chute of some kind into the depths below the floor. The sound quickly faded, then stopped.

Wincing, Reuben got up onto his knees again. The section of planking had rebounded off his wrists and was drifting slowly upward before him like the near end of a seesaw. He grabbed its edge, holding it steady, and peered into the blackness beneath it. He could see absolutely nothing.

He sat back on his heels, letting go of the wood. The section of floor swung down a little below the edge of the gap, then up a little, then down again, stopping level with the rest of the floor—a horizontal swinging door, flapping to a close. All was still again. Everything looked exactly as it had before.

Reuben held his throbbing hands against him, staring at the floor and trying not to scream. The Smoke's home had bitten him. That's what he was thinking. The Smoke's home had bitten him, and swallowed his watch.

Reuben set out at once in search of a staircase. Beyond the cabinet, the hallway led to a pair of great oak doors, then stretched away to the right. He flipped a light switch, less cautious now in his desperation, and another range of fake candles flickered to life. He moved down the second length of hallway, testing the floor ahead of him with each step, pushing down tentatively with his toes as if gauging the temperature of bathwater.

He was concentrating hard, keeping his bearings. He remembered the once-grand staircase back in the entranceway. Its banisters had been draped with cobwebs like gauze curtains. He was somewhere behind it, he reckoned, when he found the cramped set of servants' stairs leading down. He located the light switch and, clinging to a dusty rail, made his way down dusty steps.

There had been no sound of impact at the end of the watch's scraping descent. Reuben kept imagining it plummeting into a pile of old laundry, perhaps because the only chutes he'd ever heard of in houses were laundry chutes. He so badly wanted to believe that the watch had landed on something soft. What if it was broken? Or what if it was lost for good?

"Don't think that way!" he whispered, then remembered that he'd resolved to stop talking to himself. He thought about The Smoke giggling and saying, "Oh my goodness! Oh my dear!" It would have seemed silly if it hadn't seemed so creepy.

At the bottom of the stairs was a closed door. Reuben braced himself. It is always a nervous business opening closed doors. But this one swung open to reveal nothing more frightening than a furnace, a hot-water tank, and an electrical panel crowded into a dark room that stank of mildew. He reached up and pulled a lightbulb chain.

Now he saw, in the opposite wall, another door.

What Reuben discovered on the far side of that door he did not at first comprehend. When he did, he suddenly understood several other things, too. A man like The Smoke—one of the watch's twin hunters—was not only searching all his life for the other watch. He also spent all his life being afraid that the other hunter would catch him unawares. Was it any wonder that the tension between longing and fear had such strange consequences?

The Smoke had gone to a lot of trouble and expense. Reuben had never been in a jail, but he had seen plenty in old-time westerns he'd watched with his mom. He wondered if The Smoke had taken inspiration from the same movies. The steel bars rose from floor to ceiling. He took hold of two bars and pulled. It would take a bulldozer, he thought.

The homemade jail was much larger than the ones in the old movies. It occupied almost the entire basement. It also had a bizarre feature: a fine black net, the sort used to catch tightrope walkers, had been strung a few feet above the floor. The net spanned the whole jail cell, its lead lines secured to the walls and the steel bars.

And in the middle of the net was Reuben's watch. The sight of it made him wobbly with relief. He held on to the bars to steady himself. It occurred to him that since the first moment he'd found the watch on that alley ledge, he had never been separated from it by so much as a room's length.

Soon Reuben began methodically testing the bars, taking care to pull on every single one of them. He wondered if he should be disturbed that such a weird scene made sense to him. For he had to admit that The Smoke's logic seemed clear enough. If the other hunter came looking to steal The Smoke's watch, he was also giving The Smoke a chance to steal *his*. Even if the intruder didn't have the watch himself but had been hired by someone who did, he might have information that would lead The Smoke to the other watch. That was the reason for the net—to protect this captured intruder, to prevent him from knocking his head on the floor when the chute deposited him in this jail cell. The Smoke needed to be able to question him, after all. To bribe him, threaten him, trick him—whatever it took to get that other watch.

All the steel bars were solid. Reuben glanced around for a key to the metal door, hoping that perhaps it hung on a nail nearby. Finding nothing, he yanked on the door. It rattled in its frame, but he could tell it would never budge. He eyed the bars of the jail cell. He turned sideways, gauging. The Smoke seemed to have thought of everything—except that the hunter might be a child.

This was going to hurt, Reuben thought. Yet there was nothing for it but to try.

And in the middle of the net was Reuben's watch.

His small boy's body squeezed through with little problem. His head was a different matter, though. It felt like his ears would be stripped right off. He whimpered—he couldn't help it—and tears started to his eyes. But then he was through. Just like that, he was in. He grabbed the edge of the taut net and hauled himself up onto it. With his arms at his sides, he rolled to the middle of the net, which sagged only slightly under his weight, and snatched up his watch.

Reuben lay on his back, inspecting it. The metal of the watch felt greasy but was not even scratched; no, it was perfectly intact, including the watch key, which was still inserted. He polished the watch with his sweatshirt, held his breath, and pulled out on the winding key. The room went black. Never had he felt more grateful for darkness. He let his breath out in a rush. Everything was still in order.

Reuben pushed in on the winding key. The ceiling reappeared above him. Now that he knew the watch was fine, he noticed something that, in his anxious hurry, he had overlooked before. There was not just a single opening in the ceiling, but several. At least a dozen. A dozen openings, a dozen chutes. The trapdoor in the hallway had been only the beginning. The entire *mansion* was a trap, designed to capture anyone who trespassed.

Reuben thought of all the dream homes he and his mom had cooked up together. The Smoke had made his own dream home a reality. Only his dream was a very bad one indeed. His was a nightmare.

Reuben crawled back to the bars and got down from the net. He didn't give himself time to dread the pain but forced himself to squeeze through the bars again straightaway, whimpering again as he did so, tears once again springing to his eyes. Afterward he checked his ears, twice, to see if they were bleeding. Even if they had bled, though, he would have been in high spirits.

He had his watch back. He had avoided the first trap, and now he knew about the others. He also knew that The Smoke had designed his homemade jail to hold a full-grown adult. It couldn't hold a child.

Reuben was smiling as he switched off the light and headed back upstairs. He had the advantage. The Smoke was never going to know what hit him.

ℰ

Reuben was looking for two things. The first was a safe. People who lived in mansions always had safes, at least in the movies. What better place for The Smoke to keep his watch when he wasn't using it? If Reuben could find the safe, he might also be able to find a hiding place nearby, a vantage point from which to spy on The Smoke as he entered the combination.

The other thing Reuben was looking for was a bathtub. The Smoke surely put the watch somewhere safe and dry when he bathed. Was it too much to hope for an antechamber, a little room outside the bathroom proper, where The Smoke might leave the watch temporarily unguarded?

Reuben started with the cabinet in the first hallway. It did not contain a safe. There was a very old pair of soft-soled black shoes, a worn black overcoat, and two hooks. One of the hooks was empty. Hanging by a short strap from the other one was another miniature billy club, wrapped in black electrical tape, like the one Reuben had seen The Smoke put up his sleeve. He wondered how many night watchmen had awakened with headaches, with knots on the backs of their heads, to discover that the bank vault was empty or the jewelry store cleaned out. Or how many perceived enemies of The Smoke had suffered similar fates in their own homes, waking to a mystery and a note of warning.

But such things would have happened many years ago,

Reuben realized. The Smoke had long since run the city now. He no longer needed to steal paintings from museums or sneak into the homes of his enemies. He had the city under his thumb. All he had to do was keep up his weird charade as the Counselor. The Directions brought him whatever money he needed. He could spend all his time trying to find the other watch. And looking out for the other hunter.

The cabinet doors had not been perfectly closed. Reuben was careful to leave them exactly as he'd found them. Now that he thought about it, the cabinet had been an unlikely place to find a safe. If he had a safe of his own, and he kept his watch in it, where would he want that safe to be? Somewhere close to him. A room that he spent most of his time in. His bedroom.

That, really, was where he should begin his search. The Smoke's bedroom. Reuben didn't have time to inspect every nook and cranny in this whole mansion. He needed to be smart, check the most likely places first.

The great oak doors at the end of the hallway opened onto a long, narrow dining room. Dusty paintings lined the walls. A dusty grandfather clock stood in the corner, not ticking. The beautiful old table, as dusty as everything else, was surrounded by beautiful dusty chairs. From the doorway, Reuben could just barely make it all out, with the light from the hall seeping in around him and casting his faint shadow on the floor. Should he cross the room on the table? Or was the floor safe? He needed better light to inspect the floorboards.

The switch wasn't by the door, where he would have expected to find it. It was a few feet in along the wall. He almost thought nothing of it. Then he reminded himself that he should be wary of anything out of the ordinary. He tested the floor. It seemed sturdy enough. He peered at the wall and noticed a discolored spot in the plaster where he'd expected the light switch to be. Had the original switch been moved?

Clinging to the doorframe, Reuben leaned into the room, his arm outstretched. He flipped the switch and quickly pulled back. A few lights flickered on in the chandelier over the dining room table. Nothing else happened. He was about to step into the room when he heard a barely discernible whirring sound, accompanied by an intermittent clicking, as if there were beetles under the floorboards.

Directly beneath the light switch, a trapdoor fell open with a bang. Reuben gaped at the opening in the floor, his pulse racing. He shook his head, first in amazement, then with a rising sense of—well, what exactly *was* he feeling? Joy? If not joy, then something close to it. A kind of amused thrill. This was like a big game, and The Smoke was losing. The trapdoor needed maintenance. There should have been no delay between the throwing of the switch and the opening of the door.

But even if Reuben had fallen through, even if he had plummeted down the chute and into The Smoke's homemade dungeon, he could have squeezed out through those bars again, just as he'd already done. The traps were scary, but they posed no real danger to him. He even wondered if sliding down one of the chutes might not be fun.

He leaned in and threw the switch again. Gears clanked loudly as the trapdoor rose back into place. No, the only thing Reuben had to worry about now was time. The mansion was big, and his cautious exploration would be slow. He'd better not waste a moment.

Beyond the dining room lay another hallway lit by fake candles in sconces. He had decided earlier that the candles' weak, flickering light helped mask irregularities in the floorboards. But in this hallway not much of the wooden floor was visible. A faded carpet runner depicting scenes of an old English fox hunt ran the length of it, all the way to another set of grand old doors. There were also a couple of doors opening off the hallway to the left and right. No long table, just a few odd pieces of furniture here and there—a simple straight-backed wooden chair; a low set of shelves displaying china plates on stands; a larger, upholstered chair; and a wooden footstool that looked as if it went with the chair but had been moved away from it.

Reuben didn't trust the carpet runner. It could easily cover a hole in the floor. To walk on either side would be difficult, though, because of the furniture. He tested the floor near the doorway, found it solid, and made his way over to the wooden chair. Its seat was scuffed and worn. He tried to move it. The chair didn't budge. It was nailed to the floor.

Once he was standing on the chair, Reuben thought he understood. The low shelves displaying china plates were only a few feet away. The plates were all on the lower shelves. The top of the shelves was empty, and only slightly higher than the chair. An easy jump. But what if one of the plates fell off and broke? Hiding the pieces would do no good, for The Smoke would surely notice if a plate was missing. They were a warning system in disguise, Reuben thought, a way of knowing if an intruder had passed down this hallway.

But if that was true, then how was he to proceed? He could see no safe way to do so. Reuben considered, then considered some more, and then thought, *They're meant to put you off the track, to make you try a different path.* It seemed crazy, but it was the only thing that made sense to him.

He jumped.

He landed on top of the shelves as lightly as possible. A heavier landing wouldn't have mattered, though: the shelves didn't even tremble. Nor did the china plates. He knelt down to get a better look at them. He even reached and tried to take one from its stand, without success. The plates were all attached to their stands, and the stands were secured to the shelves. Reuben had to admit it was a clever idea.

He shouldn't have touched that plate, though. What if he'd been wrong? He'd done it without thinking, confident of what to expect. But it had been an unnecessary risk. He had more than enough necessary risks to take without adding unnecessary ones to the list. Next time he would be more careful.

From the shelves, Reuben had to leap across the runner to the big upholstered chair, whose springs squeaked beneath his weight. Now he could see through an open doorway opposite him into a kitchen. He saw a refrigerator, a sink, part of a counter. He moved on, jumping to the footstool, which almost certainly would have tipped over if it hadn't been nailed down. Now he was positioned outside the other doorway, this one opening onto a library full of armchairs and side tables, with bookshelves built into the walls. He was curious about what books he'd find on those shelves, but he resisted his impulse to go and see. The room had trap written all over it. No way.

Reuben got down from the footstool. Avoiding the carpet runner and testing the floor with every step, he made his way over to the grand doors at the end of the hall. They were made of a beautiful dark wood, almost black. Their brass knobs were tarnished, though, and almost black themselves. He knelt and peered through a keyhole. He could make out only a sense of open space, faintly lit as if by sunlight from windows.

He turned one of the knobs and pushed gently. The door swung open. Reuben stood a long time in the doorway, taking it all in.

The ballroom was easily the largest room he'd ever seen, even bigger than his school gymnasium. Shafts of light from very high, very dirty windows slanted down through the vast empty space, illuminating swirls of dust motes that Reuben had stirred up with the opening of the door. Two enormous chandeliers hung from a ceiling marred by great peeling strips of plaster and paint. In the far corner of the ballroom stood a dusty grand piano. In the nearer corner, off to Reuben's left, was an old bar from which drinks had once been served, the tall shelves behind it still bearing an array of bottles that, although of widely varying shapes and sizes, all wore the same uniform shade of gray, the accumulation of years' worth of dust. Projecting outward from the wall on the right was a balcony from which, once upon a time, high-society guests could gaze down upon the dancers below.

All of which seemed normal enough, as far as abandoned ballrooms went. What did *not* look normal—what in fact looked downright bizarre—was the fireman's pole. Descending from the ceiling high above, it passed within a few feet of the balcony and ended in a pile of dingy pillows on the ballroom floor. Reuben was in awe. He had always dreamed of having a fireman's pole, had almost always included one in his designs for a dream home.

Reuben approached the pole, testing with his toes as he went. The ballroom floor was made of a dark tan-colored wood, which looked still to be in good condition. It wasn't even dusty, he noticed, and with a quick curious glance around, he spotted a warehouse broom in the shadows beneath the balcony. The wall and the doors under there were lined, Reuben could see, with mounds of dirt and broken plaster. Evidently, The Smoke found it desirable to sweep the ballroom floor, but he found no use for a dustpan. Hard to blame him for that, Reuben thought. Who liked using a dustpan? Still, he wondered why The Smoke bothered to sweep in here at all. There seemed to be no accounting for the man's eccentricities.

The pillows piled around the fireman's pole numbered at least twenty, and they were a motley assortment—some with pillowcases, some without, some meant for sleeping on, some smaller and decorative. At the base of the pile were a few big couch cushions, their zippered edges poking out. Reuben looked up at the balcony. He imagined himself up there, climbing over the low wrought-iron railing. It would be an easy jump to the pole, little more than a giant step. The balcony wasn't so high, perhaps fifteen feet; the pillows seemed unnecessary. Then again, if you lost your grip on the pole, you'd be glad for them. Perhaps The Smoke had learned that the hard way.

Reuben stepped on a couch cushion and balanced against the pillow pile to touch the pole. The metal was covered in a thin film of grease. He'd been thinking of climbing it, seeing if he could reach the balcony. So much for that. The pole was unclimbable, a one-way route only.

He took care stepping off the couch cushion, not wanting to disturb the arrangement of pillows. Only then did he notice the rope ladder. From the doorway, the dangling ropes had appeared to be part of the decorative fluting on one of the balcony's support columns. Reuben frowned, disconcerted not to have realized his mistake sooner. He would have liked to blame the general gloom, but the truth, he knew, was that he'd been too distracted by the fireman's pole.

And now a rope ladder.

He stared at it, his frown deepening. Why didn't The Smoke use the stairs? There had to be a second-floor entrance to the balcony, so why not use it?

Because you can't climb stairs and then pull them up after you, Reuben thought, and he knew at once that he was right. If you did that with the rope ladder, and if you'd booby-trapped the stairs and boarded up the balcony doors, you'd be safely out of reach of stealthy intruders, like a bird secure in its nest.

In this entire gigantic mansion, The Smoke made his home on the balcony of an abandoned ballroom. That was where he lived.

Reuben began to quiver with excitement. The fireman's pole was all but forgotten now. He was close. He was very close. He extended a foot toward the ladder, tested the floor, put his weight on it. Extended the other foot, did the same. Cautiously he proceeded, scanning the floor with each step. Just when he reached the bottom of the ladder, the floor creaked beneath his foot, and he froze. He stepped back, the floor creaking again when he took his weight from it.

It might be nothing. In fact, Reuben thought, it was *probably* nothing. The Smoke had stepped onto that part of the floor every day for years. Little wonder there should be a loose floorboard. And it had borne his weight, hadn't it? He waited, listening for any unusual sounds, then stepped carefully forward again. The creak sounded again. The floor held. It was nothing.

Reuben gazed up along the lines of the ladder. The ropes appeared to be in good shape. Why, then, did he feel so uneasy? Unlike the trapdoors, there was nothing hidden about the rope ladder. On the contrary, it called attention to itself. It wasn't a secret. It was simply the way The Smoke got up to the balcony. Some things simply couldn't be hidden.

Reuben reached out to one of the rope rungs. His hand hovered over it. *Couldn't* the rope ladder have been hidden, though? At least mostly? He thought about the window blinds in his apartment, how they could be drawn down or raised up with a slender cord. If it had been him, he would have arranged something like that with the rope ladder. A single dangling cord, especially a transparent one like fishing line, might well go unnoticed. Reuben lowered his hand to his side. Something wasn't right.

If The Smoke used the rope ladder, why did he need the fireman's pole? Just because it was faster? Just for fun? Maybe. But maybe there was another reason, too.

Reuben backed away from the ladder. He wanted to get a better look at the balcony if he could. But as he turned and walked carefully out toward the middle of the ballroom, it was the floor that confirmed his misgivings.

Beginning just to the side of the rope ladder, a narrow, roughly rectangular span of scarred wood ran all the way out to where Reuben had stopped. It seemed much like the path he had followed along the tabletop, but here the wood wasn't just worn—the varnish was completely ruined, the grains of the wood battered and chipped and scraped. It was as if someone had taken a hammer to it. The rest of the floor looked pristine in comparison. Reuben had no idea what to make of it.

He scanned the ballroom again. Huge faded tapestries hung beneath the high windows, obscuring much of the wall. One of them, near the bar in the corner, did not seem to hang quite flat. Reuben went over for a closer look. A tall metal ladder had been stowed behind it, propped against the wall. Draped over one of the lower rungs was, of all things, a long blue cotton robe.

Reuben held the robe out in front of him by the shoulders, wondering. The material felt weirdly greasy beneath his fingers. He lowered the robe and peered across the ballroom at the fireman's pole—and everything came together. He got it.

Each night The Smoke climbed up to the balcony using this metal ladder. Then he kicked it away from the railing so that no one could sneak up on him. The ladder banging down every night was what had scarred the ballroom floor. Sure, an intruder could set it up again, but not without making considerable noise, not with a metal ladder like this. The Smoke would have plenty of warning if anyone tried that.

The rope ladder had to be a trap, then. No question about it. As for the robe—Reuben eyed the greasy garment again. Yes. Every morning The Smoke slipped this robe on over his clothes before zipping down the fireman's pole. At the bottom he set the pillows back in place, then took off the robe and hid it behind the tapestry, along with the ladder. Naturally, any trespassers sneaking into the ballroom during the day would be drawn to the rope ladder, and thus into The Smoke's trap.

Not Reuben, though. He found himself grinning again. He'd put all the pieces of the puzzle together.

The ladder was chained and padlocked to a bracket in the wall, but this didn't discourage Reuben. On the contrary, he was glad. That the ladder couldn't be used by his enemy must give The Smoke all the more reason to feel confident. It was a false confidence now, though, for Reuben already knew how he was going to reach the balcony, and he already had a plan.

REUBEN THE THIEF

The first part was even easier than Reuben had expected. The distance between the wall beneath the balcony and the nearest marble support column was perfect. His feet braced against the wall, his hands pressed against the column, he began to make his way up. Right hand, left hand. Right foot, left foot. Six inches at a time. He was careful but quick, remembering how he had tired that day in the alley. It seemed strangely perfect that he should acquire the second watch in the same way he had found the first one. More than perfect—fated. Destined. That's how it felt to Reuben, as if he had been *supposed* to find the first watch and then, having discovered its secret, use it to reclaim its twin from The Smoke.

Fated or not, the next part of his climb was tricky. At the top of the column, the marble flared outward in a decorative scroll that Reuben found difficult to navigate with his hands. By the time he'd worked himself into position, with his back against the underside of the balcony edge, he was sweating heavily. Now he had to try to swing a hand up and grab the bottom of the iron railing above him. If he missed, he would fall, as simple as that.

Yet he would only get weaker the longer he hesitated. And so, with a quick-whispered "One two *three!*" Reuben reached up as high as he could—and felt, just as his other hand slipped free, his fingers touch metal.

In the next instant Reuben's legs were swinging beneath him as he clung to the bottom of the railing. He used their momentum to his advantage, swinging them back and forth like the pendulum in a grandfather clock, until with one straining stretch he got a foot up onto the balcony edge. After that it was easy again. A few seconds later he was up over the railing, standing safely on the balcony, breathing hard.

Reuben checked his watch, put it away again, and looked around. As he'd predicted, the balcony doors had been boarded over. A small bed, sloppily made, stood at the back, its headboard against the wall. Beside it was a nightstand. There was also an antique wardrobe, a dressing table, and a chest of drawers.

And yet, despite the furniture, The Smoke's balcony home seemed empty to Reuben. It took him a minute to understand why: there were no pictures. No photographs hanging on the wall, none standing in frames. He wondered if The Smoke had never cared about anyone, or if he had once cared too much and didn't wish to be reminded. Whatever the case, he seemed to be living the loneliest existence imaginable.

Reuben found himself thinking of the people he cared about—his mom, and Mrs. Genevieve, and Penny and Jack—and imagined having none of them. Having nobody. It was awful even to contemplate.

He knelt to inspect the rope ladder. Its ends were not secured to the railing but instead to levers on a control box, painted black to resemble the wrought iron. Wires stretched across the tile floor of the balcony, disappearing into a drilled hole in the wall. No doubt they connected with a triggering device beneath the ballroom floor. If Reuben had put any weight on the rope ladder, he would have pulled the levers and sprung the trap beneath him. The levers themselves were probably designed to break clean off the box, so that clinging to the ladder would have done him no good.

Reuben wondered if The Smoke had been some sort of handyman in his early life, in his time before the watch. Or had he learned how to do all these things since? The amount of work he must have put into designing and building the trapdoors, the chutes, the jail cell—it was astonishing.

Reuben stooped to check under the bed. Nothing but dust bunnies. He went to the nightstand, and there he found exactly what he'd been looking for. He hadn't known what it would look like, but this was clearly it: a pedestal supporting a red velvet cushion, in the center of which was a round indentation formed, Reuben knew, from all the nights—years and years of nights—of bearing the weight of The Smoke's most prized possession.

Of course. The pedestal made more sense than a safe. The Smoke wanted his watch always to be at hand. He needed to be able to use it at a moment's notice, not have to fiddle with a combination lock. If The Smoke woke to the sound of an intruder, he could simply reach over and vanish, as quick as that.

It was just what Reuben would have done himself. Withdrawing the watch from his pocket, he lowered it, ever so gently, into the impression in the velvet. A perfect fit. It looked beautiful there, too, like jewelry on display. Beside the pedestal on the nightstand was a lamp, and Reuben imagined that The Smoke had spent countless evenings lying on his bed, gazing at his watch, admiring how it gleamed in the lamplight.

When he lifted the watch from the pedestal, so carefully that it made not the faintest sound, Reuben imagined it was not his own watch he was taking but The Smoke's. Flushed with excitement, he tucked it away.

He had yet to be wrong about anything. He'd known that the balcony was The Smoke's home. He'd known that the rope ladder was a trap. He'd expected the doors that had once led onto the balcony to be closed off, and sure enough, they were completely boarded over. The Smoke was taking no chances. It would be impossible for anyone to sneak onto the balcony while he slept.

But Reuben wouldn't have to. No, when The Smoke climbed up to his balcony and kicked the ladder away, Reuben would already be up here, invisible, waiting.

⌒

It shouldn't be difficult to pull off. In fact, it would almost be easy.

He would hide under the bed, invisible when necessary, until The Smoke fell asleep. Then he would creep out and steal the watch. He would move stealthily to the railing, stealthily climb it. If anything went wrong, if at any point The Smoke woke up, Reuben would forget stealth and make a dash for it. Either way, The Smoke would probably hear him when he hit the fireman's pole, so whatever happened before then, his plan once he landed on the pillows was to run like mad.

At that point Reuben would have both watches. The only advantage left to The Smoke would be his knowledge of the mansion. He knew the way out, and he had years of practice navigating the traps. What Reuben needed to do now, therefore, was find a different way out, some way The Smoke wouldn't expect.

Let the poor desperate villain go chasing off in the wrong direction as Reuben disappeared and went out his own way.

Before he left the balcony, Reuben practiced crawling out from under the bed, stealing the watch, and making his way to the railing. He did it several times, smoothly and quietly. Satisfied, he moved on to contemplate the jump to the fireman's pole. He couldn't do it with the watches in his hands, and in his front pockets they might bang against the pole when he jumped on. Pulling his arms out of their sleeves, Reuben shifted his sweatshirt around until the front pockets were in back. Yes, that would work. He felt the comforting pressure of his watch there as he climbed over the railing.

Sliding down the pole was every bit as thrilling as Reuben had expected. Only the bottom ten feet had been greased, and so when he hopped from the balcony, he was able to get a good grip, hugging the pole like a koala bear on a eucalyptus trunk. He slid slowly at first, then hit the greased part and shot down to the pillows in a blink. He took special care in replacing the pillows he'd dislodged. If the pile wasn't exactly as it had been before, it was very close. Yet another benefit of his well-trained memory.

Now to find his exit.

Reuben nibbled the last of his cheese, considering. The ground floor was riddled with The Smoke's traps, but what about upstairs? The prospect of someone breaking in through a second-story window was so unlikely, The Smoke probably hadn't taken similar precautions up there. Besides, to get at The Smoke's watch, the hunter would have to come downstairs anyway, where all the traps were.

An escape route, a window, and a way down—that was what Reuben needed to find, and quickly. There was no telling when The Smoke would return. Jack would do his best to stall, to give Reuben time to snoop, but he also had to make his own getaway.

Jack would have to take his best opportunity, and who knew what would happen then?

Reuben worked fast. Keeping an eye out for traps, he found the staircase that used to lead to the balcony (it proved not to be booby-trapped) and soon was exploring the mansion's second floor—a wasteland of dusty, cobwebby rooms. Time-faded paintings hung on the walls. Mice scurried out of view beneath once-beautiful old furniture. Most of the lights had long since burned out. The rooms and hallways were faintly lit by sunlight filtering through filthy windows and rotted lace curtains.

In one bedroom, Reuben discovered a chaos of leftover construction materials spread out over the floor and furniture—sheet metal, old lumber, wires and cables and rope, buckets full of nuts and bolts, nails and ball bearings—all the evidence of The Smoke's downstairs trap-building, now abandoned, dust-coated and forgotten. Reuben hefted a coil of rope over his shoulder and left the room shaking his head.

Of all the rooms, only one stood empty, the one nearest the stairs behind the balcony. This was clearly the room from which the Smoke had scavenged his furniture: the wooden floors still bore deep scratches, the telltale tracks of heavy objects that had been dragged. The man wasn't finicky. He'd taken what he needed from the most convenient room to the balcony. And then he had boarded up his doors.

Such a strange, strange man. Reuben shifted the coil of rope on his shoulders and moved on, thinking again about that little black club. It seemed like ages since he'd watched the Smoke hiding it up his sleeve. He'd been trying not to think about it, about what might happen to Jack. He chose to believe that Jack would find a way to escape. Perhaps he'd already done so. Perhaps even now he was talking with Penny and Mrs. Genevieve, all of them worrying about Reuben, wondering when he would return.

The last bedroom on that hallway had a window overlooking

the grounds behind the mansion, and in the property's perimeter wall Reuben spied one of the holes he'd noticed earlier. Unlike some of the others, this one was not entirely choked with brambles but was instead only partly obscured by overgrown rosebushes. From the mansion to that hole was a straight shot. Reuben could manage it easily, even while invisible.

The only trick was getting down. With a bit of straining, he confirmed that the window could be opened. Squinting in the sunlight, he could make out distant rooftops, glimpses of homes beyond the trees of the neighborhood. He spotted the church spire, which oriented him in the direction of the park. There was not a soul in sight. He looked at the ground, fifteen feet or so below. He would come down behind a wall of overgrown shrubs, but he could see a place where the growth was thin enough for him to press through.

Yes, this would be his escape route. The fact that it was the last bedroom on the hallway made it even better. He wouldn't have to count doors in the darkness, wouldn't dart into the wrong room by mistake. Just one straightforward pell-mell flight to the end of the hall, and here he'd be. From the fireman's pole to this spot—Reuben figured he could make it in under thirty seconds. Maybe even faster. The Smoke might still be rubbing his groggy eyes, fumbling for the switch on his lamp, and Reuben would be long gone.

He let the thin curtain fall over the window again. He tied one end of the rope securely to the leg of the canopy bed, hiding the coil under the bed skirt. Then he retraced his steps along the hallway and went downstairs.

అ

During all this time, Reuben had not allowed himself to consider the last remaining question, a critical element of his plan.

He'd told himself he needed to focus on the task at hand. But now that he had his escape route, now that he had his plan, the question had to be answered: *When are you going to do this?* And now that he thought about it, Reuben understood why he hadn't wanted to do so sooner.

Because the answer was today. Right now.

The answer was now.

Reuben put a hand to his head. He broke out in a sweat.

Never again would he have such a good opportunity. He was already inside the mansion, and The Smoke believed that the second watch was elsewhere, in the hands of a man who didn't know its secrets but only wanted money for it. His wariness and suspicion, his fear of a twin hunter in the night, would be at their lowest.

Reuben's stomach was in knots now. Yes, he had to go through with this. When The Smoke returned, Reuben would have to act fast. He would watch from one of the entranceway windows, and at the first glimpse of the limousine, he would race back to the balcony and settle in for his long wait.

Reuben stood in the ballroom, peering up at the balcony with a feeling of anxious resolution. So this was it. From this moment forward he would be carrying out his plan, one way or the other. He took a deep breath. Was he ready? He had to be. *You're the expert*, he thought.

And no sooner had Reuben thought this than all the problems with his plan suddenly exploded in his head like fireworks.

How could he just go back up there and wait until The Smoke went to bed? He needed to call his mom! And what about Penny and Mrs. Genevieve? They would be worried out of their minds! And what about Jack? What if he hadn't gotten away? What should Reuben do then?

Reuben stood frozen in place, horrified by every new thing that occurred to him. He reached behind him and took his watch from the sweatshirt pocket. After gazing at it for a moment, he began to calm down. The simple fact that he could still turn invisible if something went wrong was remarkably reassuring.

He just needed to check in, he decided. Call Mrs. Genevieve. Maybe Jack was already there. Maybe Jack could even call Reuben's mom, put her at ease the way he'd done with Mrs. Genevieve. It could all be figured out. And he could talk to Penny, too. Hearing her voice would shore up his resolve.

Reuben hurried toward the front of the mansion, retracing his furniture-hopping path in the nearest hallway, running through the dining room, scurrying across the long table in the last hallway, and finally arriving in the parlor. He listened a few moments, then darted into the office. He went straight to the desk, put his hand on the phone—and hesitated, suddenly struck by new doubts.

It was an old-fashioned phone with no digital display, but perhaps this was yet another ruse. Perhaps The Smoke had some secret way of knowing when it had been used. Probably he did. Probably he could track the calls that had been made on it. After all, he knew where people called *from*, didn't he? He knew that Jack had called from a pay phone—and now that Reuben thought about it, he understood how The Smoke had known to move his search to the Lower Downs: Reuben had stupidly called him from a pay phone in the library there.

So now, after all that hurrying, Reuben was left to stare at the phone on the desk. Did he dare risk it? How could he not? What else was he supposed to do?

"Oh, you stupid phone!" he whispered, putting his hands to his head.

At that very moment, as if responding angrily to his insult, the phone rang—a loud, jangling ring that sent Reuben leaping back, his nerves jangling to match it. "Oh man," he muttered, shaking his head. The phone continued its angry ringing.

Reuben wiped his brow with his sweatshirt sleeve. He remembered Jack chuckling to himself after the cuckoo clock had startled him. Reuben almost smiled. He would have to tell Jack about this when everything was over. When they'd gotten through it all and everyone was safe and sound, they would surely laugh about it together. First the cuckoo clock, then the phone. What next? he thought as the phone rang and rang. What other simple household sound would suddenly scare the wits out of him?

Even as he thought it, Reuben heard the front door slam.

THE RACE AND THE CHASE

The sound of the door slamming was followed by that of a man running—not walking, *running*—across the entranceway. Reuben, in his panic, instinctively reached toward his belly, his hands searching for the sweatshirt pocket that was no longer there. The phone jangled again, a hideous alarm. He darted forward and scrambled under the cabinet just as the door flew open. The Smoke's shoes flashed by as Reuben fumbled behind him for the watch. He found the winding key and vanished. The ringing phone was cut off mid-jangle.

"Have you found him?" The Smoke's voice snarled into the darkness.

Of course, that was why he'd been running—to pick up the phone before it stopped ringing. And now, despite the fierce buzz of alarm in Reuben's head, a wonderful thought managed to make itself heard: *Jack got away!*

The Smoke, breathing hard, was listening to the person on the phone. "I see," he said after a moment. There was relief in his voice. "Good. No, not now. Are you certain he doesn't know? You're absolutely sure. Then no, not yet. See where he goes, then call me. But if he spots you, take him. Do not risk his getting away again."

Reuben's relief evaporated, replaced by horror. This possibility hadn't occurred to him—Jack, on the run, being followed without realizing it. What if he went to Mrs. Genevieve's shop? They had been supposed to meet at the park unless something went wrong, in which case they would rendezvous at the shop.

This definitely qualified as something going wrong.

The Smoke sighed impatiently. "Our employer already knows who did his duty and who failed," he said. He was speaking in his guise as the Counselor, of course. "But yes, should you happen to succeed in this, I will make a point of commending you. Bear in mind that if you fail, there will be little I can say. Do you understand? Yes, yes, I have no doubt that you will make your best effort. There's no point in saying so. Simply do not fail. I can give you no other advice." The phone slammed down. "Fool," The Smoke muttered.

Reuben's skin tingled painfully, as if he were being stung all over by ants. Just like that, everything had changed. He would have to come back. He had no choice. Right now he had to get out of here, had to warn Penny and Mrs. Genevieve. Everything else would have to come later.

The Smoke flung open the door to the parlor and stalked out. He hadn't taken time to close the door when he stormed in from the entranceway—this was Reuben's chance. He crawled from beneath the cabinet and felt his way out.

He was creeping invisibly across the entranceway when he heard the front door burst open, heard the Directions coming inside, and heard the door close again. The men headed straight for him, arguing in low voices. Reuben skipped sideways, out of their path. This was good. Once they were in the office, it would be easy to get away.

But then The Smoke's voice called out from the office. "Morrison, a word with you."

"Oh man," whispered a troubled voice, presumably Morrison's.

"Good luck," one of the other men muttered.

Morrison entered the office and closed the door behind him.

"Better him than me," said one of the Directions.

"That's real big of you, Quigley."

"Well, I wasn't the one to let the guy go."

"I have a feeling you'd have let go, too, if you got hit like that."

"Tell me again why *you* didn't grab him, Clark?"

Clark sounded nervous. "I was—I was too far away. The guy was quick. And Morrison was in my way."

"Morrison better just hope they bring the guy in."

"They will. They have a tail on his car."

Reuben couldn't leave by the front door. The men would definitely notice a door opening of its own accord. He might get away, but if The Smoke found out he'd been here, he'd never get another shot at executing his plan. Next time The Smoke would be ready for him. Did he dare to wait? He didn't think so. For all he knew, every second counted.

Reuben found the grand staircase and began to mount the steps. Some of them creaked, but the men were still talking and seemed not to hear. Then he was at the top, feeling his way forward into a hallway, out of view of the entranceway. He reappeared at once, glanced around to get his bearings, and took off. Moments later he was raising the window in the bedroom. He dropped the heavy coil of rope behind the shrubs and climbed out.

It was a struggle, and it wasn't quiet, but with the window ledge biting into his knees, Reuben managed to get the window mostly closed. There was nothing he could do about the rope. From a distance, against the backdrop of this enormous building with its myriad details, the rope seemed unlikely to be noticed. It also seemed unlikely that The Smoke and his men would come back here inspecting things at a time when they were so preoccupied with Jack. Reuben hoped so. The rope would give him a way back in.

With his feet braced against the wall, he climbed down. The rope hurt his hands, but Reuben scarcely noticed, and soon he was crouching behind the shrubs. He had seen no one, heard no one approaching. He moved to the spot where the growth was thinnest, fixed the hole in the wall in his mind's eye, and disappeared. He pressed out through the scratching branches into open air, trotting uncertainly over what used to be flower beds but was now more of a weedy lot. When his groping hand closed painfully around a thorny stem, he knew he was close. He flickered into sight, spotted the hole to his left, and vanished again.

Then he was beyond the wall, hurrying invisibly across the street, reappearing behind a tree. He set his eyes on another tree, disappeared again, hurried again. In this way he left the mansion behind. As soon as it was safe to do so, he put the watch away and ran as hard as he could.

Beyond the park and the church was a street lined with shops, a post office, a fire station. He and Jack had driven down it on their way here. Now Reuben hastened along the sidewalk, his chest heaving painfully, until he spotted an old pay phone booth. He got change at a newspaper kiosk, staggered into the phone booth—and stared in disbelief at the little sign taped to the phone: *Out of Order.*

He kicked the side of the phone booth half a dozen times and came out gasping. The man at the newspaper kiosk was looking at Reuben disapprovingly, but Reuben ignored him, already distracted by the sight of a city bus at the corner. He peered desperately at its sign, wishing it would say *Middleton.*

The letters came into focus: *Middleton.*

Reuben blinked in disbelief. He could still do this.

Ten minutes later he was leaping from the bus steps. He was only a few blocks from Mrs. Genevieve's shop. He moved fast, keeping a lookout for Jack's car. He didn't see it. No Directions, either. From the alley across the street he peered toward the shop. The sign in front still said *Closed*, which could be good or bad. Reuben couldn't make out what was going on inside.

He vanished, hurried across the street, and pressed his nose to Mrs. Genevieve's shop window. He reappeared only for an instant, but in that instant he found himself staring directly into Penny's anxious green eyes, not two inches from his own.

Reuben yelped and disappeared. He heard Penny's own startled cry, muted by the glass. Then he heard her running to open the door, heard her stage-whispering his name. "Come in!" she hissed. "The coast is clear!"

He found her arm—it was trembling like his own—and let her lead him back to Mrs. Genevieve's sitting room. "It's Reuben," she announced as she closed the door. "He's right here with me. He nearly gave me a heart attack."

Reuben reappeared. There stood Mrs. Genevieve, looking unnerved as ever by his sudden materialization. Recovering, she grabbed him by the shoulders and squeezed, as if she wanted to compress him like an accordion. As if she wanted to shake him. Instead, she leaned forward and kissed him on the head. "I am so glad," she whispered. Then, evidently overcome, she sat down heavily in a chair.

"Where's Jack?" Penny asked. "What happ—"

"We have to get out of here," Reuben interrupted. "Right now. Mrs. Genevieve, sorry, but please get up."

Mrs. Genevieve looked stricken. "What do you mean?"

"Now, Mrs. Genevieve. Please!" He turned gravely to Penny. "Jack's being followed and doesn't realize it. We need to leave right away. He could be here any minute."

Penny gaped at him, uncomprehending. "They're following him? But how—?"

"No time to explain. We have to go. We—"

Penny's hands disappeared into her hair. "They're *following* him? We have to help him! What should we do?"

Reuben grabbed her elbow. "Listen to what I'm saying, Penny. If Jack shows up and we're still here, it's *over*. Do you see? We'll be trapped. We have to go!"

Mrs. Genevieve had risen shakily to her feet, her face gone pale. "Where will we go?"

"I don't know," Reuben said. "Anywhere. We'll figure something out. Mrs. Genevieve, please, what are you doing?" The watchmaker had opened the door to the bathroom. "Mrs. Genevieve!"

"Give me a moment," Mrs. Genevieve said in a hoarse voice. "I must bring my pills. Only give me a moment." She opened her medicine cabinet, fumbled for her glasses. She was taking deep breaths.

Penny had started to cry. "But can't we help him? Can't we do something?"

"I'll write him a note," Reuben said, casting about for his backpack. He found it and dug out pen and paper. "We'll put it on the counter and leave the door unlocked. I'll tell him he's being followed. He can make a break for it."

"But how will he find us again?"

Reuben had begun to write. He stopped and looked up. That question hadn't occurred to him. "I...I don't know."

Penny's face crumpled. She covered her eyes with her hands and began to sob.

"I'll think of something!" Reuben said, desperate to calm her. But nothing occurred to him. All he could think about was their need to flee. He was gripping the pen so tightly it hurt his fingers, trying to squeeze an answer out of it.

Penny suddenly gasped and looked at him with shining eyes. "Wait! I have it! We don't have to leave. We can put a sign on the door that says *Keep walking, you're being followed*. We'll watch from behind the counter. If he comes, we'll see him read the sign and move on. Then I'll run and tear the sign down. The Directions won't ever see it!"

"And then we can hide out back here," Reuben said, nodding excitedly, "and he'll find some way to contact us when he knows it's safe. Okay, let's do it!" He tore a clean sheet from the notepad and began to write.

Mrs. Genevieve had emerged from the bathroom. "What is this you are saying?"

Penny grabbed her by the hand. "We can stay, but we have to put up a sign to warn Jack! Do you have a roll of tape?"

Mrs. Genevieve, her face awash in relief, squeezed Penny's hand. "Yes, of course!" She moved quickly toward her workshop, was reaching for the knob when the doorbell sounded.

Someone had entered the shop. Even though the sign said the shop was closed.

Penny's eyes were huge. "I forgot to lock the door!" she whispered. "Do you think it's Jack?"

The three of them stood looking at one another, their faces full of dread. They had no idea what to do now. They didn't even know what to hope for.

A light tapping sounded at the door. Then it opened, and in walked Jack, smiling. He saw Reuben and raised his eyebrows. "You're here already? Did you get something good?" His voice was astonishingly casual. He dropped a handful of envelopes onto a side table. "These were in your mail slot, Mrs. Genevieve." He looked around at them. "What is it? What's wrong? Why do you all look so sad to see me?"

It was Penny who recovered first. She rushed to him, saying, "Oh, Jack! Reuben says you're being followed! We were going to warn you! But now I think we have to run!" She looked over at Reuben. "Right? We should run?"

"Right!" Reuben said, snapping to. "We have to get out of here, Jack! Mrs. Genevieve, are you ready? Let's go!"

Jack extended his palm toward Mrs. Genevieve. "It's all right, Mrs. Genevieve, we don't have to go anywhere." He wrapped his arms around Penny and gave her a reassuring hug. "Take it easy, redbird. No one followed me here."

"But that's just it!" Reuben exclaimed. "They said you didn't know you were being followed!"

"Well, they *would* say that," said Jack with a lopsided grin, "because they didn't know I knew. But I did. They followed me all the way to the Southport ferry—which is where I had to ditch my car, unfortunately, but at least I ditched those jokers in the process."

Jack sounded so confident that everyone instantly relaxed, even though no one fully understood him. He told them all to sit down—they were making him nervous, he said, standing there looking ready to bolt.

"For a while I tried to shake them," he explained. He was leaning back against the door, his ankles crossed, his hands in his pockets. "But then I realized that my car's too recognizable, anyway. It's no use to me now, at least until all this is over. So I headed down to the river port and circled around the neighborhood until the next ferry started to board. Then I got in line and drove on board along with a hundred or so other cars, and those guys followed me on."

"But you didn't stay on the ferry," Reuben said.

"My *car* did," Jack said. "And *they* did. But me, no. I got off. Surreptitious-like. Believe me, I've been all eyes since then. Nobody followed me here."

The others were so relieved that for a few minutes they were positively giddy. There was no discussion of what had transpired at the mansion, or of what still lay ahead of them. Instead, they rehashed what had just happened, chattering loudly and laughing at every turn.

"We were so scared!"

"I was trying so hard to think what to write! But I couldn't think of anything! And then Penny—"

"Oh, the look on your face, Mrs. Genevieve, when the doorbell sounded!"

"No, the look on *your* face!"

Jack sat down on the sofa with Penny, grinning as he listened and looked around at them all. Nothing they said could actually be very funny to him—such experiences generally being funny only to those who have shared them—but he was clearly amused by their excited jabbering and laughter.

"And, Reuben," Penny said with a frown and a snicker, "why on earth are you wearing your sweatshirt backward? With the hood in *front*? You look ridiculous!"

Reuben glanced down in surprise. With everything happening so fast, he hadn't thought to turn the sweatshirt around again, despite the awkwardness of having to reach behind him for the watch. He grinned and pulled the hood up over his face. "This is how I wear it!" he said, his voice muffled. "It keeps my nose warm!"

This, too, they all found hilarious, and eventually everyone but Jack was wiping away tears of laughter. And then at last their laughter was spent, and they began to compose themselves.

"Wow," Reuben said, sighing, his arms hanging limply at his sides, "I needed that."

It was true. He felt a million times better. It wasn't just the laughter, though. The way both Mrs. Genevieve and Penny kept looking at him, as if they were so grateful and happy that he was okay, gave Reuben a sense of well-being he couldn't remember having before. What was more, though he'd tried to be brave about the prospect of going through with his plan alone, the relief he felt now made him realize just how scared he'd been. Here in Mrs. Genevieve's sitting room with his friends, with the watch in his pocket and a plan in mind, Reuben was hopeful again.

When the time came for him and Jack to share what they'd found out, Reuben didn't know where to begin, didn't know how to explain to Mrs. Genevieve that he—not Jack—had been the one to sneak into the mansion. He was hoping Jack would take the lead, and indeed it appeared as if Jack was about to speak when Mrs. Genevieve held up both hands.

"Before you begin," she said firmly, "let me ask you to please do me the courtesy of telling the truth. Penny and I spoke a good deal while you were gone. Your sister is an admirable girl," she said with a piercing look at Jack, who instantly caught her meaning.

"But an atrocious liar," he said sheepishly. "Right. I should have guessed."

Penny looked embarrassed but defiant. "It's not like I set *out* to tell her! But it was impossible to keep a secret like that when we were both so worried!"

"I don't blame you a bit, redbird," Jack said mildly, and, inclining his head to Mrs. Genevieve, he said, "I apologize for the fabrication. We didn't want to worry you more than we had to. For the record, I would have liked to do it different myself, but the kid here is running the show."

"I'm sorry, too," Reuben said. "I won't lie to you again. I promise."

Mrs. Genevieve accepted their apologies rather stiffly—she was not at all pleased with the thought of Reuben having taken such a risk—but then, expressing her relief that they were both safe now, she put the subject aside and asked them to proceed with their account.

"You go first," Reuben said.

"Right," Jack said, standing up to face them all. "Well, as the kid here already knows, the first part didn't go particularly well, though I did learn something about the Counselor." He looked at Reuben. "Did you pick up on my hints?"

"He's the man from the subway," Reuben affirmed.

"The creepy one?" Penny cried.

"I'm sure of it," Jack said. "The kid's description of him was pretty perfect. Anyway, that was about all I figured out before he had his thugs manhandle me. He demanded that I lead them to my imaginary rendezvous with my imaginary associate, so I took them all the way across town, to a park I know there.

"I was kind of in a pickle. I had the Counselor and two of his men in my car with me, and two more following in a limousine. I also noticed, driving into the neighborhood, that there were an awful lot of those guys—the Directions—on the streets around there. I got the feeling that the Counselor had made a private call. They were going to set up a perimeter to keep me and my associate from giving them the slip. But here's the thing: these guys aren't pros. It's clear they aren't used to having trouble with people. I guess that's the benefit of having everybody scared to death of your boss. But then when you *do* have trouble, you're completely unprepared."

"How did you get away?" Penny asked, tugging anxiously at her hair, as if Jack hadn't already escaped.

"Well, I'd told them I was supposed to leave the Counselor's briefcase by a particular bench in the middle of the park. But then, just before we got to the park, the Counselor made me stop the car, and he got out. He said he would put the briefcase there himself.

"I was still playing a role, so I had to argue a little, but actually I was thrilled. I knew that with him gone I had my best chance. Anyway, he told his men to keep an eye on me and took off. After that it was fairly easy. I gave it a minute, then fired up the engine and started driving fast. The two guys in the back couldn't believe it—they didn't know what to do. They were yelling at me to stop, but what else could they do? Grab me? Not if they didn't want to crash.

"After a few blocks I slammed on the brakes, jumped out, and started running. Naturally, they jumped out to chase me. When I spun around and ran straight back at them, the first guy was so surprised he got out of my way—I didn't even have to touch him. The other one had been a few steps behind, so he had a second to recover and try to grab me."

"Morrison," Reuben interjected. "That's the one you hit."

Jack looked at him, impressed. "I think that *was* his name, yeah. What, were you there?"

"No, I heard about it afterward."

Mrs. Genevieve and Penny were looking at them expectantly.

"It didn't take much," Jack continued, "just a little pop on the nose. I got back in the car and took off. The limousine was pulling up by that point. Morrison and the other one jumped in and they followed me. The trouble was, every time I managed to shake the limo—which wasn't hard—some other group of Directions on a street corner would spot me. They were all on their radios gabbing it up. Sure enough, here would come the limo, cutting me off at an intersection, and the chase was on again.

"This went on long enough for someone to get the idea of following me in a different car, one I wouldn't recognize. I saw more Directions pointing at my car and talking into their radios, but that limo never showed up again. So I kept my eyes on the mirror until I spotted the tail—a van with tinted windows, probably chock-full of the Counselor's men. I took it on a wild-goose chase, nice and slow, like I didn't realize I was being followed, and finally ended up on the ferry. That's the story. You know the rest."

"Wow," Penny and Reuben said at the same time. They looked at each other. Jack seemed so nonchalant about all of it. He seemed, in fact, to have enjoyed it.

Mrs. Genevieve, for her part, had listened to Jack's account with a pained expression, punctuated with winces. She was tightly gripping the arms of her chair. Reuben wondered if she ought to take one of her pills.

"But, Jack, what about your car?" Penny asked. "Won't they be able to trace it to you?"

Jack gave her a reassuring smile. "You'll be happy to know that I removed the license plate, the registration papers, pretty much everything that would link it to me. Took me all of two minutes."

"Wow," Penny said again, and Reuben could only shake his head.

And now they were all turning to him, wondering what tale *he* had to tell.

"I was trying to buy you time to do some snooping at the mansion," Jack said. "I don't suppose you got any leads on The Smoke?"

Reuben couldn't help it—he broke into a grin. "Well," he said, "as it so happens…"

MORTAL CARES

T hat dog!" Jack cried when Reuben told them the Counselor's secret. He sounded angry but also impressed. "What a trick! I can't believe it!"

"It never would have occurred to me..." murmured Mrs. Genevieve. She reached reflexively for her glasses and squinted at them, as if a defect in the lenses had prevented her from seeing the truth.

Penny had drawn her feet up under her with a look of revulsion, as if she'd spied a snake on the floor. "It's so creepy. It reminds me of Bartholomew."

"Faug's no Bartholomew," Jack muttered, agitated. He leaped

up from the sofa and began to pace (three steps one way, then three the other, for that was all the room he had). "He's crafty, I'll give him that, but he's only halfway on his rocker. If I'd only known! I was *this* close to him! I could have clocked him and taken the watch right then and there!"

"I'm glad you didn't try," Reuben said, and told him about The Smoke's little black club.

Jack, frustrated, would have none of it. "A blackjack? That wouldn't have done him much good once I knocked him out," he muttered. "I had the jump on him. I just didn't know to jump!"

"You're being ridiculous, Jack," Penny said. She reminded him about the four Directions who would have intervened—and none too gently—if Jack had attacked their employer.

"That's a good point," Jack admitted, and he stopped pacing. He actually looked relieved. "Okay, thanks, Pen. That makes me feel better. I guess I probably couldn't have done it after all."

"We're going to get his watch regardless," Reuben said. "I saw how it could be done."

Mrs. Genevieve stared at him, aghast. "You can't be serious," she said sharply. "After all this?"

Reuben gave her an apologetic look. "I know you're worried, Mrs. Genevieve, but think about it. We know his *secrets* now. That was the whole point of going there—to figure out where we could find The Smoke. But this is even better! Not only do I know where he lives, I know where he puts the watch when he's sleeping—and I know how we can get it. I have a plan."

"Let's hear it," Jack said, suddenly all business.

Mrs. Genevieve *wouldn't* hear it, however. Not just then, at any rate. Reuben's account of sneaking around inside the Counselor's mansion had upset her very much. With a despairing look at him, she shook her head and said she needed to lie down. She rose so unsteadily that Jack sprang to her aid and helped her into her bedroom.

"I'm worried about her," Penny said quietly when the door had closed.

"She's just worried about *him*," Jack said with a nod toward Reuben, who lowered his gaze. What could he say? He knew it was true, and he felt bad about it. But one way or another he was going to have to face The Smoke. Wasn't it better to do it on his own terms?

"How would you feel if you were her?" Penny was saying. "Her hands are tied. She doesn't know what to do."

Jack grimaced and scratched his bristly red scalp. "I know. But once this is all over, she'll be fine. Even better than fine, because the kid'll be out of danger and The Smoke will be out of business." He turned to Reuben. "So tell us how we're going to do that."

Reuben leaned forward. "Okay, the main idea is simple, anyway," he said, and told them his plan.

Penny and Jack blinked a few times, looked at each other, then looked back at Reuben.

"He keeps it on his *nightstand*?" Penny said. "You're sure?"

"I'm sure."

Jack looked at him askance. "And you're just going to hide under the bed until he falls asleep? That's it?"

"I've left out some important details, but yeah," Reuben said. "The thing is, getting away might be tricky. I was hoping you could hide somewhere close, Jack, in case I need help. I haven't thought it through yet, but—"

Jack reached out and swatted Reuben's shoulder, a gesture evidently meant to reassure him. "Of *course* I'm going to be in there with you! We'll find a good hiding spot for me, and then if the least little thing goes wrong, I'm there."

"That's great," Reuben said, and heard the relief in his own voice. There was no masking it. He didn't even resent the swat, which had actually stung his shoulder quite a bit.

"Oh, it makes me so nervous!" Penny said. She was clutching her knees, which were jouncing up and down. "But I want to help. What can I do? And don't say I can stay here and keep Mrs. Genevieve company."

"You can stay here and keep Mrs. Genevieve company," Jack said.

"But that's not helping you! It's nice, but it isn't helping."

"I know something you could do," Reuben said, and then to Jack: "It's too risky to sneak into the mansion while The Smoke is there. We need to lure him away, then sneak in and get ready while he's gone. It would really help to have a lookout, someone who could warn us when he's coming back."

"Yes!" Penny said triumphantly. "A lookout! I'm perfect for that. He's never seen me before. To him I'm just some random girl. I can be skipping rope down the sidewalk or looking for my lost puppy or something. He won't even notice me."

Jack was scowling. "He won't notice a girl skipping rope on the sidewalk after dark?"

"Actually," Reuben interjected, "we should sneak in during the day. I have to show you some things, and I don't think we should use flashlights or lamps—someone might notice the lights through the windows."

"Okay, but still. How exactly would she warn us?"

"We can figure something out!" Penny insisted.

"It really would help," Reuben said, "if we can find a good way to do it."

Jack looked away. He was silent for some time. Then he grunted and said gruffly, "Fine, we'll think about it. Maybe. But only if we can come up with something that's completely safe. In the meantime," he said, turning to Reuben, "what are these things that you have to show me?"

"Oh yeah," Reuben said, nodding. "The traps."

Penny started. "Did you just say *the traps*?"

"Yes, the mansion's full of them."

"This just gets weirder and weirder," said Jack, scratching his head again. He laughed. "I guess that makes me weird, too, because you know what? I kind of like it."

ce⁓

"I will, Mom. Yeah, of course, I promise." Reuben was sitting on the floor behind the counter in Mrs. Genevieve's shop, the phone receiver in one hand, his head in the other. If he could have crawled under the floor, he probably would have. "Okay, sure, I will. And thanks again for letting me do this. No, I'm totally excited, just tired. Yeah, I'm sure we'll all sleep well tonight. Okay, Mom. You, too. Bye."

He hung up and let out a gush of breath. He'd done it. He'd asked for another night. The sleepover had been extended, he'd said—the other boys were staying another night, too, and couldn't he please stay as well? And his mom's response had been predictable. Of course she was glad Reuben wanted to spend more time with his friends. That's what summers were for, right? Just as long as he was sure that's what he wanted to do. Oh yes, he'd assured her, he definitely did.

From her tone Reuben knew that she missed him, that she was disappointed she would not see him tomorrow—but she hadn't said so. She thought he was having fun and didn't want to spoil it. He groaned. It was amazing how guilty he felt. Guilty and unexpectedly sad. At the first sound of her voice he'd realized how much he missed her.

"Good talk?"

Penny had quietly opened the door from Mrs. Genevieve's quarters and was peering around it.

"She made me promise to eat some vegetables," Reuben mumbled. "That's what she's worried about. Vegetables."

*Penny had quietly opened the door from
Mrs. Genevieve's quarters and was peering around it.*

Penny settled down next to him. "Sorry," she said. "I know you must feel terrible. I don't think I've lied to my parents since I was really little. Or anyone, for that matter. That's why it was so hard with Mrs. Genevieve. It's the Meyer way, you know."

"Not counting Jack," Reuben said.

"Not counting Jack," Penny agreed. She shook her head wonderingly. "I had no *idea* what he was capable of! Stealing a car? How does he even know how to do that?"

"Borrowing a car," Reuben corrected.

"Whatever."

At that very moment Jack was out in search of a getaway car. He didn't like the idea of trying to make their escape on foot. Reuben might manage it with his watch, but with anyone else along it would be too awkward, so Jack had said he would find a car to borrow.

Penny had gasped, guessing his meaning. "You mean *steal?*"

"It isn't exactly stealing if you give it back, right?" Jack had said with a wink.

"It isn't exactly borrowing, either!"

Jack had frowned then. "Listen to yourself. I suppose it was all well and good for old Aunt Penelope to borrow people's horses and boats without permission, but if I do the same thing with someone's car, I'm a criminal?"

Penny hadn't known what to say to that. She was obviously still troubled, though, and in the end Jack had said something halfhearted about trying to find someone who would actually give him permission. Then he'd gone out.

"You shouldn't ask him, you know," Reuben said to Penny. "If he does turn up with a car, don't ask him where he got it. You'll only feel bad."

Penny made a face. "Not talking about something doesn't somehow make it honest, you know."

Reuben made no reply to this.

411

After a short silence Penny said quietly, "You do realize I know how you feel about destroying the watches, right? I mean, that you don't want to do it. At least not yours."

Reuben felt heat spread across his cheeks and all the way into his ears. He stared straight ahead. There was no point in denying anything to this friend who could see right through him. He drew up his knees and wrapped his arms around them. "I don't know," he mumbled. "I don't know that we have to do it exactly the way Penelope said."

"Yeah, I figured that's what you were thinking," Penny said gently. "Or actually I figured you were trying not to think about it at all. Look, I get it, Reuben. Your watch—it's amazing. You think it could change your life somehow. You think it could help you and your mom. And if you don't have to worry about The Smoke anymore, you'll be safe to use it however you want."

Reuben looked at her sidelong. "That about sums it up, yeah. But now you're going to try to talk me out of it."

Penny shook her head. "Not now. Maybe later, if you still need me to do that. Right now we can just focus on getting the other watch away from The Smoke. Anyway, you already know what I think. I just want to be sure you aren't kidding yourself about what *you* think." With that, Penny got to her feet, kissed Reuben on the top of his head, and went back into Mrs. Genevieve's rooms.

Reuben sat there for some time, his cheeks still hot. Penny was right; he was good at avoiding the most worrisome questions. But didn't he have good reason to? He had so much to worry about, so much weighing on him, and it was too hard to think of everything at once—or even, sometimes, just one or two of the most important things. Sometimes what you needed most was to save those things for later.

Yet perhaps he'd always been this way, Reuben thought, even before things got so difficult. He'd never really felt bad wandering around the Lower Downs without permission, for instance. It was only when he had to lie to his mom about it that he felt guilty. He wondered now if that made him wicked at heart. He worried it might; he hoped it didn't. This entire business with the watch had left him so strangely unsure about himself. Maybe it was the pressure. Maybe it was the exhaustion.

But maybe it was him.

⁓

It was well after dark when Jack returned, and Mrs. Genevieve had yet to stir from bed. Penny and Reuben had checked on her twice. Each time the watchmaker had seemed to be sleeping. They were both concerned about her.

The only one who seemed not to worry about anything was Jack. Not only had he found several fine prospects for a car they could use tomorrow, but he'd also returned with bread, cheese, and fruit; a jump rope; and the surprising news that he'd gone ahead and "borrowed" a car—just for an hour—to make a nighttime drive around The Smoke's mansion.

"There were a couple of lights on," Jack said, tearing off a hunk of French bread. They were gathered around the coffee table in the sitting room. "Looked to me like he was home. But no guards anywhere I could see. That was one thing I wanted to check."

"Did you see the rope?" Reuben asked.

"That was the other thing. But in the dark I couldn't tell. Obviously, if it's gone when we get there tomorrow, we'll have to ditch the plan and figure something else out."

"Okay, what's the jump rope for?" Penny asked hopefully.

"You know what the jump rope is for," Jack said.

"Yes!" Penny snatched the rope from the table. "I've already been thinking about our warning system. It's pretty complicated, but if I tell you slowly, I think you boys can keep up: I'll ring the doorbell."

Reuben and Jack looked at each other.

"Right?" Penny asked, tossing her hair matter-of-factly. "If I see The Smoke coming back, I'll ring the doorbell a bunch of times. I can get in through that hole in the wall Reuben used."

"But if he sees you—" Jack began.

"If he sees me, I'll walk right up to the limousine and ask if he's seen my puppy. I'm just a little girl with a jump rope looking for her dog. He isn't going to be suspicious."

Reuben cleared his throat. "Can I just point out that you aren't the greatest liar?"

"I know, I know. But I can do this. It won't be hard to lie about a made-up puppy. Anyway, if we're lucky, he won't see me in the first place. I'll ring the doorbell and be on my way with my jump rope."

Soon they had the plan sketched out. After Penny had rung the doorbell, or if dusk approached and The Smoke still hadn't returned, she would take the bus back to Middleton and wait at the shop with Mrs. Genevieve.

Penny reached for a handful of grapes. "That will be good for Mrs. Genevieve, I think. It's going to upset her so much when we leave."

"Yeah, I'm not looking forward to that," Jack said.

They ate in silence for a while, Reuben thinking about the watchmaker, who had lived her quiet life for so long, only now to have had it disrupted in the strangest way imaginable. His own life before the watch had been relatively quiet, too. Only Jack and Penny had possessed any notion of something lurking out in the future, waiting to happen or not to happen as fate decreed. But Jack had wanted out, and Penny was only a kid, like Reuben. Now here they all were, plotting to steal a seemingly magic watch from a man known as The Smoke. It felt as real as anything, but it seemed impossible.

"You absolutely sure you don't want me to do it, kid?" said Jack, studying Reuben's face. He had already suggested twice that he could be the one hiding under the bed with the watch.

Reuben shook his head. He had felt from the beginning—and it was mostly true, he thought—that this was his to do. But it was also true that he simply didn't want anyone else to have his watch, not even briefly. At this point it would feel like lending someone the use of his head or his heart.

Jack turned to Penny, expecting her to chime in, but clearly her thoughts were elsewhere, her eyes gazing at nothing in particular. She'd been holding grapes in her hand for some time but had yet to eat one.

Slowly she became aware that they were looking at her. She put a grape in her mouth, still with a bit of a faraway look to her expression, then took it out again and said to Reuben, "Do you still remember the passage from Penelope's letter, those lines about immortality?"

"What are you talking about?" Jack said, furrowing his brow. "I never heard any lines."

"Oh, that's right," Penny said vaguely, waving him silent. "For you he only summarized it. But he actually committed this part to memory. Right, Reuben? Can you repeat it?"

"I think so." Reuben searched his memory, making sure he remembered the lines exactly. It took him a minute, but presently all the words came together in the right order. With a quick nod, he closed his eyes and recited:

"The possessor of both shall know no fear of death;
Though time may pass, he shall feel it not,
Nor feel aught pain or loss with any breath
He draws; nay, who holds these both shall have no mortal care,
Until such time as he lose possession, which God grant he will,
For it is not fitting that any man,

Be he low and wicked, or a good man or great,
Exist for long in such abnormal state."

Jack whistled. "I'm impressed, kid. You sure you're not a Meyer?"

Penny was frowning. "It doesn't sound like him," she murmured. She looked up at them. "The inventor, I mean. Why would he do this? Why would he make it possible for someone 'low and wicked' to become immortal?"

"To make the brothers turn on each other," Reuben reminded her. "At least, that's the legend."

"It seems like a terrible way to go about it," Penny said.

"Maybe once the guy realized that he could do it," Jack put in, "realized that he could, you know, create a fountain of youth in a can, he felt like he *had* to do it—just to see. To prove it to himself. A genius like that, he'd probably find it hard not to try it, especially if it was his only chance."

"But then why tell them about it?" Penny said with a look of disapproval.

Jack shrugged. "Revenge can do strange things to people. *Wanting* revenge, I mean. Maybe it just seemed like the best opportunity. Maybe he knew that the brothers would never succeed. That's probably what he told himself, anyway. And he turned out to be right."

"I wonder how it works," Reuben mused. "If it's true, I mean. I don't understand how it could work."

Jack chuckled. "*I* don't understand how you can fiddle with your watch and suddenly I'm looking at stuff *behind* you."

"Mrs. Genevieve says it bends the light."

"Bends my brain, is what it does. Eternal youth doesn't seem much weirder."

"It's just wrong in so many ways." Penny's face was still set in a frustrated expression. "Nobody should have such power, should they?" She looked to Reuben for affirmation.

"Eternal youth?" Reuben could only shrug. He honestly hadn't thought about it. "Maybe not. I know I don't want The Smoke to have it, though."

"I don't mean that!" Penny snapped. "I'm talking about invisibility! What good can a person do, being invisible? Okay, fine, it can help us get the watch away from The Smoke—but after that? All it's good for is getting away with things you don't want anyone to know about. It isn't *honest*."

"Spoken like a true Meyer," Jack observed.

Penny looked at Reuben, who was avoiding her eye, and suddenly turned regretful. "Oh. Sorry, Reuben, I just got worked up. I wasn't trying to—you know, make a case."

"That's fine," Reuben said. He did feel defensive, though. He felt sure that there were plenty of good things a person could do with invisibility. He just hadn't had time to figure them out.

"Are you two going to tell me what you're talking about?" Jack asked in the suddenly awkward silence. "No? Okay, then, not to change the subject, but let me change the subject. It's just occurred to me that we could go about this a different way. You don't necessarily have to hide under Faug's bed, kid. I could just ambush him. We could find a good place for me to hide, and then when he walks by—"

Penny gasped. "Jack, you sound like a cutthroat!"

Jack held up his hands. "I'm not talking about *killing* the guy. All I have to do is knock him out and take the watch. One or two punches would do the trick. I'm sure he's earned at least that much." He gestured at Reuben. "And then our friend here wouldn't have to take any risks."

Penny had opened her mouth to protest. She checked herself, realizing that to do so meant to insist on Reuben's taking the risks. She closed her mouth with a frown.

"It's okay," Reuben said to her. "I don't think he should do it, either. What if something went wrong, Jack? What if he sensed you were there or managed to get away from you? Once he turns invisible, the advantage is all his, and we won't have a backup plan. Right now you *are* the backup plan. You don't want to deal with The Smoke in his own home unless you absolutely have to."

"He's right, Jack," Penny said firmly.

"Well, for the record, I think so, too," Jack said with a shrug. "Just thought I should make the suggestion. But I also think you give Faug too much credit. I'm pretty sure old Aunt Penelope would have made mincemeat of this guy." He stretched out his legs and looked at Penny. "That would have been nice, huh? Our lives would have been a wee bit different."

"I just hope you're right about him," Penny said.

Jack yawned. "We'll know soon enough."

His yawn set off a chain reaction. Reuben yawned, then Penny yawned, then Jack did again. Then they all did, looking at one another in mild amusement. Speaking little now, in silent agreement, they rose and cleared the food away, took turns washing up in the bathroom, found a few blankets in a closet. Dimming the lights, they settled down to sleep, or at least to try.

Jack and Penny found places on the floor, both having insisted that Reuben take the sofa. With great care, he slipped the winding key from the watch and tucked it away in the pocket of his pants. The watch itself he closed, folded up in his sweatshirt, and placed beneath a throw pillow. He stretched out, his head on the pillow. He heard Jack and Penny shifting on their blankets on the floor, trying to get comfortable. Soon all was quiet save for the breathing of sleepers, the hum of the little refrigerator in the tiny kitchen, the whisper of cool air passing through a vent.

Reuben stared up at the ceiling without seeing it. His mind instead took him out into the city, to the Lower Downs, to the apartment where he hoped his mom would be sleeping peacefully herself. Then it took him out onto the dark streets, to the imagined homes all across New Umbra in which the Directions—who, despite everything, were people, after all—were watching television or drying dishes, some of them, perhaps, even kissing their children good night. It seemed incredible, unfathomable, that these same men would venture out in the morning to continue their search for a boy who met Reuben's description, yet he knew it to be true. What kind of people were they, really? What kind of world was this?

His thoughts traveled across the night, through a hole in a wall, through a window. They floated up in a vast, dark space, hovering over a balcony crowded with furniture to observe a bent figure in a lonely bed, gazing at an object on his nightstand, on a bed of velvet, a sphere softly gleaming in lamplight. Perhaps it seemed to him like a crystal ball, an enchanted object in which he could see his own future. Perhaps, like Reuben, he felt destiny in the air about him, a palpable feeling. Like steam. Like smoke. Perhaps, yes, when he saw the future, he saw his own name and nothing else.

IF THINGS SHOULD GO WRONG

A clink of a pan, a crack of an egg sounded from the tiny kitchen. A high-pitched splat and sizzle as the egg hit the hot metal. The sounds repeated themselves as more eggs joined the first. Reuben's eyes located the sleeping forms of Jack and Penny on the floor. So it must be Mrs. Genevieve cooking breakfast. Morning had arrived.

Reuben sat up, the iron tang of dread in his mouth. He groped for the sweatshirt and the watch and took them with him into the bathroom. When he emerged, both Jack and Penny were sitting up, both groggily rubbing the same eye. At that he smiled inwardly and felt a bit better.

"Well, today's the day," Jack said, stretching. "You kids excited?" He made it sound as if they were going on a picnic.

Penny squinted at him. "You're a piece of work," she said, her voice raspy with sleep.

"I think I smell bacon," Jack said, jumping up.

In the kitchen, Mrs. Genevieve handed Reuben a plate. "I did not intend to fall asleep," she said. She was wearing the same rumpled clothes she'd lain down in, and her face seemed rumpled, too. But her bright blue eyes were clear enough, as was the troubled emotion in her gaze. "You haven't changed your mind?"

"I'm sorry," Reuben said. "We have to do this." He looked down at his plate. Mrs. Genevieve had arranged his fried eggs and strips of bacon to resemble eyes, a nose, and a mouth. It seemed a surprisingly whimsical thing to do, given her mood.

She returned his quizzical expression with a small smile. "It is not every day I am able to make breakfast for a child I like," she said simply, and turned away.

They all ate together in the sitting room, speaking little. Afterward, Reuben and Penny volunteered to do the dishes, and Jack prepared to head out. When he returned with the getaway car, it would be time to go. Just before he left, however, while Mrs. Genevieve was in her bedroom changing, Penny caught his arm. Reuben, gathering cups from the table, sensed she was about to say something serious.

"Jack," she said, looking up at her brother. "If something goes wrong..." Her voice faltered.

"Hey, this is going to work, redbird. I have faith in our friend here," Jack said with a nod toward Reuben. "Believe me, we're all going to be laughing about this tonight."

"You, maybe," said Penny, hugging him tightly.

"All of us," Jack said. He drew back to give her a wink. "And it's going to make for quite a story, isn't it?"

An hour later they were ready to go. A nondescript gray

sedan with darkly tinted windows sat at the curb, its rear passenger door left open as if the driver was returning with something to load. Which he was. Jack stood inside the shop with Reuben and Penny, saying goodbye to Mrs. Genevieve. "We won't be back until after dark," Reuben told her. "And possibly not until very late."

The watchmaker nodded, her expression grave, and gave him a solemn hug. To the others' surprise, she hugged both of them as well. Then she returned to Reuben and took his hands in hers. "You will be as careful as you can, yes? You promise me this?"

"I promise," Reuben said.

Tears stood in Mrs. Genevieve's eyes. She shook his hands once, firmly, like a carriage driver snapping the reins. "Then go," she said, releasing him. "Save the city, change the history, all of these things, I know."

Penny took Reuben's arm. They vanished. Jack opened the door and held it as they stepped through and made their way to the sedan. Then he came out and closed the car door. By the time he had jogged around to the driver's seat, Mrs. Genevieve was standing at her window, watching them.

It was a simple, ordinary-looking scene to behold, the departure of a single car on a cloudy Sunday morning, and yet for the watchmaker it was awful. She couldn't bear to see them go but seemed unable to resist. She watched the young man jump in, close the door, and pull away from the curb almost in the same moment. And in the next moment they were gone.

Mrs. Genevieve's stomach gave a lurch, and she turned quickly from the window. She looked around her empty shop, feeling strangely bewildered to find herself alone. How had she let them go? But what had she been expected to do? It was another unsolved mystery, and never in all her years had she felt so helpless.

Suddenly she was aware of the ticking clocks in a way she had not been only moments before. Mrs. Genevieve had grown up amid the ceaseless, myriad ticking of clocks, of course; they had long since constituted a kind of silence, the backdrop to everything in her life. But now, for the first time in her many years, she felt that the sound would drive her mad. This multitude of clocks, ticking and ticking and ticking—one would think that with all this ticking, the passage of time would be accomplished more quickly. It should run infinitely faster; instead, it scarcely progressed at all.

Mrs. Genevieve began to feel a rising panic. How many hours must she wait before she knew what would become of Reuben and his friends? How many untold ticks of these clocks? These hundreds and thousands of audible, terrible moments in her empty shop?

"Oh, help!" the watchmaker gasped. "Oh, what can I do?"

And stopping her ears with her fingers, she ran into her rooms.

Jack hung up the pay phone and jumped back into the car, where Reuben was waiting in the front passenger seat. "Sounds like he bought it," he said, putting the car into gear. "He was even trying to sound agreeable. Said he understood why I got spooked and promised that this time they'll do it my way. He probably spent the night stewing over how close he'd gotten, only to lose his best lead."

Reuben eyed Jack dubiously. "But you don't actually believe he'll do what he says, do you?"

"Of course not," Jack said, running through the gears. They were moving fast now. "He was trying to seem less threatening. No, I'm sure that right now every single one of his men is on his way to Burlington again."

"Unless they're on their way here," Reuben pointed out. After all, Jack had used this pay phone in East Middleton, a neighborhood that had nothing to do with anything, precisely because he knew that The Smoke could trace the call.

"That's right. He'll probably send a few to sweep the blocks around here, just in case. But we'll already be gone. We're already gone now, in fact."

It was true. They were already halfway back to Westmont, where, with any luck, Penny would be witnessing The Smoke's departure. They had dropped her off at the park, Jack having pointed out a spot up the street from which she could watch the mansion's gates. A few small children were already on the park swings, pushed by their parents, and there were several cars on the streets, some of them pulling into the church lot beyond the park.

"Listen," Jack said, "I switched the plates on this car, so I don't expect the police to track it down anytime soon. But if it isn't here when we come out tonight, don't panic. I can find us another ride."

It took a few moments for Reuben to process what Jack had said, for whenever his thoughts turned to the car he was in, his first impulse was to leap out of it. *You're riding in a stolen car! Mom would kill you!* He'd been trying not to think about it. *Borrowed*, he reminded himself. *Borrowed borrowed borrowed.*

"What do we do if he's chasing us?" Reuben asked. "That won't exactly be the perfect scenario for car shopping."

Jack gave him a lopsided grin. "We'll have both watches then, remember? You can give me his, show me how to use it. We'll be the Invisible Duo—though don't ever tell anybody I said that. Way too corny. Anyway, we'll figure it out. Okay, here we go."

They were back in Westmont now, had passed the church and were approaching the park. At least half a dozen other cars were parked along the street. "This is perfect," Jack said, pulling up to the curb. "Lots of different cars today, not just us. Do you see her?"

Reuben had already spotted Penny's bright red hair in the distance. It was bobbing up and down—she was skipping rope. She was looking their way, had clearly seen them. She stopped skipping to pass one hand above her in a slow arc; Reuben was reminded of the way she had waved to her family members high up on the lighthouse gallery. This time, though, she was delivering a signal. A single wave was a warning; a double wave gave the all clear.

"See that?" Jack said.

"Two waves," Reuben confirmed. Penny had seen The Smoke and his men leave.

"Looks like we're in business." Jack got out a pair of dark sunglasses, considered the overcast sky, and put them away again. "So much for my clever disguise. You ready?"

They got out of the car and walked up the street, passing beneath the rather sickly ornamental trees planted along the sidewalk. Penny was ambling back in their direction. No one else was around.

"About five minutes ago," Penny said as she approached. "They left in a limousine. Turned at the first corner and drove away fast."

"Nice work," Jack said glancing at his wristwatch. "See you later."

And that was all they said. They had agreed ahead of time to speak only in passing. If by any chance they were observed, there'd be no reason for anyone to think Penny actually knew them. She might simply have been asking the time.

Good luck, her eyes told them, and she began to skip again, moving on in the direction of the park.

It would take The Smoke and his men at least an hour, Jack had told her, just to drive to the rendezvous point and back. So

Penny shouldn't expect to see anything before then, and probably not for another hour or two after that, since The Smoke, having no other leads, would feel compelled to wait for Jack to show up. For now Penny would skip her rope, eat her packed lunch, just generally be a kid hanging out around a neighborhood park. But in an hour she would drift back toward the mansion. She would be their eyes.

Reuben and Jack kept well away from the mansion's front gate, instead circling the block and coming at the property from behind. The trees in the neighborhood obscured that stretch of wall from any distant windows or other vantage points. And so, knowing themselves to be alone, they scrambled through the hole without hesitation, then crouched beside the rosebushes to study the mansion. The rope was still there.

"I'm not surprised," Jack murmured. "You can barely see it."

Reuben pointed toward the place in the shrubs they'd be aiming for. Jack nodded and took hold of Reuben's sweatshirt. "Okay," he said. "I'm ready when you are."

"Remember to stay crouched down," Reuben said. He reached into his pocket. They vanished.

Jack swore under his breath and yanked at Reuben's shirt.

"What is it?" Reuben hissed, alarmed.

"Sorry, sorry," Jack whispered. "Nothing. Just the—the going-blind part. Startled me is all."

"I told you—"

"I know, I know. Sorry. I'm good now. Let's go."

They crossed the open ground awkwardly and slowly, coming at last to the shrubs. Reuben made them briefly visible again—first warning Jack what he intended to do—and found the place where he had pressed through before. He made them vanish again until they were crouching behind the shrubs, where, for the first time, Reuben noticed that Jack's eyes were not green like Penny's but rather a pale, clear blue. His attention

427

was drawn to them because just then they were as wide as he'd ever seen them.

"That's really something," Jack whispered.

"You all right?" Reuben asked teasingly.

Jack narrowed his eyes. "I'm great," he said. "Never better. Ready to do some climbing."

The next part was riskier. Reuben couldn't climb and carry the watch at the same time; they would be briefly exposed. Jack went up first, and he went fast, his strong arms and legs making easy work of it. In no time he was balancing his knees on the window ledge, raising the window, and ducking inside. He might have been making the same climb all his life.

Reuben waited while Jack scouted from the window. He felt two quick tugs on the rope—all clear—and started to climb. The rope hurt his hands; he wished he had thought to wear gloves. He gritted his teeth and scrambled up as fast as he could. Jack reached out, caught him under the shoulders, and hauled him in.

"We're fine," Jack whispered as he pulled up the rope and lowered the window. "I didn't see a soul."

Reuben clenched and unclenched his aching hands. He shoved the rope under the bed skirt. It occurred to him that there was no need to whisper. But he wasn't about to suggest they raise their voices. Whispering seemed appropriate under the circumstances.

Jack followed him down the long, gloomy hallway, his eyes roaming left and right, taking in the empty, dusty rooms. When they reached the bedroom nearest the stairs, the one whose furniture had been removed, Reuben stopped at the doorway.

"This is where I think you should hide," he whispered. "If he's chasing me, you can step out and catch him by surprise."

Jack glanced into the bedroom. "And if something goes wrong before then? Will I be able to hear you?"

Reuben pointed to the doors near the top of the stairs. "Those are the balcony doors right there, the ones I told you are boarded up on the other side. If I call for help, you'll hear me, easy."

"Perfect. Only don't actually say 'help,' okay? No need to let him know I'm coming."

"Right. I'll just scream in terror, then."

"Yeah, that'll work fine," Jack said with a wink, and went into the empty bedroom. "So I'll be hanging out in here until the moment arrives. Too bad it couldn't be more boring." His eyes swept across the walls, taking in the dusty paintings. He cocked his head to the side and squinted. One of the paintings had caught his eye.

Reuben watched him, bemused. There were countless paintings in this mansion, all of them dusty and fuzzy with cobwebs. With his mind on other things, he'd paid them no attention. But Jack was clearly struck by this one, a small oil painting depicting an armored knight on horseback, in battle with a dragon. The dragon's scales, even beneath the dust, were a brilliant blue-green.

"What do you know?" Jack murmured. "Santo Varges's *Saint George and the Dragon*. Stolen many years ago and never recovered. Evidently, our Mr. Faug is a collector."

Reuben stepped over for a closer look. "How do you know this?"

"I did a paper on famous unsolved crimes," Jack said. "When I was about your age, actually. It might not surprise you that I was fascinated by all things untrustworthy and dishonest."

Reuben almost smiled. It was true—he wasn't surprised.

Jack had his hands on his hips, gazing at the painting and slowly shaking his head. "This was one of several stolen right here in New Umbra. Masterpieces taken from museums and private collections." He tore his eyes from the painting and glanced once more at the others. "I'll bet they're all right here in this building."

"But why did he steal them?" Reuben wondered. "He obviously doesn't care about them. They're all stuck away in these rooms, covered with dust."

"Maybe just to see if he could do it."

Reuben's mind flashed back to that morning in the narrow alley, when he had set his hands and feet against the walls and begun to climb. Just to see. "Maybe so," he conceded.

They headed downstairs. They still had lots of time. Not even twenty minutes had passed since The Smoke left. Reuben would give Jack a tour of the traps, they would make a final trip to the bathroom (better safe than sorry, as they had a long wait ahead of them), and Jack needed to see how to get to the ballroom.

"Best-case scenario, he doesn't even wake up," Reuben whispered as they descended. "Next-best scenario, I have a great head start, and he assumes I'm making a dash for the front door."

"Right. So he runs off in the wrong direction. We're long gone before he even realizes his mistake." They reached the bottom of the stairs and turned right. "Oh, I like the fake candles. Nice touch."

"But in the worst-case scenario," Reuben went on, "if you hear me scream, this is the route you take to reach me. These doors up ahead lead into the ballroom." They were approaching the intersection with the hallway that contained the scattered furniture and the red carpet runner. Reuben pointed. "That's the carpet I mentioned, so be careful. I'm not sure where the trap is, exactly, but—"

He didn't finish his sentence, for that was when they both saw the figure, crouching like a gargoyle on the footstool, looking at them.

The Trembling Rope

The nimbus of red hair was registered too slowly, the urgently whispered "Hey, it's me!" uttered too late: Reuben had already leaped back in fright, one flailing elbow catching Jack precisely in the solar plexus, and vanished. Only then did it dawn on him whom he'd actually seen.

"For crying out loud," Jack muttered, his voice strained.

Reuben reappeared to see him doubled over in pain and glaring at his sister.

"Sorry!" Reuben and Penny whispered at the same time.

"What...are you doing here...Penny?" Jack said, slowly straightening. His eyes flashed with anger.

"I'm sorry, but something important occurred to me!" Penny said. She was still balancing on the footstool, crouched like a frog on a lily pad. "What if the doorbell doesn't work?"

Reuben looked at Jack, who was still grimacing, though whether from pain or displeasure it was hard to say. "She has a point, Jack. We should test it."

Jack muttered something under his breath. He rubbed his head. "Might have been nice to agree on this ahead of time. Why didn't you try it just now, redbird?"

"And give you a false alarm? I didn't want to scare you!"

"Perfect," Jack said dryly. "And dare I ask how you even got in here?"

"The hole in the wall, same as you," Penny said. "Then I went around to the front. Don't worry, I kept behind the bushes. There was no one around, so I ran up and tried the front door."

"And it wasn't locked?"

She shook her head. "I had a feeling it wouldn't be. From what Reuben told us, I figured The Smoke might not care if someone snuck in. All the better for catching them in his traps, right?"

"Wow," Reuben said. "That never occurred to me."

"You're lucky you didn't get caught yourself," Jack snapped.

"Not really," Penny replied mildly. "Reuben told us how he got to the ballroom, so I just had to remember what he said." A sheepish look came over her face. "But you didn't describe this last part, Reuben. That's why I'm still on the stool. Do I need to jump somewhere in particular?"

"Just step right there and keep close to the wall," Reuben said. "That's what I did."

Penny did as he instructed and came over to Jack, who still looked furious. She took him by the sleeve and gazed up at him. "I really am sorry. I just didn't know what else to do. And it seemed safe enough. They haven't even been gone half an hour yet."

Jack's expression softened. "I know. I'm not blaming you, all right? I'm blaming myself for not having thought of this. We could have figured out something different." He tousled her mass of red curls. "Forget it. Let's just do this and get you out of here." With a wry look at Reuben, he added, "The front door would have been easier, wouldn't it?"

Penny, looking grateful and relieved, gestured toward the big doors. "So that's the ballroom in there, right, Reuben? That's where you should be when we test it, don't you think? To make sure you can hear it."

Reuben nodded. "Want to take a quick look?" He opened one of the doors, stepping back to watch their reactions. They led the way in, gaping all around.

"This is just how I imagined it," Penny said to Reuben. "Only weirder. You didn't mention the ceiling. It's like the sky is falling to pieces."

They walked wonderingly past the fireman's pole and its pile of pillows, and Jack knelt to inspect the damaged floor. "So this is where the ladder will be?" he said. "Okay, good, if something goes wrong up on that balcony, I have a way to reach you. Just be sure to do a lot of screaming and kicking and biting and so forth. Keep him distracted."

"I'm pretty sure that would all come naturally," Reuben said, shuddering. "But I intend to avoid getting caught, remember. Hope that doesn't disappoint you."

"Only a little," Jack said.

Penny had walked over to look at the rope ladder, though she kept her distance by several feet. "I'm impressed you figured all this out, Reuben. And is that where you'll be climbing up?" she asked, pointing. "It looks hard."

"The kid must be part monkey," Jack said, a bit distractedly. He was looking up at the high windows in the opposite wall. Dirty as they were, and given the cloud-covered sky beyond them, they didn't admit light so much as dimly, grayly glow. Scratching his cheek, now stubbly with red whiskers, he walked toward them, saying, "You'd think there'd be traps under those windows. Sure, they're way up there, but with a long rope, someone could climb right down."

"There might be!" Reuben hissed in warning. "I didn't check everywhere, only behind that tapestry. That's where the ladder's hidden."

Jack had stopped walking midstep. He lowered his foot slowly and turned to see where Reuben was pointing. "Good to know." He turned then toward the grand piano in the corner. It was so thoroughly fuzzed with gray that it looked less like an actual piano than a dust sculpture of one. "That's a weird detail, too, isn't it? You'd think it might be a trap of some kind, but then, what sort of intruder would sit down and play a few tunes?"

"Maybe he keeps something hidden in there," Reuben said.

"Or else it really is a trap," Penny warned. "Don't go near it, Jack."

"Maybe it's just there to drive us crazy," Jack said, squinting at it. He glanced back at Penny. "Don't worry, I won't get within ten feet of it. I just want to see—"

He took one step, but it proved to be one step too many. With a sound like a cash register drawer springing open, the floor fell away beneath him.

"Oh, come *on*!" came Jack's cry, hollow and booming, as he rocketed down the chute.

❧

Penny shrieked. Reuben gasped. Both raced to the spot where the floor had swallowed Jack. They dropped to their knees, peering down into the gloom. Penny called Jack's name, so loudly that Reuben winced, fearing she might be heard even from outside the mansion. All he could think was *This is bad, this is bad, this is bad.*

Penny yelled Jack's name again, and this time there was an answer. His voice floated up to them through the chute, metallic and distant. It sounded as though he was saying he was all right, but they couldn't be sure.

"There's a net, remember?" Reuben said, putting a hand on her shoulder. "He's okay. We just have to get him out of there." He mopped his brow with his sleeve. All of a sudden he was roasting.

"The rope!" Penny exclaimed. "The one you have upstairs! Is it long enough?" She looked at him entreatingly, as if he might will it to be so.

"I'm not sure," Reuben said, jumping to his feet, "but we'll try it. Stay here!"

He dashed out of the ballroom. How could this have happened? The placement of the trap seemed completely random. It was near the windows but not directly beneath them, near the piano but not connected to it—or at least it didn't seem to be. Maybe, Reuben thought as he flew up the stairs, the placement had to do with the location of support beams or something. It was a bad bit of luck, in any case.

He ran into the bedroom, threw up the bed skirt, and began frantically working at the knot in the rope. It had been pulled impossibly tight. He bit at it with his teeth. He was jittery, sweating, scared. He needed to calm down. They had time, he reminded himself, and the rope was probably long enough. It was going to be fine.

After several tugs with his teeth, the knot started to come loose. Reuben scrabbled at it with his fingers. Finally he had it all the way undone. He gathered the heavy coils of rope onto his shoulder and raced back downstairs.

Penny was pacing back and forth next to the square hole in

435

the floor, her hands lost in her hair. "Hurry!" she hissed when she saw him come in.

"I am!"

"You can tie it to the piano! It's safe—I already checked it!"

Reuben puffed past her and slid to his knees at the nearest piano leg. He got the rope tied, grabbed the coils, dragged them back over to the hole and shoved them in. The rope tumbled and slid down the chute, uncoiling as it fell away into darkness. Then, with a little tremor, all was still. They heard Jack's voice again.

"What's he saying?"

"I don't know."

They waited, straining their ears, watching the rope for any telltale movement, any twitch or tremble to show that Jack had taken hold of the end. For several moments nothing happened. Then Jack yelled up again. Penny and Reuben looked at each other and shook their heads. Neither one could make out his words.

Penny started to yell something down into the chute, but Reuben checked her. He put a finger to his lips. Then he took out the watch, vanished into blackness, and listened. Habit shifted his mind into a different mode, one in which the audible was everything. He heard Penny breathing, heard the faintest shuffling sound as she shifted her weight without realizing it, and heard a distant muttering and rustling that drifted up from the bottom of the chute. Jack yelled again. And this time Reuben understood him.

"The coils are tangled at the bottom," he said, reappearing. "He can see it in the chute, but there's no way he can reach it."

Penny gaped at him. "You understood that? Are you sure?"

"Positive." He gestured with the watch. "When the lights are off, I can hear pretty much anything."

"Okay, then we'll untangle it!" Penny grabbed the rope and

436

tried to pull it up, but though she strained until her eyes bulged, the rope didn't yield. "It's stuck!"

She tried tugging the rope from side to side, without luck. Reuben suspected it was caught in the crease of a sharp turn in the chute. "Like when a vacuum cord gets stuck," he said. "You know, when you drag it through a doorway at an angle? I think this may be like that."

"I think you're right," Penny said, and after the briefest hesitation she added, "I'll have to go down there." She swung her legs into the hole.

Reuben started. "Wait, what?"

Penny was already lowering herself hand over hand. "If I untangle it, maybe he can reach it."

Reuben started to protest, but then he wasn't sure why. It was actually a good plan. He was just anxious. He dropped to his knees to watch her climb down.

For the first few feet the chute took a straight drop, and Penny was struggling to lower herself in a controlled way. Reuben guessed that the rope was hurting her hands. But then the chute banked sharply, and as she backed out of sight, she called up to him: "It gets easier here. It's less steep." Then she was gone, and Reuben stared helplessly into darkness, listening to the funneled sounds of her shuffling and pants of exertion.

The rope trembled and jerked an inch this way, an inch that way, as Penny descended.

"Be careful!" Reuben whispered after her, belatedly. He doubted she heard him. He remained on his knees, still sweating, every muscle tense as he stared pointlessly into the darkness. He wiped his brow, glanced around the ballroom, and looked back down.

Even as he did so, Reuben's stomach clenched violently, squeezing in upon itself like a tin can being crushed in the depths of an ocean. For as he directed his eyes downward again—in that exact instant—he realized that in his glance around the ball-room, he had seen someone.

The afterimage was burned in his brain.

Reuben raised his eyes again.

Standing in the doorway, regarding him with an expression of predatory pleasure, was The Smoke.

"I'll admit it," said The Smoke, closing the door behind him. "I wish you hadn't seen me just now." He snapped his fingers. "Like that. The difference of a second." He reached into his trousers pocket and took out a ring of keys, which were bound together with rubber bands and didn't jingle at all. "Had you not looked up exactly when you did, you never *would* have seen me. You understand what I mean, don't you? I know that you do." He shrugged and turned to the door, locking it with one of the keys.

"Normally I keep this unlocked," said The Smoke, looking over his shoulder at Reuben, "for the sake of appearing careless. Under the circumstances, however..." He smiled and turned back toward the ballroom.

Reuben hadn't moved. His hand was in his pocket, fingers squeezing the winding key. His skin burned all over. His mouth felt full of cotton.

The Smoke idly, strangely, tossed the keys onto the floor at his feet. He slid his hands into the pockets of his suit coat. "There's no point in my vanishing now, is there? You've seen me, and you know how it works. You'll creep away, try to make it hard for me to find you. It will waste time. Better that we come to an agreement." His eyes traveled to the trembling rope. He smiled. "I see your brash friend has made another misstep. The last in a long series of missteps."

Reuben didn't let himself look at the keys on the floor. Why had The Smoke simply dropped them there? Then he knew. Bait. Another trap. Even if he managed to reach the keys, he would never have time to get the door unlocked.

The Smoke took a leisurely step toward him, then stopped and cocked his head. "Why do you look so surprised? Hmm?" He cocked his head in the other direction now, like a rooster eyeing an insect.

"You..." Reuben started to speak without meaning to. He fell silent again. What would he say? *Why are you here? How did you know? What will you do to us?* It was pointless to ask anything.

The Smoke shook his head and sighed. "Did you truly believe that I can't tell when someone has been in my own home?" he asked, taking another casual step forward. "As if your footprints in the dust on the basement stairs weren't enough, as if the slight disarrangement of my pillows didn't so plainly announce the fact of your visit, as if I wouldn't notice the subtle difference in the way my robe hung on the ladder, you left"—here The Smoke laughed, a short, harsh laugh—"you left a *rope* hanging from an upstairs window?" He shook his head as if in pity for Reuben and took another step.

Their eyes were locked. Reuben dared not glance away.

"Did you—what? Hope to hide under my bed, wait for me to fall asleep? Oh! I can see from your face that I've struck home. Now, now. You shouldn't feel bad. For a child, you know, you've done quite well." The Smoke continued to advance a step or two at a time, casually and slowly, as if simply to draw within easier speaking distance. They were separated now by perhaps twenty paces. "I believe you've puzzled out the secret of the ladders, for instance, though I've always taken pains to sweep the floor in here. Unlike you, I'm careful not to leave tracks."

"You mean like the scuffed wood on that table?" Reuben blurted out, though he didn't feel as defiant as he sounded. On the contrary, he only wanted to say something, anything, that

*Standing in the doorway, regarding him with
an expression of predatory pleasure, was The Smoke.*

would make him feel less helpless, would make the outcome of this situation feel less inevitable. "Or the mark on the wall where the light switch used to be? Or the banged-up floor right there? You think those aren't tracks?"

The Smoke had stopped walking. His eyes narrowed. For a moment he said nothing. Then he seemed to gather himself, his face relaxed, and he drew a little closer. The nearer he came to Reuben, the more stoop-shouldered he seemed. Was he trying to appear less threatening?

"You're right, of course," he said calmly. He offered up a shrug. "What can I say? Am I perfect? No. Yet here I stand, in my own home, outside of which is a group of men who follow my orders. I control this entire city. And you, meanwhile, are a nameless boy, desperately wishing now that you were anywhere but here. Do you see the difference between us? You are a child, and you are an amateur. The watch, for you, is a novelty, a plaything that has made you feel briefly larger than you are. Whereas for me, the watch has been an entire *life*."

At first Reuben scarcely registered any of The Smoke's words. He was trying to decide where to run. He settled on the piano. Any moment now, probably. What he would do after that, he had no idea. Even if Penny managed to get the rope untangled, it would take a while for Jack to climb back up.

Reuben noticed a faint look of disappointment pass over The Smoke's face—the man had come within a dozen steps now, close enough for Reuben to discern the subtle shift in his expression— and he realized that The Smoke's speech had not produced its desired effect, whatever that was. Perhaps he'd expected Reuben to say simply, *You're right, you're better than me, I give up.* Instead, something about the man's words provoked a question in Reuben, another possible way to stall. "Why a mansion?"

The Smoke took another step, then stopped. He frowned. "I beg your pardon?"

441

Reuben's parched mouth made it an effort to speak, but he forced out the words, croaking in much the same way The Smoke did in his guise as the Counselor. "Why do you live in this great big mansion, and why do you care about running the city, if the watch is your life? If the watch is all you really care about?"

The Smoke looked as if Reuben had just asked him where the sky was located. "But it's all the same! Do you really not see that? I've always known that the other watch was somewhere here in New Umbra. What better way to find it than to throw my arms around the entire city, to have eyes in every corner?" He gestured about the ballroom. "And if my enemy should come, what better place to capture him than this?"

"You didn't expect your enemy to be a boy, though."

"It's true. Perhaps I overprepared." The Smoke gave Reuben a thin smile. "But now to business. This doesn't have to be difficult. If you hand over the watch, I will let you go, as simple as that. Oh, I'll expect you to keep this between us, of course. Which is not unreasonable, I think. No one would believe you, anyway."

"I don't believe *you*," Reuben croaked.

"You should," The Smoke replied evenly. "It's your best option. And you should also believe that if you give me difficulty, I will punish you. There are places in this city for incorrigible children who have committed crimes. Locked facilities." Glaring at Reuben now, he began to gesticulate, anger and menace creeping into his voice. "Do you have a family? Would you care to see them again? Are you aware that I can arrange for you *not* to? Ever? What about your friend in the basement, clinging to that rope? Would he care to spend the rest of his life serving out a sentence for the crimes I attribute to him?"

The Smoke spat out these words with such venom that Reuben knew the moment was at hand. There was no changing

442

course now. "I think that's what you're planning to do anyway," he challenged. "So why should I make it easy for you?"

The Smoke was trembling, his face dark with anger. "Because if you don't," he hissed, "it will *hurt* more."

And then he vanished.

The Last Secret

Reuben ran for his life. He made for the grand piano, agonizingly aware of the sound of his sneakers striking the ballroom floor. Glancing back, he saw The Smoke flicker into view near the hole in the floor, then flicker into view again a few steps closer, running at a crouch, his eyes fixed on Reuben. Despite himself, Reuben yelped. It was a terrifying vision.

He acted almost without thinking. Darting around the piano, he vanished, ripped off a shoe, and tossed it in a high arc toward the corner. Then he yanked off the other shoe and carried it with him, padding silently in the direction of the balcony. His first shoe had landed with a soft but distinctive clattering, and now from the corner into which he'd tossed it, he heard a sharp exhalation, followed by The Smoke's irritated voice: "You must think yourself so clever! Tell me, how many shoes do you have?"

Reuben stuck the shoe under his arm and waved his free hand before him. He hoped to find one of the balcony pillars and get behind it. He might be able to peer out and spot The Smoke without being spotted himself. He had no plan other than to keep as much distance between himself and the man as possible, for as long as possible. He thought he should be getting close now. He slowed down, feeling the air with his fingers.

Another step, and he felt the side of his hand come up against not the hard stone of a pillar but the scratchy fiber of rope. He jerked his hand away as if he'd been burned. He knew it was too late, though. It was as if he'd plucked one of the strands of a giant spiderweb. If The Smoke was scanning the ballroom, there was no way he'd have missed the twitch of the rope ladder. Reuben turned and fled.

Sure enough, moments later he heard another sound of exasperation from beneath the balcony. He skidded noiselessly to a stop. He was somewhere near the middle of the ballroom floor. He considered going for the keys. That was what The Smoke wanted. He thought about the bar in the corner. He could go and hide behind it, but then what?

"I know you're close," The Smoke murmured from a few feet away. Reuben's arms prickled with fresh goose bumps. By some miracle he managed not to gasp. "I can sense you. Perhaps you should run, so I can listen to your clothes swishing. What do you think? I wonder if you realize that if I get close enough, I can see—"

Reuben threw his shoe, hard, in the direction of The Smoke's voice. He heard it smack against the man's face, heard him cry out in surprise and pain, then roar with fury. He may have lunged forward, but Reuben had already backed away, taking great, shuffling giant steps. He kept moving until he sensed that he had drawn close to the hole in the floor. He could hear the faint scratching of the rope as it jerked back and forth, and the sounds—the much too distant sounds—of someone struggling in the chute far below him. He backed away a few steps and froze, listening.

He heard nothing except the same silent scratching of the rope, now several paces in front of him. He wanted to reappear and look around, but he was utterly exposed. He listened and listened. Was The Smoke doing the same thing? Reuben wondered whose ears were better. The moments passed, each of them unbearable.

Suddenly a soft clatter sounded off to his left, and Reuben, every nerve jangling, moved quickly away from it. Yet even as he did so, he realized his mistake, recognized the sound he'd heard: his own shoe.

His own trick.

"You might as well stop right there," said The Smoke. His voice came from only a few steps away. It was moving as Reuben moved, maintaining the same distance. "I have you now. I can see you."

Reuben stopped moving. Bile rose in his throat, as bitter and horrible as the truth. For he understood that The Smoke really did see him. The man had gotten close enough that his discerning eyes could make out the faint shimmer in the air that was Reuben's invisible form, or else a certain distortion in the floor beneath his feet, or perhaps both. No one else would ever have noticed these—no one but The Smoke, who'd been looking for them. And now, no matter what Reuben did or where he went, The Smoke would follow.

"I really can hear the swish of your clothing, you know," The Smoke said. His anger seemed to have drained away, replaced by a swelling triumph. "Once I'm close enough. I only needed you to move a bit. Your shoe was very helpful in that respect, thank you." He waited for a response. When Reuben made none, The Smoke sighed and said, "I did give you options, you know. And you still have a choice. I need you to look at me so that you understand."

The last thing Reuben wanted was to look at The Smoke standing so close to him. He wanted to believe that this was all a dream. But his fingers seemed to act of their own accord, and, pushing in on the winding key, they returned him to the world of the visible. The waking world; there was no denying it.

"Ah, there we are," said The Smoke. He stood regarding Reuben in a half crouch, his awful tie hanging like a stilled pendulum, his right hand at his hip, expertly cradling the open watch. His left hand he held out from his side, as if for balance. Then, with a quick jerking motion, as if impulsively flinging something away from him, he summoned the black club from within his sleeve. The effect was that of a man snatching an invisible serpent, his touch rendering it suddenly visible, its neck black and shiny in his grip.

Reuben flinched at the movement, then held still. For some reason The Smoke hadn't attacked him already, even though he'd had Reuben dead to rights. Why was that? The question seemed of vital importance. Reuben stared at the club, which The Smoke was now pointing at him like the extension of a finger, and tried to concentrate on finding the answer.

"Use your brain," The Smoke said. He lifted the club and tapped it against his own head. "I know you have one, so use it. You can see there's no escape from me now. Hand me the watch and avoid pain. It's really quite simple."

Reuben tried to speak and failed. He tried again. "What happens then? If I give you the watch?"

"We'll discuss the future like civilized men," said The

Smoke, whose eyes had lit up at Reuben's words. "But only after you hand me the watch. That will be your gesture of good faith. If I have to take it from you, there will be no discussion, and I will *not* be civilized. Do you understand?"

Suddenly Reuben understood—not what The Smoke was trying to tell him, but rather what he was trying to keep hidden. He didn't want to attack while Reuben was still in possession of the watch. He was afraid of a struggle, afraid that the watch would be dropped and damaged. After a lifetime of searching for it, The Smoke didn't want to risk losing it in the very moment of victory.

"Yes," Reuben answered after a long pause. "I think I understand."

The Smoke held perfectly still, but his eyes seemed to dance. "And so? What will it be? Are we to be civilized or not?"

Reuben moved his mouth as if about to speak, but hesitatingly, as if trying to find the right words. What he wanted to find was a way out, but he didn't see how. His realization had bought him a minute, that was all. He couldn't get away. The Smoke would seize him if he had to; Reuben felt sure of it. And then he would be one swing of the club away from the end. He wouldn't be conscious to feel the man lowering him gently to the floor— gently, for the sake of the watch, which after all these many years he would finally claim for himself.

The Smoke lifted his eyebrows impatiently. "Well?"

"I...I..." Reuben looked down at the watch in his hand. So beautiful. He tried to give the impression that he was making his peace with handing it over. Running was out of the question. All he could do was stall and hope for a miracle to occur.

"Answer me!" The Smoke snapped. "It's a simple question. *Yes*, you will hand over the watch now, or *no*, you prefer that I use force. Answer me at once or I will assume the latter."

Reuben glanced up at The Smoke's face, the anger and

anticipation barely suppressed in his expression now, and looked away again. It was a dangerous game, one that could not go on for long. The longer Reuben held out, the angrier The Smoke would get. At some point the man would simply snap.

"I know I should give it to you," Reuben said, for he knew he had to say something. "It's just hard, you know, to…" He gave a helpless shrug, trying to present a picture of painful indecision.

"Of course it's hard!" The Smoke barked, so loudly that Reuben started and looked up. The man's face was dark and twisted with anger. "But it's over! Do you understand? It's over! Now give…the watch…to *me*."

The Smoke was sweating. He was trembling. He could barely contain his fury that Reuben might compel him to attack, and yet the fury itself made the attack seem inevitable.

"Okay," Reuben said quickly. "Okay, I'll give it to you. But first—"

"No!" The Smoke shouted. He jabbed the club toward Reuben, punctuating his words. "No, no, no! No more stalling! Hand it over immediately or pay the price! No more words!" His face had gone crimson; flecks of white spittle flew from his lips. "One!"

A countdown. So this was it. Reuben found himself cringing, crouching even lower than usual. He tried to straighten, tried to look defiant, but he knew he looked terrified.

"Two!" The Smoke was shaking his head, furious, unable to believe that the boy was going to force him to do this.

Reuben tried to brace himself. Was he really going to let this happen? But what could he do?

The Smoke took a deep breath. "Thr—"

"Wait!" Reuben cried.

"No waiting!" The Smoke screamed. *"Three!"*

And then Jack was there.

Reuben's eyes caught the movement as the young man hauled

himself into view. He tried to look away, but it was too late—The Smoke had seen it on his face. He whirled away from Reuben and charged. Reuben saw Jack roll to his feet and spring nimbly out of reach just as The Smoke's club lashed out.

Then The Smoke vanished, and Reuben fled.

In his panic he ran without thinking. Just as he'd done before, he made for the piano. He only wanted to get behind something, to hide from whatever was happening. Rounding the piano, he looked back to see Jack, an expression of fierce concentration on his face—but also a barely contained bewilderment—as he stood with his fists raised, his eyes searching, seemingly alone on the floor. Then Jack appeared to sense something and leaped to the side, his head instinctively jerking backward.

The Smoke, lunging with the club, flickered into view and out again. Jack ducked and weaved, jabbed with a fist, striking nothing. The Smoke appeared behind him, the club already in motion. Jack sensed it somehow—perhaps he heard it whipping through the air—and spun away, the weapon missing his head by inches. The Smoke vanished again.

Reuben was shaking. He wiped his sweaty palms on his shirt. He didn't see how Jack could win. His eyes roamed desperately around the ballroom. In his peripheral vision he was aware of the battle, and he could hear Jack's grunts of effort, his oaths of frustration. The Smoke popped into view and out again, always in a different place, always dangerously close with his club. *Your brash friend has made another misstep.*

Later Reuben would wonder why he didn't think of the keys. Perhaps because he would have to run past The Smoke to reach them, and his mind suppressed the idea out of fear. What he thought of instead was the balcony. He wanted to be out of reach. And so, putting the watch away, he took a deep breath and sprinted. Then his feet were on the wall, his hands on the column, and he was ascending.

His eyes flicked toward Jack in the distance, his bristled red head bobbing, his body twitching this way and that. He was backing toward the bar in the corner. When The Smoke snapped into view at Jack's side, Reuben averted his eyes. He thought it was over. He heard a noise that from this distance sounded like a thin click, followed by a cry of pain and anger. He looked again to see Jack shaking his left hand. Either the club had come down on his knuckles or he had accidentally punched it. His right fist was still raised; he was still backing up, his gaze darting back and forth.

So it wasn't over. And maybe, in the close quarters behind the bar, Jack would even have a better chance. He might be able to get his hands on The Smoke, who could attack him from only one direction. Reuben felt a flutter of hope.

He had come to the top of the column. He didn't hesitate but instantly swung his arm high, caught hold of the railing, and hauled himself up and over before he had another thought. It was almost easy; his surging adrenaline had boosted him. But now he was left with all this adrenaline and emotion and nowhere to go, nothing to do with it. What was he thinking? What should he do? Reuben held on to the railing, squeezing it hard. He didn't know.

An unexpected movement drew his eyes to the hole in the ballroom floor. A familiar tumble of red hair had risen into view. Penny! Naturally, she had let Jack bypass her and climb up first—they would have heard The Smoke talking, would have known Reuben needed Jack's help. Now she was clinging to the rope, her eyes just below the level of the floor. Reuben ran to the corner of the balcony where she might see him if only she glanced over her shoulder.

No sooner had he arrived there than Penny did just that. Her gaze went up to Reuben, waving his arms over his head as if doing jumping jacks. Their eyes met, and Reuben gestured frantically toward the door, then pantomimed turning a key in a lock. It had occurred to him that with The Smoke occupied with Jack in the corner, Penny could grab the keys and get out. And he could follow right behind her—he could use the fireman's pole and make a break for it. He had no idea what they would do then, but anywhere was better than here with The Smoke in his lair.

Penny looked frightened and uncertain, but when he repeated the gesture and pointed toward the keys, she nodded. She understood. She reached higher up on the rope, struggling to get herself out of the hole. Reuben bounced on his feet, everything in him urging her faster. She would get no better opportunity than now.

At last she was out, lying flat on the floor, her eyes fixed on the battle in the far corner. Reuben saw her work her shoes off with her toes. *Smart*, he thought. *Now hurry!*

She did. Crouching low, making herself small, Penny scuttled across the ballroom floor toward the keys. Reuben glanced toward the bar again, saw Jack standing behind it, ducking an invisible blow, then snatching a dusty bottle from the shelf. Now he had a weapon! Reuben wanted to cheer. He knew at once that Jack had been planning this the whole time, had maneuvered his way into the corner where he could not only grab a bottle but also limit The Smoke's angle of attack.

But in the next instant, a telltale clanking sound reverberated in the ballroom. The floor beneath Jack dropped open with a bang, and with a trailing "You've got to be kidd—!" he plummeted yet again toward the basement, taking with him Reuben's brief hope of victory.

The shelf of bottles had been the trigger to a trap.

The Smoke had yet to reappear. Reuben's eyes shot back to Penny, frozen in the act of stooping for the keys. The sound of the trapdoor and her brother's shout had momentarily paralyzed her. Recovering now, she bent to the keys again, reached out—and now she had them! And The Smoke was still nowhere to be seen!

Hurry! Reuben thought. *Hurry, hurry, hurry!*

Penny straightened as if to run to the door, but then she did something peculiar. She lifted her chin, as if suddenly taking a profound interest in the ballroom ceiling, and began to walk backward. "Ow!" she cried, dropping the keys. With both hands she reached toward the hair on the back of her head, which, bizarrely, had risen out and away behind her as if affected by a static charge. "Ow, that hurts!"

The Smoke appeared then, arm extended, leading Penny by the hair as he marched back toward the middle of the ballroom. He looked angry, resolute—and triumphant. He was glaring up at Reuben. Somehow, even in the midst of fighting Jack and snaring Penny, he had determined that Reuben was on the balcony. He hadn't even needed to look for him.

The Smoke marched Penny back over to the hole by the piano. The rope was not moving. Reuben wondered if Jack was hurt. They came close enough for The Smoke to glance into the hole, shaking his head angrily. He yanked on Penny's hair, causing her to cry out again.

"You and your brother," The Smoke snapped, "for he *is* your brother, isn't he? You've both caused me so much trouble, and for *what*? For nothing!"

"Oh, please!" Penny cried as Reuben looked on helplessly. "I'm sorry! Please don't throw me down there!"

"You think I won't?" The Smoke snarled.

"Please don't!" Penny whimpered. "Please, I'm scared!"

"Tell *him* that," The Smoke hissed. He gestured toward Reuben on the balcony. "Tell your friend how scared you are. Tell him that if he doesn't come down this very instant and give me the watch, I'm throwing you in." He yanked her hair again. "Tell him!"

With both hands she reached toward the hair on the back of her head, which, bizarrely, had risen out and away behind her as if affected by a static charge.

Penny's eyes locked with Reuben's. She hesitated, and suddenly he understood everything.

But so did The Smoke.

"Why do you hesitate, little girl?" he said, his voice abruptly turning oily and knowing. "I wonder. Can it be that—yes, I think it is—you *want* me to toss you in? But why would that be? Unless...Ohhh. I see! You *are* a *little* girl, aren't you? What, do you fit between the bars? I think you must. I think you knew that. Yes. You are a clever one indeed."

Penny said nothing to this, only gazed helplessly up at Reuben, who gazed helplessly back.

"My goodness," The Smoke continued, "this must mean that you tried for the keys even though you didn't need them. How noble! You were thinking only of your brother, weren't you?"

Again Penny said nothing, but Reuben knew the answer. Unlike Penny, he had been distracted by the keys, had forgotten that she didn't need them. She could have gotten away. Instead she'd climbed back up to the most dangerous place she could possibly be. Why? For Jack and Reuben, to see if she could help them. She'd gone after those keys only because Reuben had told her to. She'd trusted him.

"Speaking of your brother," The Smoke said with a glance at the rope, which had begun to twitch and tremble, "I imagine your plummeting body would interrupt his climb, don't you? And in a most unpleasant way. Naturally, I'd need to make sure you couldn't run off first, so I'm afraid you would be making your descent *unconscious.*"

The Smoke spoke these last words looking not at Penny but at Reuben, his face hard. "Is that what you'd like to see?" he called. "Must I hurt your little friend? Or will you come down this instant? How shall we go about it?" He brandished his club, waggling it mockingly. Even from this distance Reuben could see that Penny's eyes had grown huge at the sight of it.

456

At their feet the rope sawed back and forth. Jack was climbing frantically. But he had much too far to climb, and too little time. The Smoke had every advantage. He had already beaten them on every front. He could dispatch them all, one by one. No matter what Reuben did, this was going to end badly. One way or another, The Smoke would be taking the watch. It was over.

Reuben didn't think these things so much as feel them. He knew them to be true. What he was actually thinking about was his mom. He didn't just imagine her heartbreak; he felt it. He could almost hear her weeping. She wouldn't believe it, wouldn't accept that anything bad had happened to him. As if in a dream, he could see the tears on her face, and—much to his surprise—he could see how angry she was. She was *scolding* him, Reuben realized. And why?

"Because there's always another way," he mumbled, imagining her saying it to him. "There's always another way, and you didn't find it."

"What are you saying?" The Smoke barked. "Speak up! Or no, don't speak. Simply come down. *Right. Now.*"

And suddenly Reuben knew. He knew what his mom would have told him to do. The Smoke didn't have every advantage. Penelope had known that, and Reuben knew it, too. Reuben had one advantage—only one, but it would be enough. It had to be.

He stood above the rope ladder and leaned over the rail. He held the watch out before him, high above the ballroom floor, so that The Smoke could see it. "I'm going to drop it," he said simply.

The Smoke stiffened. "You wouldn't dare!" he snapped, but there was an edge of fear in his voice. "What would be the point? I would still have *mine*." Dragging Penny along with him, he moved toward the balcony.

"The point is that I'm not going to let you have it," Reuben replied. "Do you understand what I'm saying? You're never going to have this watch."

The Smoke continued his approach toward the balcony, his eyes fixed on the watch in Reuben's hand. "You won't drop it!" he growled. "It wouldn't help your friend, wouldn't help you. You think you can negotiate with me, you little fool? You—"

"I wasn't trying to negotiate," Reuben interrupted. "I just didn't want you to miss this. Say goodbye to your dream, Mr. Faug!" And with that, he let go of his very last secret, the one he'd been trying to keep from himself. He let go of the thing he had wanted with all his heart to hold on to.

He let go of the watch.

The Smoke screamed.

And then, even as his scream resounded in the ballroom, The Smoke was moving, reacting with desperate speed. In one motion he let go of Penny, flung away the club, and darted forward in a mad sprint, one hand instinctively flying to his suit coat pocket even though vanishing would have done him no good in the face of this threat, the worst threat, the destruction of the watch he'd been seeking all his life. His other hand shot out before him, fingers spread wide, and with the plummeting watch just a few feet above the ballroom floor, The Smoke dove—and caught it.

At the top of the rope ladder, Reuben threw the levers on the control box. The trapdoor dropped open even as The Smoke was crashing down onto it with a shriek of triumph. He appeared not even to notice. Reuben watched as the ballroom floor seemed to gobble the man whole.

The Smoke's delighted laughter echoed up out of the darkness of the chute. Perhaps, Reuben thought, he'd forgotten that he no longer had his keys. Or perhaps his wild excitement simply crowded out every other thought, including the fact that he was about to be imprisoned in a dungeon of his own making.

Reuben stared down into the darkness after him, after the watch that he would never use again. He was aware of Jack clambering out of the other trap, could hear Penny telling him to pull up the rope, but still Reuben stared down into that darkness. And still he could hear The Smoke's laughter. It drifted up out of the hole as if the darkness itself were mocking him.

But it was The Smoke, he reminded himself. A man who had yet to comprehend that he'd been trapped by his own dream.

"Enjoy your eternal youth," Reuben muttered, and tore his eyes away.

THE OPPOSITE OF MIDNIGHT

No sooner had Reuben plunged into the pillows at the base of the fireman's pole than his friends were on him, laughing and hugging him in relief and amazement, flinging pillows away as if freeing him from a cave-in of cushions. The three of them stumbled away from the pole, tripping over pillows, holding on to one another, all of them talking at once. In their excitement they kept speaking too loudly, shushing one another, then speaking too loudly again. They soon got hold of themselves, however, and became aware of the silence now issuing up from below.

"He stopped laughing," Penny whispered. She was still trembling, still shaken from her terrifying encounter. Even when laughing and hugging Reuben, it had seemed as if she might burst into tears at any moment. "Maybe he's trying to get out."

Jack was already heading for the ballroom door, stooping on his way to snatch up the ring of keys. "Good luck to him. More likely he's just realizing the fix he's in. But I should go and check." He stooped once more, this time taking up The Smoke's discarded club. His tone and his movements were so casual he might have been cleaning up trash after a party. But his expression was tense.

"We'll all go," Reuben found himself saying. He could hear in his own voice how anxious he was, every bit as anxious as Penny, who quickly nodded her agreement. Neither wished to be separated from Jack.

"All right, but keep behind me," Jack said with a somber glance over his shoulder. "I'm sure it's fine, but—"

"We'll keep behind you, don't worry," Penny said.

"That's not going to be a problem," Reuben agreed. He was glancing around for his shoes, but he would have to come back for them. Jack was already unlocking the ballroom door.

Reuben pointed the way to the basement stairs. Moving cautiously, keeping close together, they descended. In the furnace room at the bottom, among the shadows cast by the dusty lightbulb, they stood listening. A steady dripping came from the rusted water heater in the corner, while overhead the lightbulb made rustling, crackling sounds and gave off the scent of burned dust. From beyond the opposite door there was silence.

Jack spread his arms to keep the children behind him—an unnecessary gesture, as it happened—and murmured, "Nobody gets within six feet of those bars, understood?"

Penny and Reuben nodded. They hadn't needed to be warned, either.

Jack crossed the room and eased the door open a crack. He

waited, listening and peering through. He held the club high, ready to swing. After a few moments, he opened the door a bit further and waited again. Then in an alarming rush he threw the door open and shot through the gap.

Penny gasped, and Reuben made an extremely loud squeaking sound, and then they heard Jack calling out to them.

"It's okay!" he was saying. He poked his head back in. "Oh," he said, raising his eyebrows and suppressing a grin, "sorry if I scared you. I just didn't want to be ambushed. It's fine, though. He's still locked in."

Penny and Reuben were clinging to each other, wide-eyed.

"You should warn us," Penny hissed.

"*Seriously*," Reuben said.

"My apologies," Jack said, though he still looked amused. "So are you ready?"

Reuben and Penny did their best to collect themselves. Nervously they followed Jack through the door into what appeared to be an empty basement, with a big empty jail cell in front of them. The Smoke was nowhere to be seen.

"Are you sure?" Penny whispered.

Jack pointed. Beyond the bars the net sagged in the middle as if bearing a weight, and looking closely one could see that a large, circular swath of strands there appeared to be missing.

"Do you care to say anything?" Jack called out, to no reply. He smiled and looked around at Reuben. "I think maybe our friend is feeling a little frustrated."

Reuben felt none of Jack's nonchalance. He imagined The Smoke crouching in the net, listening to them. Perhaps he knew something they didn't, something Reuben hadn't counted on. Perhaps he was plotting something. Readying himself for some terrible, unforeseeable act.

"It's over, you know," Jack said, projecting his voice. "You won't be getting out of there, not with those watches, anyway. Don't you want to, I don't know, swear at us or try to trick us into letting you out? Maybe you want to bribe us? No? Nothing?"

"Why is he being so quiet?" Penny mumbled, in her nervousness being very quiet herself.

And that was when Reuben understood. Or thought he did, anyway. Penny noticed the look on his face and asked him what the matter was.

"We need to be very quiet, as quiet as we possibly can. Give it fifteen minutes. Okay?"

Jack and Penny exchanged glances, looked back at Reuben and nodded. Penny checked her watch.

Reuben didn't need a watch to gauge the time. His mind was already in the habit of tracking the minutes. Only three or four had passed since they had noticed that The Smoke had fallen silent. That meant that in ten or eleven minutes Reuben would know if he was right.

They waited, straining their ears for any sound, watching the net for any telltale trembling. It was an unnerving wait, for it seemed that at any moment The Smoke might leap into action, charge toward the bars, or burst out with a bloodcurdling scream. They all knew that the watches rendered one blind, and yet they all felt as if The Smoke was watching them, waiting for his moment.

Reuben felt it—but he didn't actually believe it. He closed his eyes and gave over all his attention to listening. If The Smoke reappeared even for an instant, Penny or Jack would see him. Reuben, meanwhile, waited for the sound he knew as intimately as his own breathing, the tiny ratcheting of a watch spring being wound. He didn't expect to hear it, and indeed he didn't. The tense period of waiting ended. He opened his eyes and looked at the others.

Jack shrugged. "Nothing."

"He didn't reappear," Penny said. "But he ought to have, right?"

Reuben turned to stare again at the sagging net. "I don't think so."

"So what, then?" said Jack. "You think having two watches gives him extra time?"

"No," Reuben said. He thought about it again, just to be sure. He was. "I'm going in," he announced. "Leave the door locked just in case. I'll squeeze through the bars."

Jack had him by the elbow before he could take a step. "I can't let you do that."

Reuben looked up at him, and whether it was the certainty in his eyes or the sadness, something in them won the argument before it began. Jack frowned, troubled, but he released his grip.

Penny didn't try to stop him, either. Reuben had a feeling that she had begun to understand, too. He walked forward, felt her touch him lightly on the arm as he passed, but that was all.

Bracing himself for the pain, he squeezed through the bars. He held his stinging ears for a moment, then wiped the tears from his eyes and climbed up onto the net. Slowly he crawled toward the middle, and just when he reached it, everything went black.

"Reuben!"

Penny and Jack had cried out at the same time.

"It's okay," Reuben said. He found his way forward until his hand brushed against The Smoke's body. He flinched, froze, gathered himself. He pulled his hands inside the sleeves of his sweatshirt and began his search, patting his way up and down the man's arms.

The right hand clutched a watch. The left hand, too.

So he was right.

The words had been running through Reuben's mind for almost fifteen minutes now:

The possessor of both shall know no fear of death;
Though time may pass, he shall feel it not,
Nor feel aught pain or loss with any breath
He draws; nay, who holds these both shall have no mortal care,
Until such time as he lose possession, which God grant he will,
For it is not fitting that any man,
Be he low and wicked, or a good man or great,
Exist for long in such abnormal state.

"You were right about the inventor, Penny," Reuben said, sitting back on his heels. "That poem of his was every bit as tricky as everything else he made. Having both watches doesn't give you eternal youth. It drains you of all your energy. It's too much. And the safety mechanisms, the springs—they stop working. So the watches keep going and going."

"Is he . . . dead?" Penny asked, her voice hushed.

"No, I can hear him breathing. He's just lying here, holding on to the watches. And he won't ever let them go. We'll have to save him."

Reuben sat in his private darkness. The others wouldn't see him if he touched his watch one last time, felt its smooth metal under his fingers, imagining its beauty. He could see it perfectly in his mind's eye. How he had loved it.

"You okay in there, buddy?"

"Reuben?"

He kept his hands inside his sleeves and moved away, back into the world of the visible, where his friends could see him.

"Do you have the watches?" Jack asked.

Reuben shook his head. He crawled to the net's quivering edge and knelt there, gripping one of the bars for balance. "I think Penny should take them, if that's all right with you two. I think he'll be too weak to move, but we should tie him up first, just to be safe. Then I'll kick the watches out of his hands, and, Penny, you can grab them—I'll explain how to do it so that nothing happens to you. And then you'll hold on to them. Just you, okay? No offense, Jack."

Jack gave him a long, searching look. "No," he said at last. "That's okay. That's smart. Penny, are you up for it?"

"Yes," Penny breathed. She had tears in her eyes. She looked as if she'd just been given the greatest compliment in the world. And indeed, from Reuben's point of view, she had been. "Of course. I'll do it."

But for a minute none of them moved, only gazed at the spot where they knew The Smoke to be lying, holding on to both his precious watches.

"Do you think he could tell what was happening?" Penny murmured.

"Maybe," Reuben said. "Though it obviously happens fast."

"But why would he hold on to them? If he felt that happening, why didn't he drop them?"

Reuben knew the answer, but it took some time to find the words. "If you've been carrying the watch long enough, you think of it as your special protector," he said finally. "If something scares you, your instinct is to reach for the watch, to hold on to it. Letting go is the last thing that occurs to you."

Reuben felt pressure against his hand. Penny had reached through the bars and taken it. He looked at her, then looked away again. He sighed. "Yeah," he said, giving her hand a grateful squeeze. "The very last thing."

෧෧

After they had accomplished their respective tasks, Reuben and his friends lingered in the basement long enough to give The

Smoke a final regard. He was still breathing but had yet to regain consciousness. In his ill-fitting suit, curled up on his side, Cassius Faug—or whatever his true name was—looked to Reuben like both an old man and a little boy. And perhaps he really was both.

"Time to go," said Jack.

They agreed that The Smoke had probably left his Directions guarding the gate. He wouldn't have wanted the men inside the mansion, where they might accidentally discover his secrets. And so when Reuben had reclaimed his shoes and Jack had coiled up the rest of the rope (he'd needed only a short length of it to bind The Smoke's hands and feet), they proceeded to the upstairs bedroom at the back of the mansion.

Arriving at the window, however, they immediately saw Directions standing inside the hole in the property wall—and not just one group of them, but two. They formed a curving line from rosebush to rosebush.

"Looks like he called in some extra help," Jack said. "This does not make me happy."

Reuben studied the men through the curtain. "See how he has them arranged? You couldn't sneak past them even with the watch."

Beside him, Penny was swiping at locks of hair that clung to her damp forehead. She wore Reuben's sweatshirt now and was fairly sweltering in it. "Maybe we could just go out and explain things to them?" she suggested doubtfully.

"Okay," Jack said. "I'll go and tell them that their terrifying boss was just a man who could make himself invisible, and they don't have to worry about him anymore because we took away his magic watch. I'm sure they'll let us go then."

"Well, wasn't that our original plan? To take away his watch and then call the authorities?"

"The plan was to call them from somewhere *else*. I'm a wee bit concerned about getting bludgeoned."

"I'll go myself," Penny declared, with, Reuben thought, an admirable degree of bravado. "They aren't going to bludgeon a young girl."

Jack looked just as impressed as Reuben. Still, he turned Penny to face him and said, "Maybe not. But do you think I'm going to let my little sister approach a group of dangerous men? All of them nervous? Probably with orders to tackle anyone they see, anyone at all, anything that moves? The answer to that is no. I am not."

"Let's have a look at the front," Reuben said.

The front was worse. No fewer than twelve men lined the gate. Reuben recognized Frontman and his crew among them. All the Directions in the city were gathered on the property now, covering every possible exit. The Smoke had been taking no chances.

They turned grimly from the entranceway windows.

"I don't see a good way out of this," Jack admitted.

None of them did. Penny pointed out that they might safely make phone calls from inside the mansion, but even if they convinced the authorities to come, there seemed to be no way to avoid getting caught up in the investigation, no way to leave the premises unnoticed.

"Let's don't make the phone calls just yet," Reuben said. He was pacing now, rubbing his temples, trying to work up an idea, any idea. "There has to be another way. There's *always* another way."

"Um, guys?" Penny said. There was a note of wonder in her tone. She had turned back to the windows, was pressing her nose up against the glass. "You're going to want to see this."

Jack followed her gaze. His eyebrows lifted. "Well, what do you know? Looks like we have your other way right here, kid. For better or worse."

Reuben hurried back to the window. What he saw beyond it was at first confusing, then exhilarating—but also thoroughly

469

unsettling, for it was clear to him, as it surely was to the others, that their lives were about to get very messy.

Just then the neighborhood church bells began to clang furiously, their brassy clamor reverberating even inside the mansion. Coinciding as they did with the pandemonium at The Smoke's gate, Reuben at first had the impression that they were sounding a public alarm. But then he realized that they were simply announcing the hour.

Noon, he thought. *The opposite of midnight.*

Full light.

The Open Gate

They would all learn later how it had come to pass. How after they had parted with Mrs. Genevieve, she had felt herself at the brink of a breakdown. How she had moved agitatedly about her quarters, from wall to wall, as if in search of an exit.

She had made tea. She had dusted. She had tidied her rooms. Nothing helped, but she continued to busy herself. She kept thinking, *What were you supposed to do?* And she kept answering herself: *Stop them. You should have stopped them. You should have found another way.*

What had stopped her from stopping them?

Fear.

Mrs. Genevieve knew this, but she kept trying not to know it. Until, finally, she looked straight at it. If she hadn't been afraid, the watchmaker asked herself, what might she have done? No. That wasn't the question to ask herself now. It was too late for that. The question to ask herself was this: *If you weren't afraid, what might you do* now?

The answer came slowly. The first part was that she must rely on her own judgment, not on the judgment of children, however well-meaning they might be, nor on that of a reckless young man who, however good-hearted, was clearly too desperate for excitement to be relied upon. It had all happened so fast! If they'd had more time, if Mrs. Genevieve hadn't been afraid, what might she have done?

No, she reminded herself. What might she do *now*?

Then the rest of the answer came to her, and she had to sit down. She thought she could feel her galloping heartbeat in every part of her body—her face, her hands, her feet. Her plan would require her to be braver than she'd ever been. But for this did she not have Reuben as inspiration? And the little girl, as bold as her dramatic red hair? If nothing else, the children had understood that there could be no solution without boldness.

Therefore Mrs. Genevieve must be bold, too.

Even as she was gathering herself, the watchmaker found something—something unexpected—that bolstered her courage. It was as if she were being rewarded for having resolved to do the right thing, no matter the cost. It was a very strange and good feeling, she thought, as she picked up the phone. To feel happy despite being afraid.

❧

"Here. Yes. This is perfect."

When the watchmaker stepped out of the taxicab in the

neighborhood of Westmont, she looked to be physically ill. She had been trembling as she paid the cabdriver, and for a moment she clung to the open door as if for balance. The driver rolled down his window and asked if she was all right, but Mrs. Genevieve didn't answer, only forced herself to march up the steps to the church. For a moment she leaned against the doors, steadying herself. Then readying herself. And then she swung one of the doors open and burst inside.

An organ had been playing, but the music stopped abruptly with a squelch of dissonant notes, for the organist had been startled by the banging door and the sudden shouting from the direction of the nave. Every face in the congregation turned toward the shouting Mrs. Genevieve, who strode down the aisle waving her arms frantically.

"Help!" she shouted. "Oh, help! A child is in danger! You must help me, all of you!"

For a moment no one moved. The members of the congregation looked at one another with questioning expressions, as if unsure whether to trust their own eyes and ears. Then, at exactly the same moment, two mothers sprang to their feet and hurried toward Mrs. Genevieve, their own children and husbands immediately jumping up to follow them.

That broke the spell. The entire congregation was on its feet now, everyone talking, some shouting, some giving directions, but all of them focused on Mrs. Genevieve, who with a sweep of her arm beckoned them to follow her out.

Moving together as a large group, feeling a rising communal anger without yet knowing the cause, they followed this unknown woman along the street, past the park, block after block, right to the very gate of the Counselor's mansion. There was no small amount of misgiving as it became clear where they were headed, and no one but Mrs. Genevieve understood what was happening, for she answered their questions only with the admonition that they must hurry, that every second counted. But no one faltered, no one turned back. Lacking explanations, lacking anything specific to be frightened of, all that mattered was the child in danger. This was what the watchmaker had counted on.

"Open this gate!" Mrs. Genevieve demanded, speaking to the shocked assembly of Directions on the other side of the bars. The men had been watching the approaching crowd in utter consternation. They had tried to convince one another that the crowd would veer off, headed elsewhere. Now here they were, being ordered to open the gate by this elderly woman, with her flashing eyes and her little army of well-dressed families.

"This instant!" Mrs. Genevieve shouted. "Open the gate this instant!"

The Directions were all gaping at her, every one of them. Their eyes moved from her face to take in the crowd, all the expressions of concern, alarm, and anger, then returned to her face, her stern expression and her startling blue eyes commanding them to do as they'd been told.

"Oh," said one of the men. "Um…"

Another found his voice. "Sorry, ma'am. We can't do that. Under orders of the Counselor."

"Then go and get him!"

"We've been instructed not to do that, ma'am. Not under any circumstances. We're not to leave this post until we hear from him."

Those around Mrs. Genevieve, having heard this exchange, began to pass the word that she wanted the gate opened and that the Directions were refusing.

"Open the gate!" a mother's voice shouted, immediately echoed by another, and soon the entire crowd was chanting, "Open the gate! Open the gate! Open the gate!" The chant grew very loud, and it had a markedly shrill, piercing quality, for the voices of several children, who had by far the most enthusiasm for loud chanting, could be heard above all the rest.

The Directions looked helplessly at one another. It was clear from their faces that they wished they were anywhere in the universe but here.

Then it was noon, and the church's bells started ringing, and there came the sound of sirens, too, sirens growing louder by the moment—such a clamor and commotion the likes of which no one present had ever experienced, certainly not in Westmont in the vicinity of the Counselor's mansion. The crowd was growing angrier and louder. And then the police began to arrive. Two cars, then three, then more and more.

Out of the first leaped a determined-looking young officer with walnut-colored skin, shining buttons on his faded blue uniform, and perfect posture. He didn't hesitate but marched straight up to the gate, the crowd parting for him without needing to be asked. The chanting died away, everyone shushing everyone else so that they might hear what was said.

(Looking out through the entranceway windows with his friends, Reuben recognized, of all people, Officer Warren from the Lower Downs. If he had been surprised to see Mrs. Genevieve, he had at least understood how she'd known to come here. But Officer Warren? Reuben was baffled.)

The young policeman held up a sheet of paper. "Open this gate immediately," he said, raising his voice for the benefit of the crowd. "I have an emergency warrant to search the premises."

None of the Directions seemed to wish to be the one in charge. Some even took a subtle step backward, away from the gate. "You have a warrant to search *here*?" one of them asked, unable to contain his surprise.

"The address appears plainly in the warrant," Officer Warren declared, "along with the name of the property owner, Mr. Cassius Faug."

"How do we know that's real?" one of the Directions challenged. Or perhaps entreated. From his tone and expression, it was difficult to tell whether the man was desperately hopeful or desperately afraid.

"You think I'd be foolish enough to show up here with a fake warrant?" Officer Warren coolly replied.

"I don't know!" the Direction cried, looking to his associates for help and receiving none. "I mean, even if it's real, do you not realize whose home this is? Why on earth would you want to risk this?"

"I'll tell you why!" shouted a voice from the crowd. The person who had shouted was jostling to get through the packed group, which, after making way for Officer Warren, had immediately closed in again. Now, however, everyone leaped aside, including Officer Warren himself, as a woman surged forward and thrust her hand through the bars of the gate to point furiously at the man who had spoken. "Because my *son* is in there! The Counselor has my *child*!"

Reuben's jaw dropped.

Penny gasped. "Reuben! Is that your *mom*?"

"I like her," Jack said with an approving grin. "She's spunky!"

The next half hour passed in near-total confusion—Reuben bursting out the front doors, forgetting all caution and plans, all hopes of avoiding trouble, letting go of everything but his mom, who was charging through the gates now—one of the Directions (who turned out to be Lookback) having hurried forward to open it at her words—and throwing her arms around Reuben as if he were life itself. Which, to her, he was, and Reuben felt it in a great rush of warmth from head to toe.

He clung to her, burying his face in her neck, and began at once to weep. Everything—his fear, his guilt, his relief, his love for her, everything—it all came gushing out in the form of tears.

"Are you hurt?" his mom kept asking him. "Are you okay?"

476

"No, I'm fine," Reuben kept answering her, and "Yes, I'm okay!"

"You're fine?"

"I'm fine!"

But for several minutes he continued to cry. It ought to have been embarrassing. But Reuben didn't care.

Eventually, Reuben would ask his mom how she had found out, and she would tell him that Mrs. Genevieve had called her. "Evidently," she said, "you sent her a letter with our phone number in it?"

Reuben was dumbfounded. So the letter had taken only a single day to be delivered from Point William. He'd had no idea that was possible. He recalled Jack walking into Mrs. Genevieve's sitting room with the pile of envelopes he'd found in her mail slot. They had been set aside, and as the watchmaker would later confirm, she did not find his letter until this morning, when she'd been preparing to go out. That was what had bolstered her courage: she'd been able to call Reuben's mom and tell her everything, including her plan to lead a crowd to the mansion gates. And Mrs. Pedley, ferocious in her fear for Reuben, had urged Mrs. Genevieve to hurry.

"I'll be there as soon as I can," she'd said, speaking through anxious tears, "and I'll be bringing help. I am going to rain holy fire on these people." Then she had slammed down the phone, and Mrs. Genevieve, startled, had felt her spirits soar.

"Did she really say that?" Jack wanted to know. "Did she really say she was going to 'rain holy fire on these people'? I think I want to marry her."

Reuben shot him a warning look.

"Easy, easy." Jack laughed. He raised his palms. "Just a

manner of speaking, kid. Believe me, I don't want to marry anybody. Not even your mom."

These conversations were all pieced together over the coming hours and days, with Reuben hearing different accounts from Mrs. Genevieve and his mom, then relating to Penny and Jack any details they'd missed. For instance, although the mansion grounds were soon swarming with police officers, it would be quite some time before Reuben understood that his mom was responsible—that she had gone straight to Officer Warren, whom she trusted, and that Officer Warren had immediately called a dozen other officers, scattered about the city, with whom he had been in secret communication. The officers—as well as a single trusted judge—were all men and women without families to worry about, only themselves. Men and women who felt free to be brave, given the chance.

"The plan was always to wait for the moment," Officer Warren had told Reuben's mom. "We never knew if it would come, or even what it would look like. But if it did come, we swore to one another that we'd be ready to act. One officer might have no chance, but a dozen? We thought we could turn things. We just needed the opportunity—and now you've given it to us."

In the end it was far more than a dozen officers who came. Others followed their lead, and still others followed theirs, until at last almost the entire police force descended upon Westmont. The streets were filled with blue uniforms, as if the neighborhood were hosting a parade.

Conspicuously absent were the Directions, every single one of whom had slipped away on his own—alone, not part of a group, so as to be less noticeable. Few had any idea what was going on. But it was obvious that everything was changing and that their best hope was to disperse, to go home, to be quiet as mice and cross their fingers that judgment wouldn't follow them. Or that, if it did, it would at least be tinged with mercy.

In the immediate, chaotic aftermath of the gate's opening, though, and the sudden appearance of Reuben bursting out the front door of the mansion (an appearance wildly cheered by the crowd)—during this time, the only thing that concerned Officer Warren and his associates was the apprehension of one Cassius Faug. And to this end Reuben and his friends were hastily questioned as they gathered, Reuben still in his mom's protective embrace, near the bottom of the front steps.

Reuben was too emotional to help much, and Penny excused herself to run to the exhausted-looking Mrs. Genevieve, hugging her tightly, then taking her by the arm and leading her to one of the squad cars. (And in short order Mrs. Genevieve was whisked away and cared for with much kindness and appreciative admiration—for the watchmaker had already achieved a sort of legendary status among the swelling crowd.) In the meantime, therefore, it fell to Jack to explain things to the officers.

That was when Reuben began to understand that Jack Meyer was every bit as good a storyteller as any Meyer who ever lived. The difference with Jack was that his stories weren't always true. After years of keeping secrets from his own family—a family uniquely gifted with the ability to read people—Jack Meyer had become an expert. He had become, in other words, an incomparable liar.

Given the urgency of the moment, Jack began with the truth, telling Officer Warren exactly where to find Cassius Faug, otherwise known as the Counselor, who also happened to be the infamous man known as The Smoke.

"We know," Officer Warren replied. "Mrs. Pedley told me. And to some of us, anyway, it explains a lot. But I'm not sure I heard you right, Mr. Meyer. The basement, you say? In a *net*?"

"Strange but true," Jack affirmed breezily. "And listen, you'll want to tell everyone to look out for the traps."

"*The traps?*"

"Oh yes. Here, I'd better explain...."

Jack's easy authority and friendly manner was rather like Officer Warren's own, Reuben realized. He positively radiated trustworthiness. In a matter of minutes, everything he said that could be proved true was indeed proved true—Cassius Faug was where he said Cassius Faug would be, as were the bizarre traps, as was the long-missing stolen painting *Saint George and the Dragon*—and without quite realizing it or saying so, the police officers all naturally trusted him. And so, over the next minutes, hours, and days, when Jack began to alter and even to fabricate significant details of the adventure, everyone was inclined to believe him.

The tale Jack told was one of a well-intentioned boy who found an antique watch, a watch that happened to be coveted by a sinister and powerful man but actually belonged to the Meyer family of Point William. In returning the watch to its rightful owners, Reuben had unwittingly placed himself in danger, and Jack had committed to helping him out of it. Thus ensued a complicated tangle of events and negotiations and double crosses that had resulted in the loss of the watch (accidentally dropped into the river from the Southport ferry) and, finally, this most unpleasant encounter with Mr. Faug, who had summoned Jack to his bizarre home only to attack him. Penny and Reuben— brave and impetuous children that they were—had slipped away from Mrs. Genevieve's shop without permission, arriving at the mansion just in time to help Jack bind the hands and feet of Mr. Faug, who had stumbled into his own trap and—perhaps from the shock of it—fallen into the net unconscious.

Reuben, listening along with the others, was as astounded as they were. More than that, he was grateful, for he never would have known what to say.

But Jack Meyer certainly did, and over the coming days, though there were conflicting details in the various accounts of what had happened, the only verifiable evidence confirmed all of Jack's most important assertions. Not only was Faug's mansion stuffed with stolen paintings and other items, many of which bore his fingerprints, but it also reflected a devious and unstable mind. The maps! The traps! The fireman's pole! All of it seemed too preposterous to be true, and yet the mansion itself proved otherwise. Cassius Faug had perpetrated the biggest fraud in the history of New Umbra, and he'd been doing it for years and years. How he had pulled it all off, no one could ever say. But nothing the man said would ever be believed.

And everything now was going to change.

Not long after Jack gave his first account to Officer Warren by the front steps, he and Reuben and the others watched as paramedics exited the mansion. Accompanied by several officers, they were bearing a still-unconscious Cassius Faug on a stretcher. Officer Warren went to make sure that Faug would remain well guarded in the ambulance, and for a time the little group was left alone by the steps.

The instant they were alone, Jack murmured to Penny, who was holding him by the arm, "You told her what I said? And she agreed?"

Penny nodded. She was still quite shaken—even her freckles were pale—and Jack leaned over and kissed her forehead. "You did great, redbird. You really did."

"Told who what?" Reuben asked.

"Yes, what are you talking about?" his mom asked. "And what in the world is going on? All of this that you've been telling Officer Warren and the others—it isn't what Mrs. Genevieve told me on the phone."

"I had to change a few details," said Jack, turning to her with a wry smile. "This son of yours just did something a whole lot more important than anyone else will ever know, Mrs. Pedley. And he's going to explain it all to you later, aren't you, Reuben?

In the meantime my version needs to be the official one. I'm doing my best to manage it. After Reuben ran out to meet you, I asked Penny to go to Mrs. Genevieve and tell her not to speak with anyone until we've had a chance to talk."

Reuben's mom shook her head in bafflement. She kept looking at Reuben, who was still so relieved and grateful—and, like Penny, so shaken up by all that had happened—that he couldn't find any words that seemed suitable for the moment. Instead, he just hugged her again, which, as it happened, was all that his mom seemed to expect or want.

Officer Warren returned to inform them that Faug was coming around. He was conscious but evidently delirious, for he was babbling about his watches, going on and on about them, saying that he needed them, he needed them, they were his.

"We'll get it all sorted out eventually," Officer Warren said with a sigh. "In the meantime it seems that there are more traps than the ones you indicated, Mr. Meyer. Four different officers have fallen into that net in the basement. Between you and me, I think a couple of them did it on purpose, just to see what it was like. I know for a fact that some have been trying out the fireman's pole." He chuckled and shook his head. He appeared to be in an excellent mood.

Reuben found his voice. "Thanks for everything, Officer Warren. Thanks for coming when you did."

Officer Warren put his hands on his hips and regarded Reuben. "Can't thank me for doing my job, young Pedley, any more than I can thank you for trespassing and worrying your mother to death. But I do appreciate the courtesy. And I will say that you have really brightened my day. Yes, you have. Speaking of which"—the young officer removed his sunglasses and extended them to Reuben—"I believe I promised to lend you these when I got a new pair, which I intend to do this very afternoon. Go on, take them. Let's see how you look in them."

Reuben put the sunglasses on and smiled up at Officer Warren. And it was strange: despite everything he had accomplished, and despite Jack's wondrous storytelling that promised a happy conclusion to his harrowing adventure, only now as he and Officer Warren exchanged appreciative glances did Reuben feel that everything, after all, was going to be okay.

Officer Warren smiled approvingly, then shaded his eyes and looked up toward the sun, which until a few minutes ago, it was true, had been hidden behind a mass of clouds. "Yes indeed," he said. "Things are getting brighter, aren't they, young Pedley?"

"Yes, sir," said Reuben, still grinning. "Yes, sir. I think they are."

THE MOST MYSTERIOUS THING IN THE WORLD

The light had changed. Autumn was coming on, and in Point William, just as he had in New Umbra, Reuben felt the difference not only in the temperature but in the quality of light, in the cast of shadows, in a hard-to-describe change in the colors of an afternoon sky. The trees along the sidewalks had begun to appear more golden than green, and the streets and boardwalks were roamed by restless local children wishing they could cling to summer. Penny had already introduced Reuben to a few of these, and when school started next week, he would meet many more, for he was now a local child himself.

He felt the familiar flutter of nerves in his belly whenever he thought about going to the new school. But having Penny there would make a world of difference. And considering what he'd been through that summer, being a shy new kid at school seemed like an easy-enough challenge. In fact, Reuben welcomed it. He was nervous, but he was ready.

He felt the same way about today's task, which in comparison was far more momentous. Although with the passage of time he might come to forget the details of meeting new classmates and teachers, Reuben knew he would never forget a single detail about today.

After yet another boisterous meal in the great room—another crowded affair with at least a dozen Meyers present—Reuben and Penny, clearing the table, came into the kitchen to find Jack waiting for them. He had entered quietly through the back door. Reuben thought he struck quite a figure. He was wearing a wool jacket and fisherman's cap and had grown, with remarkable swiftness, a bushy red beard. Something about all the extra red around his face made his eyes seem more piercingly blue, like marbles in a fire.

"It's time," he said in a low voice. "Are you ready?"

Penny looked anxiously over her shoulder. "Let us finish bringing in the dishes," she said. "Otherwise they'll notice."

"They'll notice regardless. We need to move. The suits are on their way."

"Already?" Reuben said. "I thought they were coming this evening."

"So they said. I think they like to show up early and catch people off guard. Penny?"

Penny was peering out into the great room, looking fretfully at the half-cleared table. Her mom and Reuben's mom were laughing about something, exchanging amused glances like old friends or sisters might. Luke was telling a story to one of his little cousins, and everyone else seemed to be talking over one another. This was exactly how every meal had gone since their return. Pandemonium, served up three times a day.

Penny turned. "Right. Okay. I'm ready."

She and Reuben grabbed jackets in the anteroom, and they all slipped out the back door. Penny ran to the oil house and returned with her backpack. Then they made their way down over the granite boulders and into the rowboat, which Jack had left tethered near the hidden entrance to the smugglers' tunnels. No one spoke.

Jack rowed them out into deeper water, to a mallard-green fishing boat he had anchored there. Even before they'd climbed aboard, Reuben was struck by the strong smell of fish. It reminded him of his mom, though it had been well over a month since she'd stopped working at the market. These days she just smelled like soap and lotion, which Reuben loved. But the smell of fish would probably always remind him of her and of all those dinners together in the Lower Downs.

That part of their old life, anyway, had been nice. And fortunately, it could also be part of their new life. They'd been staying with the Meyers in the keeper's house, but they were going to move soon, into a little cottage that Mr. Meyer had arranged for them to rent at an affordable price. Dinners with the Meyer family were raucous affairs, very entertaining to Reuben and his mom alike, but they were looking forward to some quiet dinners alone. Curiously enough, the kitchen in the cottage resembled almost exactly the one in their old apartment. They had both laughed when they saw it.

"The more things change..." his mom had said, shaking her head. "But I'll bet the stove works better." It did. So did everything else. And when they had finished looking around the place (which took only a minute), she'd asked Reuben what he thought of it.

"I think it's my dream house," he'd replied with a grin.

Jack rowed them out into deeper water, to a mallard-green fishing boat he had anchored there.

"Oh yeah?" said his mom, and she grinned, too. Reuben had never seen her so happy. "Even though there's no trapeze?"

"Well, I assumed we'd be getting one."

"Okay, good. Because I think a trapeze would really tie this place together."

Although she'd often been upset during the weeks that followed that fateful day at The Smoke's mansion, these days Reuben's mom was in high spirits almost all the time. Not only were they going to have the cottage, but they could afford to pay for it because she'd been given a good job in town. As with the cottage, the job had come to her by way of the Meyer family. Despite the recent controversies, the Meyer name still counted for a great deal in Point William; virtually every family in town had at one time or another—in the current generation or in generations past, and often in both—been helped in some significant way by the Meyers. So it was that on the strength of the lighthouse family's recommendation (not to mention a few favors called in) Reuben's mom had been offered not just a fine job but a *choice* of fine jobs.

"I can't believe this," she'd said to Reuben privately. "Make sure you never tell anybody that I'd have taken the worst job in town. Let's pretend I've always been haughty and prideful, okay?"

"Like we have to pretend," Reuben said.

"There you go again. You were almost out of trouble, too. You must love being in trouble, I guess." She was pretending to look severe.

"I learned it from Jack."

"Who is a *terrible* influence," his mom said, rolling her eyes. "Did he really call me spunky, by the way? Or did you just say that to make me crazy?"

Reuben laughed. "He really did."

His mom sighed. "The more things change..." she said again, now pretending to look dejected.

No, Reuben thought, he had never seen her so happy.

And now on this sunny, brisk early-autumn day, Reuben found himself hoping that his absence wouldn't worry her. There were enough places he and Penny might have gone off to—Jack's old room in the attic, the oil house, the lighthouse tower—that she probably wouldn't even realize they'd left the island. And they wouldn't be gone long. Jack had said the entire trip would take only an hour or so.

Once Reuben and Penny were safely aboard the fishing boat, Jack cast the rowboat loose and let it drift. He would round it up later, he said. In the meantime the suits would be compelled to find other transportation to the lighthouse island.

"Won't they be mad?" Reuben wondered. The "suits," as Jack called them, were government investigators. Making trouble for them didn't seem like a great idea.

"For all they know, the rowboat just slipped its moorings," Jack said, ushering Reuben and Penny into the wheelhouse. "Accidents happen." He started the motor, and the flooring thrummed beneath their feet.

Penny glanced around with a look of growing apprehension. "Wait a minute, whose gillnetter is this? It looks like Mr. Harsch's."

"It *is* Mr. Harsch's," Jack said as the old boat began to plow forward.

"What? But he hates you! You said you were borrowing a boat from a friend!"

"Our friendship is kind of a secret," Jack said, turning the wheel. "Nobody knows about it but me."

Penny covered her face with her hands.

"Don't worry, redbird. I think Old Man Harsch only pretends to hate me."

"Why does Mr. Harsch hate you?" Reuben asked, somewhat absently, for he was only partly listening. He'd never been in a motorboat and was preoccupied by the rumble of the engine, the smell of exhaust fumes now drifting astern, the lovely rush of water along the sides. "Or, I mean, pretend to hate you?"

"Who can say?" Jack replied with a shrug. "Maybe because I keep borrowing his boat."

They traveled a long time, out of the bay and into open seas, the choppy water sparkling blue and white, with occasional cloud shadows moving swiftly across the surface. It was a most beautiful, most melancholy day, the last day of a time that Reuben would come to think of as "the aftermath," and the first day of what he would come to think of as his true Point William life.

Reuben and Penny had not been brought into the early investigations. Nor had they been called upon to participate in the hearings or speedy trial of Cassius Faug. Their testimonies weren't necessary to convict him of his numerous crimes, and it was agreed all around that, as children, they should be protected. Thus their knowledge of what was going on had been limited to what they were told and what they read in the newspapers, which boasted such headlines as *The Counselor to See a Counselor*—for Faug had been not only incarcerated but also prescribed routine sessions with a psychiatrist.

Mental health professionals had suggested he might never come to accept that his "watches of invisibility" were the products of his imagination. He might, however, eventually accept that he had to live without them. Regardless, it was hoped that one day a true accounting would emerge of how he'd accomplished such strange and seemingly impossible things—and not only *how* he'd done them but *why*. Perhaps it would. Perhaps it wouldn't.

Reuben figured he was the only person in the world who actually hoped the psychiatrist would help Faug. Sure, he was glad the man was locked up. Yet he also wanted him to find peace. Reuben wouldn't have imagined that he could feel both things about the same person, but he did. Not that his feelings had any bearing on the situation. He had set Faug's final fate in motion, but it was no longer up to him.

Meanwhile New Umbra was getting cleaned up. The big city was a big mess. It would be years before it was operating the way a proper city should—which is to say, messily, but more or less freely and honestly, with its citizens accountable to one another and to those they've chosen to represent them, rather than to entities, spectral or otherwise, whose own interests are not in the interest of the people. In other words, being a city is hard enough without someone like The Smoke running the show. New Umbra was never going to be perfect, but it was definitely going to be a lot better. It was going to be fine.

Reuben still found it hard to believe that he no longer lived there. He and his mom had moved to Point William only last week. Or rather, they had *been* moved—by the Meyer family, who had made the initial and very persuasive invitation (it hadn't taken Reuben's mom long to accept) and then come down together to pack, load, and transport all the Pedleys' things. Several residents of Reuben's apartment building had stood in their doorways, gawking at the cheerful, bustling, almost entirely redheaded family of movers.

It had been an exciting day for everyone, including the young building manager, upon whose desk Reuben left the following note:

The cat is in the storage room. (I closed the window.) Maybe try milk or tuna fish? Good luck making friends. I'll bet you can do it.

He had spent a lot of time the previous week luring the cat with milk and tuna, so he knew what he was talking about. And when that morning he had successfully trapped it in the storage room, he felt a most gratifying sense of resolution. Closing that window in the alley, he was closing an entire chapter in his life. He'd signed the note to the building manager with his full name and even left his forwarding address in Point William. He was glad he did, too, for just yesterday he'd received a thank-you card from the young woman, along with a photograph in which she stood, beaming, with the cat in her arms. The cat didn't look especially happy—in fact, it looked quite cranky—but it *was* letting her hold it, which actually was much better than Reuben would have predicted. Sometimes things just worked out that way.

In the same batch of mail, Reuben had received a letter from Mrs. Genevieve. It was not much of a coincidence, really, because they had agreed to write to each other every week, and indeed Reuben had already written to the watchmaker twice. She would keep him apprised of developments in New Umbra, she promised, if he would keep her posted about life in Point William. She might have to forfeit a little sleep to do so, for ever since that day at the mansion she had received a great deal of attention and a significant uptick in business. She had more customers than ever before, she wrote, many of them kind and charming people who were always wanting to do things for her.

This is wearisome but not unwelcome, Mrs. Genevieve wrote. *And when I do crave privacy, I have only to flip the "Closed" sign on my shop door until I'm feeling sociable again. Everyone should have such signs on their doors, don't you think?*

Hiding in the oil house so as to read Mrs. Genevieve's letter in peace (in the house one couldn't go anywhere without bumping into a Meyer), Reuben had begun composing his reply. *That's a great idea about everyone having signs*, he wrote. *I think we should even wear them around our necks and flip them over when we don't feel like talking.*

He had a feeling that this idea would amuse Mrs. Genevieve.

And just like that, it occurred to Reuben that his correspondence with the watchmaker was going to become, for him, very much like the times he'd spent with his mom designing dream houses. He could just tell. The thought pleased him immensely.

The boat droned on, its hull thumping rhythmically against the choppy seas. Spindrift blew across the bow, creating tiny rainbows that vanished almost as soon as they appeared. It happened again and again.

A most beautiful, most melancholy day.

They had bypassed a number of small islands, Jack giving them a wide berth. It was well known that there were dangerous shoals among them, he said, and Reuben reflected on this awhile. From the boat the shoals were invisible—as was almost everything else beneath the water's surface. The ocean was the greatest secret keeper of all. Some of its secrets, like the hidden shoals, could be discovered, but most would never be known. Thousands upon thousands might be revealed, yet there would always be more that remained hidden. The ocean was probably the most mysterious thing in the world, Reuben thought, except for a person.

The mainland coast was now a smudgy line behind them, far beyond the little islands, which themselves had fallen far astern. Penny nudged Reuben with her elbow and pointed ahead. Reuben, squinting behind his sunglasses, spotted two dark forms in the distance. Twin islands, more vertical than horizontal, rising up from the sea like gateposts leading nowhere. As they drew nearer, he could make out sand, scrub, rocks—and not much else. A few birds circled the desolate mounds, which otherwise looked to be devoid of life.

"Is that where we're headed?" Reuben asked Jack, who nodded.

Penny checked her watch. "It's already been almost an hour, Jack."

"Yeah, sorry about that. The whole trip will probably take us closer to three." Jack gave them an apologetic look—or a halfway-apologetic one, anyway. "I said one hour because it sounded easier, and I didn't want to worry you. Relax, I'll take the heat for both of you. It isn't your fault you were misinformed."

Reuben shook his head. He continued to marvel at this new Jack Meyer, who seemed always to know what to say, or not to say, to accomplish what needed to be accomplished. He had, for instance, expertly navigated the handling of the Meyer family's questions about the clock watches. They had all read Penelope's letter but couldn't possibly know whether the watches still existed. Thus Jack had instructed Reuben to say nothing whatsoever, and Penny to answer only certain questions, until the whole business was done. And it was Jack himself who determined the questions that the Meyers could ask Penny. (Having proved that he could fool them, he knew that his own word wouldn't suffice.)

"Ask her if I have either of those watches," Jack had urged his parents when, after much hubbub, argument, and difficulty, they were all finally alone.

They did ask her, and Penny confirmed that Jack did not. And of course they believed her. She couldn't have deceived them if she tried.

"Ask her if we intend to tell you the truth about everything soon, but that first we have to do something—something perfectly safe but very important—and that in the meantime we need to keep everything private among the three of us. Otherwise we'd put you in a bad position and might jeopardize the important thing we need to do."

Penny confirmed that everything Jack said was true.

"Ask her if she thinks you should trust me to do the right thing," he said at last, and this question caught them all off guard, including Penny. For despite everything they now knew about Jack—that he was an accomplished liar, a fighter, a reckless driver, an unauthorized borrower of cars and boats—despite all of this, not one of them doubted for a moment that Jack would do the right thing. They were all excellent judges of character, and though it had taken recent events to reveal Jack's character for what it truly was, they were convinced now that they knew him. They didn't fully *understand* him—it was hard for the Meyers to see how Jack could be both an unrepentant liar and an honest man, but they knew it to be true.

In the end, after receiving assurances that this secret business would be wrapped up soon and having made absolutely certain with Penny that it was safe (they were wise enough to realize that Jack's idea of safety probably didn't align with their own), the Meyers had agreed to let Jack, Penny, and Reuben do whatever it was they needed to do, without interrogating them further. Jack had already managed to come to the same understanding with Reuben's mom (which still amazed Reuben), and so he and the children were able to hold their private discussions and make their private plans.

It might have been today, regardless. They had been waiting for fine weather. But the arrival of government investigators in Point William had sealed it. Jack had known they'd be coming. He'd received a call from Officer Warren, who had wanted to let him know about the questions the investigators had been asking him. Evidently, somebody in the federal government was aware of the legend about the watches. Somebody thought it worthwhile to investigate, to follow up on any leads. No doubt there were people working in intelligence or in the military who thought that such watches, if indeed they existed, could be put to good use.

"But how could we be sure they'd never be put to *bad* use?" Penny had asked when Jack informed her and Reuben about the phone call.

"My question exactly. I think we stick with our plan. How about you, Reuben?"

Reuben couldn't even think about their plan without a twinge of sadness, but he believed in it. He didn't hesitate. "We stick with our plan."

The twin islands were drawing nearer. Gray-and-white terns darted over the ocean surface between them, slowing abruptly to hover in one place, just for a moment, before plummeting into the water after fish. The sea breeze ruffled the leaves of the hardy scrub that dotted the islands, and waves crashed spectacularly against the rocks all around.

"The Devil's Waste," Jack announced. "Or The Devil's Waist, meaning the two islands represent the devil's legs, I guess. I've seen it spelled both ways. Have you heard of it, redbird?"

Penny's eyes widened. "*That's* where we're going? But you promised me it was safe. You promised Mom and Dad, too! You made *me* promise them it was safe!"

"Easy, Pen. It's safe enough. You just don't go between them. You approach the one on the left from the mainland side. There's a channel that leads right up to a little spit of sand. That's where we're headed."

Reuben was nervous now. "Are there dangerous currents or something?"

"You could say that," Jack said. "But only between the two islands. Everyone knows not to try to navigate between the islands. Certainly nobody would ever try to dive there."

"But why here?" Penny asked, somewhat mournfully. She looked disappointed in him, as if he had tricked her to no good end.

Jack put a hand on her shoulder. "Don't you want to look back and remember this day, Penny? Don't you want to be able to picture it?"

Penny thought about it. So did Reuben. Both nodded.

"That's what I figured," said Jack. "And that's why here. Anybody asks you, you just say 'the ocean.' That's true enough. Or you refuse to answer. But Mom and Dad aren't going to let anyone question you, anyway. Any talking that has to be done, I'll be the one doing it."

"But you're leaving!" Penny cried, and tears suddenly sprang to her eyes, as they had done time and again in the days since Jack had informed them that he'd be leaving Point William as soon as they had accomplished today's task. He was going to set sail, he said, going to see the world. He'd already sold his car for traveling money. His plan was to finagle a cheap berth on a merchant ship.

"But what happens after that?" Penny had asked fretfully.

"Only one way to find out," Jack had replied. "But whatever happens, you'll be the first person I tell about it."

Just like Penelope, Reuben had thought. *He's going to be an adventurer!*

It was true. One day Jack Meyer would be known in many of the world's darkest corners—but also in many of its brightest. He would be loved by some, hated by others. Some would call him Jack the Red, and some Meyer the Liar. He'd be known by other names, too. He would acquire and lose more than a few fortunes, often in the most painful ways. In short, he was going to be very happy. And through it all he would be the faithful correspondent of one Penny Meyer, who once again was crying at the thought of his departure.

Jack put his arm around his sister. "I won't go until I've got it all straightened out with the suits. And when I do go, I promise to write every week, no matter what. I'll use squid ink and papyrus if I have to. Point is, I'll always write, okay? International mail is much faster and more reliable these days, you know. You'll get a letter every week. And I'll be back to visit, don't you worry."

Penny nodded through her tears. She hugged him, then pulled away to open her backpack and dig something out of it.

She handed the tiny object to Jack, who gave a surprised and happy smile. Reuben stepped closer for a better look.

It was one of the winding keys.

Jack closed his fingers around it. "I'll keep it always, redbird. Thank you. Do you have the other one?"

"I thought Reuben should have it," Penny said, and sure enough, there it was in her hand, which she extended toward Reuben.

He hadn't laid eyes on either of the watches since that day at the mansion. He gazed at the winding key now with a curious mixture of sadness and pleasure that added up, somehow, to that same feeling of melancholy. Still, the gesture meant a lot to him, and he looked at Penny fondly before shaking his head. "You should keep it. You should each have one."

Penny started to protest, saw that Reuben was determined, and threw her arms around him. "You can look at it whenever you want," she said. "I'm going to keep it in a secret place in the oil house. I'll tell you where."

"Okay," Reuben said into her hair, which was tickling his nose. "I'll hold you to that."

Jack had found the hidden channel. The water was surprisingly calm, and he eased the fishing boat quite close to the shore before cutting the engine and dropping the anchor. He produced a small inflatable raft from below, and soon the three of them, their legs all knocking against one another's, were paddling the remaining distance to shore. Jack leaped out and pulled the boat up onto the spit of sand, tethering it to a stunted evergreen the size of a fire hydrant.

"There's no path," he told them. "You just make your way up however you can."

It wasn't very difficult. The hill was steep, but Jack quickly identified where the footing was best, and in single file the three of them made their way up. A few lizards scampered out of their way. Some kind of large insect buzzed past Reuben's ear and headed out to sea. He watched it disappear. Maybe it knew of another island, he thought. Or maybe it was making a big mistake.

At the summit of the hill they were greeted with a stronger breeze—Penny's hair was flying all about—and a view of the ocean around them, an endless sparkling expanse. Between the two islands the water churned menacingly but was a beautiful shade of green. Penny knelt by her backpack and took out, first, a cap with which to tame her hair. She wrestled it onto her head. Then she reached in again and came out with what appeared to be two softball-sized rocks.

She had disguised the watches. They were hidden within an exterior of concrete, painted with pitch and mixed with bits of shells. They looked as if they belonged on the bottom of the ocean. Not even a fish would doubt it. But inside them were the fabulous inventions of a mind more brilliant than any other, inventions with secrets of their own.

"Secrets within secrets," Penny said, and Reuben and Jack nodded appreciatively.

Jack withdrew, leaving the children to their tasks. The wind blew and blew. They moved to different points on the bluff overlooking the water, and after only a few paces Reuben could no longer make out the words Penny was saying to him; the wind in his ears was too loud. But he could tell from her expression and gestures what she meant. They should throw the watches at the same time. Together.

They regarded each other for a long minute, and then, as if reading each other's minds, they both nodded. They counted together, though Reuben could hear only his own words. One. Two. Three.

He turned and flung the watch out over the water. It seemed

to fall for a long time, and then it plunged through the surface. In the immensity of water the splash seemed tiny, the most minuscule of disturbances. And then it was gone, as if it had never happened, as if Reuben had done nothing.

But I did, Reuben thought, and he turned back to rejoin his friends. *Nobody can see it, but I did it.*

ACKNOWLEDGMENTS

I would like to thank Rivendell Writers' Colony, in particular
Carmen Toussaint, for offering me precious time and a beautiful
space to work on this book; my friends Paul and Bridgett Galvin
for a snowier version of the same; and my editors Megan Tingley,
Bethany Strout, Kheryn Callender, and Barbara Bakowski for
their wise counsel in bringing this particular secret to light.